the aRt of the SWaP

Kristine Asselin & Jen Malone

ALADDIN

New York London Toronto Sydney New Delhi

This book is a work of fiction. Any references to historical events, real people, or real places are used fictitiously. Other names, characters, places, and events are products of the author's imagination, and any resemblance to actual events or places or persons, living or dead, is entirely coincidental.

ALADDIN

An imprint of Simon & Schuster Children's Publishing Division

1230 Avenue of the Americas, New York, New York 10020

First Aladdin paperback edition February 2019

Text copyright © 2018 by Kristine Asselin and Jen Malone

Cover illustration copyright © 2018 by Julie McLaughlin

Also available in an Aladdin hardcover edition.

All rights reserved, including the right of reproduction in whole or in part in any form.

ALADDIN and related logo are registered trademarks of Simon & Schuster, Inc.

For information about special discounts for bulk purchases, please contact Simon & Schuster Special Sales at 1-866-506-1949 or business@simonandschuster.com.

The Simon & Schuster Speakers Bureau can bring authors to your live event. For more information or to book an event contact the Simon & Schuster Speakers Bureau at 1-866-248-3049 or visit our website at www.simonspeakers.com.

Book designed by Laura Lyn DiSiena

The text of this book was set in Berthold Baskerville Book.

Manufactured in the United States of America 0319 OFF

10 9 8 7 6 5 4 3 2

The Library of Congress has cataloged the hardcover edition as follows:

Names: Asselin, Kristine Carlson, author. | Malone, Jen, author.

Title: The art of the swap / by Kristine Asselin and Jen Malone.

Description: First Aladdin hardcover edition. | New York : Aladdin, 2018. |

Summary: When twelve-year-olds Hannah and Maggie switch places, Hannah must prevent a famous art theft in 1905 and Maggie must cope with modern life until they can switch back.

Identifiers: LCCN 2017030041 |

ISBN 9781481478717 (hardcover) | ISBN 9781481478731 (eBook)

Subjects: | CYAC: Mystery and detective stories. | Impersonation—Fiction. | Art thefts—Fiction. | Mansions—Fiction. | Museums—Fiction. | Time travel—Fiction. | Newport (R.I.)—Fiction. | Newport (R.I.)—History—20th century—Fiction. |

BISAC: JUVENILE FICTION / Mysteries & Detective Stories. | JUVENILE FICTION / Historical / United States / 20th Century.

Classification: LCC PZ7.1.A88 Art 2018 | DDC [Fic]—dc23

LC record available at https://lccn.loc.gov/2017030041

ISBN 9781481478724 (pbk)

For all the strong, smart, persistent girls out there, and to one special one in particular, Katie, who sparked this story idea

Chapter One

Hannah

S O, IF YOU EVER NEED THE PERFECT setting for a life-size version of the board game Clue (you know, Miss Scarlet in the conservatory with a lead pipe?), look no further. It's my house. Because we've *got* a conservatory. And a ballroom. Hall? Dining room? Library? Check, check, double check. Kitchen? Obviously.

Plus, if you want alternate murder locales (not real murders, just board game varieties), there are forty-two other room options. Like one devoted entirely to making ice, called—wait for it—the ice-making room. No, seriously. An entire room devoted to . . . ice.

There are also sunken gardens with teahouses, and

statues, and murals painted right onto the ceilings, and walls covered in silk, and marble floors, and sitting rooms, and carriage houses, and an underground railroad track from the street into the basement, and columns, and arches, and so much gilded gold, and, and, AND!

I live in a mansion.

(Which definitely doesn't suck.)

After slipping my shoes off when I hit the back terrace, I tuck my fingers through my sandal straps so that they dangle from my right hand while my left pushes open the glass door. I step into the hallway. The ceiling is so high, three other me's could stand on my shoulders and still not reach the top . . . and I'm pretty tall for twelve.

Tiptoeing across the marble floor, I head for the grand staircase, but I hear a voice in one of the nearby rooms that I just can't ignore, no matter how many times I've been told to please, please try. I should keep walking. I know this.

But I don't.

"And of course, here we have the ballroom," the voice is saying, in a kind of snooty tone. "Step inside, step inside, everyone. This is the largest room in the home and was host to glamorous evenings of high-society entertaining. You are standing in what was considered *the* most fashionable house on *the* most fashionable street in *the* most fashionable resort during America's Gilded Age."

I creep behind a woman in a red sundress who raises her hand.

"How many people would this space accommodate?" she asks.

Oh, um, I might have forgotten to mention that our house is sometimes open for tours. What with being *the* most fashionable house on *the* most fashionable street blah, blah, blah. I don't mind. It's pretty cool to show off the amazingness I get to live among every single day.

"Hundreds," Trent answers. He's my least favorite of the docents. He has silver-white hair he is forever smoothing down with a palm he licks first, and he stands way too straight for anyone who's not a statue.

"When the home was completed on August 30, 1902," Trent says, "Mr. and Mrs. Berwind played host to more than a hundred guests for a seventeenth-century cotillion. Two famous orchestras performed, and there were even monkeys scattered about the gardens."

Okay, once again, I know I shouldn't do this. I know, I know, I know. But it's like one of those mischievous monkeys is sitting on my shoulder, poking me. I clear my throat, and then . . . I do it.

"Ahem. Excuse me? Trent? I don't mean to interrupt your tour, but I'd like to clarify a few things you just said. The house was completed on August 30, 1901, not 1902. Cotillions were an *eighteenth*-century formal ball. Also, there were more than *two* hundred guests who attended, and actually the monkeys were really over-the-top for the Berwinds. I don't want anyone on the tour to think that was a typical occurrence. Although, the Berwinds did entertain a lot. Like, A LOT a lot."

Trent stares daggers at me. Then he remembers there are people watching and forces a smile that doesn't quite reach his eyes.

"Ladies and gentlemen, please pardon the interruption. We have a young history buff here." His words are pleasant, but he says the words "history buff" the same way I might say "we're having sauerkraut and undercooked liver for dinner." If he feels that way about the past, maybe he shouldn't be giving historical tours. Just saying.

He adds, "Allow me to introduce Hannah. She's our caretaker's daughter."

Oh. I might also have forgotten to mention that. Although technically speaking I do live here inside this mansion, called The Elms, I sort of left out the part where my dad and I have our rooms upstairs in the former servants' quarters/current caretaker's apartment. Which, I guess, doesn't make us that different from servants, only we don't really serve anyone so much as keep the place looking perfect for all the visitors who roll through here every day to admire how the mega-super-rich used to live back in Newport's heyday. The state of Rhode Island might be extra tiny, but the "summer cottages" around here are anything but.

Visitors go home at the end of the day. And me? Well, I get to stay and hold cotillions of my own in the ballroom. Who cares if my ball gown is really a nightgown and my dance partner is my stuffed bear, Berwind, aka "Windy." He's surprisingly good at spinning.

I also get to read the books in the library. (Yes, I had to get special training to handle them and they are a hundred-plus years old and therefore smell like dust and mothballs, but I suffer through that part because it's thrilling to think that the Berwinds—or maybe one of their glamorous houseguests—turned the very same pages!) And I splash all I want in the fountains or sunbathe on the rooftop anytime I feel like it. It might not *technically* be my house, but it basically is. It's the only home I've ever known. I've explored every square inch of this place, and

I know the Berwind family history probably better than any Berwind ever did. I kind of, sort of, consider them my family too. I would give *anything* to have lived back then and known them for real.

"Where is the famous Margaret Dunlap portrait?" a man in a Red Sox cap asks.

Trent turns and gestures for everyone to follow him into the adjoining drawing room. He points at a large gilded mirror. A smaller—but still pretty big—painting hangs from long wires right in front of it, almost like the mirror is forming a second frame around the first one. (It was a style back then.) "Obviously, that is the age-old question, isn't it? Here is the commissioned reproduction of the now-famous painting. As most of you know, the original was stolen in a renowned art heist on the evening of its scheduled unveiling in 1905. The room was full of high society turned out in their finest. . . ." Trent pauses for effect, and I try not to roll my eyes. "But no one ever saw the portrait hanging. When they removed the silk sheet covering the portrait . . . the painting was gone!"

The art heist is Trent's favorite part of the tour. And I get it. It's one of my favorite things about the Berwinds' history too. A mystery for the ages. The priceless portrait was painted by famed artist Mary Cassatt and commissioned by Mrs. Berwind to mark the occasion of her beloved niece Margaret's thirteenth birthday. But even though the police determined that a kitchen boy named Jonah Rankin stole the work of art, he disappeared before he could be arrested. No one has ever found the missing art.

Many have tried.

"If the picture was gone before the unveiling and wasn't ever seen by anyone, how was it able to be re-created here?" the guy in the Sox cap asks, gesturing at the painting of a serenely smiling Margaret (whom I secretly call Maggie, because I read once that her close family called her that) in a daffodil-yellow gown that billows around her as she sits with her hands folded in her lap. Her eyes twinkle like she has a secret for only me. I'm positive that if I'd lived back then, we would have been best friends. I can just tell.

But I live here and now, with a pretentious docent shooting me glares when he thinks no one will notice. Sigh.

"There was exactly one photograph of the painting, taken over Mary Cassatt's shoulder during the last portrait sitting," Trent says. "Of course, cameras were still new then—and only accessible to the upper class—so it wasn't the best image, but—"

Don't butt in, Hannah. Don't butt in. Remember how upset Dad got the last time the docents complained about you.

I know that should be incentive enough to turn and run away, but Trent always messes this part up, and I can't stand here and let people learn the wrong version of history. I just can't. Besides loving The Elms enough to care that our guests are getting the right information, I also can't help hoping that one of these days the docents will realize I'm more than some bratty kid who's always underfoot, which I swear is how they treat me. I guess not *all* of them are that bad. I mean, Trent's my total nemesis, but some of the others aren't outright dismissive. Yet they sure aren't outright accepting of me as their peer either. It sucks to be judged by something I can't control. If I could make myself older, believe me, I would.

Maybe this is gonna sound all humble-braggy, but I'm pretty used to being decent at things. Okay, maybe even a little better than decent. And I'm also kind of used to being recognized for that. Take the soccer field, for example. Everyone knows that if the ball comes my way, I'm most likely gonna block the goal. Or at school. Let's just say I get by pretty well and I have the awards to prove it, especially when it's anything related to my favorite subject: history. But somehow no one else seems to accept that I know my stuff when it comes to The Elms. I'm not expecting a trophy for it, but a teeny tiny bit of acknowledgment—or, God forbid, some encouragement—wouldn't be the worst thing in the world, would it?

But no. Never. Not when I was the one to notice that someone had nudged one of the chairs in Mrs. Berwind's bedroom, so that a corner of it was getting hit with light from the window. (Daylight is public enemy number one for antique fabric.) Not when I stayed up all night helping my dad patch a corner of the roof in the middle of a rainstorm, before any water could drip down onto the fresco in the dining room. (Actually, maybe water is public enemy number one . . . for antique *anything*.) It's so annoying. I wish that just *once* I could get some respect around here. Plus, these people are taking the tour to learn the facts, and it's only fair that they get the right ones.

I take a deep breath. I'm crossing a big line here by butting in on Trent. I know he actively hates me (as opposed to the other docents, who mostly just ignore me) and I really should just leave his tours alone, but it

KILLS me that these guests are getting the wrong information. I keep crossing my fingers that if I can get away with correcting him long enough for guests to mention all his errors on their comment cards, he'll be reassigned to the gift shop or something. Then every future visitor will leave with the accurate version of The Elms' history. I know it's just a house, so what difference does it make if some tours get a slightly wonky version of things that took place here more than a hundred years ago? But I can't help it: *I* care. It's *my* house, and even though the history isn't mine exactly, I still feel connected to it.

Last chance to reconsider, Hannah.

"Actually, about half the households in the country had a camera by 1905," I say.

Trent takes me by the elbow, and his fingernails dig in way more than necessary. Way more. I try to wiggle free, but he tightens his grip as he says, in a fake-cheerful voice, "Oh goodness, thank you *so* very much for illuminating us on the origins of photography, young Hannah. I'm only sorry you won't be able to join us for the rest of the tour. Ladies and gentlemen, if you'll please look up, I'm sure you'll marvel at the elaborate painted murals on the ceilings."

Under his breath he hisses, "Your father will be hearing about this, young lady! It might even be time to get the Antiquities Society involved. Dear old Dad's job can go away like that, you know." He snaps his fingers, and now his creepy smile makes him look like the Grinch. "And put some shoes on. You look like a street rat. Although, maybe that's appropriate, since that's exactly where you may end up, once I've had my say with your father's bosses!"

Epic sigh.

Mansion living is mostly amazing.

High and mighty docents who get half the details wrong more than 80 percent of the time and still think it's okay to get mad at *me* for basically doing *their* job are super-annoying.

Still, once my dad hears about this, I am extra dead.

Chapter Two

Maggie

ISS MARGARET." THE VOICE SOUNDS stern, but there's a hint of mirth under the frustration. "Your aunt will have my head on one of her silver platters if she discovers I've allowed you to be anywhere near the servants' staircase again, let alone come this far into the kitchen by yourself."

If she's this annoyed at me for simply standing in the kitchen, I can only imagine Mrs. O'Neil's outrage if I had slid down the banister, the way I'd wanted. Sliding down banisters is beyond strictly forbidden, even though I've seen Cousin Peter glide down every one in the house. Aunt would be livid just knowing I'd imagined doing it. I close my eyes, hoping the head housekeeper will be gone when I open them. But the impatient tap-tap-tapping of her left foot on the tile doesn't stop.

I count my blessings that I haven't been caught by the butler, Mr. Ernest Birch. He wouldn't waste time speaking to me; he'd simply march me by the ear to the breakfast room, where Aunt is finishing her tea. I'd rather avoid that particular sensation this afternoon. I'm sure my aunt does not fully understand and appreciate that *I have never* acted on a spontaneous impulse, no matter how much I might wish to. In my mind's eye I can picture her saying, "Maggie, darling. Young ladies should be able to control their emotions and behavior."

And I am Miss Margaret Dunlap, daughter of Mr. and Mrs. Sallows Dunlap of New York City, and niece of Edward J. and Herminie Berwind. I always follow the rules.

"I . . . I was just—"

"You can forget your excuses. I heard Miss Colette dare you over breakfast to come down here. By the by, since when have you stooped to her taunts? You should have more self-respect, if you ask me. You know she's only trying to get your goat." Mrs. O'Neil sighs. "Anyway, I can look the other way when you use the servants' staircase as a shortcut if it means you can manage to get to tea on time and spare me your aunt's rants. But land sakes, walking bold as brass into the kitchen . . . at your age! I simply can't allow it."

I clear my throat and try to speak like my aunt, Mrs. Herminie Berwind, the mistress of The Elms, the most extravagant summer cottage in all Newport, Rhode Island. The corners of Mrs. O'Neil's mouth turn up, as if she's trying to prevent a smile, and my resolve to stay strong wavers.

"My dear Mrs. O'Neil . . ."

The twitching of her lips as she stares me down causes me to lose my train of thought.

"Your aunt is correct, of course, in advising you to stay upstairs. It is not becoming of a young woman of your stature to be trifling with the help, Miss Margaret. It's 1905, and this house has amenities. You know that if you need something, you need only to use the call button, and the bell will ring in the kitchen." She gestures at the elaborate bell system on the wall. "One of the maids will bring it to you."

She wouldn't believe that I'd rather not have a maid do things for me that I'm perfectly capable of doing myself, so I don't bother to explain it to her.

She taps her foot a few more times, but she doesn't

make any move to push me out of the kitchen. Other servants have stopped their activities, and while no one is overtly staring, I can tell they are all waiting for my next move.

It's true my cousin Colette dared me to show my face down here. For a moment I consider taking something to prove I went through with it. But someone would be punished if an item went missing, and I refuse to stoop that low. I hope that just coming down here will keep her at bay for a few hours, at least.

I clear my throat and start again. "My dear Mrs. O'Neil. As the grand ball tomorrow evening is in honor of my portrait unveiling, I feel it is my duty to inspect the goings-on in the kitchen." I clasp my hands to stop them from shaking as I raise my voice and hope she believes me. "I would also like to procure a table setting, so that I might practice."

She must allow me this one small indulgence. Even with years of practice at tea parties, I am so afraid of making a ninny of myself at the ball by using the oyster fork for my hors d'oeuvres. Aunt doesn't seem to be worried, but she's *used to* hundreds of guests staring at her while she eats. I'm not.

I smooth down my dress and wait for Mrs. O'Neil's

reply, hoping she doesn't call for my aunt. I'm supposed to meet with Mademoiselle Cassatt today to view the finished portrait, and Aunt will not be pleased if I'm late. Uncle E. J. was my mother's favorite brother, and I'm treated accordingly, but there is a limit to how far I'll risk pushing my summer hosts.

Mrs. O'Neil stares me down. "Haven't you spent hours preparing for this, Miss Margaret? I'm sure you're more than capable of maintaining your manners." She softens her tone. "You should relax and try to have fun at the ball."

Between boarding school, a constant rotation of nannies, and my always-traveling father, I am constantly reminded to be good. Someone is always watching, ready to admonish or correct me. I have to mind my manners and act just so. All the time. There is precious little fun in my life. The ball is in my honor, but the last thing it will be is fun. At least during my summer at The Elms, there are people who seem to care for me. Back in the city my father is so busy, he barely says good morning when he's home. I might not even see him before I return to school. Even so, I don't want to seem ungrateful. But I can't stop myself from blurting, "There's nothing fun for a young woman of my stature." I sound whiny and childish, but

I don't care. "All that is allowed of me is to be still and silent. And to mind my manners."

I don't really expect Mrs. O'Neil to answer. But the shadow of a smile fades into a small frown as she turns to face me. "Miss Margaret." Her voice is drawn and tight. "The alternative is to be tired and invisible. As much as you don't want to be still, it would do you well to remember that others"—she makes a vague gesture to the girls behind her—"don't have the choice to sit at all." The scolding from Mrs. O'Neil washes over me. She's right. There are girls just a bit older than me back in the dark, hot kitchen. None of them are permitted to be seen upstairs. And no one is throwing a ball for any of them.

I wish I knew how to respond.

She turns away, leaving me to watch the staff go back to work. I've delayed their afternoon, which means they won't finish with their work until late this evening. I feel horrible. Also, she hasn't given me a table setting, and unless I want to involve Aunt Herminie, I'm not going to get one.

As I head back up the stairs, a noise catches my attention and I peek over the railing. A boy dressed in a starched white shirt and plain black pants stands quite still in the kitchen foyer, looking like he's waiting for some sort of instruction. Suddenly sounds from dinner preparation crescendo as someone drops something onto the slate floor—voices, and the pounding of feet, and the clatter of dishes. It's a noise I'd never hear from the main part of the mansion. I always think of the basement level as being like the steam engine of a train—it's loud and messy and you're not supposed to see it, but it keeps the rest of the cars happily moving down the tracks. It's an especially appropriate analogy, considering there are real train tracks down here that carry the coal from the street to the kitchen. I usually forget about the people who make the house run smoothly every day.

Mrs. O'Neil's skirts swish as she strides into the hall. "Jonah, what are you doing there? You should be taking the waste from the lady's tea to the compost."

"Yes, ma'am." The boy nods and retreats into the kitchen.

"Lord help me," Mrs. O'Neil says under her breath as she starts up the steps for what I'm sure is at least the tenth time since lunch. I briefly wonder what it's like to climb eighty-two steps ten times a day. Before she gets to the first landing, I hear her mutter, "What am I going to do with willful heiresses and disobedient kitchen boys? As if I didn't have enough to deal with."

As I rush up the stairs before she catches me, I remember an overheard conversation from last summer. My aunt was gossiping with her neighbor Mrs. Alva Vanderbilt Belmont from Belcourt Castle, one of the mansions down the street. "Can you imagine being born into a life of servitude, Herminie, dear? To spend your days elbow-deep in someone else's unspeakables?" Mrs. Belmont chuckled behind her gloved hand.

To her credit, my aunt didn't laugh. But neither did she defend the hardworking staff, from whom she demands an impeccable work ethic. I asked her about it afterward. "There's nothing to be gained by disagreeing with Alva Belmont, Maggie. You should remember that. She'd have the whole of Newport society against me." And then Aunt walked away to inspect the evening table settings for a dinner party.

I sigh and head toward the part of the house where I belong, feeling awful that I'm glad I wasn't born into a life of servitude. As the niece of the owners of the The Elms, the most magnificent summer cottage on Bellevue Avenue, I was born into a life of privilege. But for me, that privilege sometimes feels like a burden.

Such is life here. The servants have their own staircase, and I'm not allowed to be anywhere near it *or* the kitchen *or* the attic, where the thirty-five full-time servants live. During my first visit here, when I was ten, I was allowed to play with some children visiting other cottages for the summer. Now, at thirteen, I am considered almost a woman, so there's no fun anymore. Just manners. And of course speaking only when one is spoken to. And sitting quietly for portraits. And holding still. Constantly. Then there are the things forbidden for girls: sliding down banisters, of course. Also: walking without a chaperone, running, or doing anything that might result in perspiration. Aunt Herminie says it often, as if we're likely to forget. "Young ladies must not, under any circumstances, perspire."

I wish there were something more for me to look forward to than debutante balls and high-society parties.

New century, my foot; for a girl, there's nothing progressive about living in the twentieth century.

Chapter Three

Hannah

I POKE MY HEAD AROUND A GINORMOUS marble statue in the conservatory and watch the last of the day's guests make their way across the back lawn and over to the parking lot. Departing guests don't usually make me jealous, but right about now, skipping out the door and down to Newport Harbor for the night sounds a whole boatload better than an evening of dusting—my punishment for interrupting Trent's tour.

Especially after an entire afternoon under strict orders to stay put in the attic. Okay, that isn't actually the "Cinderella locked up by the evil stepmother" scenario it sounds like, since we converted the servants' quarters up there into an apartment for me and Dad, and it's really bright and airy, not dusty and dark like most attics. Plus, it has access to the amazing roof deck. So not exactly a prison sentence. But still.

I hate being told that I have to stay in one place. I'm usually given free rein to roam about all I want. But no. Not today. And all because palm-licking Trent went straight above my dad's head and complained to the president of the Antiquities Society about my butting in on his precious tour. I tried with the damage control, but this is maybe the thousand-millionth time my dad has warned me to stay out of the docents' way when they're giving tours, and it turns out the thousand-millionth time is Dad's breaking point. Who knew?

At least they didn't fire him, so there's that. I guess I'll have plenty of occasions to "reflect" on my actions while I spend the next month on extra dusting duty. And I quote: "You're going to get every painting in the ballroom, from top to bottom. Yes, all the way to the top. I don't care that you need the ladder."

I tried to tell my dad that Trent was giving the guests the wrong information, but all I got was a sad headshake and, "You forget, sweetie. I work for the Antiquities Society. They allow us to live here, but it's not because it's a requirement for the job. They could just as easily house me in an apartment downtown." And, "The Antiquities Society likes to use esteemed locals as docents as much as possible, and Trent comes from a very old Rhode Island family."

Blah, blah, blah. People (even kids!) who come from lesser-known Rhode Island families can have just as much to contribute. Just saying.

When I hear the front desk manager turn the bolt on the door, I jump into action and head for the drawing room. The stepladder hides out behind heavy curtains draping one of the windows, where guests won't see it during tours. I carry it over the carpeting, being extra careful not to drag it and damage a bazillion-dollar Oriental rug. Then I adjust the ladder in front of the sideboard below my favorite picture—the one of Maggie Dunlap. If I have to endure death by dusting, I'm at least gonna start with the best part of the room.

Even though I'm super-annoyed with Trent, I would never take any of that anger out on the house or its artifacts. As much as I might pout to Dad about the docents, I love everything else about being here. There's something about living in the middle of history that makes me feel like I'm part of something way bigger than me.

I gaze up at Maggie's portrait. It hangs above this

really elaborately painted sideboard. People back then (or at least the people who owned the Newport mansions) were pretty cool to hang their paintings in front of giant mirrors, because the backs of the frames get reflected, so they look kind of 3-D.

Maggie's picture doesn't even need that trick to feel lifelike, though. She seems ready to walk right out of the frame. I stare at her, like I always do, wondering what it would have been like to be her. Or even to be friends with her. I'll bet she was amazing. I'll bet she never felt halfway in her own time and halfway caught up in the lives of people who lived a hundred years ago. Why would she, when her own day and age must have been magical?

It's not that I don't love my dad and my friends and my life, but I'll just bet everyone who knew Margaret Dunlap respected *her* and treated *her* like her opinion mattered. What would that feel like?

I study her hands, folded neatly in the lap of her butter-yellow dress. They're so delicate. I'll bet they were soft. I'll bet she never did a day of dusting in her life. I'll bet *she* wouldn't have gotten in trouble for adding an entirely appropriate and accurate anecdote to a tour!

But this is my life, not Maggie's, and I have a punishment to live out. Even if it means spending the next two hours wiping down places that no guest will ever even see, let alone touch. Ugh. I climb up the stepladder and catch my foot in the hinge, almost toppling onto the wide lacquered top of the buffet sideboard.

"Oooopf." I grab the scalloped edge of the priceless piece of furniture that dates practically back to the days of the Pilgrims. An ancient Chinese vase to my left wobbles once, twice, three times before I can steady it with shaking fingers. Phew! If I break something . . . But that thought is way too horrible to even finish thinking. I would seriously be extinct, and Dad would totally lose his job.

This is going to be waaay harder than I thought. I whip the folded feather duster out of my back pocket and open it, but even fully stretched out, I can reach only the bottom of the gilded frame. Although, this is still tons closer than I usually get to the painting. Looking up, I can see more detail than I ever could from the floor. From this angle I can practically see into Maggie's eyes. Forget her eyes. I can basically see up her nose!

For a second I wonder if maybe Dad had ulterior motives when he dished out this punishment. He knows getting up close and personal with the artifacts is my favorite thing in the world. I just love how these objects that meant so much to people so long ago can still affect people today. I know they're just *things*, but they make me feel like the people who came before me are still talking to me through them. Ugh. That sounds super-cheesy.

"Do you think I'm loony tunes, Maggie?"

So, yes. Sometimes I talk to a painting.

She stares back, but her eyes are so friendly, I decide she doesn't think I'm crazy at all.

I sigh. "It must have been so unbelievable to live when you did. All those balls, and parties, and to-die-for dresses. I'll bet everyone treated you with respect. I'll bet you got to do anything your heart desired. *You* were an American princess, after all."

As I chat away, I use my duster to get into the tiny crevices and swirls carved into her fancy gilded frame. I don't usually pay close attention to the mirrors behind the paintings—they're just your basic ones, except for the extra-fancy frames, and cleaning all that glass is someone else's job, thank God!—but this time something catches my eye. Most of the mirrors around here have what I call age spots, little blobs of black discolorations that reflective glass gets over time. Nothing out of the ordinary about them. But *this* blob's shape looks exactly like an old-timey skeleton key, and I never noticed that before. I mean, I know sometimes people claim they see the face of Jesus in the burnt parts of their toast, but a key?

That's . . . different.

I can't make out the very right edge of the age spot because Maggie's portrait is hanging over it. I try to tilt the frame away from the mirror, but it's too dark behind there to see much.

Do I dare?

I look around to make sure I'm alone. What I'm considering doing is sooo not allowed. Taking a priceless artifact down from its hanging spot? Frowned upon. In a BIG way. As in, my dad would have an aneurysm. Then again, this *is* only a reproduction, so it's not exactly priceless, right?

Gently—so, so gently—I lift the frame off the hooks. I sway a little under the weight. Who knew frames were so heavy? Bending at my knees, I lower it carefully to the sideboard, where I lean it propped against the mirror. I straighten back up so that I'm eye level with the age spot blob. Now that I can see the rest of the design, it is unbelievably amazing how much it looks like the outline of an old-fashioned key. Which is the weirdest thing.

I reach my fingers up to touch it.

Chapter Four

Maggie

THE FOYER IS MY FAVORITE ROOM IN the cottage. There is so much promise in a room that welcomes you to the rest of the residence. The marble columns, the tapestry with the dancing unicorn, the urn from the Ming dynasty—they all beckon to guests to experience the rest of the magical house. Unfortunately, lingering in the foyer is another thing not allowed (unless you are a guest, waiting for the mistress).

My meeting with Mademoiselle Cassatt is supposed to take place in the conservatory. It's an odd relationship. I've spent so much time with her while sitting for the portrait, but she's always speaking in French to her assistant.

I have taken French lessons for years, but they speak so fast, and often in whispers I can't hear. Every time I try to ask a question, I'm told to sit still and keep quiet.

I long to be able to ask questions and get answers.

I pass through the ballroom into the drawing room, toward my appointment, and something catches my attention. A flicker in my side vision. I glance up to see my favorite Newport seascape perched over an ornate mirror. Something in the corner moved, I'm sure of it. I glance toward the conservatory, half expecting Aunt to emerge. Looking back at the picture, I see it again— movement in the corner of the mirror. Do I dare investigate? I would do anything to stall for a few more minutes, but what I'm considering is definitely against the rules.

Sometimes I catch Aunt looking at me with sad eyes. I think it's because I remind her of my mother, her sister-in-law, and I hope those tender feelings will help her to forgive me for what I'm about to do.

I know where Mr. Birch keeps the step stool for dusting the high mirrors, and it takes only a quick minute to drag out. I feel a thrill at doing something so . . . unexpected. Climbing up onto the sideboard over which the painting and the mirror backdrop hang, I admire the brushstrokes in the seascape. The harbor looks so beautiful in the painting—like I can almost reach out and touch the wispy clouds. Sometimes I wish I could escape into this seascape instead of being cooped up in the house, being obedient. I can almost feel the wind on my face. It's a shame this painting will be replaced by my portrait. I wonder where this one will go. Maybe Aunt will let me hang it in my room.

Then at the edge of my vision—between the painting and the mirrored glass underneath—something moves again. Like a shadow. I carefully push the painting, which is hanging from hooks in the ceiling, aside as far as I dare, bracing for a giant spider to be the culprit. Aunt Herminie will not be pleased if she catches me touching the artwork, let alone climbing on the furniture, but I lean closer. There's something there, a smudge, a shadow of some kind. I glance behind me to scan the room. When I look back at the section of the mirror, I get the shock of my life. Someone is looking back, like through a window. . . .

And it is not me.

Chapter Five

Hannah

OH. MY. GODDESS.

    I'm squinting into the mirror, and, yes, I'm still looking at the same ballroom behind me.

And there's a girl staring back at me in the mirror, all right. . . .

But she's *definitely not me*!

In fact, she looks like a spot-on, dead ringer for . . . Margaret Dunlap. She's wearing the same dress from the painting (except it's green, not yellow, which is hardly the strangest thing about this scenario).

Mirror-Maggie blinks in surprise and cocks her head to the side as she looks into the glass. Wait, *can she see me?*

"Great, first I talk to inanimate paintings, and now

I'm having visions. Crazytown, here I come," I mutter. "Does spicy bean dip ever cause hallucinations? Because if so, I'd better lay off any more of Dad's. Going loco is *not* going to help me get all this dusting done."

"Pardon? I . . . Are you speaking to me?"

Omigod, Mirror-Maggie is talking! To me, I think!

I . . . This . . . What . . . ?

No. Way.

Mirror-Maggie has a forehead that's as scrunched up as mine must be. She reaches a hand out slowly, hesitating before laying it on the mirror right on top of the key shape. I can't help tilting my head in the opposite direction as my own hand comes up. I place my fingertips right against hers, and . . .

Chapter Six

Maggie

AS I SIT UP FROM THE PARQUET FLOOR,
it takes a moment for me to realize I have fallen
off the sideboard in the drawing room. I scratch
my head, trying to remember what happened. I was trying to get a better look at the painting being replaced by
my portrait. I rub the bump on my head again, hoping
there's no bruise that will show.

I thought I saw something. Someone. In the mirror.
But no, that can't be right.

I don't remember slipping, but that's the only explanation for being down here, staring at the underside of
the furniture.

When my head clears, I get shakily to my feet. Aunt

Herminie expects me to report to the conservatory to meet with Mademoiselle Cassatt presently, but first I notice a framed painting tilted dangerously against the mirror above the sideboard.

"What in tarnation?" I slap my hand over my mouth. If Aunt hears me swear, I'll really be in trouble. Especially the day before the big ball to unveil my portrait.

My hand still covering my mouth, I stand on tiptoes to see the painting. It looks exactly like the one I've been sitting for with Mademoiselle Cassatt. Except . . . except my dress should be green. Not that horrid shade of yellow.

Why in heaven's name would she change the color of my dress at such a late date? And why is the portrait here and not in the conservatory, where Aunt and I are supposed to be seeing it in its finished form for the first time? I specifically remember Mademoiselle Cassatt preferring the light in there for the occasion of our first glimpse at it.

Out of habit I reach to touch my lucky locket as I sink back to the floor. It's not hanging around my neck. For a terrifying second I'm afraid I've lost it. I must have left it on my dresser. But something else isn't right.

The neckline of my dress feels strange.

A wave of fear flows over me, and gooseflesh emerges

on my forearms. I didn't notice before, but now, looking down at myself, I see that my entire wardrobe is wrong. First of all, I'm wearing trousers. Trousers? I once saw a picture in a book of a woman wearing trousers, but it's not proper. It's indecent. I feel the fabric. Denim? The only people I've ever seen wearing denim are the cowboys in the Wild West show that Father took me to when I was ten, and those men were dusty and dirty. This denim is light blue and soft. My blouse is soft too, with words written on it. It says, *Well-Behaved Women Seldom Make History.*

I rub my eyes. "How hard did I hit my head?"

Chapter Seven

Hannah

I SIT UP ON THE FLOOR. WHOA. I DON'T remember falling off the stepladder, but I must have kicked it out of the way as I crashed, since there's zip, zero ladder in sight. I rub my eyes. The early-evening sun is still strong because it's summertime, and it streams through the windows. Wait. What happened to the velvet cording that ropes off the furniture in the middle of the room so that none of the visitors try to plop their butts onto priceless antiques?

"There you are, young lady."

I turn my head to see a woman bustling into the room. Her hair is drawn up away from her face in a superelaborate arrangement of curls, and the long skirts on her fancy dress swish as she glides toward me. As far as I can tell, it's a spot-on, early-twentieth-century Edwardian-period costume. I rub my eyes again. We have character actors in the mansion only a few times a year, and I'm one thousand percent sure there are no events like that scheduled for months. What the heck is going on?

"We're waiting for you," the lady says, stopping right in front of me with her hands on her hips.

"Well?" she asks when I don't answer.

She drops down to her knees. "Are you feeling unwell, my dear?" She reaches out to touch my forehead. "You look a bit flushed. Did you have a fainting spell?"

A what? Who has fainting spells anymore? Who *is* this woman? She looks an awful lot like pictures I've seen of—but no. Not possible.

"I . . . I was trying to get a closer look at that . . ." I gesture to where Maggie's portrait usually hangs. "I thought I saw . . ." I shake my head at the memory. "And then I fell."

"Goodness, what were you thinking?" the woman asks. "Did you use Mr. Birch's stool to— Now, I know for a fact that you've been raised to conduct yourself in a manner more becoming of a lady. Climbing is for monkeys and little boys! Whatever possessed you?"

"I . . . Huh?"

"Come now." The woman stands up and holds out her hand to help me up. "We mustn't dawdle. We have an appointment that I, for one, am quite eager to keep. We'll discuss this behavior later."

I grasp her hand and wobble to my feet. It's only then that I realize that I'm wearing a sea-foam-green calf-length taffeta dress with more ruffles than the bed skirt in the Rose Room on the second floor. My feet are covered from my toes to past my ankles in dainty leather boots. In July.

And they don't feel like my feet. My hands don't even *look* like my hands. Since when have I been able to grow actual fingernails without biting them down to stubs? Since never, that's when. And I swear I got shorter.

Say what?

What is happening here?

Chapter Eight

Maggie

I HAVE ONLY BEGUN TO PONDER THE strangeness of my situation, when my hip bone buzzes. It's like an electric shock of some kind! I stumble into the grand ballroom as I scramble to find the source of the buzzing. There's a small device in the pocket of my trousers, unlike anything I've ever seen. I turn it over in my hand. A picture of a man and the word "DAD" appear on the glass. I shiver. My uncle has all kinds of new electronic thingamajigs in this house. But I've never seen someone's likeness reproduced in vivid color—and mounted on glass like this. It's as though I could almost reach into the device and touch the man's face, it looks so real.

The device buzzes in my hand, until I drop it and it slides under the gilded grand piano in the corner, where it continues to vibrate.

I must be in some sort of fugue state where I changed my clothing and don't remember. It's the only explanation. But it doesn't explain the strange device. And how am I aware of it? If I were in a fugue state, I wouldn't think I'd be alert enough to know.

I turn in a circle. The ballroom has not yet been set for the ball, but it looks the way it often does for summer entertaining—with chairs set in several groupings for casual conversations. I take in the elaborate mirrors that dominate the room, the Louis XV–style paneling my aunt loves so much, the full-size portrait of Lady Elizabeth Drexel Lehr and one of her dogs. . . .

Wait. I don't remember that portrait. I step closer. It is most definitely a glamorous portrait of Elizabeth Lehr, the mistress of the cottage across the street from The Elms. Why would Aunt put that in such a prominent location? A placard on the ornate table beneath it proclaims the artist to be Giovanni Boldini. Aunt loves to showcase her art collection, but I've never known her to advertise the artist in that manner.

I stumble away from the portrait and shuffle out of

the ballroom, through the drawing room, and cross into the conservatory. (On top of everything else, I'm not even wearing shoes. Aunt Herminie will be scandalized when she sees me!)

I marvel at thick velvet ropes that seem to delineate a walking path through the rooms. That's strange. I don't recall them being there before; maybe Aunt has just added them to remind the servants not to walk on the carpet?

Ignoring one of the ropes, I flounce onto the cushion of a chaise longue. Flouncing works so much better in my regular clothes. I close my eyes, hoping this is some sort of dream from which I'll awaken. Mademoiselle Cassatt is nowhere to be seen. She is usually set up and tapping her foot, waiting for me.

A few minutes later I crack open one of my eyes. It's no good; no matter how I try, I'm still lying on a chaise in the conservatory. The white marble floor gleams. All the cherub statues are in their places, and yet there's something not quite right. A card game is set out on a glass-topped table. Aunt Herminie would be horrified; she hates it when guests set up bridge games in such a public spot in the house.

And I'm still extremely aware of wearing trousers. This isn't a fugue state. As much as I don't want Aunt

Herminie to see me in bare feet and trousers, there's something very wrong with me and I need to find her. I push myself off the chair to go in search of help.

"Aunt?" I call, walking back through the large rooms of the mansion, recalling that the last time I saw her, she was in the breakfast room, instructing Mr. Birch on the proper care of a new tea set.

I have to pass through the dining room, and as I do—ignoring the fact that it is not yet set for dinner and there are no servants in sight—I notice a small device on the ceiling flashing a red light. More of Uncle E. J.'s fascination with electricity, but I've never noticed that before. Incredible. This new century is certainly a time of rapid technological developments.

Up till now I have managed not to panic. Aunt will know what is happening to me. I just need to find her. But as I feared, she is not in the breakfast room. I dash into the pantry and then back through the dining room and out into the foyer.

I stand there, absolutely still. There is no sound. The house is silent.

"Aunt Herminie?" I run up the grand staircase, marveling—even through my growing panic—at how easy it is to move in trousers. Aunt insists that proper young ladies do not run; she never minds when visiting children run on the grounds, but even so, she says I'm "getting to an age." Right now I don't care. I just want to find her so she can tell me this is all a nightmare.

There's no one. Anywhere. There are a half dozen guests staying here this weekend and several more in the guesthouses on the other side of the estate. And at least forty servants preparing for the ball tomorrow night. But all the bedrooms are empty. And they all have that strange rope across their entrances. And the smell. Or really, no smell. Instead of the fragrant hint of Aunt's favorite roses, there is a distinct lack of smell. Like these rooms are not occupied at all.

Taking a deep breath to stall the hysteria bubbling up inside me, I resist the idea of going to bed in my own room. This horrible nightmare started in the drawing room when I looked at the mirror behind the seascape, so I decide to go back downstairs. I scratch at the spot on my head where a bump the size of an egg has blossomed.

That's it.

I hit my head when I fell, and this is just a dream. Clearly that is what is happening. I must be dreaming. Maybe if I go back downstairs, I'll wake up and all will be right. I need to see that mirror again.

Chapter Nine

Hannah

SOMETHING THAT *FREAKY FRIDAY* MOVIE I watched at my best friend Tara's sleepover last winter neglected to hammer home: walking around in someone else's body feels super-weird.

That's about the extent of what I've been able to piece together about this crazy-whoa-I-don't-know-what that's happening right now, but it's the only explanation that makes any sense. Because how else could I explain why I'm suddenly shorter and paler, with hair that's way curlier than mine has ever been? Speaking of eyes, whoever belongs to this body should probably see an optometrist about this nearsighted thing she's got going on. Plus, she must have had a *whole* lot of water to drink recently, since I'm getting pretty uncomfortable here. I'm trying to hold it, because using the bathroom in someone else's body feels like it would be a huge violation of her privacy, but . . .

Like I said, it's all pretty weird.

Something else I've figured out all on my own: corsets = barbaric torture devices. No wonder no one is smiling in old-timey pictures.

My brain is working overtime as I trail the lady in the long dress into the conservatory, where another woman is hovering over a framed painting propped against an easel. It's turned around so that the back of the picture is facing us.

"Ah, *c'est bon*! You have arrived! I am so eager for you to see the finished result. I pray you will be more than satisfied. This young lady was a wonderful subject!"

She lays a whopper of a smile on me, and the other lady pats my arm gently, before saying, "We're thrilled that you accepted our commission. It will be quite the honor to have your work hanging in our home."

If it weren't for the whole "I think I'm in someone else's body" thing, I would easily be able to convince myself that I somehow got mixed up in a TV show filming here at the house. Maybe one of those *Downton*

Abbey rip-offs. It would make perfect sense. The Elms has been used as the setting for bunches of Hollywood stuff. Once they even shot a Victoria's Secret commercial in our boiler rooms, only Dad wouldn't let me hang around the set because all the models were in their underwear and he didn't think it was "appropriate."

But there are no video cameras and no directors, and these people don't seem like they're acting. And of course, there's the whole "not my own body" thing. Which puts a wrinkle in every theory I have, except for the super-weird ones. For now I'll play along as best I can until I can figure out what the heck is going on.

So I curtsy. The dress I'm wearing seems like one someone should curtsy in.

Both women smile, and the lady next to the easel picks up the frame and carefully turns it to face us.

I gasp!

It's the portrait of Margaret Dunlap!

And everything about it matches the one I've visited every day of my life, except for the color of the dress. Which is not daffodil yellow but sea-foam green. The same sea-foam green of the dress I'm wearing right now. The same dress *entirely* as the one I have on now.

Does that mean . . .

"Oh, Mademoiselle Cassatt! It's breathtaking!" the lady next to me exclaims.

Mademoiselle Cassatt? As in Mary Cassatt?!? As in the artist who painted Maggie's portrait?

"Maggie, pet? Are you going to gape with your mouth open, or do you have some words for Mademoiselle Cassatt about your portrait? Do you simply adore it, as I do?" The woman nudges my arm, gently at first, and then with more force when I don't respond immediately.

"Um, yes. It's, er, wowza!" I manage to sputter, because my brain is tripping over thoughts now.

The woman by my side scrunches her forehead and whispers, "Wowza? What in the heavens kind of expression is that, Margaret, and whomever did you pick it up from?"

I open and close my mouth like a fish, thoughts still whirring.

Finally one clear thought floats out of my brain muck: *You're Maggie Dunlap.*

I'm Maggie Dunlap?

I'M MAGGIE DUNLAP!

Chapter Ten

Maggie

WHEN I GET BACK TO THE DRAWING
room, the first thing I notice is a small stepladder next to the sideboard. Disregarding
the fact that it is not made of wood, as it should be, I
climb up to where the seascape is supposed to hang. But
instead it's that portrait of me—which isn't to have been
unveiled yet—off its moorings, leaning against the mirror it should be hanging in front of.

I crawl onto the sideboard to get a better look, and
almost fall off the edge again at the sight of a girl staring
back at me from the glass. She's got *my* face and she's
wearing the clothes I remember putting on this morning.

But she's not me.

"There you are!" she exclaims. She seems to be trying for a whisper, but it comes out a good bit louder. "OMG . . . finally! I've been crossing fingers supertight that you'd come back to the mirror! You can hear me, right?"

I sit up straighter. "Of course I can hear you. This is my dream, is it not?"

"What?" she asks with a nervous titter. But then she looks around with a panicked expression. When she turns back, she seems relieved, but she's no longer laughing. "Quickly, before your aunt comes back. You *are* Maggie Dunlap, right?"

I nod. "No one except Aunt Herminie and Father calls me Maggie. But yes. And who, pray tell, are you? And why are you talking with my face?"

"This is so whackadoodle." The odd girl shakes her head. She looks as bemused as I feel. "*You're* talking with *my* face. Did you know?" When I don't answer, she continues. "The only thing I can figure out is that somehow we've traded places. I live at The Elms with my father—in the twenty-first century. We're the caretakers, and it's a historical museum maintained by the Newport Antiquities Society."

"That's preposterous." Although, with all the strange

happenings, this is an explanation that makes as much sense as anything else I've thought of.

"I know, right? But I think we, like, time traveled. You've zoomed forward. I've jumped backward." The girl with my face looks around again as though she's nervous about being caught.

I perk up at the mention of something I recognize. "You mean like that wonderful story by H. G. Wells? *The Time Machine* is one of my favorite books. But that's just made up."

"Believe me, I thought the same exact thing. But how else can we explain how *I'm* here and *you're* there?" She lowers her voice. "I dunno how it happened; I just touched that black spot on the mirror, and presto bingo, I ended up here."

"I remember now!" I shout at her, and then instantly cover my mouth with my hand before saying more quietly, "I thought I saw something flicker in the mirror behind the seascape, so I moved it to see better—then I saw you looking back at me! I tried to touch you, but then I fell!"

The girl nods. "Yep, same for me. Okay, your aunt will be back in a sec, so listen up. I don't know about you, but I've dreamed my whole life of seeing this place when it was actually lived in. I was even wishing it right before we switched. So, I mean, when fate delivers, you gotta embrace that, right?"

I can barely process her words. What is she suggesting?

"I—" I begin, but she talks right over me, as if she's never had an etiquette lesson in her life.

"I'm just saying, this had to have happened for a reason, so I say we go with it for a day before we swap back, ya know? You can totally explore the future and I can see if your time is everything I imagined. Perfect, right?"

I'm not feeling perfect about this at all, but I'm so taken aback, I can only nod.

She grins. "Okay, so from here on out, you have to be me and I have to be you, so no one suspects a thing. My dad will probs be calling you for dinner soon. Then we usually watch TV till we crash. Just go with the flow. Let's meet up here at . . ." She pats at the pockets of her—no, *my*—dress. "Man, it sucks not having my phone."

Did she just call me a man? She gazes over at what I'm sure is the clock on the mantel on her side of the mirror. "Meet me here at seven a.m. It's gotta be before the house opens for visitors." She smiles. "You look like me, but you sure don't talk like me. Just try to keep your head down and stay out of trouble until we can chat again."

Just then she gasps, says "Gotta go," and jumps off the sideboard.

She's gone. I don't even know her name.

She said to keep my head down? How is that going to help? And what in heaven's name is TeeVee?

I slide off the sideboard and spin around in a circle, taking in the antique Chinese vase, the crystal chandelier, the expansive parquet floor, the marble-topped sideboards, the winged cherubs on the ceiling, the seventeenth-century furniture. It looks exactly as it should, so my first impulse is to believe that I am still having that same dream and the girl in the mirror is just some sort of figment of my imagination. She said it was the twenty-first century. One hundred years into the future. Can it be true? As much as I love Mr. Wells's book about time travel, I can't believe it. It's just foolishness. Maybe the clams in Chef's chowder at lunch didn't agree with me.

But then I remember the ropes and the red light on the ceiling and the emptiness of the house. And the device I found in my pocket and tossed away. I run back into the ballroom and glance under the piano; it's still there. It's not ladylike, but I don't care about what my aunt would say right now; I crawl underneath to retrieve it and misjudge how much space I have. I bang my head on the exact spot of the bump. Is it possible that the new body I'm in is taller than my own?

Tossing that thought aside, I crouch under the piano with my elbows on my knees and turn the object over in my hand. It's about the size of a deck of cards. Where did the picture go? When I touch the glass front, it lights up again in full color. With shaking hands I stuff it back into the pocket of the trousers. Twenty-first-century technology isn't something I can manage right now. I have a sudden need to find a person. A real, live, in-the-flesh person. As though the universe hears me, a voice booms from the foyer.

"Hannah!"

I freeze. The girl's name must be Hannah. She mentioned her father. This has to be him. Do I dare pretend to be someone else? I consider my options. If this is a waking dream, what does it matter? On the other hand, if I have really traveled forward in time and look like Hannah, pretending to be her might be my only way back home.

"Here I am." I crawl out from under the piano just

as the man enters the ballroom. He kneels down so we're at the same level. His soft brown eyes remind me of Uncle E. J. His blouse is the same fabric as the one I'm wearing, and the words across the front exclaim, *Life Is Good*. He's also wearing denim trousers.

Do all people wear denim in the twenty-first century?

"You all right, Bug?" he asks, a small smile lighting up his face. When I don't answer, he continues, "You know how much I hate to punish you."

He leans forward, trying to make eye contact. "I just need you to promise me you'll stay away from the tours. Even though we both know you could be a better docent than some of them. Do we have a deal? You'll keep away from them? Promise?"

This sounds like an apology, but I can't make any sense of his meaning. So I don't say anything. He's waiting for a reply, though, so I smile back and nod my head slightly. Hopefully it will be enough.

It seems to do the trick.

"Tell you what!" He slaps his thigh, which makes me startle, and he jumps up, holding out his hand. "I'm commuting your sentence for the evening. We'll do delivery. I'll order a giant pie from Nikolas Pizza. The regular? Half cheese for you and the other half Hawaiian for me?

And your favorite Greek salad, dripping with olives? We'll settle in for the night and watch some *Doctor Who*."

He is speaking English, I know that. But I have no idea what he means by "delivery." I do understand "pizza," however. I had a slice last fall when Father took me to the World's Fair in Saint Louis. I loved it.

"That sounds delightful." I take his offered hand and stand up, brushing myself off. "But why do we need to see a doctor?"

Hannah's father laughs, a deep throaty one that makes me smile despite my confusion. He tousles my hair. "Fabulous, buddy. Just wonderful. But I think you need to work on your British accent. C'mon!"

He leads me through the foyer and down the hall toward the servants' staircase. When I grab the smooth wood, I cringe at the memory of Mrs. O'Neil's scolding just a short time ago.

We continue past the butler's pantry and still we climb, past the second floor, where my bedroom and all the other private quarters are located.

I've never in a million years dared use this stairwell to go all the way to the third floor, which is strictly off-limits, so when we start climbing toward the upper floors, I have to hide my surprise. Normally at this time of day, this corridor is bustling with lady's maids and valets going up and down from the kitchen to the living spaces to help the guests dress for dinner.

We finally emerge in a simple hallway. I know this is the servants' quarters, though I've never been this high in the house. Hannah told me the mansion is a museum in the future. The caretaker and his daughter work here.

Oh my goodness. Am I a servant?

Chapter Eleven

Hannah

FOR AS LONG AS I CAN REMEMBER, I'VE daydreamed about what it would be like to live at The Elms during the Gilded Age. I've endured endless teasing from my friends for my obsession with all things early twentieth century, and I've watched every movie and read every book set in this time period. I pick Theodore Roosevelt for every school project we do on presidents. Last Halloween I trick-or-treated as his wife, Edith, which was cool even if no one could figure out who I was. So, now that I'm actually here, I'm for sure going to make the most of it.

Of course, it would be a lot more enjoyable if I were having tea on the terrace with the Berwinds, whom I at least know tons about, so I could fake it till I make it with them. Instead they're off dressing for some musicale (this gathering at someone's house where everyone stands around and listens to people play or sing), and I'm stuck hanging out with Maggie's cousin Colette and our nanny. I know absolutely nothing about either of them from my research into the family. Ugh.

My strategy is to keep as quiet as possible. Can't bust me if I don't speak, right? Luckily, Colette seems to want nothing to do with me. She's annoyed about some kind of dare, but I can't ask about it, because I'm sure Maggie would already know, and I have to *be* Maggie. Colette can't be that much older than me—maybe fifteen?—but I'm getting the distinct impression that she and Maggie aren't exactly the Taylor Swift and Selena Gomez BFF power duo of their time.

I play copycat, though, and lift my teacup to my mouth the same way she does, with my pinky finger out all fancy-like. It feels sort of weird to just sit here and look out over the lawn, while none of us are also scrolling through Instagram on our phones. Also, tea? Let's just say it's no caramel Frappuccino, even with all the sugar I dump in whenever the nanny turns away.

"Are you excited for the ball tomorrow, Miss

Margaret?" the nanny asks in her formal British accent.

Am I? I mean, *I* personally am *beyond* . . . but would Maggie be? Or is attending balls something she does every other night of the week? "Um, yeah, totally," I mumble.

The nanny gives Colette a weird look, and Colette just smirks back. Something tells me this woman came from New York with Colette and not with Maggie. She's treating me like I'm mostly a stranger. Which actually works to my advantage; maybe she won't notice how un-Maggie-like I really am.

I swipe at my sweaty forehead with the back of my arm, and the nanny gasps.

"Manners, miss!" she scolds.

What? It's mega-hot out here, and it's not like the AC is blasting inside either. Plus, between my dress with a billion layers underneath it and its long sleeves AND the white gloves I have on, it's a miracle I'm not melting into the stone terrace. I sigh and pretend to be realllly interested in my tea while Colette and the nanny start gossiping about some couple who tried to pass themselves off as members of the Four Hundred—which I know is the term that the "best of society" call themselves—at a horsing event and got super-busted by someone who actually was a member, and now the couple are social pariahs, whatever that means.

Ick. But at least they're ignoring me, so now I can spend some time thinking. The thing I can't get out of a loop in my head is *How did this happen?* And not just how, but *why* did this happen? Am I here for a reason? Like, in the *Freaky Friday* movie, the mom and kid switched bodies so they could learn to appreciate the other person's perspective and stop fighting so much. I know I might sometimes chat at Painting-Maggie, but I've never, ever raised my voice at her. I mean, please. Last winter Dad and I had an eighties movies day, and we watched *Back to the Future*, his favorite movie from when he was my age. That kid had to make sure his parents met and fell in love, to guarantee he'd eventually be born. But no one in my family tree even lived in Newport in 1905. So, what, then? Am I just here to see what life was like, the way I wished, or is there more to it?

I start by making a mental list of everything I know.

It's 1905. In the history of The Elms, this year is famous as the one when the painting of Maggie is stolen.

I landed in not just the same year but on the same *weekend* as the heist. That canNOT be a coincidence.

If it's not a coincidence, what does it mean?

I know when the painting is stolen, so I could stop it from happening.

WAIT. I'm so stupid. Of course, that HAS to be it.

That's why I'm here! That's what I'm supposed to do! It has to be, because it would be way too big a coincidence otherwise, and I don't believe in coincidences. (I also didn't believe in time travel before today, but whatevs.) I'm right—I feel it in my gut.

"Are you planning to sit like a bump on a log all evening, or do you intend to join our conversation?"

With Colette's words, I snap back to reality. Or, you know, this whackadoodle version of reality I'm currently stuck in.

"Huh?" I ask.

She cocks her head at me. "What on earth is 'huh'? You're acting entirely bizarre, Margaret." Colette practically spits my name.

"Huh? Oh, um, yeah, sorry. I mean, uh, what? Um, excuse me?" *Jeez, Hannah. Get it together. You know how people talked back then. Or would it be "back now"? Either way, you know how formal things are, including language.*

The nanny squints her eyes at me. "It's true; you're not acting yourself at all, dear. Shall I fetch you some cold water and some crackers?"

"No thank you. I'm sorry," I mumble. "I—I think it must be the heat."

"It is quite warm," she says. "Perhaps you should lie down for a spell inside."

"Perfect idea!" I say, springing up from the table.

Both of them shoot me a weird look.

Whoops. Maybe that was a little too enthusiastic, but now that I've figured out my goal, the next day and a half is all laid out in front of me like a giant adventure. I only hope Maggie is going to be okay sticking around in the future, because I *have* to do this. Even if no one in my time will ever know, because to them it will be as if the painting was never stolen in the first place. It doesn't matter. *I'll* know. And it will feel amazing to not just learn about history but to take part in it, in a real way! Glory will be mine . . . just as soon as I get my inner Nancy Drew on and solve this theft.

I wonder if I can make this a permanent gig, traveling through time to stop heists from happening. I've always wanted to see the Ming dynasty. We have a vase from that time period in The Elms. It's never been stolen, that I know of, but I'll bet something from back then was.

This is the coolest.

Really, it should be like stealing candy from a baby,

since I already know exactly who did it. All I have to do is stop this Jonah guy from being in the same room as the painting during the ball . . . and I have a plan for that already. I'm gonna find him and stick to him like glue for the entire day. He won't get within ten feet of the painting. Easy peasy lemon squeezy.

I ignore the little voice in my ear that whispers, *But, Hannah, you never believed it was Jonah who stole the painting.*

I mean, sure, I've always had my doubts about that particular theory put forth in all the history books. It's true he was the prime suspect, because he skipped town the morning after the heist and was never heard from again. Neither was the painting.

But if you read all the eyewitness accounts—and believe me, I have—every single person interviewed who knew him said they could never imagine someone as quiet and sweet embarking on a life of crime. No one could figure out how he'd have access to enough money to disappear so completely. Or who he could have been working with.

And then there is the kicker. Jonah was young. Not young from my perspective, because I happen to believe twelve-year-olds are capable of greatness as much as anyone else (and I'm not at all biased). But. Even I have to admit, twelve is pretty young to be the mastermind behind a huge, complicated theft and cover-up.

But he's the best—the only—lead I have, and I plan to investigate for myself.

As soon as I excuse myself from the World's Stuffiest Tea Party and am out of sight, I skip down the hall and veer right at the staircase. The room where Maggie's staying is most likely on the second floor by the Berwinds', but I'm not headed there. Nope. I'm going to trust that the nanny will be too busy continuing her gossiping to check on me anytime soon, so instead I point myself to the basement level, where the servants prepare meals. Where the kitchen boy works. Luckily, the coast is clear, because I'm guessing that fraternizing with the help might be frowned upon.

Obviously, I know Maggie wouldn't spend much time here, but in the movies the president is always sneaking into the White House kitchens for a midnight snack, and in those British upstairs-downstairs dramas I'm obsessed with, the lord and lady of the house slip down to visit the servants from time to time. So hopefully my showing up won't be a giant big deal or anything. I'm sure Maggie must come here sometimes, because, just going by her eyes in the portrait, she doesn't seem like someone who'd get all caught up in class differences or anything. I mean, I know it's not her fault that she lives in this day and age, when servants are totally treated like, well, servants . . . and I can't imagine Maggie being like that.

"Miss Margaret!" A woman wearing a black dress with a white collar and a cardigan sweater gasps loudly when she sees me. "I thought we talked about this!"

Um, okay, so maybe Maggie doesn't do the whole "just popping in to say hi" thing on a regular basis.

"Hello!" I say, nice and cheerfully. "I'm, uh, I'm just looking for . . . for . . ." *Think, Hannah, think. What would Nancy Drew do?* "Well, the thing is, I need someone strong to help me with . . . with . . . moving a desk in my room, and I've heard there's a guy named Jonah who works down here and might be able to lend some muscle to the job."

The woman turns pinker than that Zombie Pigman in *Minecraft*. "Beg pardon, Miss Margaret, but I don't believe it would be appropriate for Jonah to accompany a proper young lady such as yourself into your chambers."

Oh, ugh. Didn't think that one through.

"Heavens no!" I say, trying to sound positively scandalized. "When I said 'my room,' I really meant the hallway outside of it, of course."

A kid about my age steps out from behind the stove, a wrench in his hand and dirt on his face. "I'm Jonah, miss."

This is Jonah? I mean, I expected him to be young, but not so shy and timid. He looks like the kind of person who'd rescue spiders instead of squashing them. His hair is floppy and nearly covers his eyes, which are soft and quiet and very *un*-criminal-like.

I stretch out my arm for a handshake, and he blushes about ten shades of red before wiping his dirty palms on his pant legs. He stares at my hand and hesitates, then finally ignores it and gives a little bow instead.

"Pleased to make your acquaintance, miss."

He shuffles his feet and glances at the woman in the apron, who gives him a small smile and a nod. Then he exhales and begins turning the wrench over and over in his fingers, like I make him nervous or something.

I am having a really tough time believing that the history books got this one right, but I force myself to be objective. Just because someone seems shy and very, very normal doesn't mean they're not hiding a devious side.

And it's up to me to discover it.

Once again I ignore the little prickle on my arms and that whispery voice in my ear. The one that's saying, *But, Hannah, what if the history books got it wrong?*

Chapter Twelve

Maggie

A HALF HOUR LATER, AFTER A YOUNG man delivers food to the back door (Hannah's father handed me some money and sent me back downstairs to pay the boy for the food—imagine!), we are seated on a comfortable divan in what he calls the living room. The twenty-first century is odd; my father would never in a million years imagine sitting with me so informally and eating without a proper place setting.

"May I have one more piece, please?" I ask, dabbing at the corners of my mouth with my paper napkin and returning it delicately to my lap. At least I can maintain some pretense of manners.

He furrows his brow as I fold my hands, waiting for his answer. "Well, I'm not the maid," he says finally with a chuckle. "Help yourself." He points to the box holding the pizza on the low table in front of us.

I pause, but since he's right—there are no servants in sight—I reach for another piece of the pizza. This time I feel brave enough to help myself to a slice of the other side, the one with the pineapple and cubes of ham.

A bemused expression crosses the father's face. "Since when do you like Hawaiian pizza?"

When I don't answer, he frowns. "Are you feeling okay? You've been awfully quiet tonight. And your manners are shockingly impressive." The tiniest of smiles plays on his lips, but I'm not sure if he's making fun of me or if he's serious.

I stop, slice of pizza poised in front of my mouth, still wondering what he means by "Hawaiian." He can't possibly mean this pizza comes from the new United States territory in the middle of the North Pacific.

Blast it!

Hannah must not eat this type of pizza. My brain scrambles for a reply. I think about something Aunt said to me on our tour of France last summer, and it seems appropriate.

"It's important to try something new every day." My voice goes up at the end of the sentence, like I'm asking a question. Of course, Aunt meant it in the context of trying caviar—fish eggs—for the first time, not meat-laden pizza.

"Okay." He nods. "I like your new attitude." Then he laughs again. "I guess you were hungry too! This is your fourth piece."

Maybe it's a symptom of time travel, but land sakes, I feel like I haven't eaten in a century.

I swallow my mouthful of cheese before I speak. "It's delicious, thank you very much." Aunt would disapprove if she could see me sharing a meal with a strange man, but she'd be proud that I haven't forgotten my manners. "Even better than I remember."

I freeze, realizing a moment too late that I've said the wrong thing.

But he only nods. "I know. This is definitely better than the pizza we had down on the pier last time."

He stands up and gestures to a piece of black glass framed on the wall. "So, what'll it be tonight? Are we going with a classic *Who*, or something more recent?"

I adjust the napkin in my lap as I pretend to think about the question, which makes no sense. So I say the only thing that comes to mind. "Why don't you pick?"

"Fair enough." He seems to ponder the issue but then jumps to attention, like he's changed his mind about something. He sits back down. "Sweetheart, before we watch the show, I wanted to have a talk. You know I was very angry with you earlier." He pauses, as though he's expecting me to react, but continues when I don't.

"I hope you understand that it's not because I don't want you to be excited about history or this house. I'm thrilled that you love living here. I've been waiting for the right time to surprise you, but this might be the perfect way to cheer you up."

I nod because it seems like the proper thing to do. "I do love surprises. Who doesn't?" I say, before taking another modest bite of pizza.

Hannah's father takes a breath and then speaks again. "You know how the house is going to be shut down for a couple of weeks when the art historian does the restoration work on the murals? Instead of laying low and hanging out, I thought maybe we'd use the opportunity to take that trip to Los Angeles we've been talking about. We leave Tuesday morning!"

The glass I'm holding drops to the ground, splashing milk everywhere. If not for the carpet, the glass would have shattered. A half-eaten morsel of pineapple is lodged in my throat, and I can't swallow.

After a momentary bolt of panic, I catch my breath and swallow my food. I don't need to worry about leaving on Tuesday. I'll be back home before then; Hannah assured me.

"I know you're excited, but try not to break stuff." He rushes to the kitchen and then sprints back holding a towel. "What's up with you tonight, anyway? Everyone says the teen years are unpredictable, but you're not even thirteen yet." He picks up the glass and starts blotting up milk with the towel. "Please tell me this isn't what the next seven years have in store for me. Give me some warning at least, will you?" He stops to gauge my reaction, looking like he's not sure himself if he's joking.

"Are you going to say anything?" he asks.

I'm thinking how lovely it is for Hannah to be taking a trip with her father, but I keep my mouth closed.

"I thought you were dying to see the Hollywood sign and the Walk of Fame." He frowns, standing with his hands on his hips and staring at me. "We could drive up to San Francisco once we land, I suppose, if you'd rather. We can talk about going anywhere you like; it just has to be on the West Coast. I bought the tickets for the flight with last month's paycheck." He tousles my hair as he moves the empty pizza box to the floor next to the table. "But we don't have a choice. We have to vacate for two weeks." He sighs. "I expected you to be happy to have two weeks taken off your month-long dusting duty."

"That sounds . . . fine." I think about my own father, busy with his law firm. He travels from New York to San Francisco by train often, but even before Mother died, he rarely took me on trips. He relies on Aunt Herminie and Uncle E. J. to introduce me to faraway places. "Wait. Did you say 'flight'? Do you mean you're going to fly?"

I know men have experimented with flying machines; Uncle was excited the summer before last about some brothers in North Carolina managing to get their machine off the ground. But I'm not daft; the only ways to get to California from Rhode Island are by train or steamer ship sailing around the tip of South America.

For the first time, I imagine Hannah living in my body and wonder if she's having as hard a time adjusting as I am. I wonder if Aunt has noticed that her speech is different from mine.

Hannah's father chuckles, but this time his laughter is accompanied by a confused look. "I can tell I surprised you," he says slowly. "And I'm sorry. We can talk about this in the morning. Let's see what our favorite Time Lord is up to." He picks up a small device from the coffee table and points it at the wall on his way toward the kitchen with the towel and glass.

Light and color and pictures come alive in the frame, and for a moment I forget everything else. It is moving pictures—like a window into another world. Is this what Hannah called TeeVee? An instant later there's sound. Someone singing about constipation, of all things. Then a bunch of people dancing around a red-and-white bull's-eye while loud music, such that I've never heard, plays. I'm horrified and enthralled at the same time as I get up to examine it further. It looks like I'm watching real life through a window. More and more, I feel as though I'm in a fantastical novel—I wonder if Mr. Wells knows about this invention.

"Sweetheart?" Hannah's father catches me peering behind the screen when he comes back into the room, holding a giant bowl of popcorn. He looks at me strangely. "What are you doing?"

My heart thumps hard as I return to the sofa and sit stiffly on the edge. "Just not feeling quite myself tonight."

He sighs. "Oh, honey. I know you're upset about what happened with Trent earlier. I'll deny ever saying this, but Trent is a . . . well, he's a swampdragon."

I don't believe that particular animal has been discovered yet in my time, but it sounds as if he means it as an insult, so I raise my eyebrows and nod.

"And," he continues, "I understand how badly you want to be treated like the docents' equal. You *know* I'm on your side here, and I wish they could see the same mature young woman I do, but, Bug, some of this is going to take time. You just have to be patient. Besides, no growing up too fast. As your dad, I forbid it."

He leans over and kisses the top of my head before dropping next to me on the couch and reaching his hand into the popcorn bowl.

Of course I haven't the faintest idea what he's talking about, but I do understand the part about things being forbidden, and part of me sympathizes with Hannah a little more. It's quite odd to have this stranger thinking I'm his child (even if he seems perfectly nice and caring), so it takes a bit of time before I relax and start watching the pictures.

I ascertain that *Doctor Who* is a serial about a time-traveling alien. The pictures are so lifelike, it's almost like he's in the room with us.

Every time Hannah's father gets up to retrieve a

snack or to answer a communication on his little device, I move closer to the TeeVee to see if I can figure out how the machine works. All I know is that it's plugged into the electrical circuit.

Uncle E. J. is proud of the electricity that runs through the mansion—he even has an electrical icebox. But I've never seen anything like this.

"You're not dusting behind the TV, are you?" the man says as he returns from the kitchen. Then under his breath, so I just barely hear, he mutters, "Who are you, and what have you done with my daughter?"

I jump back quickly, my heart pounding. He suspects I'm not her. What do I do?

"I know how much you were looking forward to dusting all the portraits." He laughs as he says this, and I gather from his tone that Hannah likely does not enjoy dusting at all. Since I've never tried it, I wouldn't know. "But let's give you a break tonight."

I stand stupidly in the middle of the room, not sure how to proceed. I'm not doing a very good job of pretending to be her.

Before either of us speaks again, Hannah's communication device (her father calls it an "I-phone") buzzes on the end table. Words appear on the screen this time, instead of a photograph like before. Is it possible that telegrams in the twenty-first century appear this way, rather than by courier?

I glance at the words. The name Tara Lopes appears above them.

Will be at Elms tomorrow. R you around before the game?

"Aren't you going to answer her?" Hannah's father pops a piece of popcorn into his mouth and looks from the device to me, and back again.

"No, thank you." The machine intrigues me, but I have no idea what the message means. It's almost like it's in code.

He looks troubled as he sinks back into the sofa. "It's not like you to ignore your best friend. Did you guys have a fight?"

He thinks something is wrong. I can tell. What if he's worried that Hannah is sick? Or insane?

I stifle a yawn, sitting on the edge of the sofa and folding my hands in my lap. Not insane. Just not his daughter, which might be hard for him to understand. "I think it's time for me to go to sleep."

I suddenly feel as though I've been awake for a hundred years. The twenty-first century is exhausting.

After I wander down the hall and arrive in what must be Hannah's bedroom, I turn in a circle slowly, trying to understand everything I'm seeing. Affixed to the wall is a huge photograph of five young men with their arms thrown casually around each other, laughing at something behind the camera. They are all wearing very tight-fitting shirts. I wonder what the words across the bottom mean: "The Five Heartbeats." The image is so clear and colorful. It looks like they could just step out of the picture. I think they must be friends of Hannah's, but it shocks me to see men so indecently dressed hanging on her wall.

A shelf full of books with colorful bindings catches my eye. I pluck one that looks interesting: *Harry Potter and the Sorcerer's Stone*. Flipping the pages, I spot my aunt's name, spelled slightly differently. Hermione. It makes me miss her. I put the book on the desk; it's a shame, but I won't have time to read it.

A pink stuffed toy bear leaning against Hannah's pillow is soft and worn. It makes me think of my own Teddy Bear, all furry and stiff-limbed. My aunt thinks the Teddy Bear fad will fade after President Roosevelt leaves office. But considering that he inspired the trend by refusing to shoot a real bear, I'm glad it hasn't diminished yet. Aunt hinted that he might make a surprise visit to The Elms later this summer as a favor to Uncle E. J. I curl my body around the toy and close my eyes, thinking how exciting it will be to meet the president.

Lying with my eyes closed, I marvel at the last several hours. Hannah and her father are servants in this house, but they have more electric machines than Uncle E. J. The wealth in this century must be universal.

I don't remember falling asleep, but I roll over when light streams through the curtains. For a moment I forget where I am—but a device with bright-red lights reminds me I'm not at home. It must be some sort of timepiece, because it declares a series of numbers—6:15—but it doesn't look like any clock I've ever seen. I sit up, taking in my surroundings in daylight. There's no chance of falling back to sleep, and Hannah expects to see me looking back at her at seven o'clock, so I wander out of the room and down the servants' staircase to the drawing room, and spend some time marveling at how much this part of the house looks the same. This place is so odd; I do not understand how I came to be here, and I cannot wait to get back where I belong.

Chapter Thirteen

Hannah

THERE ARE THINGS I'M FULLY confident about and things I'm a little less sure of. In the "Not So Much" column I'd definitely put my freckles, my ability to spell the word "rhythm" without using spell-check, and the likelihood that I'll get my acceptance letter from Hogwarts. (Two years late is still fine by me, Dumbledore!)

In the "Why, Yes, Of Course I've Got This" column, I'd put my knowledge of all things Newport, The Elms, and the Berwinds; the way my face looks when I laugh; the fact that I can block nearly any shot that comes at my soccer goal; and the very strong possibility that Ethan Grimes likes me.

But my having the skills to prevent a heist from happening in ONE SINGLE DAY?

Um . . .

*May*be?

Step one is getting Maggie on board with my plan for me to hang here for another day. She has to agree. HAS to. Even if there weren't an art heist to foil, the thought of switching back now is . . . No. Just no. Especially since last night was kind of a bust in terms of experiencing 1905 awesomeness, because the Berwinds and their houseguests went out for the night, and I had to spend most of my time avoiding bumping into evil Colette and trying to convince a lady's maid that I really and truly did not need help bathing or dressing for bed. Yes, I got to explore the house a little on my own, but given that in my time it's set up to look exactly like it does in this era, that wasn't exactly earth-shattering. So I'm determined not to miss one single second of today, which is why I'm awake even earlier than I ever am on a school day, much less a morning during summer vacation.

It's so super-weird to wake up in the Rose Room. I've spent my whole life looking at the pinkish-striped walls and the elaborately carved white wooden bed, but I've never experienced it as an actual living space. I mean,

I've always felt like I have the run of The Elms after-hours, and we do get to treat the museum parts as our home in a lot of ways. Like opening presents Christmas morning under the ginormous tree the museum staff sets up for the holidays in the foyer, instead of under the kind-of-sketchy artificial one in our own quarters. Or swimming in the fountains on scorching-hot mornings, before the grounds open to visitors. I've even hosted epic sleepovers for ten friends in "my" mansion. But we slept on the roof deck, NOT in the antique bed with fancy silk curtains draped over its headboard. I've never even plopped my butt onto this mattress, much less climbed under the sheets.

I blink in the early light at the completely familiar, yet somehow also totally strange, surroundings. It feels so much more *real* with Maggie's hair in the silver brush on the marble-topped bureau and her dog-eared copy of *The Wonderful Wizard of Oz* propped open on the dainty round nightstand.

The whole house even smells different. Lived-in. Alive. And it sounds different too. There were fewer echoes from the tall ceilings and more muffled footsteps and swishing of maids' skirts last night as I drifted off to sleep.

Although, at the moment it's perfectly quiet. On this level, at least. The servants are probably all downstairs already, and the other residents are still sleeping, I'd guess. There was a musicale last night at Arleigh, the mansion where Harry Lehr and his wife, Elizabeth Drexel Lehr, stay. A painting of her hangs at The Elms in my time. It's so Crazytown to know that these famous high-society people I've grown up reading about are RIGHT ACROSS THE STREET at this very second, 100 percent alive! Even the building is "alive"—in my time Arleigh has been replaced by a nursing home.

I heard the Berwinds and all their houseguests coming in way, way late, so I'm guessing they won't be up for hours.

I have to squint into the morning shadows to make out the time on the clock centered on the fireplace mantel. Obviously, it is *not* digital with lighted numbers, like mine at home. In fact, it's small and round and mounted onto a pedestal that has three spindles wrapped in gold roping connecting it to a base. That's because society is just coming out of the Gilded Age, and *everything* is, well, gilded. Plated in gold, to show off the owners' Daddy Warbucks–level mega-wealth.

Finally the hour hand creeps close enough to seven

that I figure I can make a run for the drawing room and (hopefully) Maggie. I push open the door just enough to slip through, then creep down the staircase, keeping an eye out for any servants who might spot me.

I head straight for the sideboard and climb onto it. As soon as I nudge aside the painting to expose more of the mirror behind it, Maggie's peering face comes into focus.

Her whole body relaxes when she spots me. "Where have you been? I've been waiting ages! I was positive we said seven a.m., not eight."

I scrunch my nose. "We did. It *is* seven. At least according to the clock in your room and . . ." I pause and glance down at the mantel. "This one too."

She holds my iPhone up to the mirror to show me the display. The numbers read 8:01.

"But that makes no sense," I say. "I traveled a century *plus one hour* into the past? It doesn't—" And then it hits me. "Yes, it does! Daylight saving time! The United States doesn't begin using it until—"

I catch myself just before I blab the words "World War I." Maggie doesn't need to know she's less than ten years away from half the planet going to battle. Instead I mumble, "Sometime next decade."

She's still looking baffled, so I give her a quick run-down on setting clocks forward and back, and she visibly relaxes. "I spent the entire hour fretting that the mirror didn't work anymore and I'd be stranded here forever. I mean you no offense, but—"

I hold up my hand. "I get it. I would have been really freaked too."

Literally no one else on earth could get how weird this entire experience is, except the two of us, and we share kind of a bonding smile over it. But then she leans in again and gasps. "Land sakes, what are you wearing?"

I glance down. "Um, your nightgown? Is that not okay? I kind of figured we were going with the 'what's mine is yours and what's yours is mine' idea. Speaking of which, please tell me you wore my night guard last night. You might not have to worry about braces in your time, but I just got mine off, and I'm pretty desperate to keep them that way."

She blinks at me a few times. "I . . . What?"

"Never mind. It's not that important, I guess. Wait, why are you still looking at me funny?"

"You're—you're rather indecent to be wandering about. If Aunt sees you or—or, oh heavens, if Uncle E. J.—"

"No worries. They're snoring harder than Geppetto in *Pinocchio*. Oh, wait. You haven't seen that movie, so of course that won't mean anything to you. Actually, you haven't seen *any* movie, have you? So weird. And what do you mean, 'indecent'? This nightgown reaches my wrists *and* my ankles! Plus, it's kind of stiff. You're soooo gonna love fabric softener, whenever *that* gets invented."

Maggie continues to blink at me even worse than before. Hmm. It's possible she is not rolling with this whole time-traveler thing as well as I am. Which I guess makes sense. I never lived in this time, but I've grown up learning all about it and surrounded by reminders every day. She probably feels like she's been dropped into a whole new world, instead of just a whole new century.

"If you want, I'll go grab a robe or something," I offer.

Maggie shakes her head quickly. "No. I don't know how much time we have. With the ball taking place tonight, the staff is surely up and about already, even if Aunt and Uncle are not. And I think I heard your father stirring as I slipped downstairs. We should hurry and switch back."

She raises her hand and presses her fingers to the age spot on the mirror. When I keep my arms by my side, she tilts her head and says, "I believe we both have to do it at the same time."

My eyes find hers. "Um, but I thought last night we agreed it would be good for both of us to have time to explore, since we've been given this crazy opportunity."

Her eyebrows shoot up. "It was all happening so quickly, and I was trying to process the situation. I don't— That is, I assumed we'd swap back first thing this morning."

I sigh. Not how I was hoping she'd respond. I make my voice soft and pleading. "Okay, so hear me out here. I'm not asking for much longer. Just today."

She gasps. "Oh no. No. No. That's simply not possible. Tonight is the ball, and I must be there. My portrait is being revealed to all Newport society."

I scrunch up my nose. "I only need the day. We could switch back before the ball starts. But about that reveal . . . Sorry to be the one to tell you this but, not so much. Your portrait is stolen on this day in history. In a matter of hours, actually."

She gasps again, and I'm quick to add, "Only, I'm not going to let that happen. That's what I wanted to tell you. I think I figured out why I'm here—to solve the heist!"

"Whatever do you mean?"

I fill her in on exactly what's about to go down at the ball tonight—or at least the version I know from the history books—and she clutches her throat. "Heavens!"

"I know, right?"

"I glimpsed that Jonah boy only yesterday. Just before . . . just before this all happened. I'd not seen him prior."

"Yeah, well, I met him yesterday too."

"Met him? You talked to him? But he's—he's a kitchen boy. I'm—*we* are not permitted in the basement." She narrows her eyes. "Please tell me that you did not enter the servants' area. After Mrs. O'Neil expressly forbade me! Where did you see him?"

Uh, exactly where you'd expect to find a *kitchen* boy? Only, I don't say that to Maggie, of course. One, because even though I know a whole lot about 1905, I'm not sure how sarcasm worked then, and I don't want her to think I don't like her, when I'm actually totally thrilled we're talking like this, even if it's under super-weird conditions. And two, because I'm not entirely sure she won't fall off her version of this sideboard if she finds out I went down to the staff area of the house.

"Oh, just . . . about," I tell her. "To be honest, he seemed really nice. And young. I—I actually thought he was pretty cool."

"Cool? I don't understand. You felt his skin?"

I bite my cheek to keep from laughing. It's not her fault she doesn't know our slang. I have to remember to dial it down, but half the time it just slips out. "No. Sorry. I just mean I thought he was sweet. And shy. Not at all how I would picture a criminal mastermind. Although, I can't say I've encountered all that many criminal masterminds, so maybe more of them have dimples and hair that won't stay smoothed down than I realize."

Maggie looks scandalized, like she just found out about the existence of bikinis or something. But she definitely aced etiquette school, because I can literally see her face rearrange itself into something more bland and ladylike right before my eyes.

"Or perhaps he is not the thief?" she suggests mildly.

I can't help jumping at her words, because they're so exactly what I was thinking yesterday. And last night as I was trying to fall asleep. And this morning when I woke up. Maybe the reason no one ever found the painting is what I always suspected—because they were looking in the wrong direction. Or at least for the wrong person. If I stick like glue to Jonah all day—to prevent him from getting close to the action—and it turns out I'm right that he's NOT the thief . . . then what's been the point of all this? If the real culprit steals the painting instead . . . why was I ever here? No matter who ends up being behind the theft, I have to solve it one way or another.

Maggie is patiently watching as the wheels turn in my head, waiting for me to get back to her.

"Okay, so what if he's not?" I finally say. "That means it could be anyone. Wait. You probably have some insider information! Quick. Who else would want to own a priceless piece of art?"

Oh, ugh. That's kind of obvious; the answer to that is "almost anyone."

Maggie shakes her head. "But the portrait of me isn't priceless. Of course, Aunt has ensured a lovely souvenir of my thirteenth year. And she does hope to impress Newport society with its unveiling . . . but Mademoiselle Cassatt is not Renoir. She is just a woman."

"'Just a woman'? *Just a woman*? Maggie! I can't believe you said that! We need to get you up to speed on Girl Power. Where you are now, girls can do anything boys can do. We can command military troops, design skyscrapers, run for president." I want to shake my fist at her. If she's gonna hang in my day and age, she'd better start flying her feminism flag higher than that.

Maggie's gasp is about as loud as a hurricane. "You have a female *president*? Of the *United States*!"

I drop my grin. "Well . . . not yet. But we got super-close. And we will again. I have faith."

"Goodness," she breathes. "I can't even imagine men allowing us to vote, much less that men would trust us to run the entire country."

I sigh, then mumble, "*Some* do. There, um . . . there might still be some ground to cover, although we *do* have the right to vote. People are always telling us girls we can be and do anything, and we can. It's just that I guess we don't always get the same respect guys do. Most of the time women get paid less for doing the same exact work. Or, like, girls will read books about boys no problem, but lots of boys refuse to read books with girls on the cover and stuff like that. So now it's more like we have equal rights on paper but we still have to earn them in people's hearts. I dunno." I shake my head and laugh. "Wow, that got heavy. Yikes."

"Still," Maggie says. "I can't begin to imagine what it would be like to dream of a career and know it could actually happen. Or to even be permitted to have an actual say in things, instead of just going along with anything my future husband wants me to."

"Wow, I guess I never thought about it like that. And on the bright side, we might not have a female president *yet*, but there are already women governors and representatives and senators. Plus brain surgeons. And CEOs of companies. And rocket scientists. You should Google some of them. I mean, if you agree to stay for the day." I cross every finger and toe.

Her forehead crinkles. "Beg pardon?"

Oh, right. If her mind is blown by the idea of a woman running for president, just wait until she discovers the Internet and endless hours of "baby hedgehogs getting massages" videos. It's a shame I can't be there to witness it.

Although, technically she hasn't agreed to let me hang here for another day yet, and even though I could just completely refuse to put my fingers to the age spot, I'd prefer not to, like, steamroll all over her or anything. One, because I'm not an evil person, and two, because the girl is currently occupying my body and what if she gets revenge by chopping off my hair with toenail clippers? For now I plan to plow ahead until she screams "Stop!"

"Okay, let's circle back to Girl Power later," I say. "Just in case it might be someone other than Jonah, I need you to tell me any possible person who might have a motive to steal your portrait, or who might have it out for your aunt and uncle. Or you. Anything you can think of, big or small, could help. If the ball starts at ten p.m., I have to use every last hour to solve this thing."

She seems a little dazed, but she nods. Wait. Does that mean she *is* agreeing to this plan? Officially? I try to stay all casual, even though I'm doing internal jumping jacks. "Suspects?" I prod.

She takes a deep breath and looks me in the eye. "Well, there are the Gilmores. Only the other afternoon at Bailey's Beach, I heard Mrs. Gilmore whispering to Mrs. Lehr something nasty about Aunt being 'new money.' As if more than half of Newport doesn't share the same distinction. She's merely jealous that her houseguest chose to accept the invitation to our ball, rather than accompany her to Saratoga Springs this afternoon. Although, now that I puzzle it out, if she's to be on a midday train, then of course she isn't going to be able to steal a painting in Newport tonight. I suppose I would only make a note to keep an eye out for her appearance, should her plans change."

I nod. "Gilmore. Got it. Who else?"

Maggie grimaces. "Colette. My cousin. Did you cross paths with her yesterday?"

I make a face. "Ohhhhh, yeah. What's with her, anyway? She's, like, the biggest 'mean girl' ever."

Maggie sighs. "She resents how Aunt favors me."

"Got it. Adding her to the list. Can you think of anyone else?"

Maggie closes her eyes, concentrating hard, but soon opens them. "I'm afraid I really cannot. Aunt is a darling of society and charms all who know her. The household is highly regarded."

Yup. I know this from all my studying up on them too. "Okay, well, at least I have some starting points. Not sure how things are gonna play out on this end, but let's plan to meet back here at six tonight. Six in *1905* time. Seven in yours. Although, I'm guessing they'll be setting up in the ballroom by then. Do you think it would attract attention if I shut the door between the two rooms?"

She blinks at me. "Of course not. I often close it when I read in here. You'll be left alone."

Right. Just because it's permanently open in my time doesn't mean it would be in hers. This is a home for these people, not a museum.

She's chewing on her lip, though. I hope she's not reconsidering.

"Um, is everything okay?" I ask. I really don't want to

though. Don't sail on the *Titanic*. Grab your money out of the stock market before 1929, but when you get back into it, remember these three words: 'McDonald's,' 'Disney,' 'Apple.' Oh, and also 'Hitler' equals 'Very Bad Man.' If you could manage to get a message to any and all of your German friends about that sometime before the end of the thirties, that would be extra amazing."

Maggie is doing the whole blinking thing again. Oh, man. I've totally overwhelmed her. To her credit, she rolls with it pretty well, because a second later she recovers.

Except then her face falls. "Only . . . well . . . what is it I'm to do while I am here?"

"Have fun! Explore! Party like a rock star! Just don't go too crazy wild and get me grounded for life or anything, because then I'd have to find a way to get back here again and strangle you."

When I catch her expression, I say, "Kidding. Totally kidding. I always imagined we'd be best friends if we lived at the same time. Us getting to talk like this? It's seriously giving me life!" I'm quick to add, "I love it!" just in case she wasn't following along. I know I could probably dial down on the slang—and I'll be way more careful when I'm trying to pass as her the rest of today—but I'm so excited to be talking to Maggie that I don't want to have to censor myself around her. I just want to be the same way with her that I would be around any of my friends.

She gives me a small smile but then goes back to biting her lip. "Explore. Yes, that would be logical. I mean, I suppose you think I'm crazy for not leaping at the chance. *You're* brave enough to jump straight into solving a crime, for land sakes. But . . . girls in my position are not encouraged to be the exploring type. We are trained to act quiet and peaceful and to follow the expectations laid out for us."

I know all this from studying the history of this house so much, but hearing the wobble in Maggie's voice when she says it makes the reality hit home. I mean, I just took for granted that my dad would give me two thumbs-up when I told him I wanted to start a YouTube channel of coding tutorials for kids. And that, instead of rolling his eyes at me when I announced out of the blue that I wanted to give up meat, he'd go to town on an awesome veggie chili recipe. So yeah, maybe I get to do a bunch of things I want to do, without having to worry about scandalizing society. But does that make me brave? I don't know about that. If I'm being honest, I haven't even let myself think through any of the details about actually foiling a criminal, because when I start to, I get this acidy taste in the back of my mouth. But a part of me really likes that she sees me that way, and I don't want to change her opinion of me.

Besides, if she thinks I'm brave, maybe I can use that to convince her she needs to act that way too, to keep everyone believing she's me.

"Look, I get it," I say. "Girls in my time are raised to have a totally different mind-set from what you're taught. Everyone tells us we can do anything. Maybe you could just adopt a whole 'when in Rome' approach."

"'When in Rome'?"

"It's an expression. 'When in Rome, do as the Romans do.' I don't even know where it came from, but just . . . just pretend you've been told your entire life that you can do whatever you put your mind to, and then . . . act accordingly."

She looks pretty doubtful, but at least she's stopped biting her lip. She even smiles a little. "All right. I will endeavor to do that. Wish me luck."

"Luck!" Then I toss in one other thing. "Little tip, though. If you *really* want people to buy into you being me, maybe skip using the word 'endeavor,' huh?"

"I shall endeavor to. I— Oh! That is to say, I shall do my best."

"Great!" I tell her, trying my hardest to look extra encouraging and supportive. I briefly consider mentioning that she should slash a line through the word "shall," too, but I skip it. She'll probably decide to lock herself away in my room if I make her too self-conscious, and she deserves to soak up this experience too. Even if it means I have to run a little damage control when I get back.

After all, how badly can she mess things up for me in one measly day?

Chapter Fourteen

Maggie

HANNAH. JORDAN."

The man says Hannah's name in a clipped tone. Almost like he's done it that way before. It makes me wonder about what sort of trouble the real Hannah gets into.

But I'm not her. And they can't blame me. I've been trapped in the future since yesterday, and the last hour is the only time I've spent in the pink bedroom with the carved headboard and silk drapes that Aunt Herminie keeps for me. Me! Not anyone else.

Even though I promised Hannah I would endeavor to be brave, I needed to find a place to think. I just want to shut out everything that is not from my own world.

I pray to be back at *my* Elms. Not this strange version. Prayer doesn't seem to work, though.

I think about what Hannah told me earlier from the other side of the mirror. The portrait Mademoiselle Cassatt has now finished painting of me—stolen and missing for more than a hundred years. And Hannah seeking to speak to that boy in the kitchen! If she's caught, Mrs. O'Neil will have no choice but to tell Aunt this time. But I certainly wouldn't want someone blamed for a crime he didn't commit. If there even is a crime. Oh, mercy! I just want to hide in my room and pretend like I am back in my own time. I pull the musty coverlet over my head like I did as a small child when Father was cross. But back then Mother was around to comfort me and make things right again.

"Hannah Jordan!" the voice says again. "This is the last straw. You know you are not allowed to touch the furniture."

I open one eye and peer at the man framed in the doorway. His short silver hair sticks up at odd angles, as though he's run his hands through it several times. A group of people stand behind him, looking at me like I'm a canary in a cage. His glasses are askew, and his face is the color of beets. A stray bit of spittle glistens at the edge of his lips.

With a sigh I stand up and smooth down my dress . . . er, trousers. There is no one here to comfort me. I need to be brave, like I promised Hannah. If I don't pull myself together, these people will think I'm hysterical, and then who knows what might happen. "I'm sorry, sir. You're right. I just couldn't help myself. I do love this room." I step over the red rope and bow my head, hoping it will be seen as apologetic. "I meant no disrespect."

"Well, uh . . ." He runs his hand through his hair, making it stick up that much more. "Um, I—I guess I can overlook it this time, but—but don't let it happen again." He stammers like he can't think of what to say or doesn't know how to react to an apology.

"Thank you, sir." I am tempted to curtsy, but I sense that girls in the twenty-first century have lost that particular custom. I push past the tourists and run away from him as fast as my legs will go—even though it is against all the rules. At the grand staircase I pause, before bounding to the bottom. Suddenly the house is stifling, and all I want is to get outside. I know the perfect place for some fresh air to help me breathe and consider my options. I skip across the marble foyer and out the front door, almost crashing into a girl and four adults.

"Watch it," one of the men says, grabbing the small

girl and pulling her out of the way. A gasp escapes my lips. Never in my life have I ever been so rude to anyone, and it feels wrong. But pretending to be someone I'm not, in a time I don't understand, feels worse than being rude. I can't pretend for one more second! I turn and run down the concrete steps. I need to think—and I don't care how impolite it must look. Skirting around another small group of visitors, I run the length of the mansion to the back of the house. What greets me stops me in my tracks, and my heart sinks even further.

The gardens! And the trees! The elm trees are all gone. The spacious back lawn is supposed to be lined with elm trees. They're what give the house its name, The Elms.

Why would someone remove all the elm trees? There *is* a row of nondescript trees lining the space between the drive on my left and the vast expanse of green lawn, but they don't feel right. And then I spot it. One large tree, separate from the others, at the far edge of the lawn, just in front of where I hope the sunken gardens still exist.

It's here. *My* tree.

I breathe a sigh of relief and make a beeline across the massive expanse of grass for the giant weeping beech, almost falling in my haste to find something familiar. I duck under the canopy of branches that skim the ground. It's bigger than I remember, but it feels as right as my bedroom. As I sweep aside the soft curtain of leaves, I say a prayer of thanks that no one is under here.

Normally I sit under the canopy and think or read against the tree. Aunt Herminie has no idea that I sometimes come here, and as long as I keep it secret from Colette, Aunt won't ever find out. Sitting outside isn't expressly forbidden, but it is not exactly proper. I look up, wondering if I dare. Climbing a tree would be firmly on the list of things a girl of my station should not do. But . . . maybe girls in this century are encouraged to climb trees? If what Hannah said is true about what girls can do, then I don't even have to feel guilty for breaking the rules. My heart gives a little thrill as I grip the tree and begin to climb. Higher and higher I go, hoping to reach a place where no one will find me.

About ten feet from the ground, there's a sturdy limb. I tuck my feet close to me and hug my knees to my chest. At first when I look down, I'm a bit dizzy and I can't quite believe what I've done. But after a few minutes I get my bearings, and it's amazing. From this vantage point I can watch people entering the clearing below me, but I don't think anyone can see me up here. I close my eyes and consider my options.

How did I end up in this time? How is it possible that I've traveled so far into the future? I think about my aunt and uncle and the things I love—my pony, all my books, the smell of the rose garden in the morning. But being able to climb trees, and run, and get dirty? I think of all the things I'm not ordinarily allowed to do, and wonder how many of them girls are allowed to do in this time.

Out of nowhere, something catches my attention, and I glance up. Between the top branches a small spot of blue sky is visible. I see a sight that almost causes me to fall from my perch. An object that is not a bird soars far above my head. It is glorious. Spectacular! A miracle of technology! Now I understand how Hannah and her father will fly to California. Uncle E. J. would be thrilled to see this.

I have one day in the twenty-first century. I will be back at *my* Elms by evening, enjoying the ball given in my honor with Aunt Herminie and Uncle E. J.

I can do this. I can pretend to be Hannah for the day. In fact, it might be informative to see what the future has in store. Though if a giant flying machine is any indication, I may need to brace myself. And, it occurs to me, I might find out what girls are allowed to do in the twenty-first century that I can't do in 1905. And maybe I'll experience a few of them for myself.

Finished with feeling sorry for myself, I rub my eyes with the back of my hand. *It is refreshing not to have petticoats impeding my legs,* I think as I scramble back down. I jump the last five feet and stumble at the landing.

"There you are. I've been looking everywhere for you." A girl about my age stands with her mouth open, incredulous at my sudden appearance from above. "Are you okay?"

I brush the dust off my trousers and shrug. "Yes, I am. Thank you. It is amazing what a little tree climbing will do for the heart and soul."

She scratches her head. Her skin is tanned brown, and her curly black hair is cropped very short. Her clothing is strange. She's wearing short pants like my cousin Peter wears, and across her front are the words *Newport Girls Soccer.* Her socks come up almost to her knees, and she's holding a white-and-black-checkered ball. "Um. Sure. Whatever you say." She looks up at the tree branches with a smirk. "You know the director of buildings and grounds would kill you for climbing one of the antique trees."

I feel myself go pale at the thought of such violence

over climbing a tree, but I tell myself she must be exaggerating. "Well, of course. But I was just checking to make sure no one had already gone up there and broken the rules. Someone has to do it." I give her a small salute and turn on my heel, wondering if I've misunderstood the extent of things girls are permitted to do.

"Wait. Hannah." The girl trots behind me, out from under the canopy of the tree, back onto the great lawn, and into the sun. "It's not like my mother's rules have ever stopped you before."

I don't slow my pace. Now that I've decided to take advantage of this situation, I've got no time to lose. "Your mother?" Because of the way she's dressed, I assume this girl must be a servant, and for a moment I cannot for the life of me understand her informality. But then I remember, Hannah is a servant as well. I stop to let her finish.

"What do you mean?" The girl's smile falters, like she's not sure if I'm joking. "Wait. Are you still mad? Is that why you didn't text back last night? I said I was sorry about the thing with your phone. You have to be kidding." She looks like she's about to cry.

I'm such a ninny. This girl is probably a friend of Hannah's! I try to remember seeing her face in one of the photographs in Hannah's room.

"I'm not mad at you. Why would I be kidding?" I ask, walking around the side of the house nearest the kitchen. "What did you do?"

She laughs nervously. "Now you're teasing me. I was just joking around. You know, my mother took my phone for a week, so when you left yours at practice the other day, I just thought I'd have some fun. I wanted to apologize when I got mine back last night, but you didn't answer my text."

I don't understand what she did wrong. But she seems sincere. "Well, then. I accept your apology. I was going to take a walk. Would you care to join me?" It suddenly occurs to me that having a guide from this century might help in making sense of all this.

She looks around as though perhaps I'm speaking to someone else. "What are you talking about? We have a game today." She nods at the ball she's carrying.

"A what?" I stop to stare at this strange girl.

"Soccer . . . Duh. Are you sure you're okay? Why aren't you changed yet?"

"Oh, how fun!" I clap my hands. I have no idea what "soccer" means, but the chance to play a ball game is almost too good to be true. Apparently girls play ball games in the twenty-first century.

Now that I really think about it, her outfit puts me in mind of the boys who play baseball in the dusty field near the harbor. My aunt won't let me anywhere near their game, but I've seen them walking home sometimes. They are usually covered in dirt and muck, but they always sound like they've had the most fun. I can only imagine being covered in dirt, since I'm not allowed. If Aunt—and my father as well, for that matter—ever caught me climbing the weeping beech, I'd likely be sent to bed without dinner. The only sport I'm permitted to play is lawn tennis, because Aunt considers it a socially acceptable activity. But only if I don't exert myself more than necessary.

And what fun is a game like that if one does not exert oneself?

The girl tosses the ball, and it bounces off me.

"Ouch. Why did you do that?" I rub my arm.

She rolls her eyes. "Sheesh, Hannah. I'll help you get your stuff." After picking up the ball, she grabs my arm, drags me into the servants' entrance, and practically pushes me up the stairs to the apartment.

What am I thinking? I have no idea how to dress for her game, let alone play it. As much as I want to make an effort, I don't want to look foolish. I try the ruse that sometimes works with my aunt when I don't want to accompany her on a social visit. "I'm not feeling well," I say, putting my hand to my cheek at the first landing. "Look, I'm all flushed. I can't possibly play."

"Not good enough. Coach will throw you off the team if you bail today." We enter the bedroom, and she scans the floor. "Here's your bag! Now get your uniform on and let's go."

The girl, whose name I don't even know, leaves the room and closes the door. I notice she has a large number twelve on the back of her shirt. It seems like I do not have a choice. So, as Hannah said, "When in Rome." I dump the contents of the bag onto the floor. A shirt and short pants, identical to the girl's—except this shirt has seventeen on the back—fall out. Even though Hannah told me to pretend to be her, I cannot believe I'm going through with this. But I vowed to myself that I wasn't going to let this opportunity pass. I pick up the shirt between my forefinger and thumb and sniff. "Girls play sports in the twenty-first century," I whisper to the bear sitting on the bed.

I cannot believe I am about to break all the rules of civilized society. My aunt thinks any sort of exertion will damage me in some way. She has never been specific, so I'm not sure what she thinks will happen. But when I perspire too much—even if I'm just sitting on the terrace drinking lemonade—she rolls her eyes and tells me that no man will want to marry a woman so immodest.

The uniform isn't terribly hard to figure out, so it takes me only a few minutes to change. It's incredible. There are no fasteners, so I don't even need any help. I open the door to show the girl, hoping I've dressed correctly. "What do you think?"

She laughs. "You look like you always do." She runs into the room and grabs the bag. "You're out of it today! You'll be in big-time trouble if you forget your cleats."

"Of course. Lead the way." Feeling proud of myself, I link my arm through hers and drag her back down the stairs. At the bottom I remember that I don't know her name, but I take a chance. "You're Tara," I say tentatively, remembering the name that appeared on Hannah's device the night before.

She furrows her brow. "That's my name, don't wear it out." She dips into a low curtsy and then holds out her hand to shake mine, but then pulls it away before I have a chance to grasp hers. She mutters under her breath, "I said I was sorry. You don't have to drag it out."

"Please accept my apologies as well, Tara." I sigh, not

even trying to make up an excuse. "It has been a sort of long morning. I'm not really feeling like myself."

I can't tell if she's mad or not. I hope she thinks Hannah is just teasing. She sort of winks at me as we come out of the building onto the sidewalk.

I'll have to figure out some way to make it up to her. I'm lost in thought when we reach the sidewalk, and for a second I lose my bearings. I have to contain the gasp that threatens to escape my lips. Automobiles like I've never seen line the street, whizzing past faster than anything I've ever imagined. No horses. No buggies. A few people walking, but they do not look like the ladies I am accustomed to seeing in the coach parade every afternoon.

How on earth am I going to be able to go through with this?

Chapter Fifteen

Hannah

*L*ITTLE TIP TO ANYONE CONSIDERING time travel: it's super-helpful to be a total history buff on the exact era and location you land in. Super-*duper*-helpful.

For example, I know just how to skirt around the Berwinds and their houseguests for now, because I have a pretty good handle on exactly how their day will shape up. It will probably be the same as almost every day, for almost every member of the Four Hundred who spends the summer season in Newport.

It would normally start with breakfast at eight. Though, after their late night, and judging from how quiet it is in the house, I think the Berwinds slept through this today. I'm also guessing no one went out for the hour-long horseback ride that would usually follow, but I'm not taking any chances. For now I'm holing up in my—*Maggie's*—room until I'm sure the coast is clear.

After the ride, if they end up going for part of it, they'll change out of those clothes and into their day dresses so that they can catch a horse-drawn carriage to the casino for lawn tennis or a public reading or maybe a play.

Then they'll change *again* into swimming costumes (seriously, these are like wool from neck to toe, and it must be like wading into the ocean in blankets) and head to the beach. The private, only-our-snooty-kind-is-allowed beach, called Bailey's.

I'm pretty sure I'm totally off the hook about taking part in any of this, because they don't drag their kids around to these things. Or anything, really. Children are usually just foisted off on the nannies and tutors, except for maybe an hour or so every day when they *might* get to hang with their parents (if Mom and Dad aren't off traveling or doing something more interesting or important than actually, you know, parenting their offspring). I can't even imagine if that were normal in my time. Dad would basically be a stranger. But that was pretty normal for every kid in Maggie's class.

Anyway, it means no forty-seven outfit changes for me. But I'm guessing that British nanny from last night has something up her sleeve for me and Colette today, and I need all the unsupervised solve-an-art-heist time I can get. Hmm . . . I think I might be feeling a little *cough, cough* under the weather.

Most likely the Berwinds will head off to someone's yacht from noon to two for a luncheon (meaning another new dress), and then to the polo fields from two to three to watch a match from their carriage. Then another change of clothes so that they can all promenade up and down the streets in their carriages and leave calling cards for their neighbors. I never got the point of that one, to be honest.

From there on out I'll have to be more careful to keep to the shadows for my lurking, because they'll probably be back for tea on the terrace at five, and then into their bedrooms to switch dresses (again) for the ball.

(I'm pretty sure that if anyone asked any of these people what they did for a living, they'd have to answer, "Change clothes.")

I need to quit "regrouping" and find Colette. The

sooner I can figure out if Miss Hoity-Toity hates Maggie enough to steal the portrait, the sooner I can work through my list of suspects.

I creak open my bedroom door again. The house is still almost as quiet as it was earlier this morning, but I can hear the far-off clinking of silverware from the dining room below and light footsteps from the servants' quarters above. My throat closes as I picture the top floor the way I know it—as my home. In the here and now it's filled with enough beds for a good percentage of the forty-three people responsible for keeping this household running like clockwork for eight weeks of summer. It still kills me that this crazy-fancy house will just sit empty the other ten months of the year. Maybe I should sneak in a talk with Mrs. Berwind about that before I swap back. (Or maybe not.)

I tiptoe across the hall. I'm guessing Mrs. Berwind would put her weekend visitors in the three guesthouses on the property, but since Colette and I are family and are here for the whole summer, I'm assuming Colette also has a bedroom on this floor. There are *only* seven to choose from. Sigh.

Although, Mr. and Mrs. Berwind's (separate) bedrooms count for two, and then, obviously, I'm in one.

So that gives me a one-in-four shot. I start around the corner from mine, as far as possible from the Berwinds' suites. The Green Bedroom is empty, its door wide open. The Van Alen Room across the hall is decorated way masculine, so I doubt that would be super-girly Colette's first pick. And if those are her snores coming through the closed door, more power to her, but I'm thinking not so much. I creep to the door of the Satinwood Room and lean my ear against it. It's mostly quiet, but I think I can make out some rustling inside. I give a tentative knock and immediately hear "Enter!" in reply.

Yaaaasssss! Colette is sitting at her dressing table, peering into the mirror above it. In the reflection she catches my eye, and then she claps her palm to her chest as her focus widens.

"Your hair!"

On instinct I raise a hand to my head and run my fingers along my ponytail. It's probably pretty droopy, considering I had to use a scrap of ribbon in place of a cute elastic (it's the littlest inventions I'm missing the most!), but it can't be so bad that it's clutch-your-heart-worthy.

"What about it?" I ask, trying not to sound defensive.

"It's up! What are you playing at now, Margaret?" she asks in a voice dripping with snarkiness. "You know quite well that only women of age are permitted to wear their hair off their necks!"

Oh, right. I remember reading that. But, um, seriously? I have so, so many questions about this, but I can't exactly ask them, because I'm Maggie and these are things Maggie would already know. I'm here to see if Colette is acting suspicious, not to make *her* suspicious of me.

"Of course. I only tied it up for a second because I was feeling a little . . . flushed."

Colette squints at me, then rolls her eyes. Ha! I guess being eye-rolly has been a thing forever.

"I don't know how you expect to find a suitable husband if you can't be bothered to conduct yourself like a lady," she finally says when her eyes get back from their trip around her sockets.

Husband? *Husband?* Um, hello. I'm TWELVE. Any wedding of mine is, like, decades away. *If* I even decide to get married; I might not. I know most upper-class girls at the turn of this century got hitched at eighteen, but even that's five long years away for Maggie, who is just turning thirteen. Why would she have to be worried about husbands now?

I try to hide my true feelings and keep it to a simple, "Mmm."

Colette ignores this and goes back to running her brush through her perfectly straight hair. It's clear she doesn't have anything more to say to me, but I'm here to get my sleuth on, so probably I should ask some questions myself.

I start to say "um" at the beginning of my sentence and cover it quickly with a cough. Colette's look says, *Girl, you are acting cray-cray.*

"So, do you have anyone in mind for a . . ." I pause to cough. It's so weird to ask a kid this question. "Husband?"

"Of course you know I don't. Though, I do think this is the summer I will begin laying some groundwork with Theodore Willory. He's heir to a railroad fortune, and his mother seems lovely. She admired my embroidery last year when she was to tea."

I nod. This whole conversation is surreal. Colette can't be more than fifteen. Sixteen at the most.

She keeps right on yapping. "Mommy said I can go with Auntie to Paris next spring so I can begin to scout out which shops I'd like to order my debutante dresses from the following year. I can hardly wait! Not that you'd understand. You're such a child still."

Exactly! That's why this hubby talk is so super-strange. Time for a subject change anyway. I smooth my skirt and say, all prim and proper, like people spoke back—well, now, "What are your plans for today?"

She snorts. In a very unladylike way, I might add.

"Same as yours, obviously. Nanny is taking us to Providence for the day for some shopping."

"Right. I don't believe I'll take part in that."

She blinks a few times and then crosses her arms. "*I* don't believe that's up to you to determine."

"It's just, I—I'm feeling a little . . . off. Nothing too serious." I don't want to say I'm *too* sick, because, once we switch back, I don't want Maggie to have to miss out on the ball. "It might just be nerves about the unveiling, but I still think I'd better lay low and conserve my energy for tonight."

Colette does that one-eyebrow-up thing, then shrugs. "I suppose I shouldn't attempt to dissuade you as it would mean more attention at the stores for me."

Gee, nice to know she's so concerned about Maggie's well-being. But Colette's being self-centered works perfectly for me in this instance. I exhale. I've laid the groundwork for my "get free from supervision" plan, and now it's time for a little intel gathering on my first potential suspect.

"We got to see it yesterday, you know. The finished painting. I can't believe how perfect it is!"

Colette doesn't perk up or get shifty-eyed or do anything to indicate any interest whatsoever. In fact, she yawns.

"Mmm. That's nice. Of course, Mommy and Auntie have already plotted out my debutante portrait. Auntie says she's spoken to John Singer Sargent about a commission. Can you imagine? He's only *the* most famous portraitist of our time. Though I'm sure Mademoiselle Cassatt's painting will be quite serviceable."

Serviceable? Really? The woman's work is taught in classrooms the whole entire world over, but whatever. Although, I guess it does take a while for Mary Cassatt's talent to be appreciated here in America. At this point in time she's probably only famous in France, where she lives. John Singer Sargent's fame, on the other hand? Gobs bigger.

If it's true that he's all lined up to paint her, and if she's going to be in Providence for the whole day, she'd have zero reason—or chance—to steal Maggie's portrait. The disappearance would only increase interest in it, and I'm guessing Colette would way rather have Maggie's gift unveiled, only to fade into the background entirely.

That would let hers make the biggest splash of all.

Which means odds are extra high that she didn't have anything to do with the heist. I'm thinking I can cross her off the list.

Except, unless the Gilmores bag their trip to Saratoga Springs, that means I'm down to just one suspect again: Jonah.

Chapter Sixteen

Maggie

W E ARE OUT OF THE GATES AND A block down Bellevue Avenue before I realize I don't know where I am and I struggle to get my bearings. Things don't look right, and I pace back the way we came a few feet.

"Wha—" I can't even form a sentence after I notice the building across the street. It's a low, brick structure that spreads across the entire block. Just yesterday I was in the parlor of Arleigh, the mansion where my aunt's neighbor's dogs nipped around my feet. They are the most irritating little creatures, but the thought of them dead for a hundred years makes my eyes tear up more than anything else so far.

Arleigh is gone. I run down the sidewalk, but I get only a few yards before my shock turns to agony at yet another sight. Villa Rosa, the mansion closest to The Elms on the same side of the avenue, has disappeared as well, replaced by an ugly two-story monstrosity. I can't keep a groan from escaping my mouth. I cover it before Tara notices.

I realize it is going to be harder than I thought to maintain the pretense that I am Hannah. Since The Elms still stands, I assumed that all the houses on the street did as well.

I lean over and try to get control of my breathing. I've seen houses razed by fire or by vanity, and new structures blossom from summer to summer, but realizing that so many of the cottages I know are gone—modern buildings in their places—it is almost too much. It's all familiar, but not—like there's a layer of gauze covering the real Newport. It appears as though there was a feeble attempt to match the approximate style of the properties on the street, but the modern replacements are just faint imitations. They lack the grandeur and spectacle of summer cottages like The Elms and The Breakers.

Is this what time travel means? You get to see how

future generations replace everything you love and care about?

After a couple of minutes Tara breaks the silence. "Are you sure you're okay?

I inhale and scratch my bare leg. It feels strange to have any part of my extremities exposed, let alone all the way up to my thigh, but most of the young women walking along the avenue are wearing short pants or skirts, with their legs showing.

I remember Hannah's words, "When in Rome . . . ," and I try to pull myself together. "I guess I'm just a little nervous."

"Well, that's understandable." She chuckles. "We're playing the number one team in the league today. I know nothing usually makes you nervous, but I'm glad to see that you're not superhuman after all." She awkwardly pats my arm, and I realize she's trying to help. She looks at her device. "You got dressed so fast, we have time before Coach wants us there. Let's take a walk and you can try to relax? The new owners of Belcourt Castle are retiling the slate roof. My mother asked me to take a look. If we walk fast, we can make it."

My heart brightens when I realize what she said. Belcourt still stands. I find myself nodding. I definitely want to see something familiar, even if it's Alva Belmont's mansion, where my aunt's nemesis holds court.

I follow her lead and we start walking. "Why do you care about the roof?" I ask.

She purses her lips and waves her hands a little, like she doesn't quite know what to do with them. "My mother wants me to start getting more familiar with the architecture at The Elms. She thought it might help me build up my portfolio if I could compare what the other properties are doing. All I've got so far are a couple of Spanish-style colonial buildings from my visit to my grandparents in Mexico last month."

She mistakes my silence for disapproval and inhales sharply. "I guess you're right. They're such different properties. I'm not sure the comparison makes sense."

"No, that's not what I meant." I shake my head. There were too many questions flying around my brain to form a coherent sentence. "You're from Mexico?" I'd never met anyone from there.

"Um. No, I'm from Rhode Island." She stares at me with an unreadable expression, like I've crossed a line. "But my family is Mexican."

"Please forgive me." Things are different in the twenty-first century, that's for sure. I've never known anyone from her culture—I've never really thought about why. I start again. "You're studying architecture? That's amazing. I've never really paid any attention to how the buildings are designed. They are just there. But someone has to think about it." I wonder who cares for the building exterior at The Elms back in my time. "I'm sorry, Tara. I think it's so . . . cool . . . that you like architecture." I wonder if I've used the term "cool" correctly. "Your mother likes it too?" I stare at her, hoping my apology is enough to change her expression.

"Well, she better!" She smirks. "She'd have a hard time as the director of buildings and grounds for The Elms if she didn't!" She purses her lips. "You know that, though. What is your problem today, Hannah?"

I slap my forehead. Not only have I offended her, I'm making Hannah look bad in the process. I need to pull myself together and not act so surprised by things that are different in this time. I try to think of something comforting to say so Tara doesn't suspect that something is wrong.

"I do apologize, Tara. I *am* teasing you. I meant no offense." I hope my apology is enough. I've been trained well to be polite. In my time people like to gossip; I pray that is still the case. It might help Hannah's investigation if I ask Tara some questions. "How much do you know about the theft of the Mary Cassatt portrait of Margaret Dunlap?"

"Only what you've told me. I'm not sure why you're so obsessed with that thing. Some hoity-toity heiress who used to live at The Elms," she says, swinging her arms.

I'm not exactly sure what "hoity-toity" means, but it doesn't sound nice.

"Please do not speak of her like that." The tears threaten to return, and I brush at my face. I hate the thought of history painting me as spoiled and useless. After all, I am not Colette.

She frowns and pokes my arm. "Why are you talking like that? Are you practicing for one of those reenactment events coming up in the fall?"

I think about Hannah's odd way of speaking, and I know I'm not doing a good job of mimicking her. "Yes." It seems like the easiest answer.

"Oh. Phew. You had me going. I totally thought you were losing it." For a moment she looks like she might turn around and run the other way, but after a brief pause she continues swinging her arms as we walk. We're headed down Bellevue Avenue, and I'm pleasantly surprised at how familiar the area feels. There are many new structures, but there are also a lot of houses that look the same. Or close to the same. It makes me feel less like crying. I take a steadying breath, trying to get control of my emotions.

"I get why you love history, Hannah. You know I do. And all those costume dramas. And the books. But seriously, you have to tone it down." She sounds genuinely concerned. "People will start to think you're weird," she adds, almost like an afterthought.

I find myself trying to put words into Hannah's mouth, though I have no idea how she would reply. I don't know Hannah well enough to know how her friends view her, but I know what it's like when people—specifically my cousin Colette—pick on me because I'd rather read than attend a social outing. "Everything that happens in the world today is a result of something that happened in the past. The whole world is based on what has come before."

She nods knowingly, like I've shared some sort of deep dark secret. "Like breaking the glass ceiling."

"What?"

"You know, like a woman can be CEO of a company or be an ambassador or a senator or run for president of the United States." She taps my arm. "If women hadn't protested over the years for equal rights, the world wouldn't have so many women in positions of leadership. And someday," she says, an expression of confidence on her face, "a woman will *be* the president of the United States."

I nod, having no idea if this theory is correct or not, but it's the same thing Hannah said this morning. "Maybe. Yes."

It's so confusing. Some things have changed for the worse—beautiful buildings being replaced by ugly structures. But many things are better—like women playing ball games and wearing trousers. And being able to vote. And running for president.

I think about the women I know. My own dear nanny at home in New York, Mrs. O'Neil, my cousin, my aunt. All the socialites from Newport. I've overheard some of them whispering about fighting for women's right to vote. When I get back to 1905, I must be sure to ask them what they would think about a woman running for president.

Chapter Seventeen

Hannah

I AM A CHAMPION LURKER.

It comes from all the shadowing I do of the docents' tours so that I can "fact-check." I mean, *someone* has to make sure all the accurate historical dates and data are being passed along to visitors. Okay, so maybe interrupting with my corrections usually ruins the lurking part, but I can be quiet when I really need to be.

Turns out, this is an invaluable skill when time traveling and trying extra-super-hard not to call attention to yourself.

At the moment I think I've probably gone one step past lurking to full-on stalking. I'm flattened against the wall in the coal tunnel, trying not to worry about how much trouble Maggie is definitely going to get into when someone catches sight of the back of this pale-blue dress. Coal dust, tunnels, and silk do not play nice together. (But I couldn't find anything more low-key in her closet, and even if I had, it would have been impossible to convince the lady's maid who insisted on helping me dress—which was extra weird, lemme tell you, even if it wasn't technically my body that the maid was seeing.)

Edward Berwind made his fortune in coal, so it's only logical that his mansion would have an entire underground tunnel—complete with railroad tracks— off its basement. It runs all the way to Parker Avenue, where a delivery truck can open a hatch in the street and dump its load of fuel down, down, down into a giant cart waiting below.

The cart travels along railroad tracks back to the house, ending in the furnace room, so all that coal can get dumped in. Kind of genius, really. When I was a kid, this was my go-to spot when Dad and I played hide-and-seek. The tunnel is brick and about half a mile long. It's (somewhat) lit by a string of dim lightbulbs in cages, but even with the lights on, the tunnel is pretty spookily dark.

And empty.

Meaning it's the very best place to corner Jonah alone.

I happen to know one of his jobs as kitchen boy would be getting the coal, so he has to be here eventually. Sooner would be especially awesome. It's like there's a tiny clock ticking alongside my heartbeat, counting down the hours until the ball. (It's only midmorning, so I have some time, but still.) I can only hope and pray that no one is stealing the portrait at this exact second, because that would just be the worst luck ever.

Maybe I need to be more "take charge" about things, to speed this up a bit. I creep a few steps toward the light at the end of the tunnel (ha—so philosophical!), and then press hard against the bricks when I hear an odd shuffling.

RAT?!

STRANGE PERSON?!

Which would be preferable right now?

A small cough lets me know it's most definitely a person (unless we're talking about an XXL rat . . . with a head cold), and I hold my breath tight in my lungs.

The cart begins traveling down the track, and I flatten even tighter against the wall by instinct, even though I know perfectly well there's plenty of room for it to pass by me. The person walking alongside it, though? Maybe not so much. At first all I can make out is a shadowy outline, but it's enough that I can tell it's someone close in size to me and wearing pants, which means definitely a boy. No pants for girls in 1905.

Please be Jonah, please be Jonah, please be Jonah, please be—

I screw up all my courage and whisper, "Jonah?"

The shadowy figure jumps about forty-seven feet and stumbles on his landing. "What in the dratted blazes!"

"Sorry," I say in my normal voice, rushing forward to help. I peer into the boy's face as I crouch next to him, and relax a little. It *is* Jonah.

Jonah does the exact opposite of relax when he sees it's me—er, Maggie. He springs up faster than my old cat Muffintop used to when she heard me shake a can of treats.

"Apologies, miss. I didn't . . . That is, I . . . ," he stammers. "Please forgive me for using such language in front of a lady. I never expected . . . No one is ever . . . Much less someone who's not a servant . . . and I—"

"Oh no, please. It's my fault. I'm sorry for scaring you like that," I say, hoping my smile looks reassuring and friendly and not more like, *Sound the alarm. There's a crazy person in the cellar.*

He squints at me in the weak light.

I exhale. Here goes nothing. "I was waiting here to talk to you. I didn't want anyone to spot me, but I guess I didn't think things through enough to realize I'd scare the pants off you."

His eyes blink extra fast at that expression, and he does a quick check of his waistband, to make sure it's in place. Oops! I have *got* to be better about the slang thing.

He recovers quickly, though. Enough to ask, "Waiting to talk to *me*? But . . . but . . . why *me*?"

Okay, so did I say "here goes nothing" before? Nope. Here *really* goes nothing. "I know this is going to sound strange, but I have undeniable proof that there's going to be an art heist at the ball tonight."

I kinda sorta skip the part where he's the one blamed for it by the history books.

"An art heist?" he repeats. His voice sounds a little dazed. He's probably in shock. It's bad enough to come across this girl who's basically his boss—and who he talked to for only the first time yesterday—in a coal tunnel under the house. In the dark. Unexpectedly. But then she goes and opens her mouth and starts talking about an art heist that hasn't even happened yet.

If I were him, I'd probably be checking to see if I was on some hidden-camera TV show.

Of course, there aren't hidden-camera shows in 1905. Or *any* TV shows. Or video cameras, for that matter.

So maybe it's not surprising that instead of looking around, he plops down on the brick floor and shakes his head a few times to clear it. I watch him closely to try to determine if he's in shock because someone (me!) is onto his devious plan to take the painting, or if he's merely extra surprised by the combo of finding his employer's niece in the coal tunnel and all the info I dropped on him.

After a couple of seconds he takes several breaths, then looks up. "How can I help you prevent this from happening?" he asks, his eyes much clearer and calmer now.

I mean, really. What kind of a criminal mastermind would have *that* immediate response? He's so not the one. I just know it. My gut has never steered me wrong before, and it's practically screaming at me that Jonah isn't the thief.

Even so, I'm going to stick to my original plan, which is to keep Jonah close while I rule him out. If I can do that while finding a way to keep my eyes on the portrait for anyone *else* who might try to take it, I'll be #winning.

I don't feel like I can tell Jonah about the whole *Freaky Friday* body-swapping, time-traveling thing just yet. The poor guy has had enough of a shock for one day, and I'm positive that hanging out with the niece of his employers is probably blowing his mind quite enough, thank you very much. So I'll just stick to the very basics here and hope they're enough to make him go along with my plan.

"Do you believe in psychics?" I ask him, sticking out my hand to help him stand up. He stares at my palm, eyes wide, before hopping to his feet on his own. I can tell I'm gonna have to get him over this whole "you have the power to fire me" thing sooner versus later. But for now I wait on his answer.

"Do you mean as in fortune-tellers?"

"Sure, close enough."

Jonah pauses for a second, like he thinks maybe I'm asking him a trick question and I'll run and tell Maggie's aunt if he fails my secret test. I smile to let him know that's sooo not what's going on here. He winces a little at my grin but then answers, "I—I guess so? Do you?"

"Pretty much." Technically I don't, but that's not important right now. "The thing is, one of the house parties I went to last week had a carnival theme, and there was a psychic who set up shop in this tent in the backyard."

People back then—I mean back *now*—are forever throwing ridiculously over-the-top parties. One couple had a giant papier-mâché watermelon wheeled in that opened up, and a *person* sprang out of it and gave all the attendees gold cases and watches as party favors. (Totally beats the make-your-own lip gloss kit I got at the last birthday party I went to, and I was pretty psyched with that, actually.) But anyway, it's entirely possible there was a carnival party. And if there wasn't, Jonah would never be in a position to know that.

Which is why he's nodding along right now.

I continue. "So this woman was super-convincing, even though her crystal ball was a little sketchy looking. She said that the portrait set to be unveiled tonight would be stolen before the ball began."

His mouth drops. "And you—you believe her?"

I nod like I'm a bobblehead, which seems to convince him. Or maybe it's just that he would never contradict his employer. Either way, he's definitely on my side. Yes!

"Do you think maybe you could help me?" I ask, biting my lip. It's not for show, either; I really am nervous about his answer. I don't know what my plan will be if he says no.

Jonah's nodding himself now, though, almost before I finish asking the question. "Of course, miss. I'd be honored."

"Oh, whoa. You don't have to do the whole 'miss' thing. Han— I mean, 'Maggie' is fine."

It's pretty dark in the tunnel, but I'm positive that this makes him blush. "Of course, miss," he answers. "Whatever you'd prefer."

Okay, so clearly I'm gonna have to work on getting him to relax around me, but for now I'm just grateful to have an ally. Turns out adventures are a thousand times less overwhelming when you have a plus-one along. And while the real Maggie is on my side in this mission, it kind of doesn't count when she's a hundred-some years away.

"Great!" I exhale a big sigh.

He clears his throat. "Er . . . did this psychic give you any further indications as to the nature of the theft?"

Man, people talk so old-timey in this century. It's one thing to read their letters from back then in the archives, but to hear the words spoken . . . I stifle my giggle, though, and give him a straight(ish) answer. "She didn't. All I know is that sometime in the next few hours the painting of me that's hanging hidden under a sheet in the drawing room is going to disappear forever, and I need to make sure that doesn't happen, or else . . . Well, let's just leave it as 'or else.' I could use a second brain on this one."

"Well, what if you just sat in the drawing room all day? No one would attempt to steal it out from under your nose, would they?"

He's probably right, and that was basically my plan, even though preventing the theft from happening by just plopping myself in one of the armchairs and reading a book sounds anticlimactic. And way too easy. I mean, could it really be that simple?

"That's what I was thinking too," I answer.

Pride flickers across his face, but he hides it quickly. "Well, miss, I'm happy I could be of service."

He begins to push the cart along the track, heading deeper into the tunnel.

"Wait!" I call to Jonah, whose shape has nearly been gobbled up by the shadows as he walks away from me. He pauses and turns.

It can't be that clean-cut. Whoever made this time-traveling thing happen, however this happened, there's no way I switched places in time to stop an art heist just by . . . sitting around. What if spotting me on the couch prevents the theft today but the culprit returns tomorrow to snag it? Or the next day? No. Not good enough for me. I have to actively catch whoever it is in the act and make sure justice is served.

"What if I don't want to just prevent it?" I begin, taking a few steps toward him. "What if I want to solve it?"

He tilts his head; I'm close enough now that I can see a flicker of something in his eyes before he forces his expression back to something way more neutral. Intrigue? Aha! Jonah has an adventurous streak. I totally relate. I can already tell we'd be good friends if I lived now. I mean, if I lived now as someone who was allowed to hang out with servants, that is. Sigh. It's glamorous here, but there's lots that these people have to learn about how to treat others like equals. Although, if I'm being honest, I guess the same could be said about my time too. We just aren't usually as obvious about it . . . which might be even worse.

Jonah is quiet for several long seconds where the only sound in the tunnel is some clanging from far off in the kitchen. Then he asks, "What if you pulled a bait and switch?"

Okay, this is more like it! I have a partner in crime. I mean, a partner in crime-*busting*. "I'm listening. . . ."

He starts to talk faster now, clearly getting into his role as chief crime-stopper. "You could swap out the painting and replace it with some other piece of art. With the sheet covering it, no one will know the difference.

You could hide behind the curtains and wait for the thief to arrive, and then apprehend him."

"You mean 'we'?"

"Pardon?" Again with his head-tilty thing.

"*We* can hide behind the curtain and *we* can apprehend the thief," I say.

He glances at the floor. "Oh . . . I . . . With all due respect, miss, my place is down here."

"Well, what time do you get off? I mean, they can't work you all day, can they? You're just a kid."

I know I'm really lucky to have the life I do and that there are kids in my time who live in poverty and probably *would* work full-time to help their family if our country didn't have child labor laws against it. But of the kids I know personally, if any of them do have a job, it's just occasional babysitting or something, and mostly to get money for in-app purchases instead of because they have to, like, put food on the table. I help out on tours all the time—much to Trent the Evil Docent's dismay—but it's not like it's a *job* job. If I have a soccer game or something else I want to do, it's no biggie to skip out on the tours.

But right this very minute, if I got into a horse and carriage and ventured out of this neighborhood, I could find kids working in factories, in terrible conditions.

Jonah probably figures if he gets fired from here, that's exactly where he'll end up. It makes me both sad for him and kind of ashamed that I get to live this carefree childhood that he never will.

I've followed along on our Servant Life Tour countless times, and I know how hard the staff worked back then . . . er, back *now*. Regular hours were seven in the morning to eleven at night, six days a week. But it could be even later on nights when there were special events, like tonight's ball. Would a kid have to work that long too?

"I . . . well, to be honest with you, today is technically my day off. Once I finish up from taking delivery of the coal, that is. And I'll be back to help during the ball tonight, of course. It's always all hands on deck for those, and there will be all sorts of vegetables to clean and prep for Chef for the midnight supper."

"So you have to work all kinds of hours on your day off too?" Wowza. That stinks.

He ducks his head. "I don't mind. I'm grateful for the employment. It's an honor to work in a home as fine as this; my mother is proud."

And I get that. It *is* a good job for a kid who's not well-off in this day and age. But you know what would be even better? School. And summer vacation. I mean, it's not like I loooove math tests or annotating assigned reading or any kind of homework ever, but those still beat nonstop chores all day long, for next to no money.

I shake my head. "Well, now I feel extra bad about asking this, but any chance you'd want to stick around this afternoon and help me? I mean, but, you don't have to. I know I'm technically, like, your boss or something, but please don't feel like you have to say yes, if you have plans. And, um, I could see that you get paid for the time if you do decide to stay." Mental note: make sure to tell Maggie so she can take care of that once we switch back.

I watch him closely, trying to be calm about it, but inside my brain is a constant chant of *please say yes, please say yes.*

"Do you mean . . . upstairs?" he asks, with a touch of wonder in his voice.

When I nod, he says, "All due respect, miss, but I've never even been up there."

He works in this house for, like, fourteen hours a day, six days a week, and he hasn't left the basement level?

"Never?!"

He shakes his head. "I enter and exit from the service entrance, which is also where I receive the food deliveries for putting away in the pantry. On occasion I will run an item to the butler's pantry on the ground floor, but it is attached to the servants' stairwell, so I've never set foot in any of the rooms where you live. I'd never have a purpose to do so."

I can tell that he's nervous at just the thought of it, and I try to reassure him. "Don't worry, it's not that different from down here. A little brighter, of course. Although, except for this tunnel, it's fairly cheerful down here, too. All the white tiles in the kitchen? And all the copper pots and the stove shining. It's nice."

Jonah ducks his head. "I'm flattered you noticed all that, miss. I spend most of every morning cleaning the stove and a good part of every afternoon polishing the pots. I've developed this paste of flour, salt, and vinegar that—" His hand flies to his mouth. "Beg pardon. Surely you don't have an interest in drudgery such as this."

I hold out my hand and add a finger to each point. "First of all, it's Maggie, remember? Second of all, I *do* want to hear. I find it fascinating. I've always, always wondered who you were." I stop abruptly because I almost just blew my cover. Jonah can't find out that his name is known to someone a hundred years in the future, and, for that matter, he can't know that *I'm* from that time. I rush to cover my mistake. "I mean, every summer I've visited my aunt here, I've been curious about what went on down here and who did it. Um. Anyway, so yeah, upstairs. I think you'll like it. Less coal dust. A few million dollars' worth of art and adornments. You know, about what you'd expect."

Jonah looks like he's not at all sure what to make of me, so I try another tactic. Maybe if I can get him to feel invested, then he'll be on board. "Any suggestions for somewhere we could hide the real painting during the bait and switch?" I ask, slipping the "we" in and hoping he doesn't argue with my including him before he's actually agreed to help.

To my relief his face lights up. "I've already been thinking about that!" he says, squeezing carefully by me and striding deeper into the tunnel. "Come look!"

It's even harder to see back here, where the lightbulbs are spaced farther apart, but my eyes have adjusted enough that I can make him out a few steps ahead of me. Which doesn't keep me from crashing right into his back when he stops suddenly.

"Oh! I'm so sorry!" he says, sounding horrified.

"No biggie."

"Pardon?"

Whoops. Slang alert. It just slipped out. "I'm fine, is what I meant."

He relaxes and presses his hand flat against the brick wall of the tunnel, motioning for me to do the same. "Feel around. Should be right here," he says.

"What should be?" I can't let on, but I've been in this tunnel a ridiculous number of times. When Dad's friend from college visits, his little boy is forever begging me to take him on a ghost tour of the house. (For the record, I've lived here for twelve years and counting and have encountered exactly zip, zero ghosts.) We always end up in basically this very spot near the end of the tunnel. So I've "been there, done that" when it comes to this space, and I am positive there's nothing to see or feel.

Except I'm wrong.

I catch my breath when my fingers touch a tiny, worn-smooth square of metal, and I gasp when they encounter a small jagged opening in the center of it.

"What is it?" I ask.

I can't really make out any details on Jonah's face, but his voice is super-smug when he says, "Keyhole."

Say what?

"There's a door perfectly camouflaged into the brick. The hinges are on the inside, so there's nothing to indicate that it's even here, aside from this minuscule key-hole. Amazing, isn't it?" he asks.

A door! How come I've never found it? I mean, a door in a brick tunnel doesn't ever go away, so it has to be there in my time. To be fair, it's still pretty dark in here even in the future, and I've never run my hand all along the bricks. I usually walk down the center of the railroad track, actually. But still. I'm totally shocked there's an inch of this house I don't know.

"You can get into it? What does it lead to?" I ask immediately.

Jonah's voice is smiley. "My secret break spot. Oh! I shouldn't have confessed that to you. Please don't tell your aunt or uncle! Or Chef or . . . anyone! I'd be fired immediately if they knew I was sneaking away from my duties."

I step closer, so that he can see me more clearly, then use two fingers to zip my mouth closed. I lock them with an imaginary key and toss it over my shoulder. By the weird look he's giving me, I'm gonna guess that particular kid-code for "my lips are sealed" hasn't been invented yet. Whoops. I try words instead.

"I would never do that. Your secret is safe with me. You can trust me completely."

His smile is shy. "Thank you, miss. Though, I do feel guilty relaxing when the others are so hard at work. I can assure you I don't do it for more than a few minutes each day."

"For what it's worth, I think you deserve all those breaks and then some. If it were up to me, I'd give you whole weeks or months off."

He ducks his head, either in thanks or in embarrassment. Either way, I can tell he'd rather change subjects ASAP, so I ask, "Is there a whole room back there?"

Jonah shrugs lightly. "It's more of a hollowed-out space behind the wall. It's not large, but there's enough room for someone my size to stretch out."

And more than enough to hide a painting.

I could hug him. "Jonah, this is GENIUS. You're, like, smarter than Einstein!"

"Who?"

Must. Remember. Time. Period. Albert Einstein's probably still in college or something right around now. "What I mean is, you're very, very smart and this is beyond perfect."

Jonah beams at me, and I pray it really will be beyond perfect.

"But how did you ever in a million years find this?" I

ask. "And where did you get the key to open it?"

Even in the deep shadows back here, I can see his smile dim. He sighs. "There was a man who worked on the construction of the house, and he was hired on to help maintain things after the opening. He . . . he was . . . very nice to me. He requested my help on many projects around here and even taught me some mathematics and a bit of carpentry; he said I could maybe be a builder's apprentice someday."

"Where is he now?" I ask, but I can tell from the little wobble in Jonah's voice that I'm not going to like the answer.

"He took ill," Jonah says simply. I can figure out the rest. People in 1905 only lived half as long as we do now, on average I mean.

"I'm sorry," I whisper.

"As am I." Then he shakes his shoulders, and his smile returns. "But I believe he would like to know this room is being used for such an important mission now."

I sure hope so. I even hope he's watching down on us now, because I'll take all the help we can get. This *has* to work.

Has to.

Chapter Eighteen

Maggie

TARA KEEPS CHATTERING ALL THE way to Belcourt Castle and halfway back again, and I don't say a word, mostly because I don't understand one thing she says. I'm still thinking about women fighting for equal rights. Women treated as equal to men. People from other cultures playing alongside one another. It's an amazing thought.

We pass old homes I remember, new ones I don't, and large buildings that don't seem to have an obvious purpose. Knowing that other summer cottages like The Breakers and Marble House and Rosecliff and Chateau-sur-Mer all still exist and are museums just like The Elms makes me feel slightly less ill than I've felt since this whole thing started.

"So, Alex told Cheyanne that he thought Brianna was cute. But then Cheyanne got super ticked off, 'cause you KNOW she always thought that Alex liked HER. Between you and me, he just likes to tease. It's a big mess! Bri isn't talking to Cheyanne or me! I mean, is she for real? And Alex expects me to smooth things over, just 'cause he's my cousin. I didn't even do anything!" She pauses to look at me. "You know?"

I can't begin to mimic her language, so I smile and nod my agreement. "Yes. Yes, I do know. How upsetting for you!"

Her language is so strange. I feel like I get more information from her tone than the actual words, though she is speaking English. It just comes out so fast. I believe she's telling me about a quarrel between two of her and Hannah's friends, but I can't be entirely certain.

She pulls out her device and glances at it. "We'd better start toward the field. We've only got a few minutes to get there. If we're late, Coach will have kittens." She makes a devious face. "By the way, Alex texted. He's going to be at the Tower later with Ethan. Wanna stop by?"

I hope my face does not betray my confusion. "Where?"

"The Tower, of course. As long as we don't hang too

long. I need to be home by three o'clock. But we should have time to make a quick stop." She rolls her eyes. This mannerism I recognize. It's the same one my aunt uses when she's exasperated with Colette over some indecent thing she's done.

"I know how much you've been dying to talk to Ethan after last week at the pier. Alex won't tell me outright, but he totally hinted that Ethan's got a new crush. I'm betting it's you." Tara tosses her head in a way that makes me think of Colette, and I understand. A hundred years later, and girls still make fools of themselves over boys. The thought of Colette reminds me that I'm supposed to be enjoying my time in the twenty-first century. She's the one thing from my own time that I do not miss at all.

Even though I feel like I'm getting to know Tara, my hands start to twitch. So far she hasn't really asked me too many questions, but pretending to play a game she's good at, and later having to speak to Hannah's beau? Things are bound to get much more difficult.

But saying no doesn't seem like an option. "Yes, of course. I am delighted."

"Seriously . . . you should probs put the kibosh on that old-timey talk." She shakes her head.

I try to remember Hannah's words from earlier. "I'm cool." I look at Tara, hopeful that I haven't made a huge mistake. She smiles and slips her arm through mine as we head toward Newport proper.

I can breathe. For the time being.

In the heat of the day in my own time, I would be expected to sit in the drawing room and sew. Or read, in my case. I hate—that is, strongly dislike (Aunt frowns on the term "hate")—sewing. In the afternoon my aunt makes us sit quietly to "digest" our lunch while she's out calling on neighbors. Aunt would rather I sew than read. Colette always threatens to tell when I swap my handwork for a book, but I've got enough on her to make sure she won't.

But now I am walking, as bold as brass, down the main street with only another girl my own age as chaperone. It feels like I'm breaking the law! It's absolutely invigorating. I inhale deeply and breathe in the sea air, which smells identical to how it is in my own time.

But I can't enjoy my newfound freedom. My brain keeps returning to the thought of this infernal game I'm supposed to be playing in a few short minutes. And Tara has a plan to meet some boys on the way home. I exhale. One thing at a time. I can think about only one thing at time.

All of a sudden, something looks very familiar. "The Casino!" I shout as we approach a crossroads with more modern buildings. Tara looks at me sidelong.

"The what?" She stops for a moment with her hands on her hips. She looks just like Mrs. O'Neil giving me the evil eye. "Please don't tell me you're going to make me call buildings by their old-fashioned names today." She chuckles as if this might be something Hannah makes her do regularly.

"Oh." I cringe. "No. What do you prefer it be called?"

"Well, I'm pretty sure Serena Williams would want you to call it by its normal name, the International Tennis Hall of Fame." She looks at me. "Like everyone else in Newport?"

This statement leaves me with so many questions. I stick to the most obvious. "Serena . . . ?"

"Williams, of course. She's the GOAT! You know, the greatest of all time? Jeez, Hannah. You're out of it today. Future Hall of Fame inductee? She was in town last week promoting her new clothing line; it's been all over the news." She's staring at me again like I'm a fool. "I know you're crushing on Ethan lately, but it's not like you to be so far under a rock. Especially when it comes to celebrity sightings in Newport."

"The International Tennis Hall of Fame." It feels like an appropriate name for the Casino. I wanted to see Bessie Moore play with Wylie Cameron Grant in the US mixed doubles championship at this exact spot last summer, but Aunt refused to let me attend. It was exhilarating to hear of a woman playing in such a high-stakes game, even if I'm not allowed to exert myself that much. "We could play lawn tennis later, maybe?"

She gives me that look again. "Lawn tennis? Um, sure. Maybe later. But right now we're playing soccer."

We turn right past the Casino and around another corner to where a large field opens up. The smell of cut grass envelops me. Girls of all shapes and sizes and skin color, dressed in uniforms like ours, run back and forth on the field, chasing one another, or a ball. I don't know which.

I blink at the chaos. I tell myself I shouldn't be surprised that so many of the girls look like they were born far away. They are probably like Tara: families from other places, but all from Rhode Island.

And they are all running. The girls are running. They look like they are exerting themselves a lot.

Sometimes Aunt allows us to walk on the grounds, if the day is cool enough. She always says the summer sun will damage my hair or my skin and I must preserve my good looks for my debut. Of course, running is forbidden. It will damage my insides, she says. I've never understood why it wouldn't damage a boy's insides. I realize there are a lot of questions I've not asked in my own time. About a lot of things.

As we get closer, my mouth falls open. These girls are perspiring. Some of them are soaked through their clothes. They look like they are having the times of their lives. I suddenly can't wait to run alongside them.

"C'mon. We don't have much time to warm up," Tara says. "That little detour took longer than I expected. Maybe Coach won't notice we're late." She pulls me toward her and drops her bag. She kicks off her shoes and pulls out a pair with the bumps on the bottom. "Well, are you going to get your cleats on or what?" She glances toward a woman striding in our direction. "You better hurry, Coach doesn't look happy that we're so late."

I flip off the shoes I hurriedly put on in Hannah's room, and slowly lace up the ones found in her bag. If I take long enough, maybe I can observe some of the game before I'm expected to play.

"Hannah!" Tara yells, almost like she's warning me.

A shadow looms over my shoulder. I leap up and hurry after Tara, who runs for the opposite side of the field with the other girls on the team. When we get there, one of the girls says, "Two lines. Dynamic warm-ups." I follow their lead, and before long I'm laughing with them all as we skip, hop, and kick our legs. No one seems to notice that I've never done this before. I can't believe it's so easy.

One of the girls gives a cry that sounds like "whoop," and soon everyone is yelling. I make a small sound that comes out like a quack, but when I try again, I find my voice and scream with the others. I've never had so much fun, and the game hasn't even started.

Tweeeeeet! A loud sound travels across the field. The girls freeze and look toward the sound, which comes from a woman wearing a striped shirt. "Game time!"

The smell of the grass; the wind blowing through my hair; all the girls running next to me, giddy with excitement . . . for a moment I have half a thought that I can do this.

The coach stands on the side of the field, next to the woman in the striped shirt. "Line it up."

Panting harder than I ever have in my life, I get in

line next to Tara. I have to bend over to catch my breath. The striped woman calls our names one at a time. Each of the girls steps out of line when her name is called and turns to show the big number on her back. Then she shows the bottom of her cleats and touches her sock. I can do this. It's going to be easier than I thought.

"Jordan?"

I smile confidently and stride out just like everyone else, like I know exactly what I'm doing. I turn. I show my cleat and tap my sock. I head back to the line.

"Hold it."

I freeze. No one else had to hold it. Coach stands with her hands on her hips. "Where are your shin guards?"

"My what?" I rack my brain, but I'm sure no one mentioned shin guards before just now. I look at Tara, but she seems to have abandoned me.

"Shin guards. Mandatory to play soccer."

"I . . ." I have no idea what she is talking about, but before I can say anything else, Tara runs over.

"Here they are. I forgot to give them back to you. I accidentally put them in my bag." She hands them to me, and with a raised eyebrow as if she realizes I have no idea what to do, she grabs them from me and stuffs one into each of my socks. She pats them hard and says, "Good to go." She gets up and pulls me into line. "What is wrong with you?" she mouths.

Coach shakes her head and gestures. "Bring it in, ladies." We make a tight circle. I sneak a glance around, but everyone's eyes are fixed on Coach. My stomach suddenly lurches.

"This is your game. You've been working hard and have improved so much this summer. Take a deep breath. Remember what we've been doing in practice. You're ready."

Her voice is steady, calm, inspiring. "We'll go with the regular starting lineup. Hands in. 'Team' on three." Coach puts her open palm into the middle of the circle, and all the girls put a hand in. I put mine on top. For a split second the feeling of doom evaporates and I feel something I've never felt before. Something like strength, like I'm part of something much bigger than myself. "One, two, three . . ."

"TEAM!" They shout in unison and throw their arms into the air.

Some of the girls run out onto the field, and the others go over toward the bench near the white line. Coach puts her hand on my shoulder before I have a chance to follow. "Hannah, where are your gloves?"

"Gloves?" I think about the silk pair Aunt Herminie gave me to wear to the ball. No one else is wearing anything like those.

When I don't move or say anything, Coach cocks her head. "Are you feeling okay?"

"Yes, yes, I'm fine."

"Well, go check your bag, then. Your gloves are probably in there."

I rummage around in Hannah's bag, and sure enough, I find a pair of large white gloves with a bright green stripe down the back of them.

"Gloves!" I call to Coach, and wave them in the air.

"Great," she says. "How about you put them on. We have a couple of minutes for a quick warm-up."

I feel warm enough already, but I sense that would be the wrong thing to say. I pull on the gloves. They're big but not too big; it's like they make my hands feel extra large. I like how white and clean they are.

Coach waits for me with a ball in front of the net. "Ready to make some saves? Here you go," she says, and tosses the ball at me. It hits off my stomach and down my legs and feet, before rolling back to Coach. "Sorry, I thought you were ready," she says, and tosses it again.

The same thing happens.

She stares at me, holding the ball under her arm. "Are you ready?"

"I think so."

"Well, how about trying out your new gloves?"

I'm supposed to catch the ball.

She tosses it to me again, and this time I reach my hands out and the ball hits off them. I look down to the other end of the field at the girl standing in the opposite net. She is catching every ball her coach throws.

"Do your gloves feel okay? You're a little off today."

I'm thinking she's just being kind, as this must be more than "a little off" for Hannah.

"Yes. They are quite comfortable. I'm sure I'm just nervous, ma'am."

"Ma'am?" She hesitates, then grins. "It's okay to be nervous, Hannah. Take a few deep breaths. You're an amazing goalkeeper. You've made some awesome saves in practice. Just play like you know how, and you'll do fine."

That's the problem, I want to say. I have no idea how to play.

"Your gloves are probably still a little slippery because they're new. Just spit on them and that will help."

"Did you say spit on my gloves?"

"Like you always do. Remember? It helps to grip the

ball." She demonstrates by spitting on her hands.

She watches me until I reluctantly spit on my gloves and rub my hands together.

Her patience with me is running thin, I can tell. "Okay, I'm going back to the bench. Maybe you just need a few minutes to regroup." She begins to walk away. "You've done this before. Just keep it simple!" She turns back and with a wink adds, "Make sure the ball stays out of the net." She gives me a big smile and a hearty thumbs-up.

A couple of girls shout and clap for me. "Go, Hannah!"

I give them a weak smile. I'm afraid Hannah will never forgive me if I ruin this game. My knees wobble. I think I may need to vomit. Coach, Tara, and the rest of the team are depending on me, and I don't know what I'm doing.

Coach said to take deep breaths. I take one and another and another. It helps. I look down the field at the other goalie and have an idea. I've been imitating someone else all day! I'll just do what she does. I can do this. I take a full breath and feel my heart return to a normal pace.

The whistle blows and the game begins.

The other goalie crouches a little, so I do the same.

She waves her hand now and then, so I do too. The ball is being kicked back and forth mostly in the middle of the field far away from me. It seems to go off the field a lot, which causes the woman with the whistle to blow and pause the game. *I can do this,* I keep saying to myself. All I have to do is watch. And mimic. It should be easy.

The girls from both teams seem to be fighting over the one ball, kicking at it. There are bags of extra balls next to the benches. I don't know why they don't just give one to everyone.

Across the field Tara gets the ball, and she runs fast toward the other goal and kicks the ball hard at the net. The other goalie jumps sideways with her arms all the way extended and catches the ball before she hits the ground.

I stare in disbelief. "Outstanding!" I shout, but when I start clapping, someone from my bench yells to me, "What are you doing? You don't clap for the other team!"

My heart pounds again as I realize there is no way I could ever dive and catch the ball like that girl. I couldn't even catch it standing still. Then, like a lightning bolt, understanding strikes. The goal of the game is to try to get the ball into the other team's net. They expect me to not let the other team kick the ball into our net. All at once my hands feel cold and clammy. I can't stop a ball! I can't jump! I can't catch!

Suddenly someone breaks free and runs full speed at me.

"All you, Hannah!" a girl yells from the bench. "You've got this!"

But I definitely don't "got this." My heart pounds harder. My insides are all fluttery and jumbled. I'm trying to catch my breath. I'm having a hard time not panicking. Maybe this is what my aunt has been worried about—are my insides being damaged?

My teammates chase after the girl with the ball. But she has a clear lead, and it's just her and me. My mind goes blank as soon as I realize that she has kicked the ball and it's headed like a pellet right at my face. At the very last second I wince and withdraw, collapsing to the ground.

"Goal!" announces the striped woman.

I breathe a sigh of relief. But my team has a different reaction. The girls sitting on the bench yell at me. "Seriously, Hannah?"

"Why would you duck?"

"This is a big game!"

"Are you trying to make us lose?"

"What was that?" Coach's hands are in the air, and there's a look of complete dismay on her face.

How can they be mad at me? Didn't they see that that girl tried to kick the ball at my face? What kind of game is this anyway? I loved the running and warming up, but this kicking the ball at my head is barbaric.

It gets worse.

The other team scores again when the ball hits off the bar across the top of the net and then off my back and into the goal. I try not to cry, but it stings. It may leave a mark. The next goal comes when an opposing girl practically runs me over. I stick out my hands, but I never get close to touching the ball. The girl runs right past me like I'm invisible.

The next one is close. The ball strikes me in the chest and knocks the wind out of me, but I make the save. Unfortunately, it bounces out and someone kicks it back in.

With every goal the other team scores, my team gets madder and madder. Why would Hannah want to play this ridiculous position? Why wouldn't she want to run around? Having people kick a ball at me and run into me is not my idea of fun. And now everyone is cross. I bite my lip.

At a break in the game (they call it "halftime"), Coach says, "Jenny, you're going to play net for the second half."

Now I'm trying to hold back tears of joy. I'm finally going to get to sit and rest! But before I have a chance to celebrate, Coach turns to me. "Hannah, take off your gloves. I know you feel bad about the goals. So I'm going to have you start the second half as a forward. Give you a chance to make it up. You were hitting some awesome shots in practice last week. Go rip a few."

Rip a few? Tara must know what Coach means, but I can't ask her, because I'm quite certain she isn't speaking to me right now. I assume that "forward" has something to do with trying to score.

I just want to go sit on the bench and sip water like some of the other girls. Why do I have to get stuck being on the field?

When the whistle blows to start the second half, we put our hands in again. The energy in our "TEAM" call seems to have lost its vigor. I can't help but feel it's my fault. Perhaps I can make up for it playing at forward. The other team seemed to have an easy time scoring goals on us. Maybe it is our turn now.

I jog out with Tara, and she stands next to me and the ball at the middle of the field. The other team takes their places on their side. "We have the kickoff," she says.

I grin stupidly because I have no idea what else to do.

The whistle blows. Tara taps the ball and runs away. Other members of my team sprint in various directions, leaving the ball at my feet. I pause, watching. Not moving. The other team's players start coming at me. They want the ball. I have come to learn one thing about this game of soccer: the ball is like the treasure; everyone wants it. My team is yelling at me to move, to kick the ball.

And then I have the most brilliant idea. I reach down, scoop up the ball in my hands, and hold it over my head as high as I can.

"Here!" I yell, and toss it at Tara. Yes! I can't believe it. I've outwitted these girls at their own game. They are so stunned by my brilliance, no one has moved.

But instead of catching the ball and cheering my amazing move, Tara lets it drop to the ground. She looks bewildered, more than she has all day.

TWEEEEEEEEEEEEEEEEET! The striped woman blows the whistle for a very long time. She seems angry.

"HAND BALL!" she shouts. "Direct, this way." She places the ball back down near the middle of the field and gives me an extremely odd look.

"What the what, Jordan!" someone from my team says, and elbows my ribs. "Are you wacked? Get with the program or get out of the game!" she shouts as she runs off.

My eyes sting.

"Hannah!" the coach yells. "Are you sick? What's going on with you? Hit the bench."

I take that to mean I'm out of the game. Finally.

Just watching the rest of the soccer game would have been glorious. Girls running, playing, being a part of something exciting. Exerting themselves, as Aunt would say. Perspiring, even. I would never have believed it if I hadn't experienced it. But I've ruined something for Hannah with my failure, and I can't shake that terrible feeling. I won't blame her if she hates me for it.

"Bad luck on the game, Han," Tara says as we walk away from the field among the crowd of girls. We have to dodge slow-moving automobiles as they stop to pick up players. "What was up with you out there? Are you getting enough sleep? Are you sick?"

"I . . . I don't know." I sigh. "You don't have to pretend. I was horrible. The whole team hates me."

She's not protesting, so I know I'm right. I think

about the game again. "I love running. But I didn't like being a target for the ball."

"Don't worry about it. We all have off days." Tara repositions her bag on her back and expertly changes the subject as we pass the Casino again. "So . . . are you still up for heading to the Tower to see my stupid cousin and Ethan?" She glances at me hopefully.

"Is your cousin really stupid?" I can't tell if she's serious. I certainly wouldn't call Colette stupid, though there are a lot of other words that describe my own cousin.

"Nah. You know he's my best friend—well, next to you." She flicks her finger against my arm, and winces. "He's just been really annoying since he started liking girls. It used to be great when we could all just kick a ball around, but now that he's trying to get me to give him all the inside scoop on my friends, not so much."

"Why are we going to meet them again?" After my failure at soccer, all I want is to go home and crawl under the covers, but I need to do something helpful. It's one thing for someone to be suspicious of Hannah's odd behavior. And another to lose a game. But I've watched Colette talk to boys, and I am confident I can do this.

"You really are clueless today, Han. Do I have to spell it out? I know you like Ethan. God knows why. Alex has been hinting that Ethan likes you." After shrugging her shoulders, she shakes her head and for the first time looks doubtful. "On second thought maybe you're really not up for it. Maybe it's not the right day." Her voice wavers as she stops and looks at me. "Want to wait for when you're feeling better?"

I made a fool of myself—Hannah—during the game, but maybe I can make it up to her. "No. No, of course I'm okay. I do want to see . . . Ethan."

Even though I'm too young to be courting, I've watched Colette flirt with all the boys in Newport this summer—this will be easy.

"Okay. Whatever you say. Just don't mess this up. You don't want Ethan to think you're cray-cray going into the school year." She whirls her finger in a circle around her ear. "Lay off the weird talk."

As we walk, I continue to be distracted by so many buildings and fast-moving automobiles and people, but as soon as we get near the park, things look familiar. A group of young people our age congregates on the granite next to a fence that surrounds the Tower—and I realize I know exactly where we are. The Touro Tower is the ancient remains of a windmill built centuries before my own time. It's in the same spot, even though you can usually see the harbor. The familiar appearance gives me a shot of confidence. This is still, after all, Newport.

We're only three blocks away from the ocean, and my feet are itching to see what changes have been made at the waterfront. But instead I must face a sea of unfamiliar faces.

The group appears to be having a meeting, but I cannot imagine what the topic could be. Most of them stare down at their tiny devices. I scan the group, wondering which one is Ethan—Hannah's beau. I glance at Tara for a clue.

"There you are," says a dark-eyed boy with brown hair, running at us. He punches Tara in the arm and then looks at me, shaking his head. "Hey, Hannah. Bad luck on the game."

"How . . . how do you know what happened?"

He holds up his device. "Cheyanne Snapchatted your best misses."

A girl with long black hair, held back by a headband, waves from a few feet away. I recognize her from the game. She was watching, pointing her device in my direction.

"Sorry." The boy shrugs. "Good news, though," he says, perking up. "You're going viral." He looks a little like the puppy that lives at Arleigh, like I should scratch behind his ears. I know without a doubt that this is Alex, Tara's cousin.

"I . . ." I can't even pretend. He's saying words that make no sense. "Viral . . . that's good?"

Tara laughs. "Duh, Hannah. Viral is the best!" She pauses. "Although, maybe not for those reasons."

"Nah. It's all good." Alex gestures to the five or six people loitering nearby. "You're da bomb, Han. So funny! Ethan here"—he gestures to a tall, blond boy walking toward us—"was just telling me how funny he thinks you are."

"In a good way, right, Alex?" Tara looks concerned. "You're not laughing *at* her. We've all had our bad days. I mean, you ran into the metal goalpost in the first five minutes of your first game and were out with a concussion for three weeks."

"But we don't talk about that, cuz." He scowls and waves Tara away. "Ethan!" he says, and raises his fist. The other boy bumps Alex's fist with his own. I'm not entirely sure, but I think this ritual is a gesture of manners—like a handshake—and a boost of confidence shoots through me. I understand manners.

Ethan has fair hair and pale skin, and when he smiles, I see two rows of metal attached to his teeth. His baggy shorts skim the top of his knees, and he wears a blue shirt with a pair of red socks and the number one on the front. I assume it must be his team shirt.

"Hi, Hannah," he says shyly. Alex rolls his eyes, but he takes Tara by the arm and leads her away so that Ethan and I stand alone, staring at each other. Except for his clothing, he looks a lot like one of the Vanderbilt cousins. Colette would approve, although I'm more partial to Alex's puppy-dog brown eyes.

The rest of the group chatters behind us, no doubt talking about the abysmal soccer game. A soft sea breeze blows across the otherwise hazy afternoon.

This is my chance to redeem myself. I take a breath and then hold out my hand to Ethan. I've seen Colette do this a dozen times. The boy is supposed to take the girl's hand and kiss it gently. It's a sign of good breeding.

"It is a pleasure to see you . . . again." I try not to stammer, but the words don't flow in the coquettish way Colette performs them.

"Um . . ." Instead of kissing my hand, he shakes it limply at the fingertips.

Applesauce. People don't kiss hands anymore? I'm ready to retreat back to The Elms and hide in Hannah's room for the duration of my time here. But the boy doesn't seem to be affected by my faux pas.

"Do you— I mean . . . would you like to . . . um . . . Do you wanna hang out some night?" He can't keep his feet still while he stammers out the question.

"At night?" I don't mean for my voice to come out so loud. And I can tell the boy is nervous. But that's no excuse for the most forward invitation I've ever heard. As if Hannah would go out with a boy after that pathetic excuse for a request! And at night? Aunt Herminie would forbid Colette to speak to the boy ever again.

Tara's head whips around from a few feet away, where she's talking to Alex.

"Well, yeah." His feet shuffle in the dry grass. "A bunch of us are going to see the new zombie flick down at the cineplex, and I know you like that scary stuff. And it only plays after nine." After the last word he picks up his head and stares me in the eye as though daring me. It is extremely forward of him.

I will not allow this boy, no matter how attractive, to sully Hannah's good name by offering an evening date. It would be extremely improper. She'd be lucky to ever get another invitation if she accepted such a suggestion. "Perhaps we could go for a stroll along the Cliff Walk.

Some *afternoon*." I lower my eyelashes. "And Tara could serve as chaperone."

"Well, sure. That would be okay too." He looks over his shoulder at Alex with a confused look, as Tara sidles up next to me.

"Hannah, I think you've been out in the sun too long. You're starting to sound like the reenactors from the Antiquities Society again. Let's get you home." She pulls my arm.

"Oh. Of course. Ethan, my dear." I hold out my hand again, hoping he will behave properly this time. But of course he does not. I rack my brain for the most poetic verse I know. I come up with the perfect one. "'In vain have I struggled. It will not do. My feelings will not be repressed. You must allow me to tell you how ardently I admire and love you.'"

Even Colette would be proud!

Tara succeeds in pulling me away from the boys, who look like they've been struck dumb. "Over the top, Han," she whispers. "Way too far over the top."

As soon as we get around the corner, onto the cobblestone street of a bustling marketplace, she doubles over laughing. "Did you see his face? OMG, I can't believe you had the nerve, Hannah! What was that quote from?"

Seeing Tara laugh makes me smile. "Do you not know *Pride and Prejudice*?"

"Oh, sure. I knew it sounded familiar, from when you made me read it last summer. Why didn't you tell me you were going to do that?" She's taking gasping breaths as she tries to stop laughing. I'm not sure why she's so amused.

"Was it not 'over the top,' then?"

"Of course it was over the top. But if you ask me, Ethan Grimes is a bit too high and mighty for his own good. He's cute; just ask *him*." She rolls her eyes. "And I hated to say something because I thought you had a thing for him. But taking him down like that is exactly what that boy needs."

I'm suddenly afraid I've done something that Hannah will regret even more than failing at soccer.

Chapter Nineteen

Hannah

DUST TICKLES.

I mean, for something so minuscule that it usually floats through the air undetected, when it gets into your nostrils and you can't sneeze because you're hiding behind heavy drapes in the drawing room, waiting to foil an art thief, it's a surprisingly *enormous* issue.

I scrunch my nose in a hundred different directions to fight off the sneezing fit, which works, but which also makes Jonah nearly laugh out loud as he watches me from behind the window's other curtain. I widen my eyes at him in warning. Jeez, who would have thought being quiet would be this much of a problem, especially for a self-proclaimed master lurker like me?

Except it turns out there's a pretty big difference between lurking—which usually involves (mostly harmless) eavesdropping on a conversation or (mostly harmless) spying on some kind of activity—and waiting. Which is how I've been wasting my one precious day in the past. And now I'm supposed to be meeting Maggie in less than two hours to switch back, and I have nothing at all to show for my time here.

I wish I could at least chat with Jonah to pass the time. I find his life fascinating, and he's really sweet and nice. But of course that would require something other than complete silence, so I've had to amuse myself with making faces at him to try to get him to smile. He's extra good at his poker face, but I've gotten him to at least crack one a couple of times. The rest of the time, I catch him darting his eyes everywhere, like he's trying to memorize every detail of the crazy-extravagant drawing room. He's totally fascinated by the elaborate painted mural of the god of the north wind that covers most of the ceiling.

But other than that it's been a whole lot of . . .

Just. Waiting.

Boring, mind-numbing, nothing-to-do-or-listen-to waiting.

Well, not *nothing* to listen to. The house is full of people scrambling about to prepare for tonight's ball. But none of them are venturing into the drawing room, and none of them are cheerfully calling to each other or kidding around the way our staff at home does when we're decorating the mansion for the holidays or prepping for a wedding on the grounds. This household is all quiet efficiency. Would it kill them to crack a joke here and there?

I startle when Jonah's foot stretches across the distance between our hiding spots and nudges mine. I raise *What the heck?* eyes to his, only to find him looking all freaked out. He jerks his head to the side twice, and I finally catch on.

There's someone out there!

We've had exactly three false alarms in the several hours we've been hiding back here. (Yes, hours. If my sneezing doesn't give us away, my rumbling stomach might.) The first was a maid doing a quick straightening up of furniture and a run over the wooden surfaces with a feather duster. (I felt like whispering, "It's the *curtains* you should really think about dusting!") The second was a different maid, watering Mrs. Berwind's potted ficus. And the third was a footman passing through on his way to the conservatory. Other than that the room has been as quiet as my middle school on a snow day.

But this is not a false alarm, and it's not the butler looking for the jar of silver polish. It's a man creeping up to the sideboard, where the landscape filling in for the real portrait is propped behind a white sheet.

OMG, ART HEIST IN PROGRESS!

My yawning boredom disappears in a split second because there is a man putting grabby hands on the painting, only two feet to my left!

It's really, actually happening!

I don't recognize him, but I know he's not a servant, because he isn't in uniform. He's wearing a white button-down shirt, but it's loose, and the sleeves are rolled up and there are streaks of red on his arms, almost like—

Like blood! Is he a *murderous* art thief?! No one said anything about that being a possibility, and I would like my money back, please. I didn't sign up for this!

I'm scared to turn my head to look at Jonah next to me, because what if that makes a sound? Just knowing that he's here with me is comforting, at least. (Although, I would actually prefer if it were maybe more like thirty-seven Jonahs, who were all wearing shirts with the letters *FBI* stamped across their backs.)

The man has his fingers on the edges of the painting, still wrapped in the sheet. Is he gonna just walk out with it? I mean, that's basically what Jonah and I did earlier, and we didn't encounter a soul, so I guess it's as good a plan as any, but is it really this easy to steal precious masterpieces?

Jonah's foot nudges mine again, and this time I chance turning my head toward him. His eyes stare pointedly at the camera on the windowsill next to me. Oh! Right! I'm supposed to be getting photographic evidence.

I found this Brownie camera in Maggie's room when I was killing time there this morning, and although it takes pictures more slowly than a website loads in the Wi-Fi dead zone of my bedroom, if I act carefully, I should be able to catch this dude in the act. I wonder if this is Maggie's prized possession or if it was the one thing she begged for at Christmas, like me with my iPhone. Or maybe she's got twenty of these, one for every house she visits. As much as I always felt like Maggie and I would have so, so many things in common if we ever met up, being mega-rich isn't one of them.

Wow, I get rambly when I'm nervous. My thoughts are skittering all over the place, just like the pulse in my wrist. *Focus, Hannah! Get the picture!*

I ease the camera out between the opening in the curtains and try my best to hold it steady in shaky hands. I practiced snapping a shot of Jonah earlier (he blushed like crazy, as if it were the first time anyone took his picture or something), but I only took the one because I can't tell how much film is left in the camera. I already know it doesn't take pictures anywhere nearly as fast as my phone does. But I have to work with what I've got and cross fingers that a fuzzy picture combined with Jonah's and my witness statements is enough to do the job.

The man slides the painting off the sideboard. He struggles to get his hands around both sides of the giant frame and staggers backward a little under the weight of it. One step, then two. I hear the tiniest cough from Jonah, urging me on.

CLICK!

I take the shot. The noise from the flash bounces off the walls and echoes against the high ceilings, and the man freezes.

I lower the camera.

The man swivels and stares dead into my eyes.

I can't swallow or breathe.

Jonah steps out from behind his curtain, and the guy's gaze switches to him. Jonah squares his shoulders and returns the gaze, hard. (Go, Jonah! Go, Jonah!) After a second the man swallows thickly and turns back to me. He sets the painting, still wrapped in its sheet, on the ground at his feet and smiles brightly. Too brightly to be believable.

"*Je l'avais tout simplement amené à Mademoiselle Cassatt pour une retouche de dernière minute*," he says.

"Say what, now? Try English, buddy," I order.

His forehead wrinkles. "*Je ne comprends pas.* You spoke French so perfectly during the sitting."

Okay, so:

Of course Maggie speaks flawless French. I'll bet her tutor has been drilling it into her since she was in diapers.

Are diapers a thing in 1905?

Focus, Hannah!

Sitting. He said "sitting." Is he—

"Who *are* you? Are you involved with the portrait somehow?" I ask.

His eyes squinch up. "*Mais oui.* We have been working

together for weeks now. How is it that you do not recognize me? I am Mademoiselle Cassatt's apprentice."

I dart a glance at the red streaks on his arms. Not blood. Paint. Um, *phew*! I exchange a quick look of relief with Jonah, then turn back to Mr. Frenchy Pants.

"Of course you are. I knew that. But—but why are you stealing a painting of hers, then?"

"Stealing? *Non!* I'm bringing it to Mademoiselle for a last-minute touch-up. Stealing! Ha! You have quite the imagination, young miss." He barks out a laugh that sounds faker than fake.

I'm not buying it. And the "young miss" thing is so . . . demeaning. I always assumed Maggie would get mad respect for being an heiress, but I guess, even here, money doesn't trump age. Kids never get any credit from adults for having actual, functioning brains in our heads.

I sneak a peek at Jonah. When I catch his eye, I raise my eyebrows to silently ask him what he thinks of this guy's flimsy excuse. He shrugs, but I can see a whole lotta doubt on his face. I'm guessing he doesn't feel like he can speak up, seeing as he has neither age nor money on his side.

But the thing is, it's not like we can prove anything.

My gut says this guy is lying, but that plus a nickel . . . leaves me with a nickel.

The man can tell I'm hesitating. He takes advantage of my indecision and picks the painting back up. "*Au revoir.* I must deliver this to Mademoiselle Cassatt."

He hoists the frame higher in his arms and peeks around its side to see his way to the door.

Uh-oh. Not only have I not stopped a heist, but now there's going to be deep trouble when Mary Cassatt whisks off that sheet and discovers that the portrait she worked on for months is not there. We were careful, but what if someone saw me and Jonah sneaking around this afternoon and puts two and two together? Maggie will kill me if I ruin her life in a matter of one afternoon!

I'm just standing with my mouth open, watching the empty doorway that Mr. Apprentice Guy disappeared through, when Jonah puts his hand on my sleeve. "Excuse me, miss?"

I snap, "Maggie! Call me Maggie." When he fumbles back a step, I realize what a jerk I'm being to literally the only person who's been nice to me in this entire century. It's not *Jonah's* fault I'm a total fail at foiling art heists.

"Oh my gosh, I'm so sorry," I say. "I didn't mean to say it like that. It's just that it feels weird to have you call me something so . . . so . . . formal. I mean, we're both kids, so . . ."

He looks confused. "What does our age have to do with anything?"

I know what he's getting at. We're the same age, but he and Maggie are not of the same social station, and that matters a lot here. A lot a lot. He's probably been trained since the day he started not to address the occupants of the house unless spoken to first. Most likely he's been told to even avoid eye contact with me. For him to have agreed to help me today wasn't just nice of him. It was taking a big risk with his job. And here I repay him by being totally rude. *Nice one, Hannah.*

"I really am sorry. Please. I know it might not feel natural to say, but it would mean a lot if you could call me Maggie instead of 'miss.' If you could, well, maybe think of me as"—I give him a small, hopeful smile before continuing—"a friend?"

His eyes grow wide at that, and I offer, "I know that's not really normal for two people like us, but . . ."

I trail off, and it's a second before he answers. "But it would be nice. To have a friend, I mean. I don't have much free time to spend with the others my age in my neighborhood. Most of them work too, and our days off rarely match. Of course, I'm friendly with all the kitchen staff, but they're so much older and it's not the same thing."

Once again my heart hurts for him. What kind of a childhood is that? I can't help asking, "Doesn't that bother you?"

He shrugs. "It's simply life as I know it."

My throat aches. He doesn't even sound upset, so much as . . . resigned. I spend so much time back home surrounded by the glamorous side of the Gilded Age and daydreaming about the outrageous parties and the elaborate dresses and the ridiculous wealth, but it wasn't golden for everyone. Not even for *most* people. Definitely not for Jonah, and hearing it in person really drives it home in a different way than just reading about it.

The thing is, he's right. This *is* life as he knows it, and it won't change for him either. He may work his way up to chef someday, but otherwise this is probably how his whole future will look. Working here or somewhere just like it. People like Jonah didn't have the luxury of big dreams. Which is also true of lots of people—even kids—in my time too, and that sucks just as much.

But actually, even some people with *all* the luxury didn't have the freedom to dream big. Like Maggie. Sure, she's as pampered as can be and will never want for any-thing material, but she's a girl, which means she'll never get to decide for herself what she wants to be when she grows up. She already knows she'll be a wife and maybe a mother (who only sees her kids an hour a day, because that's the custom), and a society woman who spends time visiting only with other people from her same class.

The reality is, if I actually did live here, chances are next to zero that I'd be able to be friends with Jonah. Even if he weren't a servant, he's still a boy, which means we wouldn't be allowed to hang without a chaperone. (But the servant thing would kill everything first.)

Of course, I *don't* live here. I won't even be here in a couple of hours. Maybe it's not fair of me to offer Jonah friendship.

My shoulders slump. I've made a mess of things. What was all this for, if it wasn't to solve the mystery of the stolen painting? I should have just gone exploring Gilded Age Newport, instead of lurking for eons in a dark coal tunnel and hiding out for even more hours behind a dusty curtain and involving someone who was minding his own business. Great. Just great.

And all for nothing.

If anything, I made things worse. As soon as Mary

Cassatt finds the dummy painting, the whole house will be in an uproar over the missing one, and I'll have to expose Jonah's secret break spot to show them where the real painting is hidden, and that's going to take some major explaining, and what if Jonah gets fired for helping me and he can't help his family put food on their table and they—

"Maggie?"

Jonah's voice snaps me out of my spiraling thoughts, and it takes me a second to realize he's used my (well, Maggie's) first name.

"Hey, you called me—" But I break off when I see his face and how urgent his expression is. "What is it?"

"I just thought of something. Is the paint an artist uses very different from other paint?" he asks.

"Different how?"

"Is it oil-based?"

"Not always. There are watercolors and acrylics and others, but yes, the portrait was done with oils. Why?"

Jonah fidgets with his hands and glances away. "I'm just a kitchen boy, so I don't know anything about fancy things like portraits . . ."

"But?" I urge him on.

He takes a deep breath and locks eyes with me.

"But last winter I helped paint some shelves in the wine cellar, and we used an oil-based mixture. It took three solid days before the shelves dried enough to replace the bottles. Do you think—that is to say, would it be likely that the artist would truly chance a touch-up only hours before the unveiling? I wondered if perhaps the paint would still be—"

"Wet!" I interrupt. "Jonah! You're right. She would never, ever do that." Just like that, my bad mood evaporates and my head is back in the game. "They'd put the sheet back on to hide it until the big reveal, and the paint would definitely stick to that and it would be a giant mess! Mary Cassatt wouldn't chance that. Meaning, that guy was lying through his teeth! I *knew* he was. You really *are* a genius. I don't care if you don't know who he is yet—I'm calling you Einstein from here on out. We have to find that man and confront him again. Let's go!"

I take two steps toward the hallway, but Jonah doesn't follow.

"C'mon. We have to hurry if we want to catch him!" I urge. "I know he doesn't have the real painting, but I still want to bust his smug old liar-liar-pants-on-fire face."

Jonah is frozen in place. "I cannot be caught out there," he says, eyes wide. "Not on this floor of the house.

Not on my day off. There wouldn't be a plausible explanation I could give for any of it." He looks genuinely scared, and my heart hurts for him.

"I'll take full blame," I promise. "I'll say you were helping me. That I ordered you to do it. They can't get mad at you if you were following orders from a lady of the house, right?"

Jonah shakes his head slowly. "It wouldn't be honorable of me to allow you to lie on my behalf."

It wouldn't be honorable? Boys in my century could learn a bunch from this kid. I kind of like this guy at school, Ethan, but I can tell you right now he'd never worry about something like honor.

"Well, then I do order you. There. Now it's not a lie," I say, but he doesn't look any more convinced. I puff my bangs out of my eyes and force my voice to stay soft. "How about this, then? How about we just don't get caught?"

I barely know the guy, but I'm already onto his tell. It's that tiny twinkle in his eyes when he thinks about having an adventure. I watch him closely, and grin. "So you're in?"

He keeps me in suspense for a second, but then he nods sharply. "I suppose it would be even less honorable to allow you to go after him on your own. Let's find this cad."

I'm gonna have to give him a pass on that "allow" thing because he's living in this century. And also because, even though I fully believe girls are just as capable as boys, if I'm being totally honest, I definitely would feel better about confronting the "cad" with a backup at my side. But I'm so taking the lead on things, just to prove a point.

Jonah sticks close behind me as I peek out into the wide marble hallway that connects all the rooms on this level. Empty. I figure we've wasted at least two or three minutes talking since Apprentice Dude disappeared with the painting. He could be anywhere by now.

"Which way?" I whisper.

Jonah thinks for a beat and then whispers back, "He has a head start on us, but he also has that big painting to wrestle with, so he's not moving fast. He thinks he has the real portrait, so he'll be looking to make a quick getaway, but he still has to keep up his cover story until he gets off the grounds, in case he runs into anyone else."

I nod along, and he continues, "The artist is staying in the guesthouse closest to the stables; I heard Mr. Birch instruct one of the footmen where to deliver a telegram that came for her last week. So my guess is that her assistant will keep to the path toward her cottage until he hits an opening in the estate wall that will let him out into the street. I know just where that is; it's not far from the servants' entrance."

I turn to gape at him. "Okay, forget Einstein. Your new nickname is Sherlock. Have you read any of those?"

He ducks his head and murmurs, "No. I—I don't read very well."

Drat, Hannah. You should have anticipated that. Now you've embarrassed him, when it's so not his fault that he doesn't go to school. I keep my voice light. "Well, he's a brilliant detective, but I think you might be his match. We have a thief to catch. Ready?" I swing the camera around to my back, peek into the hallway again to make sure the coast is still clear, and then signal for Jonah to follow me. I do my best Catwoman impression as we dart from doorway to stairwell, then slip out the front door. We edge along the exterior wall until we turn the corner.

"There!" Jonah says, pointing to a skinny man wobbling under the weight of a sheeted painting, far in the distance at the edge of the estate grounds.

"Run for it!" I shout, taking off down the path. Jonah

follows, and if he thinks it's weird that a girl is keeping pace with him, despite all the layers of fluffy stuff underneath my dress and a camera slapping against me, he doesn't say a word. He just huffs and puffs alongside me, pumping his arms as hard as I am.

Apprentice Dude doesn't even sense us coming. All it takes is one teensy nudge by me from behind, and he goes toppling over, getting all tangled in the sheet that comes loose as he drops the frame.

"You!" he gasps. He struggles into sitting position, then spots the exposed painting on the ground. The one that is NOT of Margaret Dunlap. "The portrait!"

His eyes dart back and forth among Jonah, me, and the canvas. Finally he sputters, "I—I don't understand."

"That's right, you don't, buddy," I say, jabbing my finger into his face. It's two against one, I'm exhilarated from my run, and he's all twisted up in a sheet; the combination makes me extra brave. "But we do. Mademoiselle Cassatt's not doing any touch-ups hours before an unveiling. That would be crazy. So you lied. Because you were trying to steal the painting. Just admit it."

He ignores my order and asks, "But where is the portrait?"

Jonah snorts.

I roll my eyes. "Wow, you really don't get it. You're toast. You never had the real painting, and you never will. Deal with it."

The man puts his face in his hands and hangs his head. "I was so close."

"Yeah, you were soooo close to stealing a worthless landscape," I say. "Gold star for you."

The man shakes his head, still covered by his hands. "The portrait's not much more valuable. It wasn't about that."

Interesting. Now I'm intrigued. "What, then?"

"I didn't want it unveiled," he says through his fingers. "I didn't want anyone to see it."

I exchange a look with Jonah, but it seems Sherlock hasn't pieced things together yet either, because he looks just as puzzled as I am.

"But you told me you were there for the sittings," I say. "And you're Mary Cassatt's apprentice. Wouldn't that make you feel proud of it? Wouldn't you want the whole world to see what she created?"

He drops his hands and looks at me, and his eyes have this weird hard look in them. "I knew that if no one had the chance to see this portrait, Mademoiselle Cassatt's bright light would begin to dim, and attention would move on to the painting world's rightful artistic virtuosos, such as myself. Everyone knows men are the ones who should be honored and acknowledged for our creative genius. She doesn't deserve glory. Not—not a weak-minded *female*!"

He spits the last word out of his mouth like it's a watermelon seed.

I drop my jaw. "Seriously, dude?"

Both Jonah and Frenchy stare at me.

"Dude? What is this 'dude' word? *Je ne comprends pas.*"

I just laugh softly. "Listen, I've got news for you. Your boss is . . . She's . . . well, let me put it this way. In a hundred years her paintings are gonna hang in museums all around the world, and schoolkids are gonna do reports on her. Who are *you*?"

"Augustus Renaldo," he answers, tilting his head in confusion.

I pretend to think hard for a second. "Yeah . . . nope. Not a single person in the future will have your name on their lips. The only way your memory is going to be preserved for all time is in the picture this camera contains. The one proving you're a spineless, gutless, sneaky *nobody*. Oh, and by the way, in case it isn't totally clear"—I drop my voice to a whisper and lean down so he can hear me—"this here weak-minded *female* just B-U-S-T-E-D BUSTED you."

There's dead silence when I stop speaking, and then Jonah quietly claps. "That was amazing."

I flash him a giant smile. "Thanks."

We both turn to face Augustus-You-Bustus, who's studying the grass.

"What were you planning to do with the painting?" I ask.

"Nothing! That is to say, I planned to destroy it the first opportunity I got."

Wow. Just wow. The guy's ignorant *and* heartless. I can't even.

"What will you do with me?" he asks.

My intention all along was to see justice done and turn the thief in, and he definitely deserves to rot in jail. But then I realize what will happen if I run yelling for the Berwinds right now. Gossip about the attempted theft will be all over Newport in an hour and cause chaos for the ball. The drawing room—aka the scene of the crime—will fill with cops and there won't be any chance for Maggie and me to switch places. That's so not fair to her. She deserves to be back for her own ball. Maybe it's enough just to know that the painting is safe and sound.

I narrow my eyes. "You're really extra lucky that I don't have time today to turn you over to the authorities, like you deserve. But if I'm gonna let you get away with this, I do have terms."

"Terms?" he asks, sounding scared.

Good. He should sound scared.

I raise my finger, as if to poke him. "You're going to leave. ASAP. Pronto. Don't say a word to anyone, do not pass Go, do not collect two hundred dollars. And don't try to figure out what that means. Just leave. And never, ever, EVER come back or try to contact Mademoiselle Cassatt, or anyone in my family, or even anyone remotely related to any of the families I might know in passing. You should probably just switch to painting houses, in fact. Or fences. Or porta-potties, whenever those become a thing. Do you get me?"

He nods so fast, I'm afraid his head might pop off his neck. Wow. This is actually kind of FUN! I feel like a superhero. Jonah looks like he's trying not to laugh, but in a supportive way, not a mean way.

"How do I know you won't use that picture you took against me the minute I leave here?" he asks.

I sigh, because he's seriously pushing his luck. I hold the camera out in front of me and flick open the door that contains the roll of film. It unspools toward the ground, ruined. "Satisfied?"

Jonah gives me a look that can only be interpreted as, *Why did you DO that?* but I just shrug. "I have my reasons," I whisper.

He nods, and we both watch in satisfaction as Augustus-You-Bustus gets up and slinks out the opening in the wall, onto the street.

I turn and high-five Jonah, who seems a little unsure of how to do it but plays along. Jeez, is the high five not even a thing yet? There sure are some major inventions coming in the twentieth century!

"What do we do now?" Jonah asks.

"We have to put the portrait back on the wall, so it's all ready for tonight."

Jonah shifts from one foot to the other. "I owe you an apology. I did not put full faith in the words of a fortune-teller, but I'm a true believer now. She said there would be an art heist, and there *was* an art heist! Or an attempted one, at least."

I blink. If Jonah's mind is blown by that, imagine if he knew the rest of the story—like the fact that I hail from the future.

A future I'm about to zoom back to. I should be

crazy-excited about solving the art heist (and hello, vindication—I knew Jonah was innocent!), and part of me is. I'm so curious to see what it will be like to go home and have the original portrait hanging there and no one talking about the art heist, because it never even happened. It's going to be so weird. At least it's one less thing Trent can mess up on his tours.

But as great as all that is, I can't help being bummed that so much of my short time here was spent hiding and waiting, when there's all this history to explore. I never even glimpsed Mr. Berwind! And I wanted more time to hang with Jonah where we could just chat.

I know I shouldn't be greedy, but I really wish this weren't all ending so quickly.

Chapter Twenty

Maggie

FTER CHANGING OUT OF MY DIRTY uniform into a pair of very soft pink trousers and a blouse I found in Hannah's closet, and then taking a short nap, I feel much better. I still cannot believe the softness of these clothes. I flip through a couple of the books on her desk and ponder how to smuggle them back to my own time. After skimming the books on her shelf, I pull out one whose title I recognize. It's a brightly colored version of *The Wonderful Wizard of Oz*, and it strikes me that there are things in this time that are similar to my own. It makes me feel hopeful that not everything fades away for something newer or shinier.

Just before seven o'clock I hover near the reproduction

portrait. I've looked at it from all angles, close, far, left, right. It is not a bad facsimile. The dress is all wrong, but the artist got the lighting mostly right. I remember how many days I had to sit still in order for Mademoiselle Cassatt to capture my likeness. If I could do it again, I would ask her more questions about her life, even if that horrible Monsieur Renaldo pulled faces at me behind her back. It's a shame all her work was for nothing, since the original was never unveiled. I hope whatever we're doing here fixes that wrong, and Mademoiselle gets the credit she deserves. I feel like she is one person from my own time who would appreciate the advances made by women in this century.

And now, more than a century later, a photograph can be taken that looks as clear as real life. I must admit that there's something about painted portraits I like better. The texture and the brushstrokes breathe a life that's different from the two-dimensional photographs that adorn the shelves across the room.

"Hannah, dear?"

"Yes, ma'am?"

An elderly lady standing in the opening to the ballroom looks from me to the portrait and back to me again. She startled me, but I try not to let it show.

"I know I've been here for only a short time, but please call me Florence. You seem to be quite preoccupied with Miss Margaret this afternoon." She steps closer and looks up at the portrait again. "Is there something new you're seeing?" Her expression is curious, and though I've never seen her before, she makes me feel safe.

I take a deep breath, knowing I need to suppress all my recent thoughts, even though I want nothing more than to confide in this woman for some strange reason. "Did you ever wonder if the artist who re-created the portrait got it wrong?"

"Actually, yes, I have." She winks as she gestures for me to come closer. "The rumors are that the dress was originally green." She stares serenely up into my face hanging on the wall.

"Wha—?" I try to close my mouth, but I approach her side and gaze up. She's right about the dress, but at that moment something flickers in the mirror under the portrait. Clearly this woman must not be permitted to see Hannah and me talk.

"Did you hear that?" I ask, turning toward the front of the house.

"Oh goodness!" she says, taking a step toward the ballroom. "I'm sure it's the bride's mother stopping down to make sure the flowers have arrived. She's a big donor, so it's all hands on deck tonight. Elaine, the wedding planner, wanted to be here when the woman arrived, but the last time I saw Elaine, she was busy trying to make sure the caterer's truck could fit under the arboretum. I'll go run interference. I suggest you keep out of the way tonight."

"There's a wedding here tonight?" I feel a thrill of excitement, thinking about what a wedding in the twenty-first century will look like, and then a jolt of reality. How am I going to switch back with Hannah when preparations for a bustling party are happening behind me?

"You could probably stay in here and watch; the wedding will be intimate and confined to the ballroom, not this room." She pauses halfway to the doorway and looks at me, as if she's about to say something else.

I nod, hoping she leaves quickly, but not wanting to be rude. "Thank you."

I am a bit nervous to tell Hannah what a mess I've made of her life. Although, I've been thinking about it all afternoon, and I am fairly certain I could get better at running and kicking, if given the chance. I need to figure out how to sneak in some running when I'm not being watched at home. My heart jumps a little at the thought of creeping around behind my aunt's back. Avoiding my father when I'm back in New York will be easier, even though there won't be anywhere to run in the city. Perhaps at least I can modify my skirts somehow and run up and down the stairs. I imagine other girls in my time being interested, and for a brief moment I construct a fantasy in which I form a ladies' running club when I get back to school. I must admit that it will be nice to get home to a place where things make sense, even if I do plan on finding ways to resist some of society rules; now that I've been here, I can see how silly they are. It makes so much more sense for women to be able to do the same things men can do.

I sigh in anticipation, knowing it is a sound that would be admonished by my aunt as self-indulgent and childish—but then I giggle recklessly at the thought of her dismay at my planned rule-breaking. I take a deep breath to try to get control of my emotions. Any moment now Hannah expects me to appear, ready to return to 1905. As Florence slides the pocket door shut, I turn to the mirror and climb slowly onto the sideboard, thankful the tourists are all gone.

I push the portrait frame aside. The mirror shimmers, and Hannah's (or rather, my) face appears in the glass.

A large painting is propped next to her on the sideboard. "Hey, Mags. There's no time to catch you up on what's been going on here, but guess what? We caught the thief! It's wasn't Jonah. He's totes innocent! It was really this dude named Augustus Renaldo."

"What? That horrible man? Now that you mention it, though, he likely should have been on my list of suspects." I think about the way he's been glaring at me during all our portrait sittings. I clear my throat. "Before you continue, Hannah, I must confess something."

"Uh-oh." Her face falls. "What'd you do? Don't tell me I'm grounded for life!"

"I—I don't think so," I stammer, though I don't know what "grounded" means.

She turns at a noise behind her and then faces me again. "Confess later. It's getting busy around here, so if you want to attend this ball, now's your chance. Unless you'd rather stay me a little longer?" Her voice sounds hopeful, but I shake my head.

"No, I'm ready to return."

She nods slowly. "Yeah, I get it." Then she gives me a big smile. "Don't worry about me, Mags. I can totally fix whatever you messed up. I'm glad we got to do this." She glances behind her again. "Are you ready?"

I nod my agreement. "It will not be easy going back to wearing stiff petticoats. Should I hold on to something?" There are no handrails, but I steady myself against the wall.

"Wouldn't hurt. Here goes nothing." She lifts her arm and places her fingers on the edge of the age spot. The mirrored glass shimmers. It looks as though someone dropped a pebble into still water. I reach out to touch the same spot, and press my fingers to hers.

And . . .

Nothing happens.

My panicked expression must match Hannah's. I remove my fingers and press anew, so hard that I half expect them to pass straight through the glass.

Nothing.

Hannah's eyes—well, mine actually, only Hannah's controlling them, of course—are as wide as saucers. "It's not working!" she says.

I am quiet, my mind racing. Am I truly stuck here? What is happening?

Hannah removes her hand and jerks it through her hair. "Think, think, think," she murmurs.

"Pardon?"

She glances up as if she'd forgotten I was here. "Sorry.

I talk to myself when I'm trying to work something out. I was so positive that our swap had to do with the stolen portrait. I mean, it has to. It's waaaaaay too coincidental that I would land here on this exact weekend. But I stopped it from happening, so . . . mission accomplished, right? All that's left to do is hang it back up and wait for the big reveal."

"Perhaps that's it!" I cry.

"Huh?"

I press my palm against the mirror. "Perhaps it's not fait accompli until the portrait is hanging in its rightful place again."

"Fate what?" she asks.

"It's French for, how did you phrase it . . . 'mission accomplished.'"

Hannah nods. "Well, that's worth a try. Hang on. Gimme a sec, 'cause this frame is heavier than fifty algebra textbooks."

She struggles to lift the painting beside her but manages to get her arms around it. The back of it comes closer to the me in the mirror, and then—

Something crashes behind me, and I turn, expecting to see Florence or Hannah's father enter and scold me for being perched on the furniture.

What greets my eyes is completely unexpected, and I blink, trying to absorb what I'm seeing. It's not Hannah's father or anyone else I've met in the twenty-first century. It's not Aunt or one of the servants from 1905, either.

Another crash catches my attention, and I look down to the floor. A small boy with wheels on his shoes whizzes past the sideboard I'm perched upon. He doesn't see me, so I quickly scramble off the edge and hide behind a large potted plant near the window.

The room has somehow transformed. The antique furnishings have disappeared. A giant divan with plush cushions takes up most of the middle of the room. An enormous TeeVee hangs on the opposite wall. Even the sideboard I was perched on is different. It's made out of some sort of metal. The only thing the same about the room is the painting that covers the ceiling, the mural of the god of the north wind being driven out by spring.

What in heaven's name is happening? I pray Hannah is still at the mirror. As soon as the boy glides out of the room into the foyer, I leap back onto the sideboard and push the painting aside again.

Hannah is peering into the mirror around the side of her frame, with a tortured look on her face. "OMG, Mags, there you are. I was so freaked that you'd disappeared! What's the deal there?"

"I . . . I don't know, but I suspect that you've changed the future by hanging that portrait. The house appears to be a private residence, no longer a museum."

"Noooooooo! Then where's my dad?" Hannah gulps, and she quickly removes the painting from its hangers. She stares hard past me as though she's trying to see through me to what's happening in the room behind me.

The mirror shimmers again, and this time when I look around, the room has gone back to the way it looked before—antiques and the sounds of the wedding preparations from the next room.

I breathe a sigh of relief. "It worked. All is as it was before."

"Okay, then. We caught the thief, but hanging the portrait back where it belongs makes the future go all wonky *and* clearly doesn't switch us back. I don't get it." Hannah takes a gulp of air. "What are we supposed to do now? If the goal wasn't to solve the crime, what is it?"

I have no answer.

Chapter Twenty-One

Hannah

THINK, HANNAH, THINK.

My skin prickles everywhere, like I'm hugging a porcupine, and my throat is so dry, it's as if I gargled cotton balls. Yes, we got back to the normal time line by taking down the portrait, but what if the only way to keep things like they should be is to . . . not switch back?

I can't believe I'm even having that thought.

Up until now this whole experience has been mind-blowing and weird and cool and intriguing. I wanted even more of it. But now? What if I really am stuck in 1905 . . . forever?

What if Maggie and I have actually done something

to the whole space-time continuum? What happened to everyone I know in that alternate-reality version of the future, where The Elms wasn't a museum? Was Dad trapped somewhere else in time? I refuse to believe, even if he was, like, king of the world in that time line, that he was happier without me. And I definitely was born in that time line too, because I didn't shimmer away to dust particles when I hung the painting. What if what we've done isn't fixable? Would I be willing to live out the rest of my days here in this century, to keep everyone I love in the future they're supposed to be having? Sure, Dad would be raising Maggie-me instead of real-me, but he wouldn't know that. And, I mean, I always wished so hard that I could see this place in its glory . . . but not for forever!

WHY IS THIS HAPPENING?

A few hours ago I was having so much fun playing detective with Jonah, aside from the boring waiting-around part. We solved a real-life art heist, for crying out loud.

But now?

Now I'm scared. Legit scared.

And I don't like it one bit. Okay, so, Slender Man is super-creepy and that *Doctor Who* episode with the weeping angel statues mega-freaks me out, and I'm dying to see that new zombie movie that just got released, but this is a different kind of fear. Those are hide-under-the-covers, tiptoes-up-your-spine, but secretly-kinda-love-the-adrenaline fears.

This is a cold, raw, brick-size-battery-leaking-acid-in-my-belly fear.

I feel light-headed, and it's not because my dress is laced too tight. It's because my whole *life* is feeling very *un*laced.

No. No, no, no. I can't fall apart. Or give up. That is not the Hannah Jordan way. The Hannah Jordan way is to choose a new plan of attack.

It's what I do on the soccer field when the opposing team's defender intentionally jabs her elbow into my side as we fight for possession.

It's what I did last summer when Trent threatened to get the Antiquities Society to say I couldn't swim in the fountain after the museum closed for the day, and I retaliated by putting on Dad's Halloween werewolf mask and hiding out in the Narnia wardrobe in the Satinwood Room until he appeared. (Let's just say he was very invested in keeping his reaction just between us.)

And it's what I need to do now.

I square my shoulders and suck in a deep breath that almost makes its way into the super-deep part of my lungs. Then I face Maggie.

"I'm good. Just needed a sec. Okay, so now we gotta figure our way outta this mess. Do you have any ideas?"

Maggie shakes her head slowly, and I drop my chin. "Me neither."

I raise my eyes when I hear her whisper. "What?" I ask. "I didn't catch that."

"I'm scared," she repeats. I can only nod, because the lump in my throat is growing by the second, much as I try to push it down through sheer will. She puts her fingertips to the mirror, and I match mine to hers. Even though I know it won't switch us back through time, it's comforting to connect with a friend at a moment like this. I wish she were here in person, so I could actually feel her touch. So I'd have a friend to turn to, instead of being stuck a hundred years in the past, entirely on my own.

Except . . . I'm not *entirely* alone. Jonah's been the very best kind of friend. The kind who helps first and asks questions later. And he's smart. Supersmart. Maybe three heads are better than two.

"Maggie, I think—I think maybe we should tell Jonah

the whole story. We don't have any bright ideas, and I just have this feeling about him. Like maybe he will."

It's so weird to watch my own face in the mirror as all kinds of expressions pass over it. But in the end, she nods. "If you feel you can trust him, I suppose it couldn't hurt at this point."

She barely gets the words out before I'm off the sideboard and racing for the kitchen, my dress flapping.

I try to make myself invisible as I sneak past and head straight for the coal tunnel. When I left Jonah after we brought the real painting back to the drawing room, he confided in me that he was planning to catch a nap in his secret spot, before reporting to work to help during the ball. I hate waking him up, but if this doesn't qualify as an emergency, I don't know what would.

I rap on the door, and step back when he opens it.

"Maggie?" He squints at me in the shadows, and I can hear the sleep in his voice.

"Can you come with me again?" I ask, gasping for breath.

He nods quickly, stepping into the tunnel. I'm head lookout as we (yet again) sneak back up to the drawing room. I breathe a sigh of relief when I spot Maggie patiently waiting in the mirror.

Jonah's reaction is . . . not quite a sigh of relief. He nearly jumps out of his shoes, and I grab his arm to steady him.

"Okay, so I know this is going to sound loony tunes," I say.

"Completely insane," Maggie adds, and Jonah jumps again.

"Who's she?" He chokes out the words, not taking his eyes off the mirror.

"She's me," I reply.

"And I'm her," Maggie adds.

Jonah sinks to the floor. I plop down beside him. I'm pretty sure I hear Maggie catch a breath at how unlady-like I am about it, but she keeps quiet.

"So it's like this . . . ," I begin. With a little help from Maggie, I bring him up to speed on the last twenty-four hours.

He shakes his head a lot. A lot a lot. I even catch him pinching his own arm to try to wake himself up. But when Maggie demonstrates my iPhone for him in the mirror, I can see him start to come around to the fact that—as crazy as it sounds—we might be telling the truth. "I—I don't even know what to say, what to think. I did puzzle at your manner of speaking," he says, looking at me in wonder, "but I told myself it was only that I didn't spend any time among the upper class."

I can't help a tiny giggle. "Nope. It's a futuristic thing. We all talk like this."

"I'm sorry if I'm struggling to wrap my brain around this. I *am* trying," he says.

I snort, which seems to surprise him. Not sure if it's because I'm not taking his apology seriously or if girls in 1905 just never snort. Or maybe both. "Like that's something to be sorry about? If some weirdo popped up in my basement and started going on about psychics and body swaps, I'd have called 911 faster than you can say, 'Hey, Siri, dial 911.'"

"I—I don't—"

"It's a phone number for the cops. You know. The po-po? The fuzz? Five-oh?"

Jonah just gives me a look and shakes his head. "The future must be a very odd place indeed."

"Oh, you have NO idea. We have Kardashians, my friend."

I don't have a chance to explain (probably best, since how could you ever explain them?), because Maggie speaks from behind me.

"It is odder than you could ever imagine."

I jump a little. I was so distracted, I kind of forgot she was still here(ish).

"Maybe, but I'm pretty eager to get back there," I say as I stand up and begin pacing the room, like my grandpa Fred does when we play chess and I have him almost cornered. He claims pacing helps him see "the big picture" and all the possible outcomes. Considering that I've beaten Grandpa Fred at chess exactly once (and even that was on a technicality), I'm thinking that pacing might work. Plus, I'm desperate to try anything at this point. "Call me crazy, but in my gut I still feel like the answer to switching back has to do with the painting. It's the only thing that makes sense with the timing, and the fact that taking it down from the mirror made us swap in the first place, and hanging it back up made the time line shift," I say.

I was mostly speaking this out loud to puzzle through it on my own, but from behind me Maggie pops up with the same follow-up question I was about to ask myself.

"But then why didn't it work when we hung the painting back in its rightful place?"

I turn to face her, my eyes big and sad. "I don't know. And how can we restore the painting to where it belongs without creating a ripple effect in the events of history?"

Jonah is quiet, leaning against an upholstered chair in the center of the room, his eyes all faraway-like. He even rubs his chin the way people on TV do when they want everyone watching to know they're thinking deep thoughts.

After a second he says, "What if you didn't have to?"

"Didn't have to what?" I ask.

He lifts his head and looks back and forth from Maggie to me.

"What if the painting could still hang in its rightful place at the conclusion of all this, but you could put it there without disturbing this time line?"

"How would we accomplish that?" Maggie asks, but my own brain is whirring.

I blurt out, "By hanging it there in the future! Jonah, I'm picking up what you're putting down! I'll say it again: you're brilliant, Einstein!"

He blushes and ducks his head. "Hardly. I have barely any schooling."

I wave him off. "Pfft. Whatevs. You have street smarts. In lots of ways that's even better."

"Might someone kindly explain what it is we're speaking of?" Maggie asks. "The two of you appear to be on the same page, but I'm afraid I have no idea at all what you're going on about. Whatever do you mean by 'hanging it there in the future'?"

I share an excited smile with Jonah, then turn to Maggie. "The only way we can be sure we're not affecting anything that happened between now—I mean, then—I mean, now for me—ugh. Sorry. This space-time continuum stuff is mega-confusing."

Maggie is squinting at me. I'm sure what I'm saying is harder to decipher than those Instagram posts that are nothing but a zillion hashtags strung together. I take a deep breath and try again.

"The future rippled because if the painting was never stolen, that fact changes the way things unfold from that moment forward. A hundred tiny things could happen differently all because Augustus-You-Bustus never took off with the portrait, and that's how we end up with a totally different time line, one where The Elms is some little kid's house instead of a museum. We changed the past, and in doing so we changed the future."

I pause to take a deep breath and make sure Maggie is still with me here. She's nodding, so I race on. "What I'm trying to say is that we have to make sure everything happens exactly the way it already does in the history books. Anything that's recorded there has to stay exactly that way. *But* we can still return the painting to the wall and set things right. You'll just have to do it in modern time. No one has written the future into any history books yet, so there's nothing to disturb. And then we get to switch back to our own times. Easy peasy lemon squeezy."

Jonah laughs. "I like that expression."

"Heck yeah, ya do," I reply.

His eyebrows come together above his nose, but then he smiles and shakes his head.

I shrug and smile back.

For her part, Maggie still looks a little confused. "But if you have the painting *there*, how am I meant to hang it *here*?"

I'm ready for that question. The answer has been bouncing around in my head ever since I caught on to what Jonah was saying. "We leave it for you to find. Somewhere where it will be safe for the next hundred-plus years. Somewhere, say, in a tunnel under the house, for example."

Jonah grins and waves the key to the tiny hidden room. "Exactly what I was thinking."

I know it's the perfect hiding spot. Clearly no one in my time has any clue that place even exists. At least I'm pretty sure they don't. Dad definitely would have mentioned it to me. It's exactly the kind of thing he'd geek out over.

The painting will be safe there.

All we have to do is hide it in the tunnel room and then hide the key to the door somewhere where Maggie can find it in the future. She'll pretend she stumbled across the hidden room, discover the painting, and alert the proper authorities. Then we'll swap back right in time for me to be the one basking in the fame and glory of finding The Elms' precious missing masterpiece. I wonder if the Smithsonian will want to interview me. Or maybe even the *Today* show! Either way, I will finally, *finally* get the respect I deserve from the docents and everyone else who thought I was just a bratty kid getting in their way. It's going to feel amazing! Honestly, this scenario is even better than just swapping back and having the painting hanging there because it was never stolen. My heart trips in excitement!

"Okay, Maggie. Hang tight. Jonah and I are going to sneak the portrait to its hiding spot and lock it up. Then we'll figure out where to hide the key so you can find it in the future."

I step closer to Jonah and gasp when I take a good look

at the key in his hand! I didn't get to see it clearly when we were in the dark tunnel, but in the bright drawing room it's clear that it's not just any key but an old-timey skeleton one that—

No. It can't be.

"Can I see that for a sec?" I ask.

Jonah nods and passes it to me. I cradle it carefully in my hand, step to the sideboard, and climb up. Maggie's eyes go wide when I hold the key so she can see it.

"It looks just like . . ."

She doesn't even have to finish, because I'm already nodding hard. "I know."

We both blink as I carefully set the key flat against the mirror age spot that Maggie and I were both touching when we swapped places. It lines up perfectly.

The key and the age spot are an exact match.

For a second I think maybe *that's* going to be the thing that switches us back, but nothing happens. Even still. It's all the sign I need. We're totally on the right track now!

Jonah and I are supersleuths as we institute Operation Hide Maggie's Portrait. Fortunately, with all the preparations for the dinner party that comes before the ball, everyone is too wrapped up in their own work in

the ballroom and the dining room to pay us any attention. We wait for the coast to be clear, then duck down
the servants' stairs and straight into the furnace area.

In less than ten minutes we're back in the drawing
room, smiling at Maggie.

"This is the best plan ever. I have a very good feeling
about this," I say. I walk her through exactly how to find
the door in the tunnel, then add, "Okay, now to find the
ideal hiding place for the key."

I look around the room carefully, noting pieces that
aren't part of the museum in my time, and ruling out
obvious spots that would never sit undisturbed for an
entire century.

"What about one of the sconces?" Maggie asks.

"No good. They're reproductions. The originals
were sold at auction when Julia—"

I break off. I don't know how much Maggie wants
to know about her future. Maybe she's been reading
the signs around the museum or taking the tours. But
maybe she hasn't. If it were me, I would definitely NOT
want to know what's coming for me and everyone
around me, and if she's the same, I don't want to be the
one to tell her the house gets sold when her other aunt,
Julia, dies in the early 1960s. A bunch of stuff inside

went to auction before the Antiquities Society stepped in and saved the mansion from demolition.

Luckily, Maggie doesn't question why I just clammed up on her, and Jonah saves the day by distracting us when he flips a corner of the elaborate Oriental rug on the floor and gestures to the sewn-on label.

"What if we slid it in between the stitches attaching this tag? No one would ever think to look here. Is this rug still there in your time?"

"It is, but I'll bet the vacuum would catch on the bump the key would make."

"Vacuum?" Jonah asks.

"Never mind. Oh! This chair!" I point to a Louis XV armchair off to the side of the rug. It's 100 percent still there in my time and is too perfect a match to be a reproduction. Plus, the arms are padded underneath the upholstery, so if we can slip the key into the padding, there won't be any telltale lump to hint that anything's inside. It's the perfect hiding spot. "Be right back. I'm gonna grab a letter opener off Mr. Berwind's desk upstairs."

That takes me less than thirty seconds, and in another two I've made the tiniest of tears along a seam in the chair and buried the key inside.

Our timing is spot-on, because I'm just saying, "Mags,

do you want to—" when voices in the hallway make me slam my lips shut.

Someone's coming!

"And then I believe we should rearrange some of the seating in the drawing room. I don't want the petals laid until just before arrivals, so they don't begin curling at the edges, and I expressly do not want anyone near the portrait, of course, so please do . . ."

It's Mrs. Berwind giving instructions to one of the staff.

I shoot a desperate glance at Maggie. Jonah is standing every bit as still as one of the statues of cherubs in the conservatory next to us. His eyes are sheer panic.

Thinking fast, I hiss, "Maggie, your aunt is coming and they're talking about ball prep for this room! It's going to be too crazy in here to get privacy now. I'm so, so sorry but we *have* to push to tomorrow for the switch. Seven a.m. your time? This is all on you now, anyway. You know what to do?"

She nods, and I turn before even making sure her image fades. I grab a vase of fresh flowers and tip it over so that the water inside splashes across the marble floor. Three steps later, I'm next to Jonah.

Mrs. Berwind enters the room with the butler, and

both stop in their tracks when they see us. Maggie's aunt's hand flies to her neck. "Margaret! Whatever is going on in here?"

"Hello, Auntie." Yikes, I hope I got that right. Colette used this term when she was talking about Mrs. Berwind before, but if I'm misremembering, I'll totally blow my cover.

She doesn't react, so I must be okay. Her eyebrows arch, though, and I realize she's still staring at me, waiting for an explanation.

"I, um, well, I accidentally spilled some water, and everyone up here was so busy running around trying to get ready for tonight, so I slipped downstairs and grabbed this boy from the kitchen to help clean it up. I didn't know what else to do!"

Please buy it, please buy it, please buy it. I don't care if I get in trouble (I'm guessing Maggie will forgive me), but the last thing I want to do is cause problems for Jonah.

Mrs. Berwind's head cocks to the side. "Oh, honestly, Maggie. That clumsiness of yours is going to be the death of us both. What does it say about a young lady of your position?"

I wrinkle my nose and whisper what I hope is a super-legit-sounding "Sorry."

"And do keep your facial expressions mild, darling. You don't want your features freezing in any of those ghastly faces you make. I've been told on quite good authority that that is a genuine possibility. What a terrible tragedy that would be, come your debutante year."

"Yes, ma'am," I whisper, hiding my grin. Probably not the time to tell her how wrong she is about the whole face-freezing thing. Because, yeah . . . *science*.

"At any rate, thank you for your assistance," she says, turning to Jonah.

Beside me, Jonah nods but doesn't speak. I can almost feel him shaking with fear.

"Mr. Birch, can you please see to it that this is taken care of? Boy, you may return to your duties downstairs, and we are grateful for your help."

Jonah scoots out the door before I can even get a good-bye in, and Mrs. Berwind turns back to me. "Now, Maggie. Shouldn't you be dressing for the evening, young lady?"

My jaw drops open. I didn't even think about that. I'm 99.9 percent sure we've solved the mystery of switching back, but if I'm not meeting up with Maggie until the morning . . .

"Margaret?" Mrs. Berwind prods when I don't answer her right away.

"Oh. Yes, ma'am. Dressing. Evening."

Annnnnnd, I guess I know what this means.

I'm going to a ball.

Lemme try that again.

I'M GOING TO A BALL!

Chapter Twenty-Two

Maggie

MY EMOTIONS ARE A JUMBLED MESS when I realize I will miss the ball in my honor. I admit I was nervous about being the focus of attention, but I *was* looking forward to it. I think about how Aunt Herminie will be so disappointed, but then I remember that to everyone else in the world, I *will* be there. There's an odd sense of rebellion in my stomach at that thought. Even if no one knows, I'm doing something against the rules.

There will be other balls. And perhaps I'll have time to read some of those books in Hannah's room. I don't have time for too much adventure, however. I have to retrieve a key that opens a mysterious room in the lower reaches of the house.

"Hey, you. Doing some last-minute dusting?" Hannah's father chuckles, catching me off guard as I'm climbing off the sideboard. He is dressed in a tuxedo, with a name badge clipped to the lapel, no doubt ready to work the evening's festivities. "Have you started packing yet?"

"No, sir." I look up and catch his eye. I have to forcefully make myself not glance at the upholstered chair in the corner, wondering if the key has been hidden under my nose the whole time.

He blinks once before he smiles. "I can tell something's going on with you right now, and I can't pretend to know what it is, honey. But you know you can talk to me if you need to." His expression tells me he's considering that statement. "Don't you?" He pauses again. "You really do need to think about packing, though, my dear Miss Hannah. Our flight is"—he checks his watch—"T minus fifty-six hours. Since you always wait till the last minute, why don't you start early this time while I'm busy with this wedding?"

I don't want to think about flying to the other side of

the country. If he makes me leave the mansion, I may never get back to where I really belong. Not to mention my abject terror at the thought of what it means to actually fly.

The tickle of a tear threatens, and I hurriedly wipe it away before he notices. I envy Hannah. She seems to be handling this time travel so well, and all I've succeeded in doing is making her father and Tara suspicious, forcing Hannah to lose her game, and frightening her beau. I briefly wonder what would have happened if Colette had traveled through time. Would she have gracefully slipped into the twenty-first century? Am I the only one who could mess things up so badly? And now I'm not even sure if I'll ever get back to my own time.

I must start searching for the key, but before that I've got time for a question that's been on my mind. Hannah's father turns to walk out of the room, and I find myself speaking. "Excuse me, Father? I mean, Dad?"

"Yes, Hannah." He sounds exasperated.

"Do you think people are much different now from how they were a hundred years ago?" I fold and unfold my hands. Finally, I clasp them behind me to stop fidgeting.

He looks thoughtful as he gazes out of the floor-to-ceiling glass door that faces the lawn.

"You know, I don't guess they are. Not really. I mean, we talk differently. We have different clothes and tools and even food. Technology, of course." He scratches his head. "But down deep? I'd guess that emotions and love and fear are mostly the same."

I stare at his face and let out a sigh of relief. My own father would have scoffed and left, with the question still hanging in the air. Would this man believe me if I told him I'm not really Hannah?

"I like that answer," I say.

"Why do you ask?" He crosses his arms across his chest.

"No reason. It's just something I think about." The idea of people essentially being the same under all their exterior appearances is comforting. It makes me feel as though things aren't really all that different.

I don't want to stay here forever, but knowing that human nature hasn't changed makes me feel less frightened about being trapped here for a little while.

"Kiddo, you never cease to amaze me." He stares at me like he's seeing me for the first time, then shakes his head as though he's changed his mind about something. "Go pack, Bug."

As soon as Hannah's father leaves the room, I scurry

to the chair and ever so gently run my fingers along the armrest. Hannah no doubt stitched up the seam, since it's no longer torn. I'm impressed that it's in such good condition after a hundred years. It's a shame I have to damage it. I pick at a loose thread along the braided cord sewn onto the fabric, and trying not to make a big tear, I slip my finger into the opening. No key.

"Well, you silly goose, you didn't really think you'd find it on your first try, did you?" I say quietly to myself. It must be in the other arm, and I cringe, knowing I've got to make another rip in the fabric.

No key.

Closing my eyes, I take a deep breath. I check the legs of the chair, to make sure it's the right one. But maybe it's not the only one. Maybe there's a match somewhere else in the house.

I run through the ballroom, around the tables that have been set for the wedding, to the dining room. I search the entire house looking for another chair that matches the one in the drawing room.

No chair.

No key.

I need help.

I've already asked a strange question of Hannah's

father, so I'm reluctant to ask him anything else right now. I'm at a complete loss for what to do. Standing in the middle of the foyer, I try not to cry as servants hustle around me, setting up for the wedding. I feel invisible. Suddenly the silver-haired tour guide from this morning walks past. He must know something about the folklore of the house. Even so, I remember our interaction in the Rose Room and brace myself for an angry response.

"Excuse me, sir?"

He stops and stares at me. "Did you just call me 'sir'?"

"You know a lot about this house, right?" I try to keep my voice from shaking.

He narrows his eyes at me. "Are you making fun of me, young lady?" He huffs. "I don't have time for silly questions."

"No, please," I say, wringing my hands. "Do you know anything about a key? Some story about a skeleton key being found in this house?"

He scowls and starts to walk away. "I know everything about this house. If there were a tale about a mysterious key, I would know it."

"But I heard . . ." I jog after him. "Are you sure?"

"Hannah Jordan. You purport to know more about this house than any docent." He wags his finger at me, and it makes me take a step back. "I'm sure I'm not going to waste my time playing the fool for something that is untrue. There is no story about a mysterious key." And he strides down the hall toward the servants' staircase.

"Is there another chair that matches the one in the drawing room?" I shout as he disappears out of sight, but he doesn't answer.

What now?

As much as I'd love to curl up on Hannah's bed and wait for someone else to fix this problem, I've got to try to find that key. There's no one else who *can* do this. It's all on me . . . for the first time in my life. Hannah's and my futures depend on it. I'm scared to death at the thought of messing this up for both of us. But instead of falling apart, I push my shoulders back and start up to the second floor, thinking maybe I missed seeing the chair the first time. As I climb the stairs, I spot the older woman from earlier. She knew the correct color of my dress in the portrait. Maybe she can help.

"Excuse me, Mrs.—" I almost curtsy, but I stop myself. "I'm sorry, I don't remember your name."

"It's okay. I haven't been volunteering here very long. I'm not surprised you don't." She smiles and holds out her hand. "Florence Ensminger-Burn. Just 'Florence' is fine."

With a sigh of relief, I say, "Can you help me with something? Or are you in a rush?"

"I was just going to get a bite to eat and then head home, now that everything is sorted out with the bride's mother. What sort of help do you need?"

My shoulders relax. "Do you know anything about a key that might have something to do with the mystery of the house?"

She looks thoughtful and then shakes her head. "I don't know anything about a key. But I do know a lot about the house—you might call it an obsession. Tell me more about what you're trying to find."

I can't help but smile. "It might have something to do with the upholstered chair in the drawing room."

A large woman pushes a cart with a wedding cake past us, and I'm momentarily distracted by the spectacle. I didn't expect something so elaborate, based on my observations of this time so far.

When I look back at Florence, she's laughing. "Oh, Hannah, you're too funny."

At the sight of my stricken face, she stops. "I'm sorry, dear. I thought you were joking. I thought for sure you knew the details about the furniture. Trent has been telling me how much you've studied the house."

As another member of the staff pushes a cart laden with table service past us, Florence takes hold of my arm. "Walk with me. Let's get out of the way of the traffic." She pulls me into the corner and guides me into the chair behind the ticket desk. "I didn't mean to laugh at you. When Julia Berwind died in the 1960s— Mr. Berwind's last surviving sibling—none of the other relatives could afford the upkeep of the house. Most of the furniture and paintings were sold at auction. It was only due to the Antiquities Society that the house wasn't bulldozed. It was quite an accomplishment by the society to save it."

I can't help but gawk. Seriously? Colette's mother inherits The Elms? I can't help but wonder why it's not me or Colette, or one of the other cousins. Part of me wants to know if Florence knows what happens to us. To me. I take a deep breath and close my eyes for just a second. At the very least, I know The Elms survives. It's probably not wise for me to know too much about what happens to my family. I shake my head to stop my thoughts from racing out of control. All that's important is finding that key, so that I can get home. So that

Hannah can get home. I try to remain calm.

"Some of the furniture is original, but not all of it?" I look past her to the ballroom, where elaborate floral arrangements are being placed on the tables.

She nods. "Most of it is original, actually. The Antiquities Society was able to buy back a lot of the original furniture over the years."

"The chair in the drawing room is original, right? The upholstered one?" I wonder if somehow I misunderstood which chair it was. But I know Hannah and I were talking about the same thing.

"A few items in the house are replicas. That piece is a spectacular reproduction. The Antiquities Society was able to commission an exact fabric match. Even the best of experts have trouble telling the difference." Florence smiles at me, as though the story is finished.

"I can't believe I didn't notice that." I feel almost as if I've betrayed my aunt and uncle.

Florence beams at me. "I know you're a history buff, my dear, but there's no reason why you would have known that. It's extremely hard to tell."

The key isn't in the house. What am I going to do? I close my eyes to control the panicky feeling in my stomach and tell myself it's fine. We'll be able to fix this.

I'll just meet Hannah in the mirror in the morning and advise her to hide it somewhere else, as soon as I find out from Florence which items of furniture are original.

Perfectly fine. No reason at all to panic.

Chapter Twenty-Three

Hannah

CINDERELLA. MIA IN *THE PRINCESS DIARIES*. Giselle in *Enchanted*.

And now me.

Ball attendees, all of us. (And here's hoping mine doesn't end in disaster like two out of those three did. Unless you count a "stolen" painting as a disaster, because I can pretty much guarantee mine's ending with that one.)

But I'm optimistic anyway. I know the painting's not actually lost forever, and I'm feeling confident in the fix we came up with, which means that, for the first time since I landed here, I can actually let myself just relax and soak it all in.

And oh my WOW is there a lot to soak in. I mean, I grew up riding my scooter past the floor-to-ceiling shelves of china dishes in the butler's pantry, and hiding in the vault that houses the silverware (emphasis on "silver"), but I've never seen the real stuff all laid out on the table the way it is tonight. We'd never dare use it for any of the events we hold at the museum.

We have an art restoration expert from Venice coming to brighten up the mural in the dining room, but I can't imagine she'll ever be able to get it to shine like it is tonight. Shining like it's brand new. Because it is. This place come to life is better than I imagined any of the zillion-and-one times I've dreamed about it.

I could probably squeak four years of college tuition out of what the Berwinds dropped on this one shindig. While I was upstairs dressing, the entire downstairs was transformed by about forty billion rose petals that form an actual carpet over the floors. The ballroom is also covered in flowers—all varieties of roses bunched in big clusters, climbing the walls. There's even a rose-covered arbor set up in the doorway between the ballroom and the drawing room. Wow. This crew did a LOT in just a couple of hours. Although, obviously, people were busy assembling this somewhere else ahead of time. Maybe for months.

Tonight's ball is also a costume one, and the theme is Venetian. For whatever reason, high-society peeps super-love dressing up. They're like the grandparents of cosplay, I guess. I giggle at that thought. But honestly, the *dresses*. OMG.

Some of them are so wide, with hoops and petticoats underneath them, that the women have to walk sideways to get through the openings between the dining room and the ballroom. It's crazypants.

And the jewels. Dripping. Positively dripping. This one lady has a pearl necklace that reaches all the way down almost to her ankles, and at the bottom is this egg-size, canary-yellow diamond that practically scrapes the floor. Whenever she moves, she has to kick it out in front of her. Like, she's just kicking this massive diamond the same way I dribble my soccer ball down the field. If I weren't so busy gaping, I'd totally be laughing.

Of course, as grown-up as thirteen was back in Maggie's day, it's still not old enough to fully participate. Maggie won't get to actually attend any balls as a real guest until she makes her society debut. So while most of the women here will toss out their ball gowns (that probably cost as much as brand-new cars in my time) after they wear them once tonight, I'm in the same taffeta dress Maggie has on in the painting. The same one I "arrived" here in yesterday. Someone on the staff has cleaned and pressed it since then, but it still feels familiar . . . comforting.

That doesn't mean I didn't have to endure hours of mad-crazy preparations that involved a team of three. There was no way I could turn away Maggie's lady's maids without looking suspicious, but lemme just say, it is super-weird to be dressed by someone else. I don't really remember my mom much, because she died when I was only three, but I'm sure she must have tugged me into clothes. Since then? Uh, yeah. No.

Too bad corsets don't cinch themselves. (I did draw the line at the maids' bathing me, though.)

The one time I was really grateful to have someone else handling things was when it came to my hair. Curly hair is all the fashion, and let's just say that curling irons are pretty, um, primitive in 1905. They don't plug in; instead they're heated in the fireplace. I'm pretty sure Maggie would not be thrilled to come back to a head full of singed hair, so I let the maids have their way there.

I would have loved to wear makeup to the ball, since Dad puts his foot down on that at home, but no one suggested it. And it's not like anyone would have seen makeup on me anyway, since the party's theme means I have a real straight-from-Italy silk Venetian mask to hold up to my face. It makes me feel like more of a spy than I already am. I can hide behind this thing and people-watch all night.

Or at least for as long as I'm allowed to stay up and take part. It's okay for me to be here for some of the stuff—and I'm even kind of a guest of honor because of the portrait unveiling—but I probably won't be doing any actual dancing.

Still.

It's the best theater around, and these people aren't even acting.

"Darling, I do wish you wouldn't, just this once," a woman gliding by me in a rose-colored dress is saying to the man next to her.

"But I love it so. At a party of this sort—" He breaks off and taps a waiter on the shoulder. "I'm in need of a hard-boiled egg and a cold glass of milk."

The waiter's mouth falls open, but I guess he's well-trained, because he snaps it shut and smiles. "Certainly, sir. I'll see to it straightaway."

The woman drops her mask for a second, and I

know exactly who she is! She's Elizabeth Drexel Lehr. In my time a life-size portrait of her hangs in the ballroom, and postcards of it are sold in all the mansions. Which means the guy with her is her husband, Harry. They lived—*live*—across the street from The Elms, but their house wasn't as lucky as ours when it came to avoiding the wrecking ball. Now the weirdo request makes sense; he was meant to be a total jokester. I'll bet he thinks it's hilarious to make the staff scramble to fill his order. Me: not so much. Maybe because I know at least one person in the kitchen, working his butt off to make tonight a success, and now he—or somebody else down there—is going to have to interrupt the carefully choreographed meal prep to make a stupid hard-boiled egg. All so this guy can get his laugh.

That's just mean, if you ask me.

I don't wait around to see how long it takes Harry Lehr to get his milk and egg. Instead I slip into the conservatory and try to blend in next to a giant urn, so that I can observe and eavesdrop. Everything I've read about this time is so right on. These people are crazy-rich and crazy-obsessed with the weirdest stuff. Two women stand with their backs to me and give solid burns about the headpieces of at least four other women walking by. I know these families donate whole chunks of their fortunes to build orphanages and libraries and schools, so they can't be totally horrible, but they'd be shoo-ins for a *Real Housewives of Newport* reality show. Yikes.

The ones I'm really hoping to catch a glimpse of are Henry Jacobs and his wife. They have my favorite story of all. Mr. Jacobs had a brain tumor that left him convinced he was the Prince of Wales, and instead of checking him into a hospital, his wife just . . . went along with it. Like, she spent half his fortune hiring actors to play gentlemen-in-waiting in his court and ambassadors from other countries, and she brought in experts from London to make sure Mr. Jacobs got exact matches to everything worn by the real Prince of Wales so he could live out his days happily in his delusion. That's love, people.

Sadly, I don't see any guy dressed like a prince. Or no, really, it's more like *all* the guys are dressed like princes, but none are calling themselves actual royalty.

It's so strange to me that this is their everyday life. And this is not even that special an occasion, since they probably all have another ball to go to next week and about a billion musicales and sailing parties in between. I can't even imagine doing stuff like this all the time. It's amazing for tonight, but every night? I live for my flannel pj's and Netflix binges too much to give them up for nonstop red-carpet living.

Of course, that thought jerks me right back to reality. Because what if this *is* my future? But no. No, no, nope. I promised myself I wasn't going to stress tonight. The key is in the chair, the painting is in the tunnel, and we're going to set everything right first thing in the morning.

I exhale a deep breath. Or at least as deep a breath as I can manage. Corsets are torture devices. Maybe it's a good thing I won't be dancing tonight.

"There you are, my sweet. Why, you're practically one with the drapery. No wonder I've had to look everywhere for you." Maggie's aunt looks so beautiful with tiny diamonds tucked here and there all over her fancy hairdo. The mask she's holding in her left hand has even more jewels catching the light from the chandelier above us. I can't believe I'm hanging out with *the* Herminie Berwind, whom I've spent my whole life hearing about.

"Are you ready for the big unveiling, darling?" she asks. When I nod, she smiles. "Now, don't be nervous. I know you don't love being in the spotlight, but everyone will be too busy looking at the portrait to stare at you."

I definitely don't say, "Or not."

But it's true. No one will be busy looking at the portrait, because you can't look at a painting that isn't there. This night is not going to go at all the way Mrs. Berwind thinks it is, and I feel bad for her. Maggie clearly adores her, and she's been nothing but nice to me, even if I'm still a little annoyed with the way she called Jonah "boy" without bothering to ask his name. It's too bad her name is about to be forever linked in the history books to the mysteriously missing Mary Cassatt portrait.

Mrs. Berwind takes me by the arm and pulls me gently into the drawing room and over to the sideboard, where that very Mary Cassatt is waiting, with a smile on her face.

When we reach her, she says, "*Bonsoir, ma cherie*. Are you ready to reveal the efforts of all these past months to everyone else?"

I feel terrible all over again, knowing how upset she's about to be, and the role I played in that. I wish so hard that I could just lean over and say, "No sweat, Mare. Your portrait is safe and sound in the kitchen boy's napping spot."

But I can't, obviously.

Because she'll want to rescue it, and that can't happen.

Not until Maggie does it in the future.

Instead I smile and nod. "I cannot wait." Not technically a lie.

The orchestra set up in the ballroom stops playing,
and I get my first glimpse of Mr. Berwind when he steps
next to us and clinks a spoon on a wineglass. He's larger
than life, just like I always imagined him. Masked guests
begin drifting in from the adjoining rooms, and in a matter of a minute there's a huge crowd. Colette is right in
front, and she shoots daggers at me—probably because
I'm on display with the Berwinds and she's blended into
the crowd. But whatever. I don't have time for her right
now. I keep my own mask fixed to my eyes and hope it
hides the panic I'm suddenly feeling. How is this going to
go down? How will everyone react when that curtain on
the wall drops and there's only a landscape of Newport
Harbor hanging there?

I don't have to wait long. Mr. Berwind clears his
throat and then talks in a deep, booming voice that
reaches the high ceilings.

"Thank you, honored guests, for joining us tonight
and sharing this special evening with us. As you may
be aware, we have our beloved niece Margaret Dunlap
spending time with us this summer, as she does each

year, and we're particularly happy to have her present now as we invite you to witness the unveiling of a quite impressive portrait of Margaret completed by our esteemed guest, Mademoiselle Mary Cassatt. We are humbled that she accepted our commission of this painting. And now, without further ado . . ."

He lifts his arm, and I gasp along with everyone else as two men roll down from velvet ribbons attached to the ceiling directly above us. When did someone hang those ribbons? Is that what all the hammering was earlier when I was getting dressed? But how did those men get up there? It's like Cirque du Soleil time! They flip and twirl above us and then begin swinging in a giant back-and-forth motion that brings them closer and closer to the painting with each swing.

Each time the men's outstretched hands nearly reach the curtain covering the portrait, the audience holds their breath, wondering what they'll finally see. And each time the men's fingertips brush the fabric, I hold my breath too, knowing what they won't.

Finally it happens. The men swing close enough to grab the fabric, and with their next arc back the curtain whooshes from the wall.

Basically everyone exhales at once, and then it's

totally quiet for about three heartbeats, and *then* the entire room fills up with confused talking. Everyone is yammering over everyone else. I hear a whole lot of "I thought it was supposed to be a portrait of the girl?" and "But that's a painting of the harbor!"

Mr. Berwind is bug-eyed, and Mary Cassatt is clutching the sideboard like she needs it to hold her up.

Mrs. Berwind faints straight to the floor, her glass of red wine tumbling out of her hand and splashing everywhere.

Yep. Just exactly as shocking as I thought it might be.

Someone calls out, "We should send for the authorities!" followed by "And the doctor!" and "Yes, I can offer my carriage."

Mr. Berwind bends over his wife, fanning her face with his handkerchief, and after a few seconds he gets her awake and into a seated position. Phew. I was pretty sure the shock didn't kill her or anything, because that would have definitely been all over the history books, but still. It's a relief to see her upright.

I'm not exactly sure what I should be doing, so I just hang back out of the way as much as I can, and pretend to be too shocked for words. Once the carriages have taken off to grab the police and the doctor, things start to calm down a little and guests begin to shuffle around, like they aren't quite sure if they should go back to partying or leave or what. Definitely no one *wants* to go, because this is the best gossip in town, and I'm positive everyone is thrilled that they'll be able to say they were here to witness it. But they all have perfect manners, too, so I can tell it's a real dilemma for them. The whole crowd seems psyched when, at some signal from Mr. Berwind, the butler dude tells everyone they should adjourn to the ballroom and promises that fresh trays of champagne are on their way up from the kitchen.

In a matter of minutes the drawing room empties out, and the butler pulls all the doors into the room closed, sealing us off completely.

"Well done, Birch. We mustn't disturb the crime scene any more than it already has been," says Mr. Berwind, looking up from where's he's still bent over, fanning his wife.

Something about the words "crime scene" sends a bitter taste straight into my mouth.

Oh. My. Gosh.

I'm such an idiot.

How could I have let myself ignore the totally obvious?

If we play out the heist the way the history books have it recorded, that means the sweet, helpful, funny, smart kid working his butt off in the kitchen right now is about to have his entire life ruined. Because JONAH IS GOING TO BE CHARGED WITH STEALING THE PAINTING.

Chapter Twenty-Four

Maggie

I ROLL OVER AND THEN CURL AROUND Hannah's stuffed bear, trying to squeeze out a few more minutes of sleep. But with the light streaming in through the high windows, I know it's time to rise for the day. Her device chirps, and Tara's face lights up the screen. I take a chance and press the square that says "talk."

"Hello? Hannah? It's Tara."

Father installed a telephone at our New York City apartment, but it is three feet tall and affixed to a wall. You have to speak into a cone to be heard on the other end of the line. I love that I can hear my aunt's voice when she is at home in Philadelphia and we're not at the summer cottage together. This century has somehow condensed that technology into this handheld device.

"Hello, Tara," I yell at the device. "How. Are. You?"

"Do you have a bad connection? Why are you yelling?" Now Tara is yelling. "You weren't answering my texts, so I thought I'd call instead." The stilted timbre of her voice makes me wonder if she's still angry from yesterday. What she says next comes as a surprise.

"I'm sorry for what I said about Ethan. You're not mad, are you? Sorry it's so early. I've been up all night worried that you're mad."

Sweet Tara thinks I'm angry with her! "Tara!" I yell at the device, hoping she can hear me. "Of course I'm not mad. Friends are more important than boys."

I hear her sigh on the other end of the line. "Are you feeling better today? Do you want to come over later and watch a movie?"

"I have to be honest. I am not feeling well. I don't think I can spend time with you today, but perhaps tomorrow when I'm myself again. I'm not mad." I make a mental note to tell Hannah how sweet Tara has been. "I'm sorry, but I have to go now."

This technology isn't so hard to manage. Between my talk with Hannah's dad last night and the way I handled that telephone call, I'm beginning to feel slightly more confident in my ability to survive in the future, but thankfully we are going to fix this today. I might even be home by lunchtime.

I start to run downstairs—but then, with a pause to make sure no one is watching, I sling my leg over the railing and slide down a stretch of banister. It is as exhilarating as I've always imagined! At the bottom I dust off my trousers and then jog the rest of the way through the ballroom, into the drawing room, and scamper onto the sideboard. The clock reads just after seven o'clock—I'm a minute late. Hannah is already in the mirror, waiting. I'm sure my face is flushed, but perhaps she won't notice, given what I have to tell her.

"Good morning," I say, breathless. "There's a slight problem. You must move the key. The chair here . . ." I gesture to the room behind me. "It is a replica. The original was sold in the 1960s. Perhaps in Uncle E. J.'s wardrobe or Aunt's desk. They are both original furnishings, as confirmed by Mrs. Ensminger-Burn."

But before I finish my thought, my eyes drift over Hannah's shoulder.

My heart plummets. "Where's the chair?"

Hannah turns around, and I see Jonah behind her.

When she faces me again, she's gone pale. "I . . . I'm not sure. They took a bunch of the furniture out to make room for everyone at the unveiling. But no . . . It was here when the ball started. The police—they were taking things for evidence, and what if—"

Jonah dashes out of the room. I turn my attention back to Hannah. The color still hasn't returned to her face, so I try to console her. "I'm sure it has just been moved to another room. It often takes some time to return everything to its proper place after a ball." I do not tell her that it's far more likely the staff would have restored everything to where it belonged after the party, even though it would have been the crack of dawn after a full work day and night when they did.

Jonah returns two minutes later. He takes a deep breath. "The chair has been sent out for cleaning! Someone spilled red wine on it last night."

"Mrs. Berwind!" Hannah exclaims. "Her drink tumbled to the floor when she fainted. This is a disaster!" She closes her eyes and leans against the glass. I wish I could say something comforting, but I can only put my hand on the mirrored reflection. Her words are hard to make out. "Omigod, omigod, omigod."

Jonah's expression morphs several times. "Miss . . . I

mean, Mag— I mean, Hannah?" He's clearly struggling with how to help—and it occurs to me that he shouldn't even be out of the kitchen, let alone in the middle of the drawing room. "I'm sorry. I was hoping to steal away long enough to say good-bye in person, and I really wish I could stay and help now, but Chef is going to notice I'm gone if I don't get straight back. I can't afford to get caught."

Hannah's face pales, as though a ghost skidded through the room.

I'm not sure what that's about, but I don't stop to puzzle it out. We don't have time to delay. "Jonah, you should go!" I channel my father's most take-charge voice. "Listen to me, Hannah. You've got to find out where that chair is going. Find it and get the key back if you can— move it to my uncle's armoire. In the meantime I'll do my best to break into the tunnel room."

Hannah finally looks up at me with hope in her eyes. "Yeah. Maybe you can get into the room without the key. Go try that now. And then meet back here this afternoon at my five o'clock, after the last tour goes through on your end."

"By the way, we don't have much time. Your father is planning a two-week trip to California. We—that is to say you—depart in two days." I jump down before she can react. I'm afraid my own fear will show if I look at her too long. If I'm to retrieve that painting before Hannah's father tries to make me leave on vacation with him, I have to find a way to open that door.

The house is quiet, and most of the evidence from the wedding is gone. The front doors will open for visitors soon. I creep down the back servant stairs to the kitchen. It's the first time I've been down here in the future, and it's as silent as a crypt. I'm used to the main floor being quiet, but here on the lower level it should be bustling with servants preparing the morning meal at this time of day. A red light mounted in the corner of the hall blinks. I know now that it's a device designed to alert Hannah's dad to intruders, so I'm not worried.

I creep through the butler's pantry and past the kitchen, briefly pausing at the framed posters under glass on the wall. I still have a hard time believing my very existence is now condensed into historical anecdotes about how things were done in the early days of the house. I resist the urge to stop and read.

Hannah and Jonah gave me very specific directions on how to find the location where the painting is hidden, and I know exactly where the coal enters the house.

Uncle E. J. brought me down here once to show me the train track coming into the basement. The deeper I get in the house, the more my teeth chatter. It's damp and cool, but I'm also afraid I won't be able to find the painting. I pull open the door that leads into the boiler room, and then I descend a set of metal stairs. As I walk between the brick wall of the tunnel and the tracks, I peer into the cart resting on the rails; bits of artificial coal line the inside, obviously to show guests what the lifeblood of this house used to be. The only light comes from a series of bulbs hanging from the ceiling.

Aunt would faint dead away if she could see me down here! But this is important.

I feel along the wall. Hannah said there was a door, but I can't see very far down the tunnel, so I have no idea how long I need to walk. When I reach the end, there's just a brick wall. No door. I think I must have missed it, so I retrace my steps. It must be here! But it takes four trips up and back in the tunnel before I'm able to feel an indent. Even with my forefinger on the keyhole, I can barely make out the door about two feet off the dirt floor, flush with the brick wall. There is so little light down here, it's almost impossible to see. There's no handle. I can't find any hinges. There's nothing to grip, but I try inserting a fingernail into the tiny crack. Hannah's nails are disgusting nubs, but even with my longer ones, I wouldn't be able to make the door budge. At all.

I'm relieved to think there is a chance that it has not been opened in more than one hundred years, but on the other hand, I have no idea how to get inside.

I rummage in my pockets, hoping something I brought with me to pick the lock will work. There weren't many sharp objects in Hannah's room, but I found a pencil, a tiny jeweler's screwdriver (I'm amazed, but apparently Hannah makes jewelry—she has a whole box of beads and wire), and a piece of metal bent into a spiral.

Nothing works.

There is no way to get into that room without the key. Or dynamite, which doesn't seem plausible. The only person I can think to ask for help again is Florence.

She's my only hope to try to track down that chair and key, if Hannah can't do it in 1905.

Chapter Twenty-Five

Hannah

TURNS OUT, IT'S NOT HARD TO FIND the chair. Well, sort of. It's not hard to find out where the chair *is*, if you know who to ask . . . which Jonah did. (He was able to slip a note—well, part note, part drawing, since he doesn't read or write all that well—into the sugar bowl of the tea service that was sent up from the kitchen for me. Don't get me started on how completely terrible I feel over getting Jonah involved in this mess, especially now that he's going to get blamed for a crime he didn't commit. It really doesn't ease my guilt that he still keeps risking his job to help me.) The problem is that the chair is nowhere near where we are. Specifically, it's on the

6:02 a.m. train to New York City, where it will get some sort of special remove-red-wine-from-imported-silk dry-cleaning process.

I can only hope the focus of their attention is going to be the stain itself and not on the whole chair. I know I tucked the key deep into the padding of the arm and Jonah stitched the rip neatly, so a surface cleaning shouldn't reveal its hiding spot, but still.

Here's praying it won't matter either way because in the meantime Maggie will have broken into the tunnel room and found the painting and all will be set to normal in both our time periods.

But at the moment I'm having a super-tough time clinging to that hope. I know how hard that room is to break into.

Because Jonah and I are currently trying to do it too. Luckily, his job involves lots of time in the coal tunnel, so as long as I'm not caught with him, he won't arouse any suspicion by being here. At least we have that going for us.

If Maggie can't get in but we can, the endgame is the same. We can find a new hiding place for the painting, she can find it there in the future, and all will be perfection.

If we can get in.

We've already tried a slew of other keys I was able to sneak out of Mr. Berwind's desk drawer, but no go on any of them. Nada.

"Maybe a hairpin?" I suggest. Even if Maggie can't wear her hair all the way up, she has a ton of these, probably to keep the sides pulled from her face. So luckily I have one handy. The only good thing about big skirts is that they come with big pockets.

"Who builds a door with hinges on the inside?" I ask, but Jonah just grunts. He's crouched eye-level with the lock, concentrating really hard on trying to pick it with the bent pin.

I answer my own question. "I guess someone who doesn't want the door to be discovered, huh? Was your, um, friend who gave you the key the one who installed it? Or do you think it was the architect's inside joke? Or maybe Mr. Berwind ordered it? It's really kind of genius."

"He did say Mr. Berwind didn't know about it. I'm fairly certain only he did. Too bad he made it impossible to break in," Jonah says, falling back onto his butt. "I don't see any way to retrieve the painting without the key itself. Besides, we'll have to clear out of here. It's almost time for the coal delivery, and this tunnel will get busy for a bit. I'll have to help with that, but perhaps we can continue to share ideas for possible solutions via notes in your lunch service."

But what possible solutions? As much as I've been dying to see things outside this house, I can't just leave Newport and race to New York City to track down a chair. For one thing, how would I get there? It's not like I can order an Uber or hop an Amtrak. Yes, Maggie lives there most of the year, but she can't just take off for home on a whim. A girl my age in this time would need a proper chaperone, gobs of luggage, *believable reasons for going*.

I have none of those things.

And forget sneaking there. As Maggie, I'd have zero chance of blending. Society women—even girls—attract attention. While I know a ton about this time period, I really wouldn't have the first clue how to get around on my own outside the walls of The Elms; I'm barely treading water inside them.

But all this worry is masking what's really making me feel like all Mr. Berwind's keys are in the bottom of my stomach, as opposed to in my pockets.

Jonah.

If we DO find a way to get to the painting and hide it somewhere Maggie can find it in the future and set things right for her and me, Jonah's life is still ruined.

And I have to tell him that he's the one who has to take the fall. I don't know exactly when he's accused, but he is. Only, how do I tell him that? I lay awake for hours and hours last night trying to come up with a plan to clear Jonah's name, but there's no possible way. We can't change what's already written in the history books. Clearing him would strand Maggie and me and alter the time line of history.

And yes, it's true that we already changed things slightly by ensuring that Augustus-You-Bustus didn't end up with the painting. But I'm desperately clinging to the hopes that in the time line where he did steal it, he followed through on his plan to destroy the painting right away to keep Mary Cassatt from getting credit for it, and then he resumed his regular life as a struggling artist, so therefore the course of his own future didn't alter based on whether he nabbed it or not. At the very least his name was never recorded in the history books, so I think we're okay there.

But Jonah's name is all over history's pages.

It totally stinks, but in order to get back to the right time line, so we can swap places and history can unfold the way it is supposed to, Jonah's gonna have to take the fall. And I'm gonna have to convince him to do it.

Jonah, who has been nothing but kind and eager to help, and who's been a true friend to me in a place where I had none.

I steal a glance at him as I trail him out of the tunnel. He smiles at me, and it's so sweet and friendly that my gut twists even harder. This guy didn't even know me before yesterday, and he has totally risked his job a billion times since to help me. He believed everything I told him when literally no other sane person would have, and his ideas and support have been the only things holding me together through all this. I don't know if I would have had the courage to confront Augustus-You-Bustus either time if Jonah hadn't been beside me as backup. I mean, I never would have known where to hide the painting if he weren't here.

And now I have to take a knife and stab him in the back.

Which sucks big-time.

Jonah holds up a hand to stop me just before we step out of the tunnel, and I crash into his arm. He puts a finger to his lips and jerks his head at the opening. Someone's there!

Once again Jonah saves the day. Couldn't he be a

jerk or something, so it wouldn't feel so terrible to tell him he's about to spend his life on the run? We ease deeper into the shadows.

"Goodness, it's distasteful," the voice is saying. Colette! What's *she* doing down here?

I hold my breath and strain my ears so hard, they hurt.

"I can finish taking your statement upstairs, miss. I can search for the kitchen boy on my own and return once I have what I need from him."

Oh God, it's happening already. I thought I had more time! Next to me Jonah gasps. I nudge him with my foot and whisper the quietest "Shh!" imaginable.

Colette must be talking to a police officer, since he said that thing about taking a statement.

"Of course it's true. My niece would have no occasion to lie, sir."

Mrs. Berwind is down here too? This is getting worse and worse.

"Beg pardon, ma'am. I certainly didn't mean to suggest otherwise. So, you were saying, you were on the staircase and saw . . ."

Oh no! What if Colette spotted me talking to Maggie in the mirror? How would I ever explain that one to the Berwinds?

"I saw a boy around my age, maybe even younger, dressed like a servant. I'd never seen him before, and I know all the upstairs staff. I mean, maybe not by name, but . . . Well, at least I recognize all their faces. He wasn't one of them."

Gee, aren't you just so wonderful, Colette? Couldn't be bothered to learn the names of the people who wait on you hand and foot. But that's okay, because you could pick them out of a lineup. Ugh.

The cop talks next. "So you didn't recognize this person?"

"I did not. Though, when I described him to Aunt, her lady's maid was in the room, and she said it sounded like I was talking about this Jonah person. She said he'd have absolutely no reason to be upstairs. None at all."

Colette sounds positively giddy as she continues. "Since I was just turning the corner on the staircase, I saw him but he never saw me. He poked his head into the hallway and looked around to make sure no one was watching. Then he darted out and dashed away. Clearly he was doing reconnaissance and planning his escape route. There's no other possible reason why he'd be in the drawing room when his place is down here. Well, that's it, then! I've solved the crime, haven't

I? I suppose the newspapers will want my interview. Auntie, I may need a new dress for the photographs."

At least it's Colette who made the accusation. It's already so easy to hate her, so I won't have to tarnish my good feelings about anyone I grew up admiring, like the Berwinds themselves.

But then it slowly sinks in.

I might not be the one placing him under suspicion, but *I'm* responsible for Jonah being charged in the first place. The newspaper articles from the time of the theft said only that a reliable eyewitness account from a member of the household put him at the scene of the crime and that his disappearance from Newport led investigators to believe he was guilty. But he never would have *been* at the scene of the crime yesterday if not for me! So it has always been my fault. My stomach churns, and I'm afraid I could throw up right here and now. I can still admire the Berwinds, but I just might despise myself.

"Just a moment," Mrs. Berwind says, jerking me back to attention. "Mr. Birch, was this the same boy who was helping Margaret with the water spill yesterday? Might that have been what he was doing in the drawing room? We did encounter him there ourselves, after all."

Beside me Jonah exhales slowly at the exact time that I tense.

No. No, no, no, no.

"Indeed it was, madam," the butler answers. "Shall we find your niece and clear this confusion up?"

"Let's be on with it, then." Mrs. Berwind leaves, and there is a rustling of skirts outside the tunnel.

"I have to get to my room!" I whisper as soon as the noises fade. "No—wait! You have to come too and hide there! We can't let them find you."

"Who cares if they find me? You'll be upstairs telling everyone I was in the drawing room helping you yesterday. On the other hand, discovering me in your room would create an entirely different sort of confusion."

I exhale, grab his hand, and pull him from the tunnel with me. "Jonah, I need you to not ask any questions right now. I'll hide you in my bedroom closet, but we have to hurry up the back staircase before they make it up the front one. So I need you to run."

To his credit he picks up the pace even as he says, "But—"

I look over my shoulder as I take the stairs two at a time. "Jonah, please. *Trust me.*"

I try not to let the lead weight that hits my stomach slow me down as I utter those words.

The fact that Mrs. Berwind is the perfect society woman means that she moves serenely and deliberately along the first-floor hallway to the central staircase and then up it. It's close, but we have just enough time for me and Jonah to reach my room using the servants' stairs, and I slam him inside my closet before there's a knock on my door.

I try to slow my gulps for air, which is not exactly easy after booking up two flights of stairs. "Coming," I manage.

Taking another deep breath, I answer. "Oh. Hello."

Here's hoping they buy my innocent act.

"Margaret," Mrs. Berwind says, following me deeper into the room and gesturing for Colette and Mr. Birch to join her. The officer lingers in the doorway, looking about as uncomfortable as I feel. "This gentleman has some questions for you regarding the boy who was helping you with that water spill in the drawing room yesterday."

"Oh. Okay. I mean, um, certainly." If ever there were a time to remember to speak like Maggie, it's now. *No slang, Hannah. You can do this.*

The policeman clears his throat and says, "Now, you

fetched this Jonah person to clean the water?"

Even though the door to my closet is shut tight, it feels like Jonah's eyes are pinned to me. I know that he's in there one thousand percent expecting me to eliminate him as a suspect and move the investigation along to someone else.

And I want to so badly, it hurts.

But.

If I do that and they clear his name, the time line shifts. The whole future changes. What does that mean for everyone I love? Jonah and I are becoming friends and he's great, but we're talking about people I love with all my heart. Like my dad.

As much as I want to help Jonah, I just can't take the risk.

I take maybe my deepest breath ever and face the policeman. "Well, I wouldn't use the word 'fetch.' After all, he was right outside the door. Almost lingering, to be honest. Which I found odd, but he was there to help with the spill, so I guess I didn't really think about it too much." I pause, making sure I have everyone's full attention. Then I add, "Only . . ."

They lean in. I squeeze my eyes shut for the quickest of seconds and say a brief prayer for forgiveness.

"Only what?" Mrs. Berwind asks.

"Well, I didn't think anything of it at the time, but he did keep glancing at the sheet covering the portrait, and . . . I'm just now remembering this! He asked me if I was excited about the unveiling, and when I said yes, he said, 'It's such a lot of money to just hang on a wall,' which was a very odd thing to say. I replied I didn't know anything about its value, and he just said, 'A custom portrait like that . . . it must be worth a lot.'"

Colette sucks in a breath. I can't be sure, but I swear I hear the softest thud from inside the closet, almost like Jonah slumped against the wall. The lead in my stomach moves all the way to my feet. I've never felt so horrible in my entire life. But I have to keep going. I *have* to do this.

"I just attributed it to him being from a different class, and I thought perhaps it's not rude to mention money where he's from, so I let the whole topic drop. But then . . ."

This time it's the officer who says, "Go on."

This is it. I go in for the kill. "Well, a bit later I decided I wanted to thank Jonah for his help, since my aunt and Mr. Birch here interrupted us before I'd had the chance, so I asked Mrs. O'Neil if she might point me to where I could find him, and she said . . . she said . . ."

"What?" Mr. Birch urges, before remembering his place and clearing his throat. "Pardon me."

I shrug. "She said yesterday was his day off, and once he'd taken delivery of the coal in the morning, there would be no reason at all for him to be in the house prior to reporting in the evening to assist with the midnight supper that accompanied the ball."

The police officer snaps his notepad shut. "I'd say we have what we need, Miss Dunlap. Thank you."

"Let's remember who first cast suspicion on this Jonah person," Colette says, pushing past me to follow the officer into the hallway. Mrs. Berwind and the butler follow. "I'll still speak to the press. Auntie, I *can* get a new dress, right?"

I close the door on them and sink onto my bed. Not only is the chair containing the key hopelessly far away, and the room containing the painting helplessly locked, but I'm dreading the moment when my closet door will creak open and I'll have to stare at those two betrayed eyes.

Chapter Twenty-Six

Maggie

IN THE FOYER I'VE JUST ABOUT WORN a trench in the marble floor. I've gone over it a thousand times. If I am to find the key, I have to determine who bought that chair at the auction. I'm not sure what time Florence arrives, but I hope it's soon—and that she knows how to help. I plunk onto the step inside the front door to wait.

"Hannah. You're not supposed to be here." It's the unhelpful silver-haired man from yesterday. "Guests will start arriving in a half hour, and I can't have you sitting here, looking like a bump on a log."

I bow my head. "Of course. I was waiting for Florence. Do you know when she arrives this morning?"

He frowns. "You should not be bothering Mrs. Ensminger-Burn. I have no idea if she's planning to be on the property today. And even if she is, she does not have time for your antics."

"What?" I stand and almost trip up the few steps into the foyer. "I need to talk to her. She's the only one who can help me."

"I do not care one iota about what you need. Your father is supposed to be keeping you out from under my feet. I suggest you make yourself scarce." He taps his foot and points toward the servants' staircase until I start to move.

I'm tempted to retreat to my tree, but I turn back. Maybe he can answer a question before he banishes me. "The chair in the drawing room. The one with the floral pattern. Do you know how I can find out who purchased the original?"

Aunt would suggest that his scowl might freeze in place if he continues to make that face at me. "No. Maybe you should Google it."

What does *that* mean?

I close my eyes as he strides away, leaving me feeling like a fish out of water. Or a girl out of time. I imagine a normal morning in my own life. The carriages passing the front of the house. Aunt getting ready to have a bite to eat in the breakfast room before she heads out to make social calls to the neighboring cottages. The morning after a ball, the rest of the house would be sleeping in, but the kitchen staff would have meals ready for anyone who decided they needed food. Colette would be being Colette somewhere. But I also remember the freedoms I don't have in my own time, and it gives me pause.

"Hannah. Are you okay?"

When I open my eyes, Florence is standing in front of me. Her white hair is perfectly coiffed, and her suit is yellow today. I'm still wearing the pink cotton pants and the shirt I've had on since yesterday. Aunt would be so disappointed in how sloppy I have become, but these pants are so comfortable that I don't know how I'm going to go back to corsets and stockings.

I can't help but throw my arms around her. "Oh, Florence. I'm so glad you're here. Mr. . . . ah . . . Mr. Trent said he didn't think you were in today. I wasn't sure what to do."

"It's okay." She awkwardly pats my back, but she returns the embrace. It makes me feel better. Stronger. "Trent doesn't know my schedule, dear. What did you need?"

I take a breath, trying to reclaim my composure. "Do you know if there is a record of who purchased the furniture at auction in the 1960s?" I don't mean to be abrupt as I say it, but we don't have much time left. I'm sure that the moment I see Hannah's father today, he's going to ask me about packing.

She tilts her head to the side, as if she's thinking. "Of course. The Antiquities Society has meticulous records going back decades. There were a few files damaged by a water main break in the seventies, but I think those were only personnel files, not auction records. Why would you need to know about that?"

For a moment I think about telling her the whole story—after all, once he got over the shock, Jonah reacted so positively when he found out about our swap—but I worry that she'll think I'm crazy and be unwilling to help. "I'm curious about who purchased it. I heard a rumor about something hidden in the fabric, and I thought it would be interesting to find out if it really existed."

She chews on her lower lip for several long minutes. "I haven't ever heard that rumor, but it doesn't mean it isn't true. Who did you hear it from?"

I am not prepared for this question. "A guest on a

tour yesterday mentioned it." I try to keep the question mark out of my voice.

She looks skeptical, but she nods. "I've gathered from talking to Trent that your, er, *enthusiasm* for The Elms doesn't always go over so well with the docents, but I happen to think there are far worse things a young lady your age could be doing with her time. And . . . well, let's just say I share your passion for this particular house." She gives me a warm smile. "Besides, history buffs like us are always up for a little treasure hunting, aren't we? I've gone down a rabbit hole once or twice before because of a long shot."

"Well . . ." I breathe a sigh of relief. "I mean, thank you. Trent said . . . but I just wanted to be sure. . . . Don't you have responsibilities?"

She nods. "I'm afraid I do. I have a number of people I need to speak to this morning at The Elms. I won't be able to slip away until"—she looks at her watch—"eleven thirty."

I'm sure my face shows my disappointment, but what other choice do I have? "Who do you need to speak to?"

"Don't worry about that. Just come back and find me then." She smiles and pats my hand. "Have you ever been to the archives at the Historical Society? It's one of my favorite places. I know the librarian there, and I'm sure he'll help us."

We walk away in separate directions just as Trent opens the enormous front doors and the first of the day's guests enter. Many of them hold devices or tiny cameras. I still can't believe that this house in which I've spent so much time is on display for all the world to visit.

I have an hour and a half to wait. I spend part of that time in the tiny gift shop near the kitchen. I'm amazed that they sell replicas of my lucky locket. On a long shot I ask the clerk if she's ever heard of a mystery involving a key. (She hasn't.) I run across the grounds to the weeping beech and back to the house four times. (I feel sure I'm getting faster.) When I get tired of that, I wander through a few of the rooms, reading the notes on the walls about the history of the house (taking care to skip over anything about what happens to the inhabitants).

Finally it's time.

Her automobile is on the side of the house where all the visitors park. It's yellow, but that's not the only thing that is unusual. "Your . . . car . . . looks different from the others."

"This, my dear"—she gestures proudly at the

machine—"is a 1953 Packard Caribbean. I'm particularly partial to the whitewall tires."

She opens the door for me, and I slide into the interior. It's made of a soft caramel-colored leather. "Did you say 1953?" It's still fifty years after my own time, but as far as I can tell, the car is a time traveler like me. "I like it," I say when she nods. "My uncle has a 1905 Buick," I say, without even thinking about it.

"Does he?" Florence gasps. "I would dearly love to see that. Is that your father's brother?"

It's too late to correct my mistake, and I have no idea if Hannah's father has a brother, so I just nod, hoping the lie won't get Hannah into trouble.

The ride is so smooth and quiet, it feels like we are riding on a piece of furniture. Riding in Uncle's automobile is bumpy and rough, although that might have a good deal to do with the quality of the roads in my time, not the car. I'm tempted to ask her to drive around a bit, but then I remember our looming deadline. I'm supposed to be back in the mirror at six o'clock to compare notes with Hannah.

"I appreciate your waiting so patiently for me, Hannah. I've been collecting some impressions on the house from some of the staff. I was able to speak to several of them this morning," Florence says casually as she eases the vehicle onto Bellevue Avenue. There are so many automobiles on the road—it seems like everyone must have one. In my time they are still a relatively new invention. She drives much more slowly than everyone else, so it's not much different from riding in Uncle's new car. Several times, someone honks and she waves good-naturedly.

"Are you a newspaper reporter?" I can't think of any other reason she would have for collecting impressions of the house from the staff.

She laughs. "Oh, nothing like that." But she doesn't elaborate, and we ride the rest of the way in awkward silence. Thankfully, the trip takes only a few minutes. We stop near the Tower, where we met Alex and Ethan yesterday. When we arrive, Florence leads me up the front steps. It's not a building I'm familiar with, but it feels like something that has been here a long time.

"Excuse me," Florence says to a clerk sitting behind a large desk. "I need to see Jeffrey."

A young man dressed neatly in a suit and tie emerges from a door behind the desk. "Mrs. E.-B.! It's always so nice to see you!" He pumps her hand enthusiastically. "To what do we owe the pleasure this morning?"

It is so obvious that this man is trying to win favor with Florence. I have no idea of his motives, but I've seen countless people fawn in the same manner over my father and my uncle when they are trying to impress them.

Florence nods patiently. "We need to see the archives of The Elms' auction in 1961."

"Well." Jeffrey clears his throat. "Of course." He leads us into a small room with a large table. He flips open an object the size of a thin book that looks something like Hannah's device, only bigger.

"So," he says, looking up and cracking his knuckles. "What do you need to know and how can I help?"

"Dear." Florence puts her hand on Jeffrey's shoulder. "We're working on a top secret project. Would you indulge an old woman who has been affiliated with this facility since you were in diapers? We just need a few minutes of privacy."

Jeffrey can't contain his disappointment. "But, Mrs. Ensminger-Burn . . ." He pauses, clearly hoping she'll change her mind. "I thought I could help you with the computer. . . ." His voice trails off.

"I'm perfectly capable of managing the technology, my dear," she says, patting him on the arm.

He sighs and stands up, as though his indulgence in

her request is exhausting. He pauses again, clearly hoping, and then with another big sigh, he quietly leaves.

Florence sits down in front of his device, gesturing for me to follow. "They digitized the records years ago. We can access decades of data archives through this."

"What else can that tell you? Information about the Berwind family?" I try to keep the quiver out of my voice.

"Yes. These archives have everything on Newport going back to the mid-1800s." Florence beams like Colette does when she has beaten me at something.

I take a deep breath. I am not here to find out about my life or the lives of my family. And I'm not even sure I would want to know how things turn out. "Right. As you know, I'm curious to find out who purchased the original of the Louis XV–style armchair reproduction in the drawing room at The Elms."

She touches the buttons on the device, and I realize it's the modern equivalent of a typewriter. I don't know how it works, but with just a few strokes to the keys, she looks up with a smile. "Ada and John Stillwater purchased that chair."

"That is astonishing." I can't keep the amazement out of my voice. "All that information is in that little device?"

She gives me a bemused look. "Well, of course not, dear. It's in the Net. Or the Web. Or the cloud. Or whatever they call it these days—it's hard for us old folks to keep up. Not like you youngsters, who were born knowing how to text those emoticon thingies."

I don't have time to ponder the mysteries of twenty-first-century technology. I'm just glad it works so quickly.

My palms are starting to perspire, and I move closer to Florence, peering at the screen. "How do we contact them?"

She cocks her head to one side. "Shouldn't be too hard." A few more swipes on the keys, and she says, "Oh no."

"What?"

"It looks like they moved in 1986." She lowers her glasses and stares at the screen.

It can't be. All this technology, and it's a dead end? How will I get back to 1905?

She makes a few more keystrokes. "Wait. Here's something."

"A Stillwater relative who contributes to the Newport Antiquities Annual Fund lives in Chicago." She smiles. "Do you want to know if they still have the chair?" She pulls out her device, and before I reply, she's entering numbers.

"Drat," she says, and holds up her telephone for me to hear a stiff voice on the other end of the line.

"This number is no longer in service. Please hang up and try your call again."

"Hello! Can you tell us—"

Florence hits the button with the word "end" before I finish asking my question. "It's a recording," she says. "It appears we haven't updated our records."

It takes three more tries with different numbers before someone answers.

"Hello? Mrs. Jones? Would you happen to be related to Ada and John Stillwater?" Florence asks, and then pauses. "Florence Ensminger-Burn from the Newport Antiquities Society. Your parents purchased a chair at auction in Newport, Rhode Island, in the sixties." She looks at me while the person on the other end talks. "No, nothing like that. We are just curious about the provenance of the chair." She grimaces. "Can I put you on speakerphone?"

She presses a button, and the laughter of a woman is amplified. "I love that chair. I'm not interested in selling it."

"Mrs. Jones," I say, remembering not to yell, and trying to keep my voice even, like Florence does. "My name is . . ." I pause so as not to stumble over her name.

"Hannah Jordan. My father is the caretaker for The Elms, and we don't want to buy the chair." It surprises me how easy it has become to pretend to be Hannah. "I'm looking for a key that might have been hidden in the armrest of that chair."

Florence raises her eyebrows at me, but Mrs. Jones gasps from the other end of the connection.

"How did you know? My brother found that key when he ripped the upholstery on the chair," Mrs. Jones whispers. "We never told anyone. We were kids playing hide-and-seek. He'd been forbidden to even touch that chair. It fell over, and the key slipped out of the upholstery on the arm."

I let out a breath. "You found it? Do you—"

She continues over me, speaking as though she's reliving a dream. "He was seven and I was nine. We thought it was magic, this big old skeleton key with a gold filigreed handle. When Todd picked it up off the floor, it was as though time stopped for just a moment." She takes a breath and goes on. "That sounds silly, doesn't it. Anyway, for years it sat on his desk, but when he was in high school, he strung it on a chain and wore it around his neck."

I glance at Florence. Even though she doesn't know

how important this is, she still reaches up and squeezes my hand. I whisper toward the phone, "Does he still have it?"

There's a sadness in Mrs. Jones's voice as she answers. "My brother died last year. But that key always brought him good luck. He wore it under his uniform when he shipped out to Vietnam in '71. He had it on when he was injured in battle. He always said it was the reason he met Genevieve in the hospital while he waited to get sent home." She sighs, and I can almost hear her wipe away a tear.

Florence clears her throat. "We are so sorry for your loss. Thank you, Mrs. Jones, for sharing your story."

"Wait!" I don't mean to shout, but I'm afraid one of them is going to break the connection. "Does someone in your family still have it?"

"It's funny that you're asking about that key. After Todd died last year and my nephew moved Genevieve into the nursing home, he gave the key back to me. We never really knew where it came from. I always had an idea that it must have been hidden in that chair for a reason."

"It was," I whisper. "And I have reason to believe that it could be the key to solving the mystery of the

Margaret Dunlap portrait heist." But as I'm saying this, I realize that if the key is with Mrs. Jones in Chicago, it will take weeks to get here. My heart starts beating as if I'm running again. I have to go with Hannah's father to California.

How can I ever do that?

"The heist, my dear?" Florence whispers, her eyes crinkling in confusion. "Are you sure?"

"Oh my goodness!" Mrs. Jones practically shouts from the other end of the line. "Really? I'm holding it in my hand right now," she says. "But I . . . I'd hate to part with it. It means so much to me."

We are so close. I can't keep the tears from forming, and I brush my face, hoping Florence doesn't notice. "I don't need to keep the key, Mrs. Jones. I just need to open something with it."

Florence inhales sharply and then looks at me with a sparkle in her eye. "Mrs. Jones. If I could guarantee that we'd return the key to you, would you be willing to let us borrow it? The Antiquities Society will cover overnight shipping, and I will personally ensure that you get it back."

Overnight?

"This all sounds so mysterious," Mrs. Jones says.

"And I do love a good mystery. If you will guarantee that I'll get it back, I don't mind loaning it to you for a while. I guess it does feel like it belongs at The Elms. I'm running out to do a few errands; I'll ship the key to you this afternoon. You'll see what I mean about it feeling magical."

I can't believe our luck. I've found the key. "We can really get it overnight?"

Now *that's* magical.

As I feared, the moment we are back in the automobile and even before she starts the engine, Florence turns and looks at me, eyes shining with excitement. "Tell me more about this key."

I bite my tongue. More than ever before, I want to tell her about the mirror and the portrait and about how I'm not really Hannah Jordan. But I can't. "Would it be okay if I told you the whole story tomorrow? I don't know for sure that anything will come of this key, but it's something I'd like to do for myself, if that's all right? I promise I'll tell you everything later, though."

"How do you know it has something to do with the heist?" she asks. I can tell she is trying to piece the puzzle together, but I just squeeze her hand. Even in the warm air, it's cool to the touch. "Where did you hear about the key again?" There's a familiarity about her that tugs at my heart, and I *want* to tell her. But I can't find a way to say the words "time travel" out loud.

"I need to be sure I'm right before I involve you more than necessary." I squeeze her hand again. "You know I appreciate your help."

She nods and starts the car. "I respect your request for secrecy, though I don't really understand it." Her tone is clipped and professional. Not at all the conspiratorial tone she had just a few minutes ago. "I've been obsessed with that portrait and the heist since I was a little girl. I've always wondered what the true story is."

We ride in silence for the rest of the drive to The Elms. I've hurt her feelings, and I feel terrible. But I simply cannot reveal the secret. If Hannah wants to, she can decide to tell Florence more after we swap back to our rightful places.

I think about how anxious I am to get home, but there are parts of the twenty-first century that are beginning to grow on me. I shall certainly miss the freedoms I have had here. I glance over at Florence driving. Tomorrow it will be back to being shadowed by a nanny and sewing with Colette and a total ban on running.

Except maybe it doesn't have to be.

Yesterday Tara said if women hadn't protested over the years, the world wouldn't have been ready for a woman to run for president. Generations of women must have taken lots of baby steps to earn these freedoms. Generations that include me. Maybe there's something I can do to help things along. I've heard Mrs. Belmont whispering to Aunt Herminie about trying to involve society ladies in a movement to help women get the vote; maybe I can join them! From there, anything's possible!

It's so very obvious to me why Hannah went back in time—she needed to prevent the heist. But I've been pondering my purpose for traveling forward. I thought it was only to clear the way for Hannah. But now I wonder. Maybe I needed to see things here to have a vision for what could be for me. My time here has been so short, but it has opened my eyes to something much longer in duration—a purpose for my whole life. My life doesn't have to be a whirlwind of meaningless balls and dinner parties; I can contribute something important. Something that will have a lasting effect.

I think I finally understand why all this is happening. I need to stop bemoaning the things I'm not "supposed" to do, according to my aunt and my father (and society at large), and start doing the things that make me happy, like running and reading as much as I want. Maybe even playing lawn tennis until I perspire and sliding down a banister once in a while. I bet there are a lot of girls my age and older who would love to get a chance to do something outside the so-called rules.

I'm suddenly beyond eager to get home and begin planning right away! I'll find out from Mrs. Belmont how to get involved. It's not going to be easy. Many people—including women—won't think that these changes are appropriate.

And no matter how outraged Aunt Herminie might be, I'm going to find a way to continue running! I will never tire of the wind in my hair and the feeling of freedom I get when I run.

My brain is whirring with the possibilities. "Did you ever play a sport when you were younger?" I blurt as Florence eases the car between the white lines painted on the surface of the driveway. It's suddenly important to me to find out more about her before I leave.

Florence looks at me in surprise, startled for a moment out of her hurt feelings. "I confess that's the last thing I expected you to want to discuss right now." She chuckles. "I'm more of an artist than an athlete. But my grandmother was a long-distance runner before it was acceptable for women to really be active in sports. She has always been an inspiration to me." There's a wistful tone to her voice, and I wonder if she's missing her family in the same way I'm missing mine.

We get out of the car and start up the path toward The Elms' front entrance, and I try to think of something to say. "Thank you for all your help."

"Oh, Hannah. You're welcome. I'm sorry about the way I acted when we got into the car. I respect that you would want to do your best to confirm a rumor before sharing it. I know you'll tell me more after the key comes from Mrs. Jones tomorrow." She squeezes my shoulder. "I need to confess something to you," she says. "I arrived the other day as a result of a complaint from Trent. About you."

I gasped. "What?"

"Now, don't worry." She waves her arms like she's swatting a fly. "The Antiquities Society knows that he is inclined to exaggerate. Actually . . ." She pauses. "He's a bit of a blowhard, if you ask me. But we still needed to investigate the . . . how did he put it? 'The bratty, know-it-all girl who interrupts my tours.'" She laughs. "*My* confession is that I never expected you to be a kindred soul with such a passion for history." She pulls me into a tight hug. "Promise me you'll never lose that passion."

I relax into her embrace; even though I can't tell her who I really am, I feel like she understands. As I pull away, I notice for the first time the edge of something silver peeking out from under her jacket.

"My lucky locket," she says, noticing my gaze and pulling it out for me to see. "It's an heirloom." She opens it to reveal a small picture of a child. "And this is my granddaughter."

My heart pounds for no obvious reason as I look at the locket. For a moment I wonder if it IS my locket, but then I remember I've left it at home. "I have one that looks very much like that, but the chain is shorter."

"The ones at the gift shop are best sellers." She tucks the necklace back into her blouse.

"Mine used to be for luck as well," I say, "but I don't need it for that anymore. Good friends are a better talisman."

Florence nods. "Good friends are a gift. That is for sure."

Suddenly I can't wait to tell Hannah everything.

Chapter Twenty-Seven

Hannah

MY DAD WOULD BIRTH KITTENS IF HE knew I had a boy in my bedroom closet.

Don't worry, Dad. This one refuses to open the door.

As soon as the coast was clear, I tried to get in to talk to Jonah, but he must have been holding the doorknob, because it refused to budge. And when I attempted to speak to him through it, he cut me off at "Jonah—"

"Please, Hannah. I can't talk right now." It sounded like he was speaking through tears.

I didn't know what to do, so I did . . . nothing.

Only, now it has been at least an hour, maybe more, and I've done my own share of crying, waiting for him to open the door. It doesn't seem like that's ever going to happen. It's perfectly quiet in there; in fact, there's been no noise on the floor at all since Mrs. Berwind poked her head in right after my big "confession." She started to fuss over me, but then Mr. Berwind showed up and hustled her out. I overheard him say she should leave me alone to rest because my "delicate female constitution can't handle all this drama, poor thing."

If I hadn't been so upset about Jonah, that would have made me scream.

Um, hello. Delicate females, my foot. Let me start a list for you of women who handle(d) the drama just fine, thank you very much:

Abby Wambach

Rey from Star Wars (fictional, but still)

Rosa Parks

Marie Curie

Susan B. Anthony

Malala Yousafzai

Wonder Woman (also fictional, but STILL)

I could go on for about ten years, but . . .

It's not what's important right now.

I slide off the bed and crawl over to the closet door again. I tap lightly. "Jonah?"

He doesn't answer.

I take a breath like I'm about to swim the entire Olympic hundred-meter dash underwater. Is that a thing? Well, whatever. I'd rather be doing that anyway. I'd rather be doing just about anything else in the world.

"Jonah, please?" It's all I can get out.

Nothing. But just when I'm about to give up and crawl back to my bed, the doorknob turns.

Jonah peers at me from the darkness of my closet, like a trapped animal. Which he kind of is. His eyes are the saddest thing I've ever seen, and he doesn't do anything more than stare at me, but the *Why?* is written all over his face.

I slide my earring from my lobe and drop it, so that I have a ready excuse for what I'm doing on the floor if anyone should barge in. *Breathe, Hannah.* "I know you don't understand—or maybe you do—but I know it sucks, and I just . . . *Do* you understand?"

He doesn't answer, just stares off into some nothingness over my shoulder.

"Okay," I say, taking another deep inhale. "The thing is, well . . ."

"I'm in the history books, aren't I? As the one blamed for the crime?" Jonah asks when I literally can't make myself say the next words. "You can't change it because it's already written." His voice is flat and dull, like he has already accepted his fate.

I nod because my throat closes up too much for me to speak. He really is so smart.

"You used me this whole time." He doesn't even sound angry, just sad. Betrayed.

"NO!" I nearly scream it, and I have to clamp a hand over my mouth. I don't want anyone coming in to check on me. "No," I repeat, more quietly but just as urgently. "I mean, I knew that history blamed you, but I always had my doubts and lots of people vouched for how nice you were and how you would never have done something like that. To be perfectly honest, when I first approached you in the tunnel, it was partly to rule you out as a suspect but also . . . well, partly to keep an eye on you in case you were the thief." I hang my head.

"I'm sorry," I whisper, before adding, "but you have to believe me. I swear I thought that Maggie and I could switch back whenever we wanted. We didn't know any of that stuff about the alternate time line until *after* you and I had stopped the heist. You know that! You were there!"

He raises his eyes to mine finally, and something

glimmers in there. Like maybe he remembers. Like maybe he believes me.

"But then you didn't say anything once you *did* realize," he says. "All last night. This morning in the tunnel. You were perfectly fine letting me continue to help you."

I take this with only a small wince. He's not wrong. "Things didn't click into place for me until the ball. What it would mean for you, I mean. And this morning I—I was trying to work up the courage to tell you when . . . when . . . well, you know. When we were interrupted."

He nods but doesn't say anything. I'm desperate to ask him if he understands how I never wanted any of this to happen, how all I wanted was to spend some time in the Gilded Age and then everything with the art heist stuff just started snowballing and . . .

I wish I'd never come here. I wish I were safe in my own room, curled up in my bed with my stuffed bear, Windy. I'm so homesick, it hurts.

But it's not about making *me* feel better. It's about Jonah.

He's quiet for a long time, and then he says, "What do the history books say? Do I go to jail for life?" He sounds totally resigned. I shake my head so hard and fast, it practically swivels off my neck. "NO! No, you don't! I promise. You—you escape Newport. You're never caught! It's like this huge century-old mystery or whatever. But I swear, you don't go to jail for it. At least, not in my time line."

Now it's his turn to exhale. About a hundred times. When he can speak again, he asks, "Never caught, huh? I'm a notorious fugitive?" There's a hint of something in his voice that kind of matches that adventure-y eye twinkle tell of his, and my heart leaps with hope.

"Um . . . I guess so?" I mean, the history books don't make him out to be Billy the Kid or anything. Mostly they just say he was never heard from again, and neither was any news of the painting, but if he wants to think of himself that way, I'm sure not gonna be the one to stop him.

"How?" he asks.

"Huh?"

"How can I possibly escape? Between my mother's and my jobs, we barely put food on the table. How would we ever afford to run away? Where would we go? How will we get new jobs without papers and a letter of recommendation from the Berwinds? I can't—I can't picture it."

"I know. We'll figure it out, I promise. This is all my

fault, and I swear I'm not going to abandon you. We'll figure it out!"

"You said that twice," he murmurs, sounding doubtful again.

"I know. I really mean it, that's why."

"Sure."

"You don't believe me?" I ask.

"I believe that *you* believe it. But you're from a different time. Everything is different for someone like you."

"Someone like me? What? It's not like *I'm* rich, like Maggie is," I say. "I *work* at The Elms in the future, just like you do here."

Only, that's not really true. Yes, I work at The Elms, or at least my dad does. But it's a hundred kinds of different. I have . . . options. I have education. And we're not rich, true, but we can afford things like vacations and new school clothes and soccer registration fees, and my dad is forever telling me I can be anything I can dream of, and I believe him.

Has anyone ever told Jonah that? Would he have any reason to believe them? Jonah definitely has serious street smarts, based on all his ideas for hiding the painting, but it's not the same. He's not a slave or anything, but he might as well be, for all the chances he has of changing things for himself in any real way. Without money and school, he's basically looking at an entire life doing exactly what he's doing at this age.

Jonah slumps farther into the closet, and my heart drops into my gut.

"I'll, um—I'll give you some privacy while I think of ways to do this escape. You probably want to, like, digest all this, I'm guessing," I say.

I leave the door cracked a bit, so at least he has a sliver of light, but he'll be safely hidden from anyone coming in. Then I cross the room and plop onto the lounging chaise. I wish these were still a thing in my time; it's like an extra-fancy version of a reclining beach chair. It's also the perfect place for a sulk.

My head hurts and my stomach cramps. It feels like every body part is encased in armor and like moving would be the hardest thing ever. Maybe I really am getting sick. Not from the drama but from how overwhelming everything feels.

I have no idea how to get to the painting. I have no idea how to help Jonah while still keeping everything okay in the future. I have no idea about any of it. And I miss home. I miss my dad and Tara and my phone and Windy and my whole entire *life*. I would give anything—

anything—to be back there now, with no worries bigger than how to get Ethan to ask me to hang out, which I couldn't really care less about right now.

I wish, I wish, I wish.

I have to wake Jonah after my lunch is delivered by one of the maids on a silver platter. I give him all of it. I don't think I could eat anyway.

I just want to go home.

"I'm really sorry about this whole entire mess," I tell him.

"Don't be. It isn't your fault."

"Um, actually, yeah, it's *exactly* my fault."

He smiles slightly. "I was trying to make you feel better. But truthfully, I didn't have to help you when you asked."

"Wrong again. What were you going to do? Say no to the niece of your boss?" I ask.

"You're very hard to cheer up, you know."

And that just makes my stomach twist even harder. Why should Jonah be trying to cheer me up when it should be the other way around?

"I really am super-sorry," I say again.

"I know."

But that's not good enough. I didn't give up last season when we were down by four goals in the second half of the division finals, did I? NO WAY! I'm not a give-up kind of girl. I've been mopey all morning, but what I should have been doing was figuring out a plan. The Louis XV armchair is gone, so there's no way Maggie can get the key in the future. It's up to me.

I begin pacing the room. I whisper, so no one (cough, Colette, cough) who might stick their ear to the door will hear talking inside, but I'm loud enough that Jonah can hear me.

"Okay, we need a plan of action to get you out of here and maybe get me home. Enough hiding and waiting. Here's what I'm thinking: I can't get to New York without attracting all kinds of attention, and you need to escape Newport, so it's only logical that we need to sneak you on a train to the city. Once you're there, you find the shop that has the chair and pretend to be Mrs. Berwind's errand boy, sent to check on their progress."

The more I get going, the more the plan just falls into place in my head. Like my brain was working behind the scenes the whole time I was sulking.

I race on. "I can disconnect the phone and intercept any telegrams, so there's no way the chair cleaners can contact the house to confirm. They'll definitely let you see the chair. Then you just have to pretend to inspect it and get close enough to sneak the key out. Okay, so maybe that's not as easy as it sounds, but I have total faith in you. I've seen how fast you think on your feet, Einstein."

Jonah blushes at that. But then his eyes drop. "My mother? I can't just—"

"I'll take care of that. Once everyone's in bed tonight, we'll sneak you out so you can get word to your mom. Can you reach her without anyone noticing?"

Jonah nods.

"Do you think . . . um, do you think she'll flip out?"

"If that means what I imagine it does, then yes, probably. But the alternative is her son in jail for a crime he didn't commit. I think given that choice, she'll go along with whatever plan we come up with. I'll make it up to her, I swear it."

I duck my head. "I know you will. You're a really good guy. And I'm really, really sorry. Again."

Jonah nods quietly.

I blow out a breath. "Okay, so then you'll sneak back here and I'll let you in. You can sleep in the closet tonight."

Even in the shadows, I can see Jonah's cheeks turn

red. "I—I believe I would be more comfortable in the tunnel."

I shrug. "Whatever. If you really don't think anyone will go down there."

I resume my pacing, but this time I'm grabbing little items here and there and tossing them onto my bed. A silver brush. A hand mirror with a mother-of-pearl handle. I take off the locket Maggie had on when I swapped into her body and add it to the pile, but then I reconsider and instead add a hairpin that looks like it might have a real jewel in the center. If she was wearing the necklace, it might mean something to her. I'm hoping she won't mind sacrificing these other things to the cause.

"I'm guessing that selling off even one of these will bring in enough money to get you around New York and back here, once you have the key. Then it's just a matter of planning how to meet up so you don't have to risk coming back to the house, and then figuring out a plan for you and your mom to skip town permanently, but that will come to me."

I pause to finally take a breath. "I really think this could work!"

Then I realize what I've just asked of Jonah. "Oh

man. I'm doing it again. Forget New York and helping me with the key; obviously, escaping with your mom is the only thing we should be worrying about right now. I'll figure out the key another way. I'm sorry. Aaaah-gain."

Jonah looks a little dazed, but after a long minute I see the tiniest hint of a smile. "Except, I've always dreamed about seeing New York City. And my mother would never set foot in all that hustle and bustle."

I bite my lip. "Soooo? You're saying . . ."

"It's risky, but I think it could work. I'm in."

"You are the nicest person in any time period ever. Seriously."

We smile at each other, and then I rush on. "Okay, so my guess is the police will be expecting you to travel under the cover of night, meaning we have to outsmart them. You should take a train tomorrow afternoon, and if you can go to the next town over to board, even better."

"You seem to know a lot about these matters."

"I've watched only about a zillion-and-a-half caper movies."

He tilts his head in confusion, but I zoom on. "Let's work on how to sneak you out tonight. In a few hours I'll meet back up with Maggie in the mirror like we planned and ask her if this stuff is okay to take. Which, obviously, she'd better say yes to. Maybe she even knows where we can get our hands on a little cash so you can get a train ticket with that. It will be way easier to pawn all this other stuff once you get to New York."

For the first time all day, the knot in my stomach loosens.

We have a plan. Forward momentum. Too much drama for a girl's delicate constitution?

Pfft.

Not *this* girl.

The afternoon feels like it takes about forty-seven years to pass, but finally it's time for my mirror chat with Maggie. Wait until she hears our perfect plan. I leave Jonah safely hidden in my closet—daydreaming about the new life he seemed to latch on to pretty quickly once he allowed himself to imagine the possibilities—and head downstairs.

As soon as I'm on the sideboard, I take the trinkets from Maggie's room out of my skirt pockets and line them carefully on the mantel, so she can approve them as soon as she appears. They have to be worth more than enough to get Jonah to New York City and then off on a new adventure somewhere. Probably enough to get him to the moon and back, actually.

The mirror shimmers.

Before Maggie can even open her mouth, I speak. "Mags, we have the best plan ever to get to the key in New York. Wait until you—"

But Maggie's grin is even bigger. "You don't need to."

"You broke into the room! Wow, I give you so many props, because we tried and—"

She interrupts me. "No, I wasn't successful with that. But I did manage to locate the key. And it will be in my hands in a matter of . . . One moment, please."

She looks down at MY phone in her hand and punches a few buttons like she's a pro at it or something. "According to this tracking app Florence installed for me, delivery is scheduled for between one and four p.m. tomorrow."

My jaw drops. "You . . . What . . . It . . . How?"

This is even better than I ever dreamed! Everything is falling into place!

Chapter Twenty-Eight

Maggie

AT PRECISELY ONE O'CLOCK I STAND in the servants' entrance outside the gift shop. I still can't believe all the books written about the heyday of the summer cottages in Newport and the reproductions of art and artifacts. There is a whole stack of postcards featuring my portrait. I feel like scooping them all together and burning them. Who would possibly want me on a postcard? I wonder what they'll do with these when the original portrait is unveiled.

It was Florence's idea to have Mrs. Jones mail the package to Hannah's attention. I still can't believe it's possible to get a package from Illinois to Rhode Island overnight, but in the three days I've been here, I've seen stranger things. I just hope I don't have to wait three more hours for the delivery.

I half expected Florence to meet me here, though I'm glad she didn't. She's been such a big help, but I'm afraid that if I talk to her any more, she'll suspect that Hannah is crazy.

A brown truck pulls into the drive and stops in front of me. I consider taking a step or two backward, but before I can act, a young man wearing all brown, from his shoes and socks to his short pants and shirt, jumps down out of the truck with a package. "You're waiting patiently this afternoon. Is there a new Harry Potter book out or something?" He grins as he hands me a device and something that looks like a pen. "Sign, please."

With a flourish I sign Hannah's name, and then, hands shaking, I grab the package. Forgetting all polite manners, I turn and walk straight through the door and back toward the coal tunnel. In my mind the ghosts of servants rush past me as I pass the kitchen and descend the metal stairs to the boiler room, then walk past the coal wagon and into the tunnel still lit by sporadically placed bulbs hung from a cord attached to the ceiling.

As I walk, I rip the envelope open and dump the key into my hand. It has delicate gold filigree and is heavier than I imagined. Mrs. Jones was right. There is something magical about it. I'm holding the key to my past. Just as it was yesterday—and for the last hundred years—the door is sealed tight. Suddenly I'm afraid. What if the key doesn't work? I close my eyes and imagine my aunt and uncle, and my father, and yes, even Colette. They aren't perfect, but I do miss them.

I miss the comfort of my books, I miss the horses and carriages that carry ladies down Bellevue Avenue to their social events, I miss the sounds and smells of my Elms. At the end of the summer I'll return to the brownstone in New York City with Father, where I'll get back to my studies. I can't wait to shock Mr. Walsh, the headmaster of my school, with questions about rights for women.

I shake my head, sweeping my thoughts aside, and fit the key into the lock. It goes in smoothly, but it takes both my hands to make it move. At first it seems like I've turned it the wrong way, but then the chamber clicks into place. Using the key as a knob, I throw my whole body against the door until it opens. I'm not sure what I expected, an illuminated room with a ray of sun pointed at the portrait?

Instead I'm looking into a pitch-black void.

For a moment I consider my options. I could go

upstairs and find help. Either Florence or Hannah's dad could probably find a candlestick or a torch or a lantern somewhere. I try to use the ambient light from Hannah's device, but it's no good, it's not bright enough. I could climb into the void and feel around until I find the portrait. But the thought of bugs or rodents or something else lurking in the crypt stops me cold.

The tunnel is dank, dim, and dusty. I haven't come all this way to fail. I shiver, but then I see it. Just down the tunnel there's a bulb hanging low. With my arm outstretched I can touch the ceiling anyway, so it takes only a couple of attempts to pull the wire attached to the bulb a little lower. If I angle it just right, it gives me enough light to see into the chamber.

Nothing. What if it's not here?

But then I angle the light a bit to the right, and I spot it. Against the wall in the corner is a tarp covering an object suspiciously shaped like a portrait. Gritting my teeth and ignoring the thought of rodents, I crawl gingerly into the room and gently pull off the tarp.

And looking back at me . . . is myself. But not in a mirror this time. The century-old portrait that hasn't seen the light of day in more than a hundred years is in shockingly good shape, considering it's been kept in this disgusting space for so long.

The only thing left is to haul it upstairs without being seen, and then wait for the tourists to leave for the afternoon, so that Hannah and I can swap back to our rightful places.

All I can think is, *Cool*.

Chapter Twenty-Nine

Hannah

THERE'S NOTHING LEFT TO DO HERE, and I know it. I'm also desperate to be home. So why am I swallowing around a giant lump in my throat?

It's okay to leave. More than okay.

Most important, *Jonah* is more than okay. He snuck off before the sun came up this morning, after about a zillion hugs from me. True, at first he was slightly disappointed that he didn't need to go to New York City. But wow did that go away fast when he told me about his decision to go all Wild, Wild West. He'll take a new name, of course. Bye-bye, Jonah Rankin; hello, Jeremiah Duncan. It turns out Jonah/Jeremiah has always had an obsession with cowboys. He wants a whole ranch, with a big farmhouse for his mom and a zillion horses for him, a totally different future from what he thought he'd have, but one with way more possibilities for adventure. Doesn't everyone deserve that? And, as it happens, just the one ruby in the middle of Maggie's hairpin can actually make that happen. Thankfully, Maggie was more than eager to donate it and all the other items to such a good cause. She doesn't even think anyone will notice she doesn't have those things anymore. (Ah, to be filthy, stinking rich.)

I love happy endings.

And now it's time for mine.

Then why is it feeling so bittersweet? Crazy key drama aside, I always wished I could see The Elms in its prime, and not only did I get to see it, I got to live it. When I land home, I'll be playing the hero for a while because I'll be credited with finding the missing painting.

So why is my stomach doing backflips, and not in the good way?

"You ready for this?" Maggie asks quietly.

"Yes, no, yes," I answer.

She rolls her eyes. "You're weird, Hannah Jordan." Then she smiles. "And thank God for that. I can't imagine spending days trapped in some boring, stuffy person's body."

I smile too.

Yup. This is why my stomach is doing a world-class tumbling routine. Because it knows that as soon as Maggie pops that portrait of herself onto the wall, I won't get to talk to her ever again. Or at least it *thinks* so. Neither of us are even acknowledging that this theory of ours might not work.

It will. I can feel it.

"I'm gonna miss you like whoa," I say.

"Back atcha."

I giggle. "Where'd you learn that one?"

"I ascertained how to work the television remote last night. I've not been to sleep yet!"

My giggle becomes a full-on laugh. She's adorable. "I wish we had gotten more time to just chat, ya know? Like, when we didn't have to worry about solving art heists."

She grins. "Or finding keys missing for decades? Or figuring out how to explain away knowledge of their existence?"

"Exactly. I think we nailed that, by the way. One last mission for when you get back, huh?"

"I've got it covered. Though, returning to your original comment," she says, "I feel as if I probably know you better than anyone else in the world, after spending three days in your body."

"Ewww. There were some weirder parts to that that I'd rather not acknowledge, if you don't mind. No offense." I shrug, and smile.

"None taken." She chews on her bottom lip before saying, "Hannah? I've been working up the courage to tell you about some, er, incidences that took place during my time here. I'm afraid I may have—quite inadvertently and with only the best intentions, of course—taken some missteps in a few areas, and I—"

I cut her off. "Stop! I don't care. Unless you got a tattoo on my butt or something, I'm sure you didn't cause any permanent damage. Besides, everyone will be so caught up in the portrait discovery that I'm sure they'll forget all about anything weird I did or said or whatever. I don't want to spend our last minutes together on apologies."

She looks so relieved that I reconsider for a second. Just exactly what did she do? But I shake it off and continue. "This is gonna sound super-cray, so just go with it, okay?"

She nods, her nose wrinkling. I should totally skip

that move in the future; it makes my face look all kinds of messed up.

"Okay, so," I say, "when I was a kid and, um, maybe possibly right up until this week, I used to talk to your picture all the time. Like we were friends or something. And I always thought . . . I always thought we totally would be, if we lived at the same time."

"Oh, I'm quite sure of it!" Maggie says, and I smile.

"Me too. More than ever. But the thing is, I don't think I'm going to be able to anymore. I'll know it's not really you in there. It won't feel the same."

"I understand. But perhaps you can try anyway. You *do* have a spare copy of the painting now. Perhaps there's a place for it on your bedroom wall, next to the oversize picture of your friends with the instruments."

I burst out laughing again. "Those aren't my friends, you nut. That's a poster of the Five Heartbeats. Rock stars? Boy band?"

"Boy band?"

She looks completely confused, and I laugh harder. "You know what? Never mind."

She shrugs. "You also have your dad to talk to. And Florence is quite lovely. Of course, you have Tara. I'd love to have a Tara in my time."

I flash her a cheesy fake-innocent smile. "What? Are you saying you don't consider Colette your BFF for life?"

Maggie's eye roll is even bigger this time. "I don't know what 'BFF' means, but don't even utter her name!"

"I know, seriously. Wish I could help you there, but yeah. She's super-ugh. So . . . what will you be doing? You know, if I want to imagine you. And please don't say anything about debutante balls or husband-shopping."

Maggie shudders. "Hardly." Her face gets this thoughtful, faraway expression on it. "I have bigger plans than that. Now that I know everything it's possible for women to do and be in your time, I'm going to be the loudest voice there is to help the progress along in mine. After all, someone has to lay the groundwork. I know that a couple of the women in Aunt's circle are already discussing this issue, and I plan to join their ranks and expand their vision of what's possible for us."

I laugh. "So, like, rock the vote and all that?"

I swear, Maggie's eyes practically twinkle. "For starters. And only for starters."

"Awesome. Um, Maggie? I don't know if you were able to resist looking at any records of what happens with your life, but—"

She cuts me off. "Land sakes! I don't want to know!"

"Got it. Yeah, I wouldn't want too many spoilers either. So I'll just say that if 'someone' was worried about returning in time and doing something with her newfound, um, *revelations* that might disrupt the history books in some way, then I would probably tell that person, whoever she might be, that she shouldn't be worried about that. At all. I'd tell her that maybe she's on exactly her right path."

She gasps and covers her ears, but then she lets her hands fall away and smiles softly. "Thank you, Hannah."

I nod, and we share a smile before she asks, "And you? How shall I picture you?"

I grin. "Kicking butt and taking names, of course." But then I get more serious. "Remember when we were talking the first time and I was saying that stuff about women in my time having equal rights on paper but not necessarily always being treated that way? I was thinking that if you're going to be working so hard here, maybe I could do some stuff on my end to keep it going. You work on the laws and I'll work on the hearts. I can't let all your future efforts count for nothing, right?"

I give her an exaggerated wink, and she grins. "I like that." Our smiles fade as we stare at each other for a second, taking mental pictures. I swipe quickly at my eyes, then take a deep breath. "I think it's time. Are we ready to do this?"

She nods formally. For just that second I can see what she's probably like here, when she's being all "young lady of the house."

I bite my lip and put my fingertips on the glass. She tilts her head, then smiles and fits her hand to mine.

"It was nice to meet you, Margaret Dunlap," I say.

"Rock on with your bad self, Hannah Jordan," she replies.

Before I can even open my mouth to ask where she learned *that* expression, Maggie drops her hand and then her face becomes blocked by the back of the frame settling into place over the age spot. Then I'm falling, falling, falling.

I wake up on the floor, my feet in flip-flops, and my hair—*my* hair—in a ponytail.

I breathe in the quiet museum air.

It worked. Oh, wow. I jump up and race to the mirror. I edge the portrait gently out of the way, and my heart falls. There's no Maggie on the other side. Not even a shimmering behind the glass. In fact, it looks like the most ordinary mirror ever. My fingers fly to where the key-shaped age spot was—but it's gone! Completely, as if it never was there to begin with.

I let my hands fall to my side, and I take a few more deep breaths before slowly turning to face the empty room. I take it all in, a grin spreading across my face. Never have I been so happy to see velvet ropes or the blinking light of the security system.

"Hannah?" my dad calls from somewhere in the house.

"I'm here. Coming!" I call back.

I'm home.

I'M HOME!

NEWPORT GAZETTE DAILY NEWS
Century-Old Portrait Recovered, Mysteries Remain

By Harold Mathews, City Desk

An unsolved art heist dating back to 1905 still puzzles investigators, but the missing portrait at the center of the theft has been safely returned to its rightful hanging spot at The Elms, onetime home of Gilded Age socialites Edward Julius and Herminie Berwind, now operated as a museum by the Newport Antiquities Society.

In fact, it appears that the long-lost portrait of the Berwinds' niece, suffragist Margaret Dunlap, painted by famed Impressionist artist Mary Cassatt, never left the home.

The artwork was recovered on Monday from its apparent century-long hiding space, a sealed room discovered off a tunnel that had been installed to facilitate delivery of coal into the house in The Elms' early days of operation.

"We're thrilled to have such an important piece back where it belongs, and we're excited to delve further into the mystery of how it came to be hidden right under our noses for all this time," says Antiquities Society president Barnaby Drumworth.

The discovery was made by Hannah Jordan, the twelve-year-old daughter of the property's caretaker. Earlier this week Jordan, who resides in an apartment on the museum's third story that once contained the home's servant quarters, discovered a piece of paper under a floorboard in her bedroom closet.

"I was packing for a trip to California we were supposed to take—before all this happened—and the handle of my duffel bag was caught on this piece of floor. So I got a flashlight, and I was on my hands and knees trying to push the board back down, when something underneath it caught my eye," Jordan told reporters at a press conference yesterday. "I got it out, and it was this note that talked about a secret door in the tunnel and a key to the door hidden in a chair in the drawing room. Basically, it was like a treasure map, and I was so, so psyched!"

Although the chair Jordan references had been sold at auction in the 1960s, she was able to track down the new owners with the help of museum volunteer Florence Ensminger-Burn, who herself has ties to the painting as the granddaughter of Margaret Dunlap, the portrait's subject.

"It ended up being way easier than we imagined. We made some phone calls, and by the next day I was holding the key in my hand. From there it was just a matter of unlocking the room and grabbing the painting," Jordan says.

She's being lauded as a hero for helping shed light on a heist that has baffled historians and museumgoers since the night the portrait went missing, at an elaborate Venetian ball thrown by the Berwinds in honor of the portrait's unveiling.

Still a mystery is how the painting ended up in the hidden room and who placed it there.

At the time of the theft, officials charged a twelve-year-old servant, Jonah Rankin, who worked in the home's kitchen, but he evaded authorities and was never heard from again. Historians long asserted that Rankin fled with the painting, but they couldn't explain how it never surfaced in any private art collections. Many had abandoned hope of ever laying eyes on it again. It is unclear whether Rankin was the author of the note retrieved under the floorboards, particularly given the fact that he was known to have been illiterate, and no records exist of his handwriting for comparison. Early analysis indicates that the note may have been written by a female.

Margaret Dunlap, who posed for the painting as a twelve-year-old, went on to make a name for herself as a prominent suffragist, using her position in society to rally influential women to the cause and gain audiences with politicians. She is pictured above at the August 18, 1920, ratification of the Nineteenth Amendment to the US Constitution, which awarded women the right to vote.

After restoration experts clean the recovered portrait, The Elms will celebrate the return of the famed piece by hosting a fund-raiser this fall, a Venetian ball that will mimic the 1905 event where the portrait was to have been unveiled.

Jordan, who has lived in The Elms since infancy and has been tapped to help create a Life of Children in Gilded Age Newport Tour of The Elms to debut at the holidays, spoke at the press conference about the significance the painting has played in her life. "I grew up looking at the reproduction of Maggie hanging on the wall, listening to tours discuss the theft, and researching the house's history for myself. The past has always come alive for me, but especially with that portrait. I just can't believe I got to be such a big part of setting things right with history. It's really so, so cool. . . . I mean, you almost can't make this stuff up!"

*T*HE ART OF THE SWAP IS BASED ON very real people. Not just famous historical figures such as Mary Cassatt, Elizabeth Lehr, and Alva Vanderbilt Belmont (who commissioned a fabulous "Votes for Women" set to serve tea on), and the original occupants of The Elms—Mr. Edward J. Berwind; his wife, Herminie; their niece Margaret Dunlap; their butler, Ernest Birch, etc.—but also the more recent occupants, a father and a little girl who was raised on the third floor of the museum, enjoying free rein of the mansion whenever it was closed to the public. In fact, a magazine article about caretaker Harold Mathews and his daughter Tara's experience growing up at The Elms was the spark that got our imagination going on this story.

In all cases we beg forgiveness for any liberties we've taken as we've reinvented these people to suit our fictional needs!

But while many of the people are/were real, the story

is not. There is no Mary Cassatt portrait of Margaret Dunlap and, therefore, no art heist and no Jonah Rankin. (If there's a magical mirror that makes time travel possible, we have yet to discover it but plan to never stop searching!)

While we took license with some things, wherever possible we tried hard to make sure that the physical descriptions of The Elms and the ways of life depicted for its occupants (the owners, their guests, *and* those who served them) were accurate reflections of the time period. Fun fact: all the ball details, from the floor-trailing diamond to the man who believed he was an English prince to the man who ordered an egg at parties, were all borrowed from actual Gilded Age–era Newport balls and residents.

The Elms is open for public tours, and we highly suggest popping in if you ever find yourself in Newport, Rhode Island. Harold Mathews remains the caretaker, though his daughter is grown and has moved away. There is an excellent Servant Life Tour that will even offer you a glimpse of the coal tunnel that plays such a big role in this story. Though, to our knowledge, there is no secret room inside it. However, in the adjoining furnace room there is an opening three quarters of the way up a wall, and Harold claims that this has never been investigated. Sequel?

For more on The Elms and the Gilded Age, we recommend the following resources:

- To plan a visit to the Newport Mansions (including The Elms) and to view pictures of their jaw-dropping interiors, go to www.newportmansions.org. This site also offers teacher resource guides on the architecture at The Elms, as well as other guides relating to the additional museums in the area, such as Marble House, The Breakers, and Chateau-sur-Mer.

- Meet Samantha: An American Girl is a series of books (and a movie) about a privileged girl living in New York State in 1904. She and Maggie likely would have been finishing-school friends!

- *The Art of the Swap* Classroom Discussion Guide (aligned to Common Core standards) and a related activities guide themed to Women's History Month are available at

www.simonandschuster.net/books
/TheArtoftheSwap.

One of the most compelling aspects of this story for us was writing about how the role of girls changed from Maggie's time to today. And while we both, as Hannah would say, "fly our feminist flags high" and are thrilled at all the freedoms that women and girls now claim, we worked on this book during a time in our own history when women's rights have once again come to the forefront of a national conversation. So in addition to including resources so that you can study more about how the women's suffrage movement gained momentum through the work of women who would have been Maggie's contemporaries, we're including resources on how we can all continue the march toward full equality. There's so much more we can achieve for all the girls and women around our world! Go, Girl Power!

To learn more about them, read these books:

- *Alice Paul and the Fight for Women's Rights: From the Vote to the Equal Rights Amendment* by Deborah Kops
- *Failure Is Impossible! The History of American Women's Rights* by Martha E. Kendall

- *If You Lived When Women Won Their Rights* by Anne Kamma
- *Origins of the Women's Rights Movement* by LeeAnne Gelletly

To get involved now, read these books:

- *Good Night Stories for Rebel Girls: 100 Tales of Extraordinary Women* by Elena Favilli and Francesca Cavallo
- *She Persisted: 13 American Women Who Changed the World* by Chelsea Clinton
- *Strong Is the New Pretty* by Kate T. Parker

And visit these websites:

- Black Girls Rock! Inc. at www.blackgirlsrockinc.com
- Girls for Gender Equity at www.ggenyc.org
- Girls Inc. at www.girlsinc.org
- Girls on the Run at www.girlsontherun.org
- Girl Scouts of the United States of America at www.girlscouts.org
- Girls Write Now at www.girlswritenow.org
- National Organization for Women at www.now.org
- Women's Sports Foundation at www.womenssportsfoundation.org

And watch these documentaries (these films are all unrated; please check with a parent or guardian before viewing):

- *Diamonds Are a Girl's Best Friend*
- *Half the Sky: Turning Oppression into Opportunity for Women Worldwide*
- *Miss Representation*

Acknowledgments

WE LOVE THAT GIRLS RUN THE WORLD over at Simon & Schuster, from CEO Carolyn Reidy at the tippy top right on down to the fantastic "Swap-esses" who worked on this book. Big thanks to publisher Mara Anastas, cover illustrator Julie McLaughlin, art director Laura Lyn DiSiena, managing editor Chelsea Morgan, production manager Sara Berko, copy editor Bara MacNeill, and the entire sales and marketing teams (which, of course, include men—to whom we're equally grateful!).

Our biggest accolades are reserved for Amy Cloud, the best editor two girls could ask for. You saw right to the heart of our story and encouraged us to add *even more* to our Girl Power subplot, and we love you for that. And a bonus thanks to Tricia Lin for all your added help!

Harold Mathews and Tara Kaukani, we are grateful for your willingness to share a window into your lives at The Elms. Hannah and her dad really came alive for us after hearing your anecdotes about living in Newport.

Alison Cherry, yours were the first set of eyes we trusted with this story, and you didn't let us down. Your notes and insight were amazing. Thank you!

Julia, Isabelle, Nora, Samantha, Nina, Jillian, and your moms: thanks so much for making an early version of *The Art of the Swap* a selection for your mother-daughter book club. Your feedback was beyond helpful!

And to all the girls reading this: keep demanding, keep dreaming, and keep bringing your brand of caring to the world . . . and we'll all be just fine!

Kristine wants to thank:

Kathleen Rushall, the best agent ever—cheerleader, support system, and friend. Thanks for believing in all my ideas and pushing me to be better.

Jen Malone—writing this book with you has been an amazing roller coaster. I've loved our brainstorming sessions, our coffees "midway," and all the joys of a shared file in Google Docs. I can't imagine writing this with anyone but you. I'm so glad we decided to drive to New Jersey together in June 2015. I can't wait to see Maggie and Hannah take on the world!

Pam Vaughan—for being my sports guru, and for helping to get Maggie's soccer game just right.

Katie—the first person in the whole world who believed in the idea of a story about a kid living in a mansion with her dad, the caretaker; and who is never afraid of asking a question, no matter how hard. I love you to the Lost Moon of Poosh and back.

Phil—for indulging me in my little "hobby" and for always giving me the time and space to write, even if it means the living room isn't vacuumed and dinner is takeout.

Jen wants to thank:

Holly Root, I'd never swap you for anyone else's agent (the pun trend continues uninterrupted!)—you are magic and that is all.

Kris—I think we make a better team than even Maggie and Hannah. Writing this with you has been so much fun!

J., B., and C.—thanks for accompanying me on research trips to Newport and letting me see The Elms through "kid eyes" (and for all the hugs and meals you deliver to my writing cave). I love you mostest mostest.

John, ten books in, and there are no words left at this point. But you already know them by now, don't you? SHMILY.

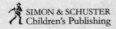

A Loving
Scoundrel

Also by Johanna Lindsey

A Man to Call My Own

JOHANNA LINDSEY

A Loving Scoundrel

A Malory Novel

DOUBLEDAY LARGE PRINT HOME LIBRARY EDITION
ATRIA BOOKS
NEW YORK LONDON TORONTO SYDNEY

ATRIA BOOKS

1230 Avenue of the Americas
New York, NY 10020

ISBN: 0-7394-4282-1

ATRIA BOOKS is a trademark of Simon & Schuster, Inc.

Manufactured in the United States of America

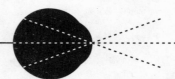

This Large Print Book carries the
Seal of Approval of N.A.V.H.

A Loving
Scoundrel

Prologue

~~~~~~~~~~

The rain didn't wash away the stench or lessen the heat. It seemed to make them both worse. Trash was piled high in the alley—boxes, rotten food, crates, broken dishes, all manner of discarded things no one wanted anymore. The woman and child had crawled into one of the larger crates on the edge of the pile of trash—to hide. The child didn't know why they needed to hide, but she'd felt the woman's fear.

It had been a constant thing, that fear, in the woman's expression, in her voice, in the trembling hand that held the child's and dragged them from alley to alley at night, never during the day when they might come across other people.

Miss Jane, the woman had said to call her. The child thought she should have known that name, but she didn't. She didn't know her own name either, though the woman called her Danny lass, so that must be it.

Miss Jane wasn't her mother. Danny had asked and been told, "No, I'm your nurse." She never thought to ask what a nurse was, though, because it sounded like something she should know. Miss Jane had been with her from the start, the start of her memories, that is, which were actually only a few days old. She'd awakened lying beside the woman in an alley much like this one, both of them covered in blood, and they had been running and hiding in more alleys ever since.

Most of the blood had come from Miss Jane. She'd had a knife stuck in her chest and had other assorted wounds from where she'd been stabbed more than once. She'd managed to pull the knife out herself, when she woke up. But she hadn't tended to those wounds. Her only concern had been the child and stopping the blood still seeping from the back of Danny's head—and getting them away from that place where they'd woken up.

"Why are we hiding?" Danny had asked at one point, when it became obvious what they were doing.

"So he doesn't find you."

"Who?"

"I don't know, child. I thought he was just a thief who went on a rampage of mayhem in order to leave no witnesses behind. But I'm not so sure now. He had too much purpose and was too intent on finding you. But I got you safely away and I'll keep you safe. He won't hurt you again, I promise you that."

"I don't remember being hurt."

"Your memories will come back, Danny lass, don't you fret none about that, though we can hope not too soon. It's a blessing, truly, that they're gone for now."

Danny wasn't upset that she could remember nothing prior to the blood. She was too young to worry about what might happen next. Her concerns were only immediate, hunger and discomfort, and that Miss Jane hadn't woken up from their last sleep.

Her nurse had seemed to think they'd

find something useful in the trash piled around them, but she'd been too weak to look yet. They'd crawled into the crate in the middle of the night, and Miss Jane had slept through the day.

It was night again and she was still sleeping. Danny had shaken her, but Miss Jane didn't stir. She was cold and stiff. Danny didn't know that meant she was dead and was what accounted for the worst of the stench.

Danny finally crawled outside the crate to take advantage of the rain while it lasted, to let it wash away some of the dried blood on her. She didn't like being dirty and so concluded she must not be used to it. It was confusing though, knowing simple things like that, yet having no memory to support it.

She supposed she could search through the trash as Miss Jane had intended to do, though she wasn't sure what to look for, what could be termed "useful." She ended up gathering a few things she found interesting, a filthy rag doll that was missing one arm, a man's hat that would keep the rain out of her eyes, a chipped plate that they could eat on—the missing arm from the doll.

Miss Jane had bargained a ring she'd been wearing yesterday for some food. It was the only time she'd ventured out during the day, wrapped up in her shawl to cover the worst of the bloodstains.

Danny wasn't sure if she had more rings to bargain with, she hadn't thought to look. But that was the last time she'd eaten. There was rotten food in the trash, but although she was hungry, she wouldn't touch it. Not because she knew better, but because she had no concept of being desperate and the smell of it was offensive to her.

She would probably eventually have died of starvation, huddled in the crate next to the body of Miss Jane, waiting patiently for Miss Jane to wake up. But she investigated the sounds of someone else searching through the trash that night and came upon a young woman. She was a girl of no more than twelve, actually, but being so much bigger than herself, Danny put her in the category of adult at first.

Thus her tone was respectful, if a bit hesitant, when she said, "Good evening, ma'am."

She'd startled the girl. "What are ye doing out in this rain, lass?"

"How did you know my name?"

"Eh?"

"That is my name. Dannilass."

A chuckle. "More'n likely only half o' that, dearie. You live near 'ere?"

"No, I do not think so."

"Where's yer mum, then?"

"I do not think I have one anymore," Danny was forced to admit.

"Yer folks? Yer people? Yer too pretty to 'ave been let loose on yer own. Who are ye with?"

"Miss Jane."

"Ah, there ye go," the girl said brightly. "And where's she gone off to?"

Danny pointed to the crate behind her, causing the girl to frown doubtfully. She took a look though, then a closer look, crawling inside the crate. Danny preferred not to go in it again herself, so didn't. It smelled much nicer out with the trash.

When the girl returned, she took a deep breath and shuddered. She then bent down to Danny's level and gave her a weak smile.

"Ye poor thing, was she all ye 'ad?"

"She was with me when I woke up. We were both hurt. She said the hurt on my head took my memories, but I would get them back someday. We have been hiding ever since, so the man who hurt us wouldn't find us."

"Well, now, that's a bleedin' shame. I s'pose I could take ye 'ome wi' me, though it's not really a 'ome, just a lot o' children like ye, wi'out folks to care for 'em. We make do as best we can though. We all earn our keep, even the youngest like you. The boys pick pockets, so do the girls for that matter, till they're old enough to earn their coins on their backs, which is wot I'll be doing soon if that bastard Dagger 'as 'is way."

The last was spit out in disgust, causing Danny to ask, "That is a bad job?"

"The very worst, dearie, sure to get ye the pox and a young death, but wot does Dagger care, long as the coins are comin' in."

"I do not want that job then. I will stay here, thank you."

"You can't—" the girl began, then amended, "Listen, I've an idea. I wish I could've done it for m'self, but I didn't know then wot I do now. It's too late for me, but not for ye—not if they think yer a lad."

"But I am a girl."

"Sure ye are, lass, but we can get ye some pants, chop off yer 'air, and—" The girl chuckled. "We won't even need to tell 'em wot ye are. They'll see ye in pants and think yer a boy right off. It will be like a game o' pretend. It will be fun, ye'll see. And it will let ye decide for yerself what job ye'll be wanting to do when ye get older, 'stead o' being told there's only one job for ye, 'cause yer a girl. So how's that sound, eh? Want to give it a try?"

"I do not think I have ever played pretend before, but I am willing to learn, ma'am."

The girl rolled her eyes. "Ye talk too fine, Danny. D'ye know no other way to talk?"

Danny started to offer yet another "I do not think so," but shook her head instead, embarrassed.

"Then don't talk at all, eh, till ye can talk like me. We don't want yer speech drawing eyes to ye. I'll be teaching ye, never ye fear."

"Will Miss Jane be able to come with us, when she is feeling better?"

The girl sighed. "She's dead. Too many wounds, it looked like, that never dried up. I covered 'er wi' that big shawl—now don't cry. Ye've got me to look after ye now."

Chapter 1

Jeremy Malory had been in some unsavory taverns before, but this one was likely the worst of the lot. Not surprising, since it was located on the edge of what was quite possibly the worst of London's slums, a neighborhood given over to thieves and cutthroats, prostitutes and wild packs of urchin orphans who were no doubt being groomed into London's next generation of criminals.

He didn't actually dare to enter the heart of that area. To do so would probably be the last his family would ever see of him. But this tavern, on the very edge of that den of thieves, was there for the unsuspecting to stumble upon, have a few drinks, and get their pockets picked, or if they were stupid enough to let a room there for the night, to get completely robbed, clothes and all.

Jeremy had paid for a room. Not only that, he'd spread his coins around freely, buying a round of drinks for the few customers in the tavern and giving a good performance of being quite foxed. He had deliberately set the stage for a robbery—his own. But then that's why he and his friend Percy were there—to catch a thief.

Amazingly, Percy Alden was keeping his mouth shut for once. He was a chatterbox by nature, and quite scatterbrained on top of that. Percy's keeping mostly quiet on this unusual outing attested to his nervousness. Understandable. Whereas Jeremy might feel right at home in this element, having been born and raised in a tavern before his father stumbled across him when he was sixteen, Percy was a member of the ton.

Jeremy had more or less inherited Percy when Percy's two best friends, Nicholas Eden and Jeremy's own cousin Derek Malory, had gone the domesticated route and got leg-shackled. And since Derek had taken Jeremy under his wing when Jeremy and his father, James, had returned to

London after James's long estrangement from his family ended, it was quite natural that Percy would now consider Jeremy his closest cohort for entertainments of the nondomesticated sort.

Jeremy didn't mind. He was rather fond of Percy after chumming about with him for the last eight years. If he weren't, he certainly wouldn't have volunteered to extricate Percy from his latest folly—getting royally fleeced by one of Lord Crandle's gambler friends at a house party last weekend. He'd lost three thousand pounds, his coach, and not one but two family heirlooms. He'd been so bloody foxed, he didn't even remember it, until one of the guests commiserated with him the next day and told him all about it.

Percy had been quite done in, and rightly so. Losing the money and coach were no more than he deserved for being so gullible, but the two rings were a different matter entirely. One was so old it was the family signet ring, and the other, quite valuable because of its gemstones, had been passed down in Percy's family for five generations now. Percy would *never* have thought to use them as betting tender. He had to have been coerced, goaded, or otherwise duped into putting them in the pot.

All of it now belonged to Lord John Heddings, and Percy had been beside himself when Heddings refused to sell the rings back to him. Money the lord didn't need. The coach he didn't need. The rings he must have considered trophies, a testament to his gambling skill. More likely a testament to his cheating skill, but Jeremy could hardly prove it when he hadn't been there to witness it.

Had Heddings been a decent sort, he would have sent Percy off to bed, instead of plying him further with drink and accepting the rings into the pot. Had he been a decent sort, he would have let Percy redeem them for their value. Percy had even been willing to pay more than they were worth. He wasn't poor, after all, as he had already come into his inheritance when his father died.

But Heddings wasn't interested in doing what was decent. Instead he'd gotten annoyed at Percy's insistence and downright nasty in the end, threatening Percy with bodily harm if he didn't stop bothering him. Which is what had annoyed Jeremy enough to suggest this alternative. Percy was quite convinced, after all, that his mother was going to disown him over this. He'd been avoiding her ever since, so she wouldn't notice the rings were missing from his fingers.

Since they'd retired to the tavern's upstairs room several hours ago, there had been three attempts to rob them. Bungled attempts each, and after the last, Percy was beginning to despair of finding a thief to carry out their mission. Jeremy was more confident. Three attempts in two hours meant there would be many more before the night was over.

The door opened again. There was no light in the room. There was no light out in the corridor either. If this new thief was any good, he wouldn't need light, he would have waited long enough for his eyes to adjust to the dark. Footsteps, a bit too loud. A match flicked.

Jeremy sighed and, in one fluid movement, left the chair near the door where he was keeping vigil. He was quieter about it than the thief had been upon entering the room and was suddenly there blocking his path, a mountain of a man, well, in comparison to the short thief, but big enough to scare the daylights out of the urchin, who immediately bolted back the way he'd come.

Jeremy slammed the door shut behind the fellow. He still wasn't disheartened. The night was young. The thieves hadn't gotten desperate yet. And if it came down to it, he'd just keep one of them until they agreed to bring him their best.

Percy, however, was fast giving up hope. He was sitting up on the bed now, his back resting against the wall—he'd been appalled at the thought of getting under *those* sheets. But Jeremy had insisted he lie on the bed, to at least give the impression of being asleep. He'd done so on top of the covers, thank you very much.

"There must be an easier way to go about hiring a thief," Percy complained. "Don't they have an agency for this sort of thing?"

Jeremy managed not to laugh. "Patience, old boy. I warned you this would likely take all night."

"Should have brought this to your father's attention," Percy mumbled.

"What was that?"

"Nothing, dear boy, nothing a'tall."

Jeremy shook his head, but said nothing

more. Percy couldn't really be faulted for wondering if Jeremy was capable of handling this mess on his own. Jeremy *was* nine years his junior, after all, and Percy, scatterbrain that he was and quite incapable of keeping a secret, had never been apprised of Jeremy's real upbringing.

Living and working in a tavern for the first sixteen years of his life had left Jeremy with a few unexpected talents. A tolerance for hard spirits that had reached the point that he could drink his friends so far under the table that they'd be passed out cold while he'd still be mostly sober. A way of fighting that could be quite underhanded if called for. And a keen ability to recognize a real threat as opposed to a mere nuisance.

His unorthodox education hadn't ended there, though, when his father discovered his existence and took him in. No, at that particular time, James Malory was still estranged from his large family and living the carefree life of a pirate in the Caribbean, or, *gentleman* pirate, as he preferred to be called. And James's motley crew had taken Jeremy in hand and taught him still more things a boy his age should never have learned.

But Percy knew none of this. All he'd ever been allowed to see was what was on the surface, the charming scamp, not so scampish anymore at twenty-five, but still charming, and so handsome that Jeremy couldn't walk into a room without every woman in it falling a little bit in love with him. Aside from the women in his family, of course. They merely adored him.

Jeremy had taken after his uncle Anthony in his looks; in fact, anyone who met him for the first time would swear he was Tony's son, rather than James's. Like his uncle he was tall with wide shoulders, a narrow waist, lean hips, and long legs. They both had a wide mouth and a strong, arrogant jaw, as well as an aquiline, proud nose, darkly tanned skin, and thick ebony hair.

But the eyes were the most telling, a mark of only a few Malorys, purest blue, heavy-lidded, with the barest suggestion of an exotic slant, framed by black lashes and slashing brows. Gypsy eyes, it used to be rumored, inherited from Jeremy's great-grandmother Anastasia Stephanoff, whom the family had just last year discovered had really been half Gypsy. She'd so captivated Christopher Malory, the 1st Marquis of

Haverston, that he'd married her the second day of their acquaintance. But that was a tale only the family would ever know about.

It was quite understandable why Percy had wanted to get Jeremy's father involved instead. Hadn't his best friend, Derek, gone straight to James when he'd had problems of the unsavory sort? Percy might not know of James's pirating days, but who didn't know that James Malory had been one of London's most notorious rakes prior to his taking to the seas, that it was the rare fellow indeed who dared stand up to James, then or now, whether in the ring or on the dueling field?

Percy had settled back down on the bed for his "impression" of sleeping. After a few more mumbles, some tossing and turning, he was then mostly quiet in anticipation of their next intrusion.

Jeremy wondered if he should mention that taking this particular matter to his father wouldn't get it settled anytime soon, that James had hied off to Haverston to visit his brother Jason the very day after Jeremy had been presented with his new town house. He was quite certain his father had gone to the country for a week or two out of

fear that Jeremy would drag him about furniture shopping.

Jeremy almost missed the shadow moving stealthily across the room toward the
bed. He hadn't heard the door open this
time, hadn't heard it close either, hadn't
heard a bloody thing for that matter. If the
occupants of the room really had been
asleep, as was to be expected, they certainly wouldn't have been awakened by this
intruder.

Jeremy smiled to himself just before he lit
a match of his own and moved it over the
candle on the table he'd placed next to his
chair. The thief's eyes had been drawn to
him instantly. Jeremy hadn't moved otherwise, was sitting there quite relaxed. The
thief wouldn't know how quickly he could
move to prevent his escape if he had to. But
the thief wasn't moving either yet, as he was
apparently frozen in his surprise at being
caught.

"Oh, I say." Percy raised his head. "Did
we finally get lucky?"

"I'd say so," Jeremy replied. "Didn't hear
him a'tall. He's our man, or boy as the case
may be."

The thief was starting to shake off his surprise and probably didn't like what he was hearing, to go by the narrowed, suspicious look Jeremy was now getting. Jeremy ignored it. He looked for a weapon first, but didn't see the thief carrying one. Of course, Jeremy had his own hidden in his coat pockets, a pistol in each, so just because he didn't see one didn't mean the lad didn't have one.

Much taller than the previous miscreants who'd tried their hand at robbing them, and lanky besides, this thief was probably no more than fifteen or sixteen, to go by those smooth cheeks. Ash blond hair so light it was more white than blond, naturally curly, worn short. A misshapen black hat several centuries out of fashion. He wore a gentleman's coat of dark green velvet, stolen no doubt, and quite grubby-looking now, as if it got slept in a lot. A discolored white shirt was under it with a few ruffles at the neck, black trousers of the long variety, and no shoes. Smart fellow, no wonder he hadn't made a single sound yet.

Very flamboyant looking for a thief, but probably because he was such a handsome young lad. And he was definitely recovered from his surprise. Jeremy knew to the second when he would bolt and was there at the door before him, leaning back against it, crossing his arms across his chest.

He offered a lazy smile. "You don't want to leave yet, dear boy. You haven't heard our proposal."

The thief was gaping again. It could have been Jeremy's smile, but was more likely his speed in getting to the door first. But Percy noticed it this time and complained, "Damn me, he's staring at you the way the wenches do. It's a man we're in need of, not a child."

"Age is irrelevant, old man," Jeremy replied. "It's skill we're in need of, so the package it comes in doesn't matter all that much."

The lad, blushing now, was insulted, apparently, and with a glower toward Percy spoke for the first time. "Ain't never seen a nabob so pretty is all."

The word *pretty* started Percy laughing. Jeremy was no longer amused. The last man who'd called him pretty had lost a few teeth because of it.

"Look who's talking, when you've got the face of a girl," Jeremy said.

"He does, don't he?" Percy agreed. "You should grow some hair on those cheeks, at least until your voice drops an octave or two."

Yet another blush from the boy and a distinct grumble: "It won't grow—yet. I'm only fifteen—I think. Just tall for m'age, I am."

Jeremy might have felt sorry for the lad because of that "I think," which implied he wasn't sure what year he'd been born, which was usually the case with orphans. But he'd noted two things simultaneously. The boy's voice had started out high-pitched, then lowered before he'd finished his speech, as if he were going through that awkward time in a boy's life when his voice started changing to the deeper tones of manhood. And yet, Jeremy didn't think it was a natural slip, it had sounded much too contrived.

But the second thing he noticed upon closer examination was the lad wasn't just handsome, he was downright beautiful. Now, the same thing might have been said about Jeremy at that age, except Jeremy's handsomeness was decidedly male, while this lad's handsomeness was decidedly female. The soft cheeks, the lush lips, the pert little nose—yet there was much more. The chin was too weak, the neck too narrow, even the stance was a dead giveaway, at least to a man who knew women as well as Jeremy did.

Still, Jeremy might not have drawn the conclusion he did, at least not quite so soon, if his own stepmother hadn't used the same sort of disguise when she'd first met his father. She'd been desperate to get back to America, and signing on as James's cabin boy had seemed to be her only option. Of course, James had known from the start that she wasn't a lad, and to hear him tell it, he'd had a great deal of fun pretending to believe she was a boy.

Jeremy could be wrong in this case. There was that slim possibility. And yet he was rarely wrong where women were concerned.

But there was no need to expose her. Whatever reason she had for hiding her gender was her business. He might be curious, but he'd learned long ago that patience reaped the best rewards. And besides, they only needed one thing from her—her talent.

"What do they call you, youngun?" Jeremy asked.

"None o' yer bleedin' business."

"I don't think he's figured out yet that

we're going to do him a good turn," Percy remarked.

"Ye set a trap—"

"No, no, think of it as an opportunity for employment," Percy corrected.

"A *trap*," their thief insisted. "And I don't need wotever it is yer offering."

Jeremy raised a black brow. "You aren't even a little curious?"

"No," said the thief most stubbornly.

"Too bad. The nice thing about traps is— you don't get out of them unless you get let out. Do we look like we're letting you out of this one?"

"Ye look like ye've bleedin' well lost yer minds. Ye don't think I'm alone, d'ye? They'll be coming for me if I don't return when I'm expected to."

"They?"

The question just got Jeremy another glower. He shrugged, unperturbed. He wouldn't doubt she ran with a pack of thieves, the very bunch that had systematically been sending their numbers in, one at a time, to rob the unsuspecting gentry who had blundered into their territory. But he doubted they'd come looking for her. They'd be more interested in obtaining the expected fat purse first, before they thought of any rescuing. If anything, they'd assume this attempt had failed, that she'd been apprehended, knocked out, or killed, and would be sending in the next thief soon.

Which meant they should wrap this up and be on their way, now that they had their quarry in hand, so Jeremy said congenially, "Sit down, youngun, and I'll explain what you've volunteered for."

"I didn't vol—"

"But you did. When you came through that door, you most surely did volunteer."

"Wrong room," their thief tried to assert. "Ye've never walked into the wrong room by mistake?"

"Assuredly, though usually with my shoes on," Jeremy said dryly.

She blushed again and swore a blue streak.

Jeremy yawned. Much as he'd enjoyed the cat-and-mouse bantering, he didn't want this taking *all* night. And they still had a good distance to travel to reach Heddings's house in the country.

He injected a note of sternness in his tone when he ordered, "Sit down, or I will physically put you in that chair—"

Jeremy didn't have to finish. She ran to the chair, practically dove into it. She definitely didn't want to risk his touching her. He forced back another smile as he moved away from the door to stand in front of her.

Percy, amazingly, injected a bit of logic into the proceedings: "I say, we could explain this on the way, couldn't we? We've got our man. Is there any reason to remain in these god-awful accommodations a moment longer?"

"Quite right. Find me something for binding."

"Eh?"

"To tie him up with. Or haven't you noticed that our thief isn't being the least bit cooperative—yet?"

At which point their thief desperately bolted for the door.

Chapter 2

Jeremy had known it was coming, one more effort to escape them before it was too late. He'd seen it in her eyes just before she flew past him. He was at the door before she could get it open, though, and rather than just lean his weight against it to keep her inside, he decided to find out conclusively whether he was right about her sex and put his arms around her instead. He'd been right. Those were definitely female breasts under his forearms, packed down flatly, but unmistakable to his touch.

She didn't just stand still there and let him discover that. She turned around, and good God, that was even better, since he wasn't letting go of her yet. The very last thing he'd expected to find that night was a pretty wench wiggling about in his arms. Now that he was positive she was a wench, he was quite enjoying himself.

"I suppose I should check you for weapons," Jeremy said, his voice lowered to a husky note. "Yes, indeed, I really should."

"I ain't got—" she started to claim, but ended on a gasp as his hands slid over her derriere and stayed there.

Rather than pat her pockets as his suggestion had implied, he gave each rounded check a gentle squeeze. Supple, soft she was, and suddenly he felt an urge to do more than just feel her with his hands; he wanted to press her loins firmly to his, pull down those ridiculous trousers she was wearing, run his fingers over her bare skin, and enter her wet warmth. He couldn't have been in a better position to do so, his hands cupping her luscious bottom. But he was already rising to the occasion, as it were, and didn't want her to know the effect she was having on him.

"Will these do?" Percy asked, reminding Jeremy that he wasn't alone with the girl.

With a sigh, Jeremy got back to the matter at hand and toted their thief back to the chair and shoved her into it. He leaned over her, his hands on the arms of the chair, and whispered, "Stay there, unless you like having my hands all over you."

He almost laughed, she went so motionless. But the glare she gave him promised retribution. Not that he thought she was capable of anything of the sort, but she probably did.

He glanced back to see that Percy had ripped up the bedsheet, having found a good use for it after all, and was dangling a number of strips from his hand.

"Those will do nicely, bring them here," Jeremy said.

He should have had Percy take over from there, but he didn't. And he tried not to touch the girl more than he had to, really he did, but he was a man who loved women and he just couldn't help himself. He held both her hands in one of his while he wound the strip of cloth about her wrists. Her hands were warm, moist with fear. She had no way of knowing that they meant her no harm, so her fear was natural. He could have eased her mind, but Percy was right, they needed to vacate the place before the next thief showed up, so the explanations could wait.

The gag was next, and he didn't mind at all leaning close to her to get it tied behind her neck. He should probably have tied her hands behind her back instead, but he didn't have the heart to make her any more uncomfortable than he had to. The fisted punch he got to his gut when he leaned over her wasn't expected, but didn't annoy him all that much since there wasn't much strength behind the punch from her current position.

Her legs he didn't trust a'tall, though. Squatting down to get the cloth around her ankles would have put him in a prime position to get knocked on his arse, so he sat on the arm of the chair instead and brought both her legs over his lap. She shrieked under the gag once, but then was quiet and still again. She had long pants and socks on, so there was no bare skin he could touch. But still, just having her legs across his lap affected him profoundly, much more than it should have. He glanced down at her when he was done, and there was such heat in his eyes, she would have had no doubt that he saw through her disguise—if she'd been looking at him to catch it. She wasn't. She was trying to work her wrists loose from the binding and had nearly succeeded.

He put his hand over hers again and said, "Don't, or instead of my friend toting you out of here, I'll do it."

"Eh? Why me?" Percy complained. "You're the stronger by far. Don't mind admitting it. No indeed, specially when it's so bloody obvious."

Much as Jeremy would love to carry the wench, he had to be sensible for the moment. "Because one of us has to make sure there are no objections to our leaving with this chap in tow. And while you might be up to the task, old man, I doubt you'd enjoy it quite as much as I will."

"Objections?" Percy said uneasily.

"We aren't exactly walking out arm in arm, the three of us."

Understanding now, Percy said abruptly, "Quite right. Don't know what I was thinking. You're better at bashing heads by far."

Jeremy managed not to laugh, since Percy had probably never bashed a head in his life.

They didn't run into much opposition.

Only the bartender was still around down-stairs, a huge, ugly fellow who would likely give most men pause if he even glanced their way.

" 'Ere, now, ye ain't leaving 'ere wi' that baggage," he growled.

"The 'baggage' tried to rob us," Jeremy cut in, attempting for the moment to be peaceable about the matter.

"So? Then kill 'im or leave 'im, but ye ain't taking 'im to the watchmen. Ain't 'aving no law come sticking their noses round 'ere."

Jeremy gave it one last try. "We have no intention of visiting the authorities over this matter, my good fellow. And this *baggage* will be returned by morning, none the worse for wear."

The big man began lumbering his way around the bar with the intention of blocking their exit. "We've rules round 'ere, gov'nor. Wot's 'ere stays 'ere, if ye catch my mean-ing."

"Oh, I'm very good at catching. And we've rules where I come from as well. Sometimes, they don't need explaining—if you catch *my* meaning."

Jeremy didn't think any head bashing would work on a head that big, so he simply lifted one of his pistols and shoved it in the chap's face. That worked very well. The man spread his arms wide and started backing off.

"Smart fellow," Jeremy continued. "Now you can have your thief back—"

" 'E ain't mine," the burly bartender thought it prudent to mention.

"Whatever," Jeremy replied on his way out the door. "He'll be returned just as soon as we've concluded our business with him."

There was no other attempt to stop them from leaving the area. And the only other person they came across at that late hour of the night was an old drunken woman who still had enough of her wits to cross to the other side of the street to get out of their way when she saw them.

But Percy was definitely out of breath after traversing four blocks with the bound thief over his shoulder. They hadn't left the coach near the tavern for obvious reasons, mainly being that it probably wouldn't have been there when they were ready to leave. Four blocks away in a safer, well-lit area had seemed a reasonable spot, but was a bit far to tote their thief. So it wasn't surprising that Percy simply dumped his package on the floor of the coach and none too gently, too worn-out to do more'n that.

Climbing in behind Percy, Jeremy saw there was no help for it, he was going to have to touch the wench again after all, to get her up on the seat. He'd been trying to avoid temptation by letting Percy carry her. It wasn't as if he couldn't have carried her *and* seen to any interference along the way. But he'd given the chore to Percy because he'd already discovered what touching her did to him. Looking was one thing. It had no effect on a man who overindulged in women. Touching, however, was much too intimate, and Jeremy reacted to intimacy on a purely prurient level.

And the simple fact was, he didn't want to want this wench. She was beautiful, yes, but she was a thief, probably raised in the gutter or worse. Her personal habits were more than likely so far below his standards that they weren't worth contemplating.

There was no help for it. Percy, poor fellow, was no doubt as exhausted as he presently looked. But before Jeremy actually put his hands on the girl, he realized that enough time had passed while contemplating his dilemma that the coach was on its way, the outskirts of the city were in sight, and it would be a simple matter to keep their prize from escaping now. So he could simply untie her and she could make herself comfortable on the seat.

He did that now, first her feet—damned dainty they were. Then her hands. He didn't touch the gag. She was able to remove it now herself and she did that most quickly. Quick, too, was the punch she threw at him as she came up off the floor.

It was the one thing he hadn't expected, though he should have, since she'd tried to punch him earlier. Ranting and raving could be expected, yes, more vulgar swearing, certainly, but for her to do what a man might do . . .

She missed, of course. Jeremy was no slouch in his reactions. And although he did get his jaw out of the way, which she'd aimed for, her fist still slid along his cheek and clipped his ear, which was now stinging.

But before he dealt with that as it deserved, Percy said in an excessively dry tone, "If you're going to beat him to a pulp, dear boy, do it quietly, please. I'm going to nap until we get there."

And that had their thief turning toward the door. Jeremy reached out and caught the back of her collar and yanked her onto his lap instead. "Try that again and you can spend the next several hours right here," he said, wrapping his arms around her so tightly she couldn't move.

She couldn't get loose, but that didn't mean she was going to stop trying. Wiggling about in his lap, however, was probably the worst thing she could have done. The position was much too sensual, producing lascivious thoughts of what he'd like to do—no, *would* do if they were alone. Stripping her clothes off slowly, finding out how she was concealing her breasts, nibbling on her shoulder as he drove into her. *Bloody hell.* If she continued to bounce on him like that, he might just kick Percy out of the coach for a while.

She must have realized her efforts were useless about the same time he realized he couldn't stand the wiggling and bouncing of her bottom on his thighs and loins anymore without becoming quite obvious in what she was stirring up. She groaned, yet to him it sounded more passionate than frustrated and had him dropping her as if he'd just been burned. Good God, she shouldn't be affecting him this strongly. He had to get it under control.

She'd fallen to the floor again, but immediately scrambled up on the seat opposite them, jerking down her coat lapels, dusting off her grubby pants, and avoiding eye contact as best she could, all the while watching for the counterattack that Percy's remark had suggested might be coming.

Jeremy waited a full five minutes, about the time it took for him to get his desire in check and hope his voice wouldn't reflect it. Finally he stretched out his legs, crossed them, leaned back and crossed his arms as well, and said, "Relax, youngun. We'd as soon not hurt you. You're going to do us a favor, and in the process make yourself rich. What could be more agreeable than that, eh?"

"For ye to take me back."

"That isn't an option. We went to a lot of trouble to obtain you."

"Ye should've obtained me bleedin' consent first—*m' lord.*"

The title was added as an afterthought, and with a large heaping of contempt.

She was glowering at him again, now that

she was relatively sure he wasn't going to throttle her. He'd tried not to examine her eyes too closely, hoping the dim light of the candle in the tavern room had misled him. But the brighter coach lamp and close proximity were his undoing. Her eyes were simply incredible and added tenfold to her beauty. Violet they were, dark, rich violet, and such a startling contrast to her white-gold mop of curls. Her eyelashes were long, but not overly dark. The brows, too, weren't very dark, merely a few shades more golden.

He tried, he really did, to find some masculinity in the face across from him, but it just wasn't there. How anyone could mistake her for a boy boggled his mind. And yet Percy had no trouble seeing a lad, albeit a "pretty" one. Her height, he supposed, was the deciding factor. It was rare, after all, to find a female who was bloody well as tall as his father was. Anyone that tall would naturally be assumed to be male.

He'd also tried, truly, not to react to her as he would any other beautiful woman he came across. But those eyes . . . He gave up the fight. He would have her in his bed, and before the night was done. It would happen. He had no doubt whatsoever.

Having given in to his prurient nature, the change in Jeremy was immediate. Some might call it charm, but it was in fact pure sensuality, and to look at him when his thoughts were carnal was to know he promised pleasures untold.

The wench reacted immediately to the way he was now looking at her, casting her eyes away from him, but not before she blushed. Jeremy smiled. He'd known she wouldn't be an easy conquest, yet that blush spoke volumes. She was no more immune to him than other women were. But he wasn't going to give away her little secret. He'd let her play her manly role for now—at least until he got her alone.

For the moment, he addressed her remark, wondering aloud, "Should you have obtained our consent before you robbed us?" That got him another blush, so he merely concluded, "No, I didn't think that was your habit. So let me just explain what's needed and why, before you get back to refusing out of hand. My friend here got himself robbed, you see, but in a legal way."

"If ye insist on explaining," she injected, "ye could at least make sense."

A mere grumble. Encouraging. Apparently she was going to listen to him.

"The 'legal' way I mention was gambling."

A snort. "That ain't being robbed, that's being stupid. A big difference there, mate."

Jeremy grinned, and the wench became obviously flustered by it, which only made his grin turn knowing. He then explained that John Heddings was the culprit who chose not to play fair and that she was going to exact retribution for them.

"We're taking you to Heddings's house in the country," Jeremy continued. "It's rather big, will be filled with servants, and thus, they'll be confident that no thief in his right mind would ever consider robbing them, and rightly so. Which is to your benefit, lad."

" 'Ow's that?"

"The doors might be locked, but the windows will pro'bly be open this time of the year. The fact that they don't expect to be robbed means they won't be on their guard for it. And it's past midnight, so the servants should be asleep and out of the way until morning. So you should have no difficulty entering the house."

"And then wot?"

"You will need to enter the master bedroom undetected. Chances are Heddings will be in it when you do, but you're quite used to that I'm sure. Like the servants, he should be fast asleep this time of night. Then proceed to do what you do best. Rob the man."

"Wot makes ye think 'e won't 'ave his valuables locked away in a safe?"

"Because he doesn't live in London. The gentry feel much more secure on their country estates."

"Wot do these 'eirlooms look like then, that I'm s'pose to be nabbing?"

"Two rings, both very old."

"I'm still needing a description, gent, if I'm to pick them out o' the pot."

Jeremy shook his head at her. "It doesn't matter, since you can't just take Percy's two rings. That would leave Heddings knowing right where to point the finger. Your job, dear boy, is no different than you're accustomed to, to take everything of value you find. Your gain is that you may keep all the rest for yourself, thousands of pounds' worth of jewelry, I'm sure."

"Thousands!" she said, gaping at him.

He nodded with a chuckle. "Now aren't you glad we insisted you come along?"

Those lovely violet eyes narrowed abruptly on him. "Yer a bleedin' idiot if ye think any trinkets, no matter how costly, makes up for the trouble I'll be in for not getting permission to do this first."

Jeremy frowned, but not over the name-calling. "You're on that tight a leash?"

"I've rules to abide by, aye, and ye've made me break most o' them."

His sigh was long and drawn out. "You *could* have mentioned this sooner."

"I figured the barkeep would've stopped ye. Didn't take 'im for no coward, big as 'e is."

"No one likes to get a bullet in their face, lad," Jeremy said in the barkeep's defense. "But he can attest that you weren't given a choice in the matter. So what, really, is the problem?"

"It's none o' yer concern—"

"Beg to differ, you've just made it my concern."

"Like 'ell. Figure it out real quick, mate,

that ye've interfered in m'life too much as is. Drop it, or we're done talking about *any*-thing."

A long moment passed before Jeremy nodded—for now. But causing their thief extended grief had not been part of tonight's agenda. He'd have to accompany the girl home now, when they were done, to get whatever trouble he'd caused her set right.

There shouldn't have been any trouble, though, and that's where this situation was getting most odd. They were offering a thief a golden opportunity. Any *normal* cutpurse would have jumped on it and been grateful to have such a golden egg dropped in his lap. But no, they had to get the one exception, a thief from a gang that was apparently so bogged down in rules that they couldn't even do odd jobs without getting permission first. Which defied reason. What bloody difference could it make when, where, or what, as long as the fat purse got brought home?

The coach stopped. Percy said with a sigh, "Finally." Then: "Good luck, youngun. Not that you'll need it. We've every confidence in you, 'deed we do. And can't tell you how much this is appreciated. It's deuced hard hiding from your own mother, specially when you live with her."

Jeremy opened the coach door and ushered the girl out before Percy's dissertation turned into his usual long-winded sort. They were parked in the woods near Heddings's estate. He took her arm and led her through the trees until the house was in sight.

"I'd wish you luck as well, but you aren't likely to need it," he said in parting. "I've seen how capable you are at what you do."

"Wot makes ye think I won't be bolting for home soon as I'm out o' yer sight?"

Jeremy smiled, though she probably couldn't see it. "Because you have absolutely no idea where you are. Because it's the middle of the night. Because we can get you back to London much, much sooner than if you try to find it yourself. Because you'd rather return home with your pockets full of dazzling gems than empty. Because—"

"That were enough becauses, mate," she interrupted in a low grumble.

"Quite right. But one last assurance. If for some inexplicable reason you are apprehended, don't panic. I'm not sending you to the wolves, dear boy. I *will* see to your release no matter what it takes. You may depend upon it."

Chapter 3

I'm not sending you to the wolves. Who did he think he was kidding? He was the bleed-ing wolf. But she could breathe normally again, now that he was no longer near her and looking at her with those penetrating blue eyes.

She'd nearly given herself away, with all those blushes, and that had frightened her, too, that she'd been unable to control what that gent made her feel. She usually dealt well with men, she was "one" of them, after all. But then she'd never come so close to one of Malory's caliber. Just looking at him flustered her, she found him so attractive!

Danny had never been so distraught in

her entire life, with possibly one exception. But she'd been too young to realize the danger she had been in then, hadn't known that if she'd stayed where she was she'd surely die, only knew that she was completely alone in the world, with no one to turn to for help.

She wasn't alone anymore, but she might as well be. She'd been living on a tightrope of anxiety for several years now because she was getting too old to hide that she'd never fill out with manly proportions like the rest of the boys eventually did. Sooner or later, someone was going to realize and reveal that she'd deceived everyone from the very beginning.

It had been easy, keeping that secret over the years, much easier than she could have hoped for, and all because Lucy had been right. Bringing her home to the pack in ragged knee breeches, a shirt too big, a coat too small, that old hat she'd found to keep the rain out of her eyes, and with her long hair chopped off to the neck had left a lasting impression that had never altered.

She quickly became "one of the boys." She'd learned to steal with them, learned to fight with them, learned everything they did—well, except when they went looking for female companionship of the type Danny didn't want to know about.

There were fourteen of them at present, and they lived in a dilapidated house that Dagger paid the rent on. There had been many houses like it over the years, even a few abandoned tenement buildings when there wasn't enough money to pay for rent.

Dagger never stayed in one place long. The current house had four rooms: a kitchen, two bedrooms, and a large living area. Dagger had one of the bedrooms for himself. The girls got the other bedroom to sleep in, or work in, if they were old enough to start whoring. Everyone else slept in the large living area, Danny included.

There was a small backyard. Though no grass grew in it, it was still nice for the younger children to play in. Danny had enjoyed backyards herself, once she got over her aversion to being dirty. Bathing wasn't an option for her, at least not in the communal tubs set up once a week in the kitchen. She snuck off to the river instead, when she could manage to. And the rain became her friend.

Lucy was her only confidante. Lucy didn't

get the pox as she'd feared, but she did end up selling her body at Dagger's insistence. Danny understood his logic, even if she didn't like it. Being a comely woman, Lucy would have gained too much notice from the victims she intended to rob. A pick-pocket had to be almost invisible to his target. Lucy couldn't be that, and how else was she to earn her keep then?

Dagger had been the oldest among them back then and he still was, so he was their leader by default. There'd only been a few rules to start with, nothing anyone could really mind. But Dagger seemed to think if he didn't add more rules every so often, then he wasn't doing his job.

Danny never argued with him. She did what she was told to do without complaint. His was the only keen eye she really worried about because, aside from Lucy, he was the only one left who had been there the day she'd arrived with Lucy, and eventually it was going to occur to him to count up the years—and wonder why a twenty-year-old man still had the face of a twelve-year-old boy.

He was thirty himself now or thereabouts, thirty and still running a pack of orphans. He could have moved on. Most of them did when they reached their high teens, wanting more than the pack offered, wanting to be able to keep what they stole, rather than turning it all over to Dagger to buy the food and pay the rent and bring home the occasional trinket to make one of them smile. Dagger could have moved on himself to more lucrative crimes, but he hadn't.

He meant well, even if he was abrasive. Danny had concluded years ago that he had a kind heart hidden somewhere in his scrawny chest. As leader, he probably thought he had to be hard and unbending. But she guessed he didn't see himself just as their leader, but also as their father. And that's why he hadn't moved on with the rest. More orphans joined them, more left. Their numbers never really got higher than twenty or so, but they never got lower then ten either. There was always someone who needed looking out for.

The number one rule of the pack was never, ever, rob the gentry in their own homes. That was the surest, quickest way to get them up in arms and to have the authorities come sweeping through the slums in search of the culprits. Finding a house full of orphans who weren't official orphans would be a dead giveaway. And the horror stories that Dagger told about real orphanages were enough to enforce that rule. He knew firsthand, since he'd escaped from one years ago. Danny was breaking that rule tonight.

Not that the gentry were off-limits, no indeed. But they were only to be robbed when they were found out and about, on the streets, in taverns, at market or otherwise shopping, where they might not even notice a few coins missing, and if they did, might think they'd merely dropped them by accident or spent them without remembering.

The second rule that served them well was that they were to stick to their own areas and never go off to steal in places they weren't familiar with. Dagger assigned each an area and changed it weekly, so the normal residents in those neighborhoods wouldn't start to recognize any of them. Danny was breaking that rule, too.

Another rule pertained only to her and a few others, since their age and height marked them as no longer children. The logic was, the taller they were, the harder time they'd have reaching their hand into a pocket. So when they reached a certain height, they graduated into the "specific jobs only" class, which meant they did no stealing on their own, only jobs that Dagger sent them to do. Danny was definitely breaking that rule.

Dagger had arrangements for these jobs with three taverns and one inn. And because Danny was very recognizable due to the color of her hair and eyes, Dagger no longer let her do any job other than "sleepers." She'd never failed before, but then, she'd never walked into a deliberate trap before either.

The trouble she was in pertained only to her though. If one of the other boys had been captured instead, she had no doubt Dagger would have called it an exception and been glad of the unexpected riches that would tide them over for quite a while. There would be pats on the back and a celebration. But because *she* was the one captured and forced to break the rules, Dagger's attitude was going to be just the opposite—because he'd been looking for a reason to give her the boot.

For over two years now, nearly three, she'd been on the outs with Dagger.

Whereas they used to get along just fine, used to joke and laugh a lot, now it seemed that he despised her. He singled her out for reprimands every chance he got. He criticized her constantly, deserved or not. He couldn't be more obvious that he wanted her gone, but she'd given him no reason to kick her out. Until now.

She didn't even know why he'd turned against her, but it had started about the time she'd surpassed him in height. It could just be that as leader, he figured he should be the tallest. But he wasn't a tall man to begin with, only about five feet seven inches. And she was flamboyant in her dress, whereas Dagger was nondescript. This impressed the children. Many of them modeled themselves after her and came to her when they needed something.

She supposed Dagger might be fearful that she wanted to take his place. She didn't. She didn't even like to steal herself, so she certainly didn't want the responsibility of sending out others to do the same. She felt it was wrong, an ingrained feeling that she'd never been able to shake. But she hadn't had much choice in the matter, living among thieves. However, she'd tried to subtly reassure Dagger that his position didn't appeal to her, without actually discussing it, but it hadn't seemed to help.

She could lie to Dagger, say they'd carted her out of the tavern to take her to jail, but she'd managed to escape, that it just took her a long while to find her way back home. Dagger couldn't kick her out just because she'd walked into a trap. She had to settle for that hope.

Her distress stemmed not just from knowing what she'd have to face when she got home. It was also him, that Lord Malory. He'd disturbed her so much she couldn't think, couldn't even breathe. But not only that, he frightened her to her core because he mesmerized her.

Danny had never in her life imagined anyone could look like him. He wasn't just handsome. His looks were so far beyond handsome, she simply couldn't find a word to describe them. The closest she could come was *beautiful,* yet in a masculine way, which was a combination that was utterly amazing—and mesmerizing.

It was a wonder she'd been able to talk to him at all, he so flustered her. And she knew exactly what it was that turned her senses to mush and stole her breath when she looked at him. He appealed to her sexually, something she'd never really had to deal with before. Other men had caught her interest over the years, but none had made her wish she could actually do something about it. Playing the role of a man meant she had to ignore such things and that had been easy enough to do. Not this time. And that's what frightened her the most about Lord Malory.

She'd spent fifteen years, her entire life, actually—at least all that she could remember of it—avoiding Lucy's fate. And she had done it only for one reason: to not end up a whore. Nor had she ever changed her opinion about it. Lucy might have settled into the job, might not have complained as much after the fact as she had beforehand, but Danny still saw it as the worst sort of degradation.

For her, it would be the end of her life, and not just metaphorically, because she would rather starve to death in some alley than suffer strangers paying for the use of her body. But here was a man who could make her jump willingly into that role. Worse, he'd looked at her as if he knew her secret, as if he could see right through to her core—as if he wanted to touch her. Surely her imagination was playing tricks on her, yet she couldn't shake the feeling that he knew, especially when his look turned so sensual, it nearly melted her on the spot.

He'd be a *lover.* Lucy's term. Lucy had put all men into one category or another, depending on how they wanted to use her and for how long. The names she gave them were mostly derogatory, and some were explicit, like the *grapplers* and the *beasts. Good-bye Henrys* she liked the best since they didn't take up much of her time, in and out in under five minutes, not there long enough to say hello to, just good-bye. Lovers, she claimed, were rare, a man who actually wanted to give pleasure as well as receive it.

A definite danger, Lord Malory was. A danger to Danny's senses, her peace of mind, her secret. The sooner she saw the last of him—well, it couldn't happen soon enough.

Chapter 4

~~~

The job those young lords sent her on was so simple in comparison to her troubled thoughts that Danny did it almost without thinking about it. Just about every window in the large mansion was open. She climbed through one on the side of the house, made her way to the hall, then up the carpeted stairs.

No lamps had been left burning, but with all those opened windows, a good deal of moonlight filtered in. Not that Danny needed light, as she was used to working in pitch-dark. But even the upstairs hall had a window opened at the end of it.

A lot of closed doors were up there. It

was a really big house, larger than anything she'd ever been in before. One side of the hall had more doors than the other, however, so she started on the side with less, thinking those led to larger rooms, the master bedroom in particular.

She was correct. It was the second door she opened. The sheer size of that room gave it away, as well as the lump in the bed. Heddings was sleeping soundly, his loud snoring making an uncommon racket. That was annoying. Danny prided herself on her catlike movements, never making a sound, but she didn't need to be extracautious with all the noise that Heddings was making.

She moved straight to the tall bureau first. The second drawer held the jewelry chest. A large chest, it nearly filled the drawer. It wasn't locked, didn't even have any means of locking it. Too trusting by half, Lord Heddings was.

She lifted the lid and was dazzled for a moment at how much glitter spread across the bottom of that chest, not just rings, but bracelets, brooches, even necklaces. In fact, most of the jewelry it contained was feminine. More gambling winnings? Danny couldn't care less.

She decided not to take the chest. It was too big and she wasn't even sure she could lift it out of the drawer, so she stuffed her coat pockets instead. She ran her hand across the bottom of the velvet-lined chest before she finished, just to make sure she hadn't missed a dull piece of jewelry. She did *not* want to have to do this again if Percy's two heirlooms weren't in this stash.

With that thought in mind, she even did a quick search through the other drawers, but found nothing else of interest. She also checked the desk, but it contained only papers. Lastly she moved over to the vanity table where she discovered a fat wad of money, a gold watch fob, and another ring that had rolled back among the cologne bottles, as if it had just been tossed on the table. She swiped those up as well, stuffing the money in her pants pocket, since her coat pockets were full.

There was nothing else to look through. The night tables next to the bed didn't have drawers, and she discounted the bookcase, reasoning that a man who left a fortune in jewelry unlocked in his bureau wasn't likely to hide things in hollowed-out books.

Relieved to be almost done, she headed

toward the door, but stopped cold when Heddings started a fit of coughing. She ducked down at the foot of his bed. The coughing was harsh enough that it could wake him. He might even get up for a drink of water from the pitcher across the room. She was prepared to slip under the bed if he did.

The coughing got much worse. It even sounded as if he were choking. The horrid thought came to her that he could die, and a vision flashed across her mind of her being accused of murder, standing before a judge, being sentenced to hang. Her palms broke out in a cold sweat. For a moment she wondered if she should try to help him. For a moment she was paralyzed with fear and couldn't move to help him even if she was temporarily that stupid.

It took still another moment to realize he was peacefully snoring again, the sweetest sound she'd ever heard. Well, actually, it quickly became an annoying sound again now that the crisis was over, and she wasted no more time in getting the hell out of there.

All was still quiet downstairs. She quickly slipped back into the room she'd first entered and was immediately yanked back against a hard chest, a hand clamping over her mouth to keep her from screaming. She had no wits to scream with her heart in her throat. She nearly fainted . . .

And then she heard hissed in her ear, "What took you so bloody long?"

Him! And her relief lasted about a second before fury took over. She jerked about, snarled, albeit in a whisper, " 'Ave ye lost yer flippin' mind? Wot are ye doing in 'ere?"

"I was worried about you," he replied somewhat contritely.

She snorted to herself. What a whopper. Worried that she was going to take off with their precious rings was more like it.

"The next time ye want to scare someone 'alf to death, pick yerself. I'm done 'ere."

"You got the rings?"

"This ain't the place to discuss it," she shot back. "I am so gone from 'ere I left yesterday."

"Quite right," she heard behind her as she headed to the window—and tripped over a rug on the way.

Falling took her by surprise. She wasn't the least bit clumsy, and that rug had been nice and smooth when she'd walked over it on her way in. No doubt Malory had bunched it up. She reached for something to prevent the fall, but the only thing nearby was a tall pedestal with a bust on it. The pedestal was heavy and did stop her from falling, but she knocked the bust off it in doing so. It hit the floor with a loud thud.

She groaned inwardly. In the still of the night, that noise had been loud enough to wake the dead, or at the least, one of the servants sleeping on the same floor. She turned back to tell Malory to get out immediately and saw the man standing in the doorway with a gun pointed at the nabob.

Danny went so still she stopped breathing. The man was fully dressed, obviously already up and nearby even before the bust had crashed to the floor. Maybe Malory had made some noise on his way in and roused the man to investigate.

He was within his rights to just shoot them and figure out what they were doing there later. That's what she would have done if she caught a pair of men sneaking around her house in the middle of the night.

Malory's back was to the door. He'd leapt forward to try to prevent her fall, but had stopped when she'd managed it on her own. He was still looking at her, but in good light now, since the man had a lamp in his other hand. She wasn't even sure if it had dawned on Malory yet that someone was there holding that lamp.

"Don't turn around," she whispered as quietly as she could. "If ye get recognized, yer in bigger trouble than if 'e shoots ye."

Gathering her wits about her, she moved around him to block him from view somewhat and told the man holding the pistol, "There's no need for guns, mate. We were just looking for a place to wait out the night. Our coach broke down in the woods nearby. M'lord 'ere thought 'e recognized yer 'ouse. 'E's foxed to the gills, so if 'e were wrong, I wouldn't be surprised none. And we did knock. Bleedin' lord wouldn't give up though when we didn't get an answer, insisted on coming inside and sleeping in the parlor. 'E said that 'Eddings wouldn't mind. Were 'e wrong? This ain't 'Eddings place?"

The man's tense expression altered immediately. His pistol lowered as well, though not completely. So Danny laid it on a bit thicker.

" 'E tried to blame that wheel fallin' off on me, 'e did, when I warned 'im just last month that 'e needed new wheels on that old coach o' 'is. Course 'e'd rather spend all 'is blunt on fancy women and gamblin', so 'e didn't pay me any mind as usual."

The man coughed. "Should you be mentioning this in front of him?"

She managed a laugh. " 'E's so foxed, 'e won't remember. Don't know 'ow 'e's still standin', I don't."

"Who is he?"

Danny hadn't been expecting to come up with any names, but considering how she ended up being there herself, one came easily to mind. "Lord Carryway o' London town."

"Why didn't you just let him sleep it off in your coach then?" the man asked next.

"Would 'ave, but I saw some movement in those woods we were passing through near 'ere. Could 'ave just been some animal, but could 'ave been some bleedin' highwaymen, too, I was thinking. Didn't want 'im adding getting robbed to the tally against me. I'd prefer to be keepin' me job, even though it means puttin' up with a lord who's foxed more often than 'e's not."

There was a long pause where Danny was sure the fellow was going to call her

bluff and laugh in her face. She was calcu-
lating which way she should run, or if she
should just dive at his legs and try to take
him by surprise.

"Bring him along then," the man said.
"We have several empty guest rooms upstairs. There's a comfortable couch in one
you can use yourself."

Danny hadn't really expected the man to
believe her. He must be no more than a servant himself, probably the butler, and so he
couldn't bring himself to kick a member of
the nobility back out into the woods. He
could have thought to lock them up until the
morning, when what she'd told him could
be verified. But he must not be a suspicious
sort, to have believed her outright.

A good opportunity to bolt through the
window presented itself as soon as the man
turned his back on them to lead the way upstairs. But he hadn't put his pistol away yet.
And with that weapon still in his hand,
Danny preferred to play out the charade and
not risk a bullet or two flying her way.
Besides, there were two of them to get out
that window, and no way they could both
manage it before one of them got shot for
trying.

The nabob hadn't said a single word, thank God. He could have spoiled the whole story if the servant realized he wasn't foxed at all. He was either smart enough to play the part she'd set up for him or nervous enough to keep his mouth shut.

No, she doubted he was nervous, at least not as much as she was. He'd handled that barkeep tonight too easily for him to be bothered by the mere possibility of flying bullets. Stupidly brave was probably what he was, and a high-handed blackguard for getting her into this mess.

She grabbed his arm now and dragged it over her shoulder so it would look as if she were holding him up, then blanched to see the pistol in his hand. He'd had it trained on the man the whole while, just hidden behind her back. Bleedin' nabob could have gotten them both killed!

She snatched it out of his hand and stuffed it back in his pocket, only to hear him chuckle at her for doing so. God protect her from half-wits!

She hissed at him now, "I 'ope ye know 'ow to play the drunkard, mate, and 'ang yer 'ead so 'e don't get a good look at ye."

It was easy to get him upstairs. She was

too nervous to take note of the closeness of their bodies, and he only rested his weight on her when the servant glanced back at them; otherwise, he was mostly getting up the stairs on his own, was in fact leading her instead of the other way around.

"In here," the servant said, opening a door. "We should be able to find someone to fix your coach in the morning so you can be on your way."

" 'Preciate it, mate."

He'd followed them in, lit a lamp for them, then headed toward the door. He still hadn't relinquished the hold on his pistol other than for a moment to light the lamp. Danny began to wonder if he'd believed her tale after all. And as soon as the door closed behind him, she threw off Malory's arm and hurried to the door to hear if the fellow was actually leaving. What she heard instead was the soft click of the lock on the door.

Chapter 5

～～

Locked in to await . . . what?

Danny lost what little color she had left in her cheeks. Had the man not believed their story, or was he simply being cautious?

She hoped he was just being cautious. After all, they were strangers until his employer verified otherwise. But if he was going to stand out there and guard their door the rest of the night, then this mess was just going to get worse.

She turned back to Malory to see him watching her curiously, one brow raised in question. She rushed back to him to whisper, " 'E's locked us in."

"Bloody hell," he growled low.

"Ye got that right, mate. So go stick yer 'ead in a pillow and start snoring, eh, and loudly. 'E needs to think we're sleeping so 'e'll go back to bed 'imself."

Having said that, she didn't wait to see if he'd comply. She moved back to the door and lay down in front of it to look under the crack. Sure enough, there were shoes right on the other side of the door. The servant was still standing out there, probably trying to listen through the door himself.

When she didn't hear any snoring starting up yet, she turned around and glared at Malory. He rolled his eyes toward the ceiling, his lips twisted in disgust, as if her suggestion was quite beneath him. And he didn't move directly to the bed but went to the window instead, to see how much trouble it would be to leave that way. He must have decided that wasn't an option because he sighed then and moved to sit on the bed, bounced on it actually, then tested out a few snoring sounds till he got one he was satisfied with and started making a lot of racket with it.

Danny almost grinned. He looked so disgruntled to be doing something so simple as snoring. Too bad. They wouldn't be locked in an upstairs bedroom if he hadn't come in the house to begin with. She would have been out of there without a hitch, instead of lying on the floor hoping a suspicious servant would get tired and go back to bed.

It didn't look as if he would. It was starting to look as if he was going to stand "guard" out there in the hall all night. She could almost hear the prison door slamming shut on her and she was getting a queasy, sick feeling in her belly.

With desperation creeping up on her, she went to look out the window for herself. Malory's sigh had been accurate. It was not an avenue for easy departure, not without a rope. No tree nearby to jump to, no ledges of any sort to use to climb down with.

They could rip up the sheets to make their own rope, which she wouldn't even have thought of if the nabobs hadn't done that earlier in the evening, but a glance about the room showed nothing heavy enough to use as an anchor to support Malory's weight. Hers maybe, but not his. The bed might work, but it was just a small one for a single guest and had a wooden frame that could break. They'd probably make too much noise trying to move it next to the window anyway.

When it finally dawned on her that the servant might be waiting for the lamp to go out, Danny could have kicked herself. Her drunk "employer" might not worry about the lamp, but why would the sober "driver" want to leave the light on to sleep, unless he wasn't planning on sleeping? She hoped that was what the servant was thinking, and sure enough, about ten minutes after the light went out, he moved off down the hall and back down the stairs.

All the while, Malory had been trying out a wide assortment of snoring sounds that would have caused Danny to bust a gut laughing if she hadn't convinced herself they were going to be stuck there all night. The servant definitely distrusted them, or else he wouldn't have stood outside their room so long. But it could have been worse. He could have gone to wake his employer, they could have checked to see if anything was missing from their house, and there'd be no talking her way out of having her pockets filled with Heddings's jewels.

She moved over and told the nabob,

"He's finally gone. We'll give him a few minutes to go back to bed."

"Then what?"

"Then I pick that lock open and we get the 'ell out o' 'ere."

"You know how to do that?"

She snorted. "Course I do, and I carry m'own picker."

She pulled a thick pin out of her hat and went to work on the door. Piece of cake. Bedroom doors usually were.

Within seconds she was saying, "Come on. And we'll use the front door. Since they already know we've been 'ere, leaving it unlocked won't matter."

She didn't wait to see if he was going to follow her. The moment she was outside she took off at a run and didn't look back or stop once until she reached the trees. Only then did she pause, but merely to catch her breath and her bearings. It took a moment to spot the coach lamps through the thick foliage. Malory caught up to her then.

He took her arm to lead her the rest of the way to the coach. She tried to jerk it away but that effort just made him put his arm around her shoulder. He obviously didn't trust her to turn over the jewels now that they were safely out of Heddings's house.

Without the danger of having a servant holding a gun nearby, she couldn't handle being this close to Malory. She'd put his arm around her earlier when they'd walked up Heddings's staircase and had felt nothing but her fear. This was nowhere near the same thing. Now she was feeling the length of him pressed to her side, his muscular thigh, his hip and his hard chest, feeling how perfectly she fit under his arm, feeling the heat coming off him—or was it her heat? She was remembering just how bleeding handsome he was, even though she couldn't see his face in the dark of the woods. She was remembering those sexy blue eyes moving over her in the coach, as if he could see right through her disguise.

If he stopped right then and there and turned her toward him, she would have been mush for whatever he had in mind. He stopped. Her heart began to pound so loudly it throbbed in her ears. He was going to do it, lower his mouth to hers. Her first kiss, and from the most handsome man she'd ever encountered. It would be sublime. She knew it and held her breath, trembling in anticipation.

He pushed her into the coach. They'd only stopped so he could open the door.

Deflated more than she wanted to admit, Danny sat back on her seat in a huff, then glared at Malory as soon as he took the seat across from her. More than half of that glare was because of what had just happened, or hadn't happened—all in her own mind, of course. But that didn't stop her from feeling disgruntled. Malory wouldn't know that though. He would attribute her look only to the topic she introduced.

"That were the most stupid thing I ever saw," she told him. "D'ye realize gettin' caught in there were yer fault! If ye were going to enter that 'ouse, ye could 'ave stolen the rings yerself. Wot did ye need me for then, eh?"

"What happened?" Percy asked, but was ignored.

"You were gone longer than necessary," Malory pointed out stiffly. "Or I wouldn't have gone inside."

"I weren't gone even ten minutes!"

"So it was an inordinately *long* ten minutes. All of which is irrelevant now."

"You could 'ave got us killed! I wouldn't be callin' that irrelevant, mate."

"*What* happened?" Percy asked again.

"Nothing the youngun here wasn't adept at handling," Malory conceded. Then to Danny, as if he hadn't just pumped up her pride with that casual compliment, he added, "Let's have a look at your findings to see if all that trouble was worth it."

"Get this coach moving first," she said, mollified somewhat that he'd just admitted she'd saved his arse. "We ain't safe till we're nowhere near 'ere."

"Good point," Percy agreed, and tapped on the roof of the coach, which signaled the driver to head back to town. "Now, please, keep me on tenterhooks no longer."

As long as Lord Malory wasn't doing the insisting, Danny saw no reason to deny his friend. She started emptying her pockets on the seat next to her, including the wad of money, then scooped up the whole pile and dumped it on the seat between the two nabobs. She even turned her pockets inside out to show them she wasn't keeping anything back.

Percy immediately pounced on one old-looking ring with the exclamation "Good

God, yes!" He brought the antique to his lips to kiss it, then with unseemly haste, stuck it back on his finger where it apparently belonged. "Can't thank you enough, dear boy! You have my—" His appreciation was cut short when his eye was caught by the jewelry again. "Oh my, there's the other!" he exclaimed, and spread the jewelry wider to snatch the second ring out of the pile.

"You have our thanks, lad," Lord Malory finished Percy's thought.

"Eternal thanks," Percy added, beaming at Danny.

"I wouldn't go *that* far," Malory rejoined.

"Speak for yourself, old chap. You weren't the one hiding from your own mother."

"I don't have a mother."

"From George then."

"Point taken," Malory conceded with a grin.

"George?" Danny asked.

"My stepmother."

"Is named *George?*" she gasped.

When the young lord laughed, his cobalt eyes fairly sparkled. "It's Georgina actually, but m'father cut that short just to be contrary. Habit of his, don't you know."

She didn't know and didn't want to. She'd

done what they'd asked—insisted—she do. And successfully, so there was no question about doing it again. She just wanted to get home now and face Dagger—and find out if she still had a home.

Reminded of that, her expression turned gloomy. They didn't notice. They were still glancing down at the pile of glitter.

Percy tapped a large oval-shaped pendant surrounded by emeralds and diamonds. "Looks familiar, don't it?" he said to his friend.

"Indeed. I admired Lady Katherine's bosom more'n once when it graced her chest."

"Didn't take her for a gambler, least not the sort to part with something like that."

"She isn't. Heard it was stolen several months ago while she was vacationing in Scotland."

"You pulling my leg, old man?"

Malory was frowning by then. "No, and this bracelet looks rather familiar as well. I'd swear my cousin Diana was wearing it just last Christmas. Don't recall her mentioning it was stolen, but I know *she* doesn't gamble a'tall."

"Oh, I say, are you suggesting Lord Heddings is a thief?"

"Looks that way, don't it?"

"But that's splendid news. Can't tell you how much guilt I was trying to ignore over this distasteful business."

Malory caught Danny rolling her eyes over that remark. She could tell he had to work really hard not to grin at her. Percy wasn't finished, however, and his next question sobered the young lord.

"But what are we going to do about it?"

"There's nothing we *can* do about it, without implicating ourselves and our young friend here."

"Well, that's too bad. Hate to see a thief go about his merry way without paying a price for . . . it . . ." Percy intercepted Danny's pointed stare and coughed. "Present company excluded, naturally."

"Let's not forget yerselves," Danny sneered. "Stealing that glitter weren't *my* idea."

"Quite right," Percy said with a blush.

But Lord Malory noted with displeasure, "No, *your* idea was to empty *our* pockets, so there's no need to be pointing fingers here."

The heat from the multiple blushes she felt just then could have lit the coach brazier. Danny hated having the tables turned on her, she really did. But under the circumstances, she was fresh out of rejoinders.

He was quick, that one, and suspicious, or he wouldn't have followed her into the house to make sure she did the job. Astute, too, and clever. She didn't doubt coming here had been his idea.

It was too bad he wasn't a half-wit like his friend. She might have called him that in her mind earlier, but she knew it wasn't so. She could probably have talked her way out of her involvement if he was. She still probably could have—if he weren't so bleedin' handsome. But she had trouble putting two thoughts together when he turned those cobalt eyes on her. Her cunning and wits had gone right out the door, leaving behind a brainless ninny, hopelessly out of her element.

Chapter 6

~~

It seemed to take much longer getting back to the city than it had taken getting to Heddings's house. Danny didn't have a watch, but she wouldn't have been surprised if the sun had soon made an appearance. She was tired, exhausted really, from so many emotions she wasn't used to experiencing. She was starting to get hungry, too. And she still had a lot to deal with when she finally got home.

Actually, she hoped Dagger would be asleep so she could get some sleep herself. It would be much easier to offer explanations, or lies for that matter, with a clear mind that wasn't muddled with exhaustion.

Percy was napping again, smart man. Danny wished she could do the same, but with Lord Malory still wide-awake, she didn't dare. Not that she thought he'd do anything to her while she slept. She just needed to be alert to watch for an opportunity to escape in an area she recognized.

She didn't doubt they were going to let her go, now that she'd done what they wanted, but she doubted they'd take her back where they'd found her. Why would they go out of their way, late as it was? And dropping her off in *their* end of town would mean she'd be hopelessly lost and wasting hours more trying to find her way home. She might have grown up in London, but it was a big town and she was only familiar with her small section of it.

She knew to the second when his eyes were back on her. Glancing at him confirmed it. He had something on his mind. The look he was giving her was much too thoughtful.

"By the by, where'd you leave your shoes?"

The question surprised her. It certainly wasn't what she'd expected to hear, considering his pensive frown. And actually, she was surprised he hadn't mentioned it sooner, since he'd had her march through the woods in her stockings. And he'd tied up her ankles earlier. He would have had to be blind not to notice she wasn't wearing normal footwear.

"These are me shoes," she replied, and lifted one foot so he could see the soft sole of leather on the bottom of her wool stocking.

"Ingenious."

She blushed slightly, but only because she was rather proud of her improvised footwear. She'd made them herself. She had a pair of normal shoes, since running around in what looked like her stockings would draw too much comment during the day. These she wore only when she worked.

"Mind if I have a closer look?" he asked.

Quickly she tucked her feet under the seat, as far away from him as she could and gave him a mutinous stare. He merely shrugged.

Then he amazed her when he added, "You're much smarter than I would have thought. That was quite a tale you told back there on the spur of the moment. Lord

Carryway?" As soon as he said it, he chuck-led.

Danny merely shrugged. "It fit."

"I suppose," he allowed, but his curiosity was still present. "Do you often get caught and have to talk your way out of it?"

"No. Never been nabbed, not once—until tonight. Twice in one night, and both times because o' ye."

He coughed slightly. But to avoid tossing around blame again, he instead introduced what was *really* on his mind.

He tapped the necklace and bracelet on the seat next to him that had been under discussion earlier and said, "Would like to return these two pieces to their rightful owners, anonymously, of course." He cleared his throat and looked distinctly uncomfortable as he added, "Would you mind, youngun?"

"Why would I mind?"

"Because this pile is yours."

She snorted. She'd already decided she wanted no part of that glitter. The vision of her being caught and hanged was still too fresh in her mind. But knowing the jewelry was twice stolen made it even more risky and she said so.

"It's one thing to get rid o' stuff like that

when it's first stolen, just a matter o' being quick about it. But trying to dump stolen goods that were already stolen goods is just askin' to get caught. Some o' that stuff, if not all, is already being looked for. I'd as soon toss it out the window as touch it again."

He shook his head. "This won't do. You were promised a fortune in—"

"Get over it, mate. If I want anything from ye, ye'll know it."

Oh, God, his look suddenly turned sensual again, heating her thoughts, turning her innards to mush. If she said anything else just then, it would be utter gibberish. How could he *do* that with just a look? And what had she said to change his expression like that? The mention of "want"? That would mean he knew she was a woman, but he *couldn't* know. No one knew. And he couldn't have guessed. She didn't even know *how* to act like a female anymore, she'd played her male role so long, and she'd made no mistakes to give herself away.

He let her off the hook by cooling his carnal stare. Was it the squirming she'd done?

He picked up the wad of money, thumbed through it briefly, then tossed it on her seat.

"Not quite a hundred pounds there, but it will do for the moment I suppose."

Why did he make it sound as if they weren't done with each other? "That's more'n I've ever seen at one time, or two, or more," she quickly assured him. "That will do me fine."

He merely smiled. She went back to staring out the window. Her eyes widened to see London on the other side now.

She didn't recognize anything, but she still said, her tone somewhat desperate, "Ye can let me out 'ere, mate. I can find m'way—"

"Not a chance, lad. I'll take you to your door and do any explaining that's needed, to get you out of the trouble you mentioned. We'll just drop Percy off first. Won't take long a'tall."

And then be alone with him and his bleedin' eyes that undressed her? Not a chance was right.

"I exaggerated," she lied. "This money will more'n make up for the time I've been missing."

"I insist," he said, not buying her lie.

"Wouldn't be able to sleep if I thought this nasty business had repercussions for you."

"Like I care if ye can sleep?" she snapped churlishly. "Yer idea o' favors is my idea o' getting buried, so don't do me any more. I'd be in even more trouble if I showed ye where me friends live. Waking up in an alley beat nigh to death would be lucky."

"You expect a beating for—"

"Not me," she cut in pointedly.

He chuckled. "All right, I get the picture. But I'll escort you back to that tavern. Very least I can do."

She didn't think he'd settle for that once he got that far, so she had no choice but to say, "No."

"Wasn't asking for permission, dear boy."

Danny opened her mouth to snarl something really nasty, but since it wouldn't accomplish anything, she decided to save her energy for what was about to come next.

Chapter 7

Danny had to wait until the nabob took his eyes off her before she made her move. When he finally did, she didn't spare another thought on it, just shot toward the coach door, jumped out, and took off at a run down the block.

Too easy, just as she'd figured it would be, though she'd underestimated how much ducking she should have done to get through the door. Not being a frequent rider in coaches, never in one so fine as his, she hadn't taken her above-average height into account when leaping out that coach door. She was lucky she'd only knocked her hat

off and hadn't knocked herself unconscious.

She'd miss the hat. She was right fond of
that hat, had won it in a fight down the block
last year. It gave her a certain "flare" that
she loved, probably because it appealed to
her feminine vanity. But it was gone now,
left on the floor of the nabob's coach, and it
would be a sorry day before she'd risk running into that young lord again to retrieve it.

She didn't slow her pace, didn't need to
as she wasn't winded yet. But a block away
she figured she better stop running before
she did wear herself out. She started to,
then finally heard someone running behind
her. A glance back and she shot forward at
full speed.

She simply couldn't believe it. The
bleedin' nabob was chasing her! And not
just a short distance either. He should have
given up after the first block, but he was still
at it.

It made no sense, since they were done
with each other. She'd done what they'd
wanted and they had gotten her back to
London. Why in the bleedin' hell would he
go out of his way just to get her closer to

home when she obviously didn't want him taking her any farther?

Three bleedin' blocks now and he still wasn't stopping! She was getting winded now. His legs were longer. He was slowly catching up to her. She almost stopped and gave up, but she rounded a corner and found a passing hack just approaching it. While she was out of Malory's line of view for those few seconds, she dove under the hack, grabbed hold of the frame to lift herself off the ground, anchored her feet to it as well to help hold herself up as close to the frame as possible, and waited until she saw his legs run by.

Pressed close to the underbelly of the coach, she was out of Malory's sight. He kept on running, in the opposite direction from her now, which allowed her to drop back to the ground when the hack turned another corner.

She was still somewhat winded, heart still racing, even more hungry now, and close to toppling over from pure exhaustion. If she didn't think it would make matters much worse to delay getting home, she'd find a nice alley to curl up in and sleep the day away.

She was lost, of course, in an area of the city she'd never been in before. And she was drawing too much attention. Without her hat to hide the white-gold of her hair, her mop of curls was like a beacon, especially in contrast to her dark green velvet jacket. She was drawing attention wherever she passed, making her more uncomfortable than she cared to admit.

It took another hour to find a landmark she actually recognized so she could stop walking around in circles as she'd been doing and start heading in the right direction from there. It took yet another hour and a half to finally reach home at the slow pace she could manage, as tired and sore as she was by then.

And she still had the feeling someone was following her. She knew bloody well she'd lost Malory, so it wasn't him. But every time she glanced behind her, she merely saw other people going about their business. There were too many alleys along the way though that someone intent on following her could slip into and just peak out of to keep sight of her. She finally concluded she was being silly, that her exhaustion and overactive imagination were just playing tricks on her.

And she was worried. That was probably the main reason why she was getting jumpy and imagining things. It was getting worse and worse, the closer she got to home, because she wasn't sure if she'd have a home after today.

~ ~

Tyrus Dyer had been unable to believe his eyes. He was either losing his mind, because he knew the woman couldn't have regressed in years to look that young again, or he was seeing the girl who was supposed to be dead. It was one or the other, had to be, and he'd rather not think he was losing his mind, so obviously the girl wasn't dead. And she'd grown up to look just like her mother.

Tyrus was the one who'd been hired to kill her—her and her father. Getting rid of the man had been no problem. The child should have been even less trouble. But she'd had a nurse guarding her, and that woman had fought like a banshee. Though he was sure he'd mortally wounded her, she'd even managed to knock him out with his own club! He wasn't out long, just long enough for the nurse to drag the girl out of the house and hide her somewhere.

When he'd been unable to find her, he thought she'd curled up in a hole somewhere to die, her body just never discovered. That had *not* satisfied his employer, however. Money was involved, a lot of it, and the fellow had been so livid over Tyrus's incompetence, he hadn't just refused to pay him, he'd tried to shoot him. But Tyrus had seen it coming and had managed to dodge the bullets and make his escape.

Tyrus had been livid himself for quite a few years after. He'd done half the job. But after that his luck had turned so rotten, it was as if that unfinished job had jinxed him. No matter what he did, he bungled it now. As a result, he'd been fired so many times he'd lost count.

But his bad luck had just showed up. It wasn't illusive anymore. It was tangible. And he'd just been given the means to actually get rid of it. This required some thought. He didn't want to be hasty and mess up again. But he knew where she lived. Hiding in the slums all these years, who would have figured! He'd be back. . . .

Chapter 8

It was too much to hope Dagger wouldn't be awake. The sun had been up for a while now. And he was sitting at the kitchen table, drinking a cup of tea Nan had made him. Six of the children were in the main room, not counting a couple still sleeping there. They all took one look at Dagger staring at her through the arched opening to the kitchen and started vacating the house.

Danny entered the kitchen and dropped down in the seat across from Dagger.

He was a plain-looking man, but the long scar on his chin and the short one under his left eye gave him a mean look. His long brown hair was mussed, his eyes bloodshot. He looked haggard at the moment. Actually, he looked about as tired as she was. She guessed then that he hadn't slept at all, that he'd stayed up waiting for her to get home. It wouldn't be because he'd worried about her. No, when she hadn't returned when she should have, he would have realized she'd given him the excuse he'd been looking for to get rid of her. He wasn't a stupid man. She could have talked circles around him if he was.

She was too tired to lie about what had happened. She'd trip herself up if she tried. Before he said a word though, she took out the wad of money from her pocket and tossed it on the table between them. None of them had ever brought home so much. A hundred pounds was a bleedin' fortune to them. She was hoping it might make a difference. It didn't. He barely glanced at it. And too late she realized it made her look as if she'd willingly broken the rules.

"Will ye 'ear me out, Dagger?" she asked. "I've not 'ad many choices since leaving 'ere last night."

"I know ye were caught, but I also know ye weren't taken to jail."

"It were still a trap. They wanted a thief to do some stealing for them."

"Ye know better, so why didn't ye refuse?"

"Why do ye think I was carted out o' there tied up?" she countered.

"But ye didn't stay tied up, did ye?" he said with a pointed glance at the money on the table. "Ye could 'ave escaped them sooner."

That was true. Tiredly she explained, "That would've stranded me in the countryside wi' no telling when I would've found me way back to London."

"Ye left London!"

She flinched at the shout. "That's *why* I didn't try to escape sooner. I've never been out o' London before. It probably would've taken me a week to get 'ome. But they swore they'd bring me back soon as I robbed the lord for them."

"A *lord!*" That shout was even louder than the last one. "I s'pose in 'is own bleedin' 'ouse, too?"

She could have lied at that point, should have. That was the number one rule, after all. But she knew, could tell by the very questions he'd been asking, that her an-

swer wasn't going to make a bit of difference.

"Pack up yer things and get out. Ye've
broken the last rule ye'll be breaking 'ere."

Danny didn't move a muscle. She'd
known she was going to hear that, that no
matter what she said, she was going to hear
it. But still she wasn't prepared for the tight-
ness filling her chest or the emotion clog-
ging up her throat. Dagger had been "family" to her for fifteen years. That he *wanted*
her gone was what hurt the most.

She wasn't going to cry. She wasn't supposed to be a female who would. She was
no longer a child who would. She was supposed to be a man who wouldn't, so she
couldn't. It wasn't something she could
stop though, so she stumbled quickly away
from the table before Dagger could notice
the moisture filling her eyes.

She went straight to her pallet on the
floor in the main room. It was hers. She'd
roll it up and take it with her, though she
couldn't imagine where she'd lay it down
next. Her sack of clothes was beside it, not
a very big sack. The outfit she was wearing
was her favorite so she wore it daily,
changed to her only other outfit just to wash

it. Her pet was there in his little box. She managed to stuff it into the sack for ease of carrying.

The two children who had still been sleeping were sitting up on their pallets now openly crying. She stopped by each to give them a hug. Ordinarily she would have tried to cheer them, but she still couldn't get any words out past the lump in her throat, so she didn't try.

Opening the door, though, she found the rest of the children lined up outside it, most of them crying, too. They'd listened at the door, knew they wouldn't be seeing her again. It was breaking her heart. She'd been their hero for the longest time. They'd probably follow her if she gave the word. But she couldn't do that to Dagger, despite how callously he'd treated her. They were all Dagger had. She tore herself away from them and headed down the street.

Ironically, she'd wanted to leave for years, to find a real job, a respectable job, so she'd never have to steal again. Dagger was just forcing her to realize that dream sooner than she'd expected. She hoped she could be grateful to him someday for that, that the hurt wouldn't last too long.

Reminding herself that this was something she had wanted to achieve wasn't helping to ease the pain. She'd wanted to leave on good terms, to be able to come back and visit, to maybe help the other children find respectable jobs, too.

"Danny!"

She swung around with a gasp, saw Dagger marching determinedly down the street toward her. The hurt eased up immediately. She'd known, deep down, that he couldn't do this to her. He'd only wanted to scare her is all, so she'd stop breaking the rules and set a good example for the other children.

He reached her and she saw that his expression wasn't conciliatory at all. Her brief burst of hope was dashed. He was still angry. In fact, she'd never seen him quite this angry before.

"Ye want to know why, Danny?" he hissed at her. "Yer too bleedin' pretty for a man. I've found m'self wanting ye, and that makes me so disgusted wi' m'self I can't think sometimes. But I'd as soon kill ye as touch ye, so the better choice was to get rid o' ye, now weren't it? Ye'll make do. I've no doubt o' that. I taught ye well. But ye'll make do somewhere else. Now be gone wi' ye 'fore I change me mind and we both end up regrettin' it."

She could have told him right then that he didn't need to be disgusted with himself for wanting her. She was a girl after all. But that confession would probably produce a serious rage the likes of which she'd never seen, because she'd deliberately deceived them all these years. And besides, he'd just admitted he wanted her. If he knew she really was a woman, he'd want her in his bed for a time, then probably set her to whoring—or both. And why had she hidden her sex for fifteen years if not to avoid that very fate?

She turned away and walked on before she said something that *she* would regret— and ran into Lucy around the next corner.

"Cor, where've ye been, Danny? I've been looking every—wot's wrong?"

It was her undoing. The tears started rolling down her cheeks. She could have controlled it, gotten away without having it all ripped out of her, if she hadn't run into Lucy. Anyone but dear Lucy, her sister, her mother, her only true friend . . .

"He did it, didn't 'e?" Lucy guessed immediately. "Kicked ye out?" At Danny's nod, she added, "Ah, luv, don't take it so 'ard. This is yer chance, ye know, to do something wi' yer life that 'as some meaning. Ye talked o' gettin' yerself a husband, raisin' some kids, teachin' them proper. Ye've wanted to do that, but ye couldn't begin while ye were still 'ere."

"I know," Danny replied, barely able to get the words out past the lump in her throat.

"Then buck up, eh?" Even as she said it, Lucy's own tears were starting. She turned her back on Danny, as if that could hide the emotion welling up in her.

"I'll send word, once I'm settled," Danny promised.

"Ye better. I'll worry m'self sick till you do. Now go. This is a good day for ye, luv. Ye 'ave to believe that."

Danny tried, she really did, to dredge up that optimism, but she couldn't. She started to hurry past Lucy. This good-bye was much more painful than she could have imagined. But the other woman's hand caught her shoulder, stopped her for one last minute.

"Be yerself, Danny lass," Lucy whispered

through her tears, as she put her arms around Danny and hugged her tightly. "It's finally time. Just be yerself, and it will all turn out right for ye."

Chapter 9

"I've a package to deliver to a Lord Malory. Would ye 'appen to know where 'e might be found?"

"Heard tell there's a Malory family lives over in Grosvenor Square."

"And where would that be?"

"New to town, are ye?"

"It's that obvious?"

A chuckle. "You'll find Grosvenor north o' here. Head down the block, then turn right and just keep going that way till you come to the rich houses."

An address would have helped, but then again, probably not. Danny would need a map for that and didn't know where to get one, wouldn't be able to read one either, for that matter. An address would have helped only if she could afford to hire a hack, which she couldn't.

She was so out of her element it was beyond pathetic. She was keenly feeling the disadvantage of her lack of education, too. She would have given up by now if her anger weren't goading her on.

She had found a nice quiet alley to sleep the day away in, but didn't actually sleep that long. Her hunger woke her much sooner than she would have liked, and the headache it was causing lent desperation to her situation.

She had to find a job fast. If she had to resort to stealing just to eat, then she'd be no better off than she had been. This was an opportunity to *better* herself, not slip back into the gutter and old habits. But it wasn't going to be easy. She knew, because she'd tried before.

Lucy used to cover for her absence when Danny would go out to look for a respectable job. The problem had always been her appearance, and her lack of even a basic education. To apply for a man's job that didn't require being able to read and write did require muscle, which she couldn't muster. To apply for a woman's job she'd need some female clothes first, which she didn't own. And no matter what job she could talk her way into getting, she'd need a roof over her head and some coins in her pocket to last her till her first pay.

She'd thought she'd had that solved at one point. The job of a maid often came with room and board, which was ideal for someone starting out completely broke. She'd borrowed one of Lucy's dresses for the interview and had been so thrilled to get hired—for all of two hours. The butler had given her the job, and only because he'd been fascinated by her looks. As soon as she met the housekeeper though, she was fired. They were a middle-class household trying to move up the social ladder, which meant they wanted only a better class of servant, at least none that sounded like gutter trash or looked like whores.

Danny had been so disappointed and discouraged by that experience, she'd stopped looking for decent work for a long time. Then when she did start looking again, she simply had no luck.

Recalling her many failures, she got angry. The fact was, she'd hunted for a job sporadically, maybe four or five times a year. She'd never done it daily because she hadn't really been ready to go out on her own. To be alone. But she had no choice now, and she didn't have the luxury of taking her time about it. She needed to find a job immediately, that very day. And she needed to find some food even sooner. Calling herself ten kinds of a fool for not holding back at least a few of the pound notes Malory had given her, instead of giving the whole wad to Dagger, wasn't going to feed her.

She didn't like being on her own. She was finding that out firsthand, but she'd known she wouldn't. She'd grown up with a houseful of children around her. She wanted that back, but she wanted them to be *her* children, so she could have a say in raising them proper. She needed a husband to help with that, though, a good man, and one with a respectable job. That had been a goal of hers for a long time, she'd just never been able to get serious about it while she was still living the life of a boy.

She wasn't going to find a husband around the next corner though. And food was a necessity, which meant a job of her own came first. Then she could start looking for a husband to start raising a family with.

She got lucky with the food. She found that one of the rings from Heddings's stash had fallen through the little hole in her coat pocket to the lining underneath. She couldn't sell it by normal means, since it might be one of the stolen pieces being looked for. But she remembered Miss Jane selling a ring all those years ago to buy food.

She hadn't thought of Miss Jane in years, not since the nightmares had stopped. She wasn't sure why they had stopped. They'd plagued her from as far back as she could remember—which was the short time she'd spent with Miss Jane. And they'd usually been the same, filled with blood and screams, until a club fell on her head to end it.

One dream she had far too infrequently was very nice and left her feeling warm and comfortable. It was a dream of a young woman, one she'd never met, but the lady had white-gold hair just like hers, though arranged in one of those fancy styles she'd only seen ladies wear. A beautiful woman, dressed elegantly, like an angel she was, walking in a field of flowers.

Lucy had figured the angel dream really was an angel calling to her because she was supposed to have died all those years ago but didn't. Of course Lucy had been fanciful. But Danny had been even more fanciful, figuring the beautiful lady was herself, something she could aspire to. The dream gave her hope.

She needed hope now, and a lot more. The ring had fetched her less than a pound note. Very disappointing, but then the best she could get from a total stranger who'd only looked as if he could afford a good deal.

Her predicament was entirely that young lord's fault. If he hadn't been so highhanded, if he'd just accepted her refusal and instead found himself someone who would have been thrilled to do what he wanted, she wouldn't be worrying about where her next meal was going to come from.

He owed her. And he could bleedin' well pay up, or she'd let Lord Heddings know where his stash of stolen jewelry had trotted off to. Well, she wouldn't *really* go that far, but Malory would get the idea.

She finished the meal she'd bought in a nice restaurant and thanked the waiter for the food and his directions. She didn't see his frown. If she had, she wouldn't have realized it was because she didn't know to leave a tip for him. Ignorance was sometimes bliss, or it could have been.

In this case, the waiter was annoyed enough that he wasn't going to let her remain ignorant. He followed her outside to shout at her, "Cheap bastard! And after I gave you directions, too, which I didn't have to do!"

Danny swung around, realized he was yelling at her, though she couldn't imagine why. "Wot are ye talking about, eh? I paid for the bleedin' meal."

"Shows how dumb you are! You think service is free? I should have known better than to let your kind through the door."

Her kind? That stung and made her cheeks bloom with color. She'd picked the first restaurant she'd come across, hadn't really noted that it was in an affluent business district, with well-dressed people everywhere she looked. A crowd was gathering because of the waiter's shouts. And she heard other angry murmurs now.

"A thief, no doubt."

"Better check your pockets if he's been working this area today."

"Better check *his* pockets."

"All I wanted was some food," Danny said quickly to the waiter. "Which I paid for. If I didn't pay enough, ye could 'ave just said so. Ye didn't 'ave to insult me."

The fellow looked as if he realized he had overreacted. But too many of his regular customers were about now for him to back down and apologize.

"Just get out of here and don't come back," he warned. "This is a respectable district. Go back to the slums where you belong."

Chapter 10

Danny walked away from that restaurant trying to hold her head high, though it took every ounce of will she had to accomplish it. She wanted to run instead, had an overwhelming urge to do so, but she had no doubt someone would try to detain her, because running would make her look guilty. They wouldn't consider that she just wanted to find a deep hole that she could crawl into and cry, she was so heartsick and embarrassed.

She'd experienced that kind of snobbery before, when she'd looked for jobs in the past. She shouldn't have let it crush her as it did. It merely pointed out just how hard it was going to be to find a decent job.

It took a while to push the hurt aside. When she finally did, it was replaced with unease, because for the second time in two days, she felt that someone was watching her, following her. This time it was probably just someone who'd been in that crowd, making sure she left their neighborhood.

But turning to look, she saw nothing out of the ordinary, at least, not close to her. A lordly type entering an office building. A delivery boy. A lady with a maid following behind her bogged down with packages, a few couples walking along arm in arm, and dozens of other people going about their business. For the next two blocks, the feeling just wouldn't go away, but every time she looked over her shoulder, she couldn't imagine who it might be. There were just too many people on the street in this part of town.

She finally ducked into a shop, then got yelled at when she kept on going, running through the back, which was restricted to employees only, and out the back door. For the next ten minutes she ran, backtracked, passed through other buildings, and finally, the feeling went away. If someone had been following her, she was satisfied she'd lost them.

It was a long walk to Grosvenor Square. Night arrived before she got there. And there was a definite lack of nice alleys in the areas she'd been passing through. There were parks, though, lots of them, some so big she worried that she'd wandered out of the city by accident. She finally curled up in some bushes to wait for morning so she could get her bearings again.

Dawn brought the hunger again, and even more anger because of it. But that was pushed aside when she actually looked around her and *recognized* the park she was in, though she'd never been in that part of town before to her recollection. She'd barely seen any of the park last night, it was so dark. But this morning, the benches along the pathway, the giant old oak shading them, the child running through a flock of pigeons to scatter them, laughing in delight. She blinked, and the child was gone, had never been there. A memory!

Danny sat back down, shaken to her core. It was the first memory of her past that had ever come back to her, and it had come

to her because it was the first time she'd
ever been to a place that she must have visited as a child. Had her parents lived in this
part of London, or had they only been visiting? There had been a hotel on one side of
that park, along with a middle-class neighborhood, though she found more fancy
houses on the other side when she left in
that direction.

She tried to remember more, to recognize other things, but nothing else stirred
any memories, and it was giving her a
headache to try. No, the hunger was doing
that again. So she hurried now, had to
question a few more strangers for directions, and finally arrived at the Malory house
around midmorning.

It was a bleedin' mansion! It stood by itself, was fenced in, even had grass all
around it, and nice flowers and shrubs,
hardly what she'd been expecting. She was
too intimidated to approach a house like
that, especially after what had happened at
that restaurant yesterday, so more time was
wasted while she waited around for someone who looked like a servant to leave the
house. A young woman finally did, dressed
in a maid's uniform—well, not so much a

uniform, but not a fancy lady's dress, so Danny took a chance and hailed her.

"G'day, ma'am. The 'andsome Malory live 'ere?"

"That's rich, dearie," the woman replied in a good-natured tone. "They're all handsome."

"'Ow many Lord Malorys are there?"

"In this household, three."

"With black 'air and—"

"No, the earl lives here, with his two sons, none with black hair. You must mean his brother Sir Anthony. His house is over on Piccadilly. Or you could mean his nephew Jeremy. Those two lords both have black hair."

"I've this package to deliver," Danny said, tapping her pet's box, the best excuse she could come up with to gain access to Malory. "It were a young lord that placed the order, around twenty-five 'e was."

"That'd be Jeremy Malory then. Lives with his father in Berkeley Square."

Danny blushed, forced to lie again to get directions. "I'm new to the city. Could ye point me to Berkeley?"

The woman did, and it didn't take all that long to find the square, which was crowded at that time of the morning with pedestrians and carriage drivers pulled up to the curb, waiting on their passengers to leave their fancy houses. So she easily got pointed again to the house she needed. It wasn't quite as imposing as the other one. She knew enough to go around to the servants' entrance from all her job hunting.

But it just wasn't her day for luck, she was beginning to fear. Jeremy didn't live there anymore, had moved out just last week to his own residence over on Park Lane, near his cousin's house. As if Danny gave a flipping hoot for all the extra information the friendly cook's helper passed on as she tried her best to flirt with Danny.

More directions, more walking. Tarnation! She'd never walked so bleedin' far in her life. It was a nice street though, that she finally reached, at least she thought it was, because one side of it bordered a park in full summer bloom. But even getting there in good time, another hour was wasted before she found someone who pointed her to the right house. Since Malory had only just moved in, most of the passing servants on the street didn't know which house was his.

Now after all that running around, she

didn't expect to find Malory at home. At the rate her luck had been going, tomorrow would be more like it, or even the day after. Which meant another night or two sleeping in parks. But at least one was near to hand. And as long as she kept her expectations low, she could keep her anger to just simmering. But that young lord *was* in for a ripping earful, when—if—she ever clapped eyes on him again.

Chapter 11

He was home! Not only that, Danny was actually let in the front door!

A young girl around her own age did so. Slightly plump of frame, with lackluster brown hair, she barely glanced at Danny, said merely, "Wait here, and don't touch anything if you know what's good for you." Then she disappeared up some nearby stairs.

Danny stood there tensely, still amazed that she'd gotten in the door. She ran her hand through her mop of curls to make sure they were orderly. Lucy always saw to her hair when they were alone, keeping it trimmed short. Lucy wasn't very good with scissors though, so the chopping she did was usually uneven. But Danny wasn't vain about her hair, and besides, not much of it could be seen when she was wearing her hat, which she missed keenly at the moment.

She wasn't going to touch anything. She didn't want to even *look* at anything, she was suddenly so nervous. This was a bad idea. Hadn't she concluded, when she was still in his company, that Malory was too dangerous to deal with? Her anger had made her forget that, but she recalled it now in her nervousness.

She turned to leave, the *smart* thing to do. But she was arrested by the mirror on the wall next to the door. Not very big, it hung over a narrow table that held only a plate with two small cards on it. The sight of herself had stopped her—and fascinated her.

Rarely did she ever get to look in a mirror. The houses Dagger rented never had them. The rooms she robbed in that old inn didn't have them, at least none that she'd ever noticed in the dark. This one showed her from the waist up, and without the debonair, manly hat, it pointed out just how pretty she really was. Amazing that anyone could still mistake her for a boy. Amazing what a pair of pants did for first and lasting impressions. Well, the flatness of her chest probably helped some with those impressions.

That had been one of her old fears, that she'd develop really huge breasts like some women did and be unable to hide them. But she was lucky. Her breasts were a modest handful, medium-sized, and thanks to Lucy, easily contained.

The easy part was because one of Lucy's rare well-to-do customers had left behind a corset. They'd laughed a bit, that men would wear them, but then Lucy got the idea that it might come in handy for Danny in a few years, and it had indeed. Instead of wearing it around her waist where it was designed to go, she was thin enough that she could wear it around her chest. She just laced it up the front instead of the back, so she could manage it herself.

It was a stiff contraption for the most part, but of a fine quality, the material that encased it so soft, she barely noticed anymore that she was wearing it. Yet it flattened her bumps nicely. That, and the slightly slouched posture she affected, was all she'd needed to look as flat-chested as any male.

The sound of footsteps coming down the stairs reminded Danny that she had decided she didn't want to be here after all, and she'd dawdled too long, ogling herself in the mirror. She didn't turn around to see who it was though. She quickly reached for the door handle again.

"Leaving?" the girl said. "Good. He can't see you now anyway. He's entertaining a lady friend. I hadn't heard them come in, but then I don't come in this part of the house often. We're short of staff, or I wouldn't have answered the door at all."

Danny swung around. She hadn't needed to hear all that, figured the girl just needed someone to complain to. Her tone had been distinctly grumbling.

"You're the maid?"

"No, we don't have a maid yet, not even a footman to open the doors, much less a butler. I work in the kitchen. And you'd best run along. Come back later today. His lady friend should be gone by then."

Danny was about to take that advice when her belly growled. Roam around starving for several hours while Malory whiled away his time in bed with some lady? Not bleedin' likely.

"I'll wait here if it's all the same to you. It's important I see him as soon as possible."

"Suit yourself. You might as well go into the parlor then, it's through there. Though don't expect to find anything to sit on. This house hasn't been completely furnished yet."

The girl walked away toward the back of the house. Danny didn't move, was still amazed at the speech that had come out of her own mouth. It was the way she used to talk! The way Lucy had insisted she forget if she was going to survive with the pack. And she'd learned Lucy's way of speaking, learned it so well, she hadn't spoken any other way in all these years.

It no longer seemed natural to talk like that. She wasn't even sure why she had just done so. Being in a fine house? Listening to a servant complain—with good speech? But it had obviously put the girl at ease with her, enough to leave her alone in their house.

As for Malory, she'd give him exactly ten

minutes to get his lovemaking over with. She'd experienced too much hunger in the last couple of days to wait any longer than that on that high-handed young lord.

Chapter 12

⤳ ⤳

"I was pleasantly surprised to run into you this early in the morning," Mary Cull said as she lazed back in the overstuffed chair by Jeremy's bed. "So unexpected. I was sure all you young rakehells were in the habit of sleeping the day away, since you stay up to all hours of the night searching for your entertainments."

Jeremy smiled at the lady as he knelt by her feet, removing her shoes. Mary was a rather young widow, the youngest he'd ever seduced. Old Lord Cull had died on their wedding night. Too strenuous an enterprise for the old boy to undertake was the consensus.

Mary was no beauty, but she was rather pretty with her round blue eyes and dark blond hair. And she had taken to lovemaking so well, she entertained a number of gentlemen in her home now regularly. Jeremy wasn't one of her "regulars," though he'd been invited three times now and had enjoyed himself each time. Today when he had run into her, they had been closer to his house than hers, and it being so new, he had the ready excuse of wanting to show it off to her. Of course they hadn't stopped to see much of the house; they had come straight upstairs to his room instead.

"I had some business to attend to with my uncle Edward this morning," Jeremy replied.

"Something to do with your family?"

"No, actually, I've been managing several of the family's investments, including one of my own."

She was surprised. "You? Involved in business? You must be joking."

"Not a'tall. I've found that I rather enjoy the managerial aspect. Wouldn't dream of trying my hand at *finding* investments. We leave that to my uncle, who has a knack for only picking winners."

"You amaze me, Jeremy. You are quite frankly the most handsome man in the city, *and* you know it. Your family is extremely wealthy. Like many of your peers, you don't need to work. Why on earth would you?"

"Bite your tongue, m'dear. I don't see it as 'work,' but as something I enjoy doing. Big difference there, don't you think?"

"Not really." She grinned at him. "But whatever suits your fancy—"

It was the wrong thing to say to a rakehell like Jeremy Malory if conversation was on your mind. His expression turned immediately sensual, his hands started rising up her skirt. Mary's heart fluttered. But when she glanced over at his bed, which was their intended destination, she frowned.

"This room is entirely too—bachelorish. Is that even a word, darling? Never mind." A sigh. "I really wish you had come home with me. I'd feel much more comfortable in my own bedroom."

Her skirt rose up her thighs as his hands continued their path and pulled her hips closer to him so she was almost lying in the chair, her legs straddling his waist. "Pretend it's your bed."

She laughed. "It doesn't look anything

like mine and you know it. Where are the satin sheets, the fluffy pillows, the things that make you want to *stay* in bed? That's a bachelor bed if I've ever seen one."

"But you won't know how nice it is until you get in it, will you? I promise you, you'll find no complaints with my bed."

It was said so huskily, Mary couldn't resist clasping his head to draw it to her bosom. And that's when the pounding started on the door and someone shouted, "Get decent, mate, I'm coming in."

Danny bristled on the other side of the door. She'd given Malory his ten minutes, more like twenty, though she didn't have a watch to confirm it. She was afraid he was one of those "lover" types that Lucy praised, that he'd be taking all day with the wench he had in there with him, and she wasn't about to wait that long. So she'd finally marched upstairs and put her ear to each door she passed until she heard voices behind one.

It didn't take long, though, for the door to get yanked open after she'd pounded on it. Malory was standing there, impatience turning immediately to surprise when he recognized her.

"You?"

"Ye got that right," she snapped, her street slang coming back in her anger.

Her tone brought back his frown. "What the deuce are *you* doing here?"

"Get rid o' the wench, then we'll talk."

It looked as if he'd momentarily forgotten about the lady behind him, and she'd taken offense at the word *wench,* was stiffly adjusting her skirts as she looked about for her reticule. Finding it, she snatched it up and marched to the door.

Jeremy quickly told her, "You don't have to leave, Mary. This will only take a moment."

"That's quite all right, darling," she stopped long enough to say, and patted his cheek to assure him she wasn't that upset to have their tryst end so abruptly. "Come and visit me later today, where we *won't* be interrupted."

With one last glare in Danny's direction, the lady left. The nabob ran a hand through his black hair in frustration and turned back into the room, heading toward the mantel over the fireplace, and a bottle of brandy and two glasses kept there. Danny followed him in, then stopped cold when she saw the bed. Where was her sense? She should never have barged into his bedroom of all places.

"I'll wait for ye downstairs," she said uneasily, and turned back for the door.

"The devil you will." When that didn't stop her, he added, "Don't make me tackle you. I might like it."

That definitely stopped her. She could have been made of stone for all the movement she was capable of at that moment. Could she outrun him again?

As if he could read her thoughts, he added the warning, "I'd have you in my grasp before you could reach the hall. You may depend upon it. So you might as well close the door and tell me what you're doing here."

She wasn't about to close the door, but she did turn around to face him again. It was galling, though, to find him not even close to her; in fact, he was leaning against the wall next to the mantel, arms crossed, ankles crossed, in that damned relaxed posture he'd used at the inn. Deceptive. He'd been no more relaxed that night than he was now.

He lifted a black brow at her. "Well? I

doubt you've come to rob me. You wouldn't have knocked. Or would you? D'you think you're that good?"

She felt a blush coming, but with it, some of her anger returned, too, which bolstered her enough to say, "I've retired from robbing. Got kicked out, thanks to ye and yer bleedin' high-handedness."

"Did you? Well, now, that's too bad. Indeed it is."

Not a speck of sympathy was showing in his expression to support his remark. He even smiled! And that smile hit her in the gut, started her pulse leaping, had her eyes so mesmerized her thoughts scattered. How was she going to blister him with a piece of her mind if her mind wouldn't function in his presence?

"Should have let me escort you home to do the explaining," he added in a slightly scolding tone.

"Wouldn't 'ave 'elped," she grumbled. "'Is mind was made up to get rid o' me long ago. Ye just gave 'im the excuse 'e needed."

"He? Your boss?"

"Something like that."

"So you were expecting this ousting?"

"Not this soon, and not without a job

lined up nor a penny in me pocket," she snarled.

"What happened to the money you earned that night?" he asked with only mild curiosity.

Another blush. "I turned it over, 'oping it would change 'is mind. It didn't."

"So you're looking for a new band of thieves to join up with? Good God, you didn't think you'd find one here, did you?"

Her eyes snapped up to find his expression as appalled as his tone had been. She should say yes and give him several reasons why he fit the role of thief, at least in her opinion. After all, it hadn't been *her* idea to rob Lord Heddings. But she'd rather just get to the point.

"I told ye I've retired from thieving. Never liked it and 'ope to never 'ave to do it again. It's a real job I'm looking for."

There was avid curiosity in his expression now. "What sort of job?"

"I'm not particular," she replied with a shrug. "Anything decent that will let me afford a roof over me 'ead and food on the table. I've been sleeping under the stars since I got kicked out. And being that's yer bleedin' fault, I figure ye owe me some."

"I find it rather admirable that you'd prefer to sleep in some alley than do what you do so well."

A third blush, but this one had her snarling, "Don't. Ye were the preferred option, since ye *do* owe me, and I would've been 'ere sooner to collect if it didn't take me so bleedin' long to find ye."

He chuckled. "Since you are determined to blame me for your dire straits, I'm not going to send you off with your pockets full and never find out if that exonerates me in your mind. And, no, before you think to mention it, I wouldn't trust you to come visiting from time to time to let me know how you're getting on."

Her back stiffened. "I were going to ask for money, but the wench downstairs says yer short o' staff here. I've decided I'll be taking a job from ye instead."

"*You've* decided?" He burst out laughing. "What would you prefer, footman or maid?"

She glared at him. He wasn't taking her seriously. That was easy to tell. And then it dawned on her what he'd just said, bowled her over actually. He knew! He wouldn't have mentioned the maid's job otherwise.

There was no point in denying it. She asked baldly, "When did ye guess?"

He left his position, strolled casually toward her—more like a wolf stalking his prey, she thought nervously. He stopped in front of her, raised a hand, was going to touch her cheek. She leaned back, even though he stopped just short of touching her.

He was smiling as he said, "There was no guessing, m'dear. I've an eye for beautiful women, no matter what they're wearing. Though truth to tell, I do prefer them naked."

Nervously she took a step back from him. "Ye won't be seeing me naked."

His brow rose. "No? Well, that's a shame and leaves us nothing further to discuss, does it?"

"The devil it don't. We're discussing the job yer going to be giving me."

He sighed. "We just did, and you turned it down without giving it the least bit of thought."

"Getting naked?" She gasped indignantly. "Ye call that a job?"

He laughed. "More or less. I'm willing to take you on as my mistress. I find you quite amusing. Don't mind admitting it. So I'm sure we'd both enjoy it for a while."

Danny's cheeks bloomed red, not with embarrassment this time, but with anger. "Forget it, mate. It's a decent job I'm wanting, and ye *will* give me one, or I'll be paying a visit to Lord 'Eddings. I'm sure 'e'd give me a job in exchange for the information I can supply 'im with, o' where 'is jewels ran off to."

The nabob was flushing with some angry color himself now. "This is preposterous. You don't know the first thing about propriety or how a household like this is run. And you talk like a guttersnipe," he said contemptuously.

"I can speak properly," Danny replied slowly.

She *did* have to think it out though, since she wasn't quite familiar with it yet. And it wasn't going to be easy, especially when she was angry or even nervous, which seemed to be the perpetual case around Malory. After fifteen years, she was much more used to the slang.

She'd managed to surprise him, but only for a moment. "So you can mimic your betters? But you don't know how to behave like them, do you? How d'you expect to get on here without embarrassing yourself as well as this entire household?"

"By learning. Yes, you heard me right. I will learn the job as well as how to conduct myself."

"Why?" he demanded in exasperation. "Why go to all that trouble when you're much more suited to—"

She took a swing at him. He ducked, but he probably got the point, that she was sick and tired of being insulted today. Just to make sure, she snarled, "Because I'm getting m'self a respectable husband and then lots of children. Those are me goals, mate. A good job, a husband, then to get started on a big family, in *that* order. And ye'll be 'elping me with the first goal or there will be 'ell to pay."

"Bloody hell," he snarled back, then sneered. "What's it to be then? Footman I suppose?"

The nabob was trying to insult her again and doing a good job of it. Or was he just stressing how difficult the task that she'd set for herself was going to be? Could she really fit into this handsome aristocrat's world, even if only as his maid?

Chapter 13

~

Jeremy was so furious he was having a hard time containing it. It was so unusual for him to be angry at a woman, but blackmail! Bloody hell, that would get a saint furious.

It boggled his mind that she had resorted to that, but he should have expected it. She was smart, after all. He wouldn't have expected that either from someone who came from the slums, but she'd proved it the night of the robbery, when she'd extricated them from a sticky, even somewhat dangerous, situation.

Remembering that he did owe her for that took a small chunk out of his anger, though only a small chunk.

This was absurd. He knew how to handle women. Where was his bloody finesse with this one? He ought to be looking on the bright side. Now that she was going to be living under his roof, he didn't doubt he'd get her into his bed eventually.

He was nothing if not confident where women were concerned. And this one was rather unique, adorable in her manly togs, amazing in her height, incredibly lovely with those big violet eyes, and not the least bit susceptible to his charms—yet.

She was attracted to him, though. He bloody well knew when a woman was attracted to him. But she gave every indication that it didn't matter. "Don't touch me, don't even get near me" was the subtle message she exuded. Was that partly responsible for his anger? Another first for him. No, he simply didn't like being blackmailed, and by a wench he'd prefer to be making love to. Bloody hell.

He sighed. The sound brought her out of her pensive state and had her informing him, "I'll take the maid's job."

"Too bad. It would have been amusing watching you bungle your way through as a footman."

She glared at him. He raised a brow. "You don't think so? And by the by, you don't scowl at your employer. You 'Yes, sir,' 'No, sir,' 'Very good, sir,' and with a smile or no expression a'tall. When you're my mistress, you can scowl at me all you like."

She started to snap something at him but turned her back on him instead. A stiff posture, full of indignation and ire.

"Counting to ten, are we?" Jeremy said dryly.

She turned back around, gave him a tight little smile, and gritted out, "Yes, sir."

He burst out laughing. He simply couldn't help it. And it removed the rest of his anger for the moment. It was going to prove amusing, after all, her attempt to "better" herself. He supposed he could tolerate being blackmailed as long as the blackmailer was going to end up as his mistress.

Still grinning, he said, "Let's get you settled then. Shall we start with your name?"

She unbent enough to answer, "It's Danny."

"No, I meant your *real* name. If you were sincere about turning over a new leaf, as it were, then you'll want to start with a clean slate."

"That *is* my real name," she replied with a stony stare.

"Truly? It's not short for Danielle or—?"

"It's the only name I 'ave any memory of. If I were given another at birth, it ain't one I'll ever be knowing."

Jeremy found himself slightly embarrassed. Of course an orphan might not know her real name, and this one apparently didn't even have a surname. Deuced odd, to go through life without a last name.

He asked hesitantly, "Would you mind if I called you Danielle?"

"I would mind. I ain't no Danielle. My friends call me Danny. Since you ain't one o' them, *you* can call me Dan."

She was delightfully amusing in her stubborn adherence to being standoffish. Wouldn't give an inch, he was guessing. Habit, he was sure. But he supposed she would have had to be defensive, growing up where she did.

"But we *are* going to be friends, dear girl, so I suppose I will get used to Danny. Actually, it's a nice name, has a nice ring to it."

"Get over it, mate," she grouched, then at his raised brow, added, "Sir."

He grinned. "Very well. On to the next

subject then. Have you any dresses in that sack you're guarding with your life?"

She shook her head. "Just my pet and one change o' clothes."

"More pants, I presume?"

"Course more pants," she said tersely. "I've been a boy for fifteen years."

"Good God, really?"

She was blushing now, profusely.

"Well, you do realize that you picked the job that will require feminine togs? My father might thumb his nose at convention, but I'm not my father. I don't expect uniforms, though," he assured her. "No indeed. This is a bachelor residence, and as such, I expect my servants to enjoy working here. No worrying about collars not being stiff enough or wrinkled skirts or the like."

"I was expecting to wear a dress," she said stiffly. "Did I mention I 'ave no money?"

"You did, didn't you?" He grinned again. "Not to worry. My housekeeper will be able to help in that regard and to get you otherwise situated and instructed. Come along. Much as I enjoy your company, I suppose I should turn you over to her now."

She followed him, but stopped when they reached the bottom of the stairs, told him,

"You'll let her know you hired me? That she can't fire me? The last time I tried to be a maid, soon as I met the 'ousekeeper I got fired. She didn't like the way I talked, or looked."

"I can imagine," he said dryly.

"No, ye can't," she snorted. "Ye've never tried to be a maid b'fore."

"Well, no, I don't suppose I have."

"Don't be laughing at me again, Malory. I won't tolerate it. And that was in a lower-class 'ousehold, not one up 'ere on the bleedin' rich end o' town."

He wiped the grin off his face. "So you *have* tried honest work before?"

"Never got a chance to. Either got fired quick or couldn't get 'ired. Can't read, ye know, which don't give me many choices for jobs."

"Would you like to be able to read?" he asked curiously.

"Sure I would, but I'm too bleedin' old for any schooling now."

"But you're never too old to learn. Regardless, you needn't worry about anyone firing you here. You didn't exactly get hired under normal means, now did you?"

He was surprised that she actually

looked embarrassed by that reminder. She wasn't going to be easy to deal with. Stepping on eggshells around her came to mind. It was that defensive stance of hers, ingrained, that so easily took offense. And she didn't have a deferential bone in her body. Cocky guttersnipe was what she was. But that was to be expected from someone who'd never had to deal with their betters before—except to rob them.

"Come along," Jeremy suggested. "Mrs. Robertson is probably in the back of the house somewhere. You'll like her. Motherly sort. She—"

He got no further before the front door opened and his cousin Regina barged in. Bad habit, Reggie had, of not knocking. Of course, she did live just down the street, and she did know that he'd yet to find a butler.

She was startled by his presence there in the hall. "Goodness, didn't expect to find you this quickly. Were you on your way out?"

"No, just getting my new servant situated."

She looked at Danny then and tossed her

a brief smile, but to Jeremy she said, "Well, that settles that."

He raised a brow at her. "Dare I ask what?"

Reggie sighed. "I came to offer you one of my footmen. Billings returned from his leave of absence. Have to have him back, of course. He's like family. But that new man who took his place has worked out splendidly, too. But I don't *need* three footmen, only two, so I was hoping you could take the new man. But you don't need two, one will do you fine. And—"

"Hell's bells, Reggie, don't write a book about it. Spit it out."

She gave him a reproachful look. "I was getting to the point. This fellow here is too young to be a butler, so it's obvious you've just hired your footman. Which is perfectly—"

Danny interrupted her this time. "I've taken the maid's job, ma'am. Decided footman would be too easy."

Reggie blinked at her, then rolled her eyes at Jeremy. "Very funny. I see why you've hired him. He'll amuse you endlessly with drollery like that. Now I must run. I've hundreds of things to do today. And don't forget you're coming to dinner."

"I am?"

"You *did* forget!" she said, appalled.

He grinned at her. "No, I'd say you did. This is the first I'm hearing about it."

"But Nicholas was going to stop by to— famous, I suppose *he* forgot. Well, never mind. Now you do know, so don't be late. Uncle Tony and Ros will be there. And Drew. Derek and Kelsey, too. I've even invited Percy."

"Drew is back in town?" Jeremy asked in surprise.

She nodded. "His ship docked this morning. And since your father and George are visiting Uncle Jason at Haverston, I imagine Drew will be at loose ends. Though I also expect George will be rushing back to London as soon as she knows her brother is here."

"So you thought to entertain him?"

"Of course. Your father might still hate his brothers-in-law, but the rest of us like them well enough."

Jeremy chuckled. "You know he doesn't hate them. He just—well, doesn't *like* them. Principle, don't you know."

"Yes, just like he doesn't *like* my husband," she grouched.

Jeremy laughed. "Well, old Nick did try to get him hanged."

"So did George's brothers, but who's counting," she huffed on her way out the door.

Jeremy almost felt out of breath after that brief visit. But Reggie was like that, a whirlwind of chatter. He glanced back at Danny to find her looking a bit dazed as well. He imagined all that rapid chatter hadn't made a bit of sense to her.

Considering the conclusion Reggie had drawn, Percy as well, for that matter, Jeremy asked her curiously, "Am I the only one who sees the woman in you?"

Her lips twisted in disgust. "Aye, you are. It's the pants. They usually serve me well, but didn't fool you none."

He took a step closer, but he only had to glance down a few inches to meet her eyes. "No, I'd guess it's the height. You're taller than many men. That's very rare."

She broadened the space between them again before she spat out, "Like I can bleedin' well 'elp that."

"Don't get defensive. It's not a bad thing

to be tall. Though come to think of it, Mrs. Robertson will probably have trouble finding you any ready-made clothes. Having you making the beds wearing your—"

He stopped that thought abruptly. Thinking of her near a bed quite undid him.

"Was that yer sister?"

A safe subject, thank God. "No, m'cousin Regina Eden. She and her husband, Nicholas, have a town house just down the street from here, though they are more often at Silverley, his country estate."

"It were easy to tell ye were related. Yer whole family like that?"

"No, most of the Malorys are big and blond like m'father. There's just a few of us who took after my great-grandmother's side, m'self included. Why, I look so much like my uncle Tony that most people who meet us think he's m'father."

"Ye look like ye find that amusing."

"But it is."

"I'll bet yer father don't think so."

He chuckled. "Course not, but then that's why it's amusing."

Chapter 14

~~~~~

Dinner was relaxed that night. It usually was
when it was just family and close friends.
Anthony had to get in a few digs at Reggie's
husband, Nicholas, of course. It was the
one thing that James and Anthony Malory
were in complete agreement on, that
Nicholas Eden, former rakehell, just wasn't
good enough for their favorite niece and
never would be. That the brothers had both
been notorious rakes themselves before
they married didn't make a bit of difference.

Reggie was special to them. All four
Malory brothers had had a hand in raising
her after their only sister died. And despite
that Reggie so obviously adored her hus-

band, James and Anthony weren't going to let Nick forget that he'd be dealing with them if he ever hurt her.

But Anthony's digs tonight were more good-natured than derogatory, and after his wife, Roslynn, kicked him under the table as a gentle reminder to behave, he turned his attention to Jeremy instead.

"So how's the new residence shaping up? All staffed and furnished and ready for a grand party?"

Jeremy coughed. "Half-staffed, barely furnished, and as for parties, perhaps by the winter season."

"You have your own place now, Jeremy?" Drew Anderson, his stepmother's brother, asked in surprise.

Jeremy grinned. "Just. Uncle Tony and m'father decided it was time for me to experience true bachelorhood."

Anthony coughed now. "Bloody hell, makes it sound like we bought him a license to debauch."

"I believe he does that very well without a license," Reggie replied with an impish grin.

"Don't encourage him, puss," Anthony scolded. "Charming scamp that he is, the idea was to introduce him to property management in running his own household, to become his own man, as it were."

"Well, he didn't need help with that," Reggie disagreed. "He's been acting the man since he was twelve."

"I didn't mean *that* sort of manly endeavors."

"Och, Tony, you're falling for her teasing," Roslynn chimed in with her soft, Scottish brogue. "We know your intentions were good ones." Then she teased a bit herself, "Though you do need to leave management out of your excuse, since he's been helping your brother manage our investments for quite a few years now."

Jeremy came to Anthony's rescue this time. "Inspecting rentals, seeing to repairs, and keeping agents honest is quite different from dealing with a household staff."

"And good servants are so hard to come by, especially those you want to keep," Reggie added. "By the by, Jeremy, how's your new footman working out?"

"Actually, I'll take your man," Jeremy replied. "Send him round tomorrow."

"Splendid. But I hope you didn't let that handsome young lad go just because I offered—"

"No, no, nothing like that."

Jeremy didn't bother correcting his cousin about the sex of his new servant. He'd installed Danny as an upstairs maid, so there wasn't much chance of Reggie coming across her again. And truthfully, he didn't want to talk about her or explain why he'd hired an ex-thief—well, *hopefully* an ex-thief—to work for him.

Thankfully, the conversation turned in other directions after that, because having been reminded of her, Jeremy became quite distracted with thoughts of his new maid. It was a novel experience, having to deal with two such opposing emotions where she was concerned, anger and desire. The anger he could control, the desire he wasn't so sure of. The anger should have canceled the desire. But it didn't, not even a little.

Being distracted around his family had its disadvantages as Jeremy found when he realized Drew Anderson was coming home with him. He wasn't sure how he got elected to put Drew up until his father and his step-mother returned to town, though it was probably because the whole family knew he and Drew had hit it off well, and now that Jeremy had his own bachelor residence, they figured Jeremy would enjoy the company. Which was true enough.

He liked Drew Anderson. They got along famously, enjoyed the same things, which was women and more women. They'd had some rousing good times together since the Anderson brothers had started coming to London, after their only sister, Georgina, had married into the Malory family. But now was *not* a good time to have a houseguest, and in particular, one as handsome as Drew was.

George had said of her brother once that Drew had a sweetheart in every port he'd ever sailed into, and that was probably true. The second youngest of the five Anderson brothers, Drew was the most devil-may-care of the lot, and at thirty-four, still a fun-loving rogue with no intention of ever limiting himself to just one woman, so matrimony was absolutely out of the question for him. Even seeing how nicely his older brother Warren, confirmed bachelor that he'd been, had settled into marriage with Amy Malory and had never been happier wouldn't change Drew's mind. Like Jeremy, he was of the firm opinion that variety was the spice of life, and the more of it the better.

Above average in height at six feet four inches, in prime shape from captaining his own ship for so many years, Drew was definitely a man the ladies cast their eyes toward. With a golden brown mane of curls and eyes so dark it was impossible to guess if they were anything other than black, he was an extremely handsome man—which was why Jeremy *wouldn't* have invited him to move in, no matter how temporarily, at least not now when a female was under Jeremy's roof that he had designs on himself.

Which had Jeremy saying as they walked the short distance to his house, "Are you sure you wouldn't prefer a hotel for a few days, Drew? My house is barely furnished yet. Beds for every bedroom are about all I've bought so far. The other rooms are still empty. I've even been eating in the kitchen m'self."

That room at least was filling up nicely, now that he had a cook and had given her carte blanche to get whatever she needed. And his own bedroom was fully furnished, thanks to George's insisting he take every-thing from his old room.

Drew chuckled. "A bed is all I need."

"It's too early for bed," Percy added. His house was just a few blocks away, so he was walking with them. "Aren't we going—"

"Not tonight, Percy," Drew cut in. "It's been a busy day for me. Docking is always a headache here with so many ships waiting in line for it. And I also spent a good portion of the day at the Skylark Shipping office and have to return there in the morning."

"You pulling my leg, old man? Thought all you sailors were eager for some female company after being at sea."

Drew grinned. "Absolutely, but I'd prefer to seek that sort of entertainment when I'm fresh and thinking of beds as other than ob-jects to sleep in. Tomorrow night?"

"Certainly. Looking forward to it. Jeremy? Are you up for—"

Jeremy decided to interrupt before he was tempted. "I'm due for a good night's sleep m'self, Percy. Still haven't caught up from coming home at dawn the other night."

Mention of their trip out of London to Heddings's house had Percy agreeing.

"Quite right. Now you mention it, bed does sound rather appealing, don't it?"

Jeremy didn't go directly to bed himself. As soon as he showed Drew to his room, he went to his own and yanked on the bellpull connected to the servants' quarters. He hoped his housekeeper had explained to Danny what the bell's ringing in her room signified. He doubted she'd be asleep this early, then again, she could be.

Actually, it might work to his advantage if she was and the bell woke her. Danny, soft and drowsy, had him thinking of things other than showing her what a lazy employer could be like. Waiting on him hand and foot had been the plan, but not if she was susceptible to his charms instead. He'd have to play it by ear, retribution or some immense pleasure.

She must have been awake because she arrived soon enough to indicate she hadn't needed to dress first. He'd been undressing down to just his shirt and pants when she rapped loudly on the door. He opened it quickly and yanked her inside before Drew investigated the noise.

" 'Ere now," she objected, and jerked her arm out of his grasp.

"Keep it down. I have company across the hall."

She raised a brow, indicating she wasn't quite buying that excuse. "Wot are ye wanting then?"

Apparently having secured a job, a roof over her head, and food just down the hall hadn't improved her disposition any. But she appeared to regret her choice of words immediately because she broadened the distance between them.

Jeremy knew well that to say what he really wanted would be a serious mistake at this point. She wasn't ready to hear it. His expression said it though, something he couldn't seem to control when he was near her.

But to put her at ease for the moment, he quickly replied, "I need a new bottle of brandy. You'll find a stock of them in the pantry."

"Ye called me up 'ere for that?" she asked incredulously. "When ye could've fetched it yerself?"

His eyes widened innocently. "Why ever would I do that, when I have a maid now?"

She started to snarl something, but snapped her mouth shut and left to get the brandy. Jeremy had a hard time keeping the grin off his face, but managed it before she returned a few minutes later, brandy in hand.

He'd made himself comfortable in one of the chairs by the fireplace. She approached and shoved the bottle toward him. He merely nodded toward the mantel where the empty bottle sat.

"Pour me a glass while you're there," Jeremy said, then continued derisively, "And I hope I don't need to add, bring it to me?"

She made a sound of impatience rather loudly and dumped nearly a third of the bottle in the snifter, much more than was needed. It was a large snifter. She obviously didn't know any better.

He sighed, showing some impatience of his own with her ineptitude, and instructed, "No more'n an inch next time."

Her back stiffened as she turned with the snifter in hand. It was a wonder the brandy didn't slosh all over him, she thrust it at him so forcefully. Too bad. He would have had her clean it up. The thought of her leaning close and dabbing a cloth over his chest was quite delectable.

"You might as well turn the bed down

while you're here," he suggested. "Mrs. Robertson did explain your duties to you, didn't she?"

"Not yet, though I doubt bed turning is one o' them."

"Of course it is, and I'll expect to find it done each evening. You'll catch on soon enough, I'm sure. By the by, how did it go with Mrs. Robertson after I left you in her care? Any trouble? You did seem to have some fears in that regard."

She seemed to relax slightly with the new subject and, with a shrug, headed toward the bed to yank down the covers. "She's a nice old bird, she is. She had me repeating m'self a few times until she got used to my speech, but she didn't seem to mind it."

"Danny, Danny," he sighed. "Look at the mess you've made. Turning down the bed is done neatly, not as if you're changing the bedding. I expect to slip under the sheets, not fight to find them."

She blushed over the scolding, but she didn't balk at trying again. That surprised him. She'd blackmailed her way into the job, so she didn't really have to take it seriously. Apparently she was going to though, which opened up numerous possibilities that he would find enjoyable, but she probably wouldn't.

"Don't forget to fluff the pillow, too," he ordered.

She stiffened again just before she slammed a fist down in the center of his pillow. Jeremy had to bite back a laugh. Retribution was *so* sweet.

"My boots now."

She glanced at him with a nervous frown and slipped back into her slang. "Wot about them?"

"Come help me get them off."

She didn't move, sounded quite nervous again when she asked, "Don't ye 'ave a man for that? Wot's the position called?"

"A valet. And, no, don't need one. I have you—to see to such minor details."

She closed her eyes. He thought he even heard a groan, though he wasn't quite sure. Was it the pause? Was he actually getting to her, despite her disagreeable mood? His own blood was warming. Seeing her next to his bed made him want to see her *in* it.

"Come here," he said, his voice turning sensual.

Her eyes opened wide, but she still

wouldn't approach him. He supposed he'd made her too nervous.

To alleviate her fears for the moment, he glanced at his feet and reminded her, "My boots? I'd like to get to bed *some*time tonight and without them." She *still* didn't move, so he said tersely, "Need I remind you that you wanted, *insisted,* on having this job?"

That got her moving. She fairly flew across the room to grab hold of one of his boots and started yanking on it. It wasn't coming off that way, of course. She tugged and yanked some more. It still wasn't budging from his foot.

He finally said dryly, "I suppose you don't know how to do this either?"

"I do," she said in her own defense. "I was just hoping you nabobs wore boots that came off easy."

"Well, no need to be squeamish about straddling my leg, dear girl. Just get to it."

She did, presenting him with her back and waiting for him to plant his other foot on her backside for the shove needed to get the boot off. But this time Jeremy was frozen. She'd come upstairs without her coat, wearing only her shirt, pants, and socks, so nothing was covering the shapely derriere that was suddenly in front of him and quite within his reach. It was probably one of the harder things he ever did, not taking advantage of that and instead putting his foot to her derriere instead of his hands.

Annoyed that she was making him want her again, he shoved a bit harder than necessary. She stumbled several feet away as the boot came off, but she didn't seem to think anything was amiss in that and she came right back to tackle the other one.

In an attempt to cool his ardor, he remarked casually, "I notice you're still wearing your thiefly garb. Couldn't Mrs. Robertson find you any suitable clothes?"

She glanced around to give him a cross look for the term he'd used, but there was no inflection in her tone. "She did. She took me to her sister's seamstress. Said it would be a waste of time to look for that new ready-made clothing to fit me. Didn't want my ankles showing, she said."

"Well, that's too bad. Showing ankles sounds interesting."

She snorted at his grin. "The first dress will be sent over sometime tomorrow, the other one by the next day."

"Only two? That won't do a'tall."

"I don't need more'n that and told her so."

"Of course you do. Can't have you washing your clothes every day. Pure waste of time, that. I'll let her know to increase the order. And how d'you like the room? Finding it satisfactory?"

The second boot came off, in time for her to turn and lift a brow at him. "And you'd be changing it if it weren't?"

He stood up and leaned close to her to say in a conspiratorial whisper, "My room is available for sharing if you'd prefer. I know *I* would."

Her back stiffened. "Not bleedin' likely, mate."

He straightened and sighed at her tone. "You need to stop being so defensive, Danny, over such harmless flirtation. Really, I don't bite, you know—well, only if it gives pleasure, which it usually does. Like nibbling on your neck." His tone got husky. "And your ear—and this might be a good time for you to leave."

Bloody hell, she did.

Chapter 15

Danny hurried down the hall to the kitchen. She'd overslept and had had to be wakened, which wasn't a good way to start her new job. And it was such a nice job. She still couldn't believe she'd be living and working in such a fine house. Even the hall in the servants' wing was carpeted! But even needing a maid, Malory wouldn't have hired her if she hadn't blackmailed him. She felt bad about that. She'd make up for it though, vowed to be a better maid than he could have found by normal means.

Thinking about him brought on a twinge of excitement that she quickly tamped down. It wasn't going to be easy ignoring

her attraction to him, but she would, because a man like that would be her downfall
otherwise.

Danny reached the kitchen. The cook
was there, Mrs. Appleton. She was a jovial
middle-aged woman, short but hefty. She
liked to sing while she was cooking and got
very loud at it, too.

She'd laughed yesterday when Mrs.
Robertson had introduced Danny as the
new upstairs maid, laughed for nearly ten
minutes, off and on, every time she glanced
at Danny. It was the clothes, at least Danny
hoped that was all that was causing the
woman such amusement. She'd probably
never seen a woman wearing pants before.

Her helper, Claire, was in the kitchen now,
too, the grumpy girl who'd let Danny in the
house yesterday. She was quick to point out
when Danny walked into the room, "You're
late."

"I know. I'm sorry."

"The food is cold now."

It was said as if that were Danny's fault.
Claire was definitely a glum sort. Dumpy of
shape, shoulders stooped, she seemed to
wear a perpetual frown—at least Danny had
yet to see any other expression cross her

face. Or maybe it just seemed so in contrast to the happy cook.

"I 'aven't time to eat it now," Danny explained with a wistful sigh as she stared at the wide assortment of dishes that had been prepared. She was hungry.

"Why not?" Claire demanded. "Where else are you going then? It's the food you're late for."

"Oh. But ain't I late for work?"

Claire snorted. "I work early, you don't. You have to wait until the master vacates his room so you can clean it. There's to be no noise upstairs that might wake him sooner than he planned to wake."

"But wot if 'e sleeps all day?"

"Then you'll be working at night, won't you. And work on your speech as well," Claire added in disgust. "Cor, you sound like a street urchin. Where do you come from?"

Danny didn't answer, was too busy blushing. She could have spoken better just then, but it would have required concentration, and it was hard to do that when she was nervous. And besides, just because she'd recalled that she did used to talk much differently didn't mean it was all going to come back naturally. The way she talked now was natural to her, had been ingrained in her for fifteen years.

The cook tsked at her helper and said to Danny, "Don't worry about it, dear. Mrs. Robertson will train you well in what needs doing and when. Just follow her instruction and you'll do fine."

The lady in question came through the doorway then, spotted Danny, and said, "There you are. All done eating? Follow me."

So she wasn't to be scolded? She had only been late for breakfast? Danny's relief was immense, but so was her hunger.

With a last glance at the wide assortment of food spread out on the table, she quickly swiped up two rolls and stuffed them in her pockets, then hurried after the house-keeper. The cook had seen what she'd done and her laughter followed Danny out the door.

Mrs. Robertson took her upstairs and into one of the unoccupied rooms to explain in exact detail what her duties would be. Even though the room was pretty much empty at the moment, it wouldn't stay that way, and so Mrs. Robertson explained what

Danny would have to do when it was fully furnished.

There was never to be a speck of dust in the house. That was Mrs. Robertson's first rule. Danny would have dirty laundry to fetch and return cleaned. Floors, windows, just about everything upstairs, fell to her to keep spotless.

The upstairs would be her domain, Mrs. Robertson had stressed. Danny rather liked the sound of that. But in the meantime, at least until the downstairs maid was hired, she'd have to help in keeping those rooms clean as well. Claire took care of the kitchen. And at the moment, most of the other downstairs rooms were empty, so keeping them dust-free wouldn't take up much time at all.

"You will wait until Master Jeremy leaves his room before you enter it to clean it, unless he needs something, in which case he'll likely call for you. If he has guests, again, wait until they go downstairs before you enter their rooms. Do not, in any case, disturb any occupants upstairs if they are sleeping. Currently a member of his family is staying with us, so two of these rooms are occupied. You do not need to do your chores in any exact order, just make sure they are all done by the end of the day."

Mrs. Robertson had a *lot* more to say, and Danny managed to retain it all, but it still didn't seem like enough work to keep her busy all day. She pointed that out.

"Wot if I finish up early each day?"

"You will need to keep yourself available if Master Jeremy is at home, in case he requires something. Otherwise you will be free to do as you like, rest, read, go out, visit friends, whatever suits you. You will have Sundays off after you make the beds and make sure everything on your floor is in its proper place. You might also wish to spend some time each day working on your diction."

"Eh?"

"Exactly. The proper response would have been, 'What is wrong with my diction?' or 'What is diction?' or even 'I like my diction the way it is, thank you.' "

"But—that's wot I said, I just tossed it all into one word."

The woman actually laughed. "Danny, lass, this is nothing personal. Frankly, I find your speech quaint. It reminds me of my younger years. I didn't always work for the

nobility, you know. But you'll find that improving your speech can only be a benefit
to you. Unless you like being embarrassed
when you have difficulty conveying your
thoughts?"

Danny was jarred by what the housekeeper had called her, *Danny lass.* It
brought back a vague memory of being surrounded by a room full of toys, someone
holding her hand and telling her, "Make a
choice, Danny lass. Your father said you
could have any toy that strikes your fancy
for this birthday."

Had her life really been that nice before
someone had ripped her from it by trying to
hurt her? Or was that just some dream
she'd once had? Her head starting aching,
trying to remember more, but nothing else
would come to her to prove that it had
been a dream—or a real memory. And
Mrs. Robertson was waiting on an answer
from her.

"I—I might know 'ow to talk better," she
said hesitantly. "It's just been so long, I've
mostly forgotten. My friend Lucy, she
wanted me to talk as I do now. She worked
'ard at it, making sure I did."

"How odd. But at any rate, I don't mind

correcting you, if you won't mind being corrected. Master Jeremy also mentioned that he would try to assist you in that regard."

" 'E did?"

"Yes, he's apparently taken quite an interest in you. This is an upper-crust household. If you were employed by tradespeople, it wouldn't matter that much. But servants of the nobility can be quite as snobbish as their employers, and you do want to fit in, don't you?"

Danny thought about that for a moment, then said, "I don't think I'm wanting to be a snob, no."

Mrs. Robertson burst out laughing again. "You're priceless, child. I haven't laughed this much in years. I wasn't suggesting turning *you* into a snob. Good heavens, no. I don't believe I'm one myself, and Master Jeremy certainly isn't. But, you will meet other servants on this street, I'm sure. And we have yet to finish staffing this house. My point was, you are likely to come across such people, and while you might look down your nose at them, just as they will at you, you don't want to stand out for ridicule if you don't have to, do you? No, of course not. No one enjoys ridicule."

Danny hadn't been expecting this type of instruction. But since it did fit right in with her desire to improve herself, she was quite grateful that the woman suggested it and said so.

"Thank ye, ma'am. I'd be beholden for the teaching."

"Splendid. Shall we devote a half hour each evening to it for a while? We'll get those *h*'s and *u*'s back into your speech in no time!"

Danny grinned. "There's fifteen years to correct. It may take more'n a while."

"Possibly. But, you aren't going anywhere, are you? So we've plenty of time to work on it."

Not going anywhere? Some of the weight just lifted from Danny's shoulders. Now if Malory would just get off them as well . . .

Chapter 16

~

"Hullo! Where is everyone?"

Danny heard the women's loud call and poked her head around the upstairs corner to glance down the stairs where the noise was coming from. Three women were in the entry hall, decked out in high fashion, beauties all of them. She recognized one—Malory's cousin Regina Eden, who'd barged in on him yesterday. Which explained how they got in when no one was around to let them in.

Danny had no intention of answering the lady's question. Her duties were fresh in her mind and they didn't include answering doors or dealing with guests. She was aware that there was no butler or footman yet to do that, but Claire was around some-where and had managed to answer the door just fine yesterday.

Danny quickly leaned back out of sight again, but not soon enough. "You there! Come here, please."

Danny didn't move. Just because it seemed as if the woman was talking to her didn't mean she was. Claire could have ap-peared. *Someone* should have by now, with all that yelling going on.

"I know you heard me, so don't run off. Come down here, please."

Danny stuck her head around the corner again. Sure enough, Regina Eden was look-ing directly at her and beckoned her forward with a wave of her hand. There was no help for it. Rudeness wasn't part of her job.

She bounded down the stairs in her usual get-to-it-quickly pace, then nearly landed on her arse on the marble floor as she slid a few feet. Bleedin' slippery floor. Her blush didn't last long though as she was boggled by the three women, now that she was closer and could see them better. They weren't just beauties, they were raving beauties.

One of them had flaming red-gold hair and gray-green eyes. She was petite, a good five inches shorter than Danny, and looked to be in her early thirties. The other new one was younger, perhaps twenty-five, with black hair that looked naturally curly and soft gray eyes. She was a bit shorter, too, making Danny feel positively huge standing next to the three of them.

Malory was related to Regina Eden, but these other two women? He'd said the rest of his family were blond, so they weren't family of his. And if he had beauties like these visiting him, maybe he wasn't out to get her in his bed after all. Maybe he had only been toying with her. She was nothing compared to these elegant ladies, and they were definitely ladies. Nobility was written all over them.

"How are you liking your new job, lad?" Regina was asking her. "My footman will be over later today. I'm sure you'll get along with him splendidly. He's such a nice fellow. But in the meantime, it looks like you're the only one available to fetch Jeremy for us. I imagine he and Drew made a late night of it after they left my house last night, not that

Jeremy is known to be an early riser in any case. He's still sleeping?"

The hour was still early, barely ten in the morning. Danny could truthfully say he was still in his room, since she'd been keeping a close eye and ear on his door, to make sure she'd be behind some other door when he left his room. Running into Malory in the hall upstairs was *not* going to be part of her daily routine.

"I 'aven't seen 'im today, so, aye, 'e's probably still abed."

That should have been their clue to leave, but, no, Regina said, "Well, run along and wake him. And do tell him to hurry. We have a great many shops and warehouses to stop in today if we're going to get this house furnished."

"Yer taking 'im shopping?"

"Indeed. Waiting for him to muddle through the process on his own will never get this place up to scratch. He has entertaining to do, but he can't do it if there isn't a sofa to sit on."

Danny wondered if Jeremy knew he had entertaining to do. She was smirking as she headed back upstairs. His cousin seemed so pushy, Danny wouldn't be surprised if the entertaining was her idea, not his.

She stopped short in the hall before his door, realizing suddenly that *she* was supposed to wake him. She'd been hoping she wouldn't have to see him today. She'd been hoping to get used to her job before she had to deal with him again. After what he'd said last night . . . she caught her breath, thinking of it, and remembering the way he'd looked at her.

She went ahead and pounded on his door, shouting, "Get up, mate! Ye 'ave company."

Then she took off down the hall to hide in an empty bedroom. Not soon enough though. The door across from his opened and a blond giant of a man stepped out to growl at her, "If that's the way you wake people, make sure you send a maid to my door, or you'll end up being tossed down the stairs in short order."

Danny could have cried at that point. Just when she'd begun to feel comfortable, she had to blow it again and get a member of his family annoyed enough to send her tossing. She turned about, ready to apologize, and forgot what she was going to say.

Big, blond, and gorgeous. And he was as surprised as she was, now that he got a look at her.

"I'll be damned, if you aren't a woman, I'll eat my ship plank by plank."

"A gut full o' splinters don't sound too appetizing," she said by way of acknowledgment.

He grinned. "I take it you *are* the maid? Or rather, let me rephrase that. I *hope* you are the maid and not one of Jeremy's ladyloves."

"I ain't no one's ladylove."

"Then it's my lucky day."

"Eh?"

"Means you're available, sweetheart."

Danny snorted. "Don't mean any such thing."

"Don't devastate me this early in the morning. I may not recover."

Since he didn't look the least bit devastated, looked nothing but confident and full of mirth, she replied simply, "Get over it, mate."

Danny turned to leave again. She wasn't used to men flirting with her. Women, yes, all the time and everywhere she went. She was very used to that, but then they saw a handsome lad when they looked at her. And she'd developed trite phrases that didn't insult, but let them know she wasn't interested. But men . . . and how the devil had another one seen through her disguise so easily?

Bleedin' hell, she'd been right to worry that she couldn't go on much longer playing the man. Twice in a matter of days she'd been figured out.

She'd gotten no more than a step away when she heard Jeremy say in a less-than-friendly tone, "My servants are off-limits, Drew—just so you know."

"So it's like that, is it? I'm not surprised. A face like that is worth giving up the sea for."

"Which you have no intention of ever doing."

A chuckle. "Not a chance."

One of the doors closed, Danny couldn't tell which. She took the chance of glancing back, hoping it was Jeremy who'd gone back in his room. It wasn't. He stood there looking at her, and he wasn't completely dressed. He only had his pants on.

She couldn't move, she even forgot to breathe for a moment, she was so mesmerized. He was more muscular than his clothes indicated, and rock-firm. Even his tan extended down his chest, implying it was his natural skin tone. And his hair was mussed from sleeping, giving him an irresistible sexy appeal that was so strong, she was almost drawn forward like a moth to a flame . . .

Oh, God! Looking for a door, any door, to dash behind, she found the closest, opened it, and stepped inside. Bleedin' hell, she was in the closet where the clean bedding was kept, along with a supply of cleaning materials! It was dark with barely any room between the door and the shelves behind her. But she wasn't going back out there to see that man half-naked again.

He rapped on the door. She groaned inwardly. "Go away. Ye ain't dressed."

"You could get used to it."

"Not bleedin' likely."

She heard his chuckle. She gritted her teeth.

"Was there a reason you nearly broke my door down waking me?"

She blushed. Hearing it put that way, she probably shouldn't have been so loud about it. Having to wake him at all, well, she supposed that task was going to fall to her occasionally and be the hardest part of her new job. She'd have to find a way to avoid it, maybe make a deal with the new footman when he arrived. She felt better already, until she recalled that Jeremy was on the other side of the door waiting for her answer. And half-naked.

"A good reason. Ye've a gaggle of females downstairs . . ."

Her words trailed off. He'd opened the door. He leaned against the frame of it, too, crossing his arms over his bare chest. It was a wide chest, tapered down to a lean waist. Broad shoulders and sculpted muscles went with it. He was put together too fine, he really was. That's probably why he always seemed so confident. He bleedin' well knew he was a prime piece to look at.

At the moment he was perfectly relaxed—and amused. She stared at his blue eyes to keep from looking at his chest.

"Having a conversation through a door is rather silly, don't you think?" he asked.

" 'Aving a conversation at all is silly, when ye've got guests waiting on ye."

"Who?"

"Yer cousin and two other ladies."

"I suppose they aren't stopping by just to say hello?" he asked hopefully.

She shook her head and, for the life of her, couldn't figure out why a smirk was in her tone when she replied, "They mean to drag ye shopping." Probably because it was obvious that he didn't particularly like to shop, or he'd have finished furnishing his house on his own.

And his sigh wasn't happy. "Bloody hell, I wish Reggie would give some warning when she makes plans for me. Course, then she wouldn't be our sweet Reggie. Be a love and fetch me a couple pastries while I dress. My cousin won't want to wait while I eat a decent breakfast."

Anything to get out of his presence!

But he didn't move! She had to squeeze past him and didn't quite manage it without brushing against his arm. That arm shot out across her waist to stop her.

"The next time you want to hide in a closet"—he leaned closer to whisper by her ear—"you might consider some company. You'd be surprised what delights can be found in cozy spots like this."

Danny didn't answer, wouldn't have been able to utter a word even if she'd thought of one. She pushed past him and bolted down the stairs. The last thing she'd heard from Jeremy was his sigh. The only surprise she had was that she made it to the kitchen without falling apart from having been that close to him.

Chapter 17

"I don't see how you're going to manage it. He's a confirmed bachelor, a rakehell even. He only comes to these affairs to please his family."

Emily Bascomb listened to her friend with only half an ear as she watched Jeremy Malory across the room. He would have stood out in any crowd, as tall as he was, but he was also so sinfully handsome, every single woman in the room had become aware of him the moment he arrived. His black evening togs fit him to perfection. His hair, which fell in thick black waves about his ears and neck, might be worn a trifle longer than was fashionable, but that just gave him a rakish air.

Both girls were debutantes that season, though Emily had been stealing all the attention with her unparalleled beauty. Jennifer was used to that, having grown up in the same shire. With blond hair and light blue eyes, petite, exquisite Emily was a smashing success and basked in so much adoring attention.

But from the moment Emily had clapped eyes on Jeremy Malory last week, she had become entranced with him and had determined he would be hers. She hadn't expected to have to work at winning him, though, was quite annoyed that he'd barely glanced at her during their too-brief introduction last week, and now that she was finally seeing him again, he was ignoring her completely, as if they hadn't even met.

It was intolerable. She had every young lord that season in the palm of her hand as she'd known she would, all except for Malory. And she had no interest at all in any of the others now—because of him.

For years she'd been hearing rumors about how handsome he was, but living in the country with her family, and rarely ever

getting to London, she'd never had an opportunity to meet him to find out if the rumors were true. They were. His looks were
positively mesmerizing.

Her friend Jennifer was still warning her,
"And the only women he pays any attention
to a'tall are"—she paused to add in a whisper—"those he knows he can take to his
bed without risk of losing his bachelor
standing."

"Jen, you don't get it," Emily replied impatiently. "I *will* marry him, even if I have to
sleep with him first to accomplish it. One
way or another, he's going to be mine."

"Emily Bascomb, you wouldn't dare!"
Jennifer gasped.

Emily made a moue with her pretty lips
and pulled her friend off to the side to whisper, "Of course not, but it wouldn't be the
first time that the rumor of an indiscretion
has brought a fellow to the altar, now
would it?"

"What rumor?"

"Give me a few moments and I'll think of
one. But I'll give him one last chance to redeem himself first. Come along. Let's remind him that he's met us."

"I haven't met him," Jennifer pointed out,

not liking in the least being dragged in on her friend's scheme.

"Then I'll introduce you."

"You can't be so bold!" Jennifer complained, hanging back. "You've barely met him yourself."

Emily tsked and let go of her friend. "How do you expect to get what you want out of life if you play the coward?" Then she sighed, "Suit yourself then, I'll go alone. It's perfectly appropriate to approach the man you're going to marry."

"But you . . . aren't . . ."

Jennifer closed her mouth, embarrassed that she was talking to no one, since Emily had gone on without her. Much too bold, her friend was, but that's what came of being the prettiest woman in all of England. It lent confidence on a par with royalty.

Jeremy saw her coming, turned around abruptly, looking for the nearest exit, but got caught by Drew, who was coming to join him. "This wasn't exactly what I had in mind for this evening," Drew was saying. "I'm much better at socializing after I've bedded a few wenches."

"Aren't we all." Jeremy grinned and took Drew's arm to steer him toward the door.

"Shall we then? This ball was Percy's idea, since he'd promised he'd make an appearance. But we've done that, so—"

"Jeremy, you can't possibly be leaving so soon. We haven't danced yet."

He could pretend he hadn't heard her, should do just that, but he simply wasn't that rude. With an inward sigh, he turned around.

"Lady Emily, how nice to see you again," Jeremy said politely if in a somewhat bored tone, hoping she'd take the hint that he wasn't interested in her.

She didn't. She beamed at him. Positively stunning when she smiled like that, with her light blue eyes sparkling, Jeremy thought. She was quite the sensation this season. And looking for a husband, which put her off-limits to him.

"And you as well," she said to him demurely. "We had so little time to talk when we met last week."

"I was late for an appointment. And I'm afraid you've caught me late for another one. We were just—"

Drew jabbed him in the ribs, said, "Aren't you going to introduce me?"

Jeremy sighed. "Lady Emily Bascomb, meet Drew Anderson, my uncle by marriage."

"Make me feel positively ancient, why don't you," Drew complained, taking the hand Emily had offered Jeremy and shaking it gently. Nor did he let go immediately. "The pleasure is entirely mine, especially if you've come here without your husband."

"Husband? I'm not married—yet."

Drew coughed, realizing his mistake, though it was understandable. Even an American knew that young, unmarried debutantes, either on this side of the ocean or his own, didn't approach bachelors without an escort in tow.

"I'm sorry to hear that," Drew replied, baffling the young lady.

Jeremy almost laughed. Drew had been quite interested until hearing that she was a young innocent.

Jeremy saved him having to explain that remark by saying, "Sorry, old chap, but you'll have to find some other time to further your acquaintance with the lady. We really need to be off. We're already quite late."

"Such a shame," Drew replied. "But if we

must . . ." And this time he did the dragging to get them out of there.

~~~

Despite her pleasure with the new furnishings that had arrived that day, a glum mood had settled on Danny and was still present when she went to bed, keeping her from sleeping. She couldn't figure out what was causing it. She should have been filled with euphoria. She'd gotten through her first day of working at a decent job and hadn't been fired. She could be proud that she was firmly planted on the straight and narrow. The job was easy. The other servants were nice. The housekeeper was even willing to teach her to talk better. And she had a wonderful room all to herself. She should bleedin' well be ecstatic.

Her new clothes had also arrived that day. They were plain and serviceable and comfortable to work in, the white blouse long-sleeved with small ruffles at the cuff, high-necked, but not tight enough to choke her. The skirt was unadorned black. A short white apron had come in her package to wear over it. It was trimmed with a tiny ruffle, but otherwise was definitely a maid's apron, with deep pockets on both sides, even a long, tube-shaped one that looked as if it would hold her feather duster.

She'd spent quite a while admiring herself in a mirror. After tucking her curls back behind her ears so they were a little more contained, she'd been amazed at how pretty she looked. No, she was more than pretty, she was every bit as beautiful as those women who'd fetched Malory. Is that what he'd seen all along when he looked at her?

The new footman had shown up around noon, about the time all the new furniture started arriving. Carlton was the new man's name. He was young, probably only a few years older than Danny, plain looking, though he had some pretty doe-brown eyes. A talkative sort, he seemed good-natured. Danny had paid close attention to him when he was introduced to the staff, a bit too close probably, since it caused him a few blushes. She wasn't exactly attracted to him, but she realized he was definitely the sort of fellow who would make a re-spectable husband, so she determined to get to know him better when she got the chance.

She still couldn't sleep. Finally she got back up and went to make sure everything was still in its proper place upstairs. It was, except for the occupants. The two young nabobs were still out on the town, probably prowling about looking for wenches to bed. That's what rich young men did. Was that what was bothering her? That Malory was out trying to find a skirt to toss because she'd put him off? That should please her. It would mean he might leave her alone. The thought didn't please her at all.

She went back downstairs, just as glum. She'd made it around the corner at the back of the hall when she heard the front door open and the tail end of an ensuing conversation.

"Then what are you waiting for? She's just a wench," Drew was saying.

"No, she's not," Jeremy replied. "And I don't want to talk about her."

"So it's like that, is it? And what about that pretty little Emily Bascomb who fairly drooled all over you tonight at that ball. Don't tell me she didn't prick your interest at all?"

"Did I seem interested?"

"Not a bit, which was my question. Why not?"

"Same reason you backed off as soon as you heard she wasn't married. In that we're quite alike, old man. I avoid debutantes having their first season, second season, or any bloody season. Emily was rather obvious that she's set her cap for me, but all she's interested in is marriage, which I'm not. I'm sure you know how that goes."

"Yes, marriage or nothing." Drew sighed. "That's too bad. Pretty little thing. And she did seem like she'd offer you a lot more."

There was a shrug in Jeremy's tone. "I don't doubt she would. Some of them don't mind putting the cart before the horse, but only because they're confident they'll get what they want in the end. I've seen more'n one lord get leg-shackled over mistakes like that."

"Eh?" A long pause. "Oh, you mean married. Well, damn, that's depressing. Think I'll stick with tavern maids and parlor maids."

"Did anyone ever tell you that you talk too much when you're foxed?"

"I'm not foxed. Might be a little drunk though. And why don't you English *talk* En-

glish? Need a blasted dictionary to understand you sometimes."

A chuckle. "Accents can get pretty strong
in some quarters of the country, but you're
probably referring to *cant*. Just a passing
phase, old man. Could be gone from the vocabulary in a year or two."

"And get replaced by something just as
undecipherable?" Drew complained.

"And you Americans have no slang?"

"Nothing that isn't perfectly understandable," Drew said with a smirk in his tone.

"Understandable by *you,* old boy, but it
would be foreign to me, now wouldn't it?"

"Try not to be logical when I'm drunk,
Jeremy, it gives me a headache."

Jeremy laughed. Danny even caught herself about to chuckle, which was a good
clue for her to take herself off to bed before
she was discovered there in the hall. And
she went to sleep immediately now that
Malory was home.

Chapter 18

"There's going to be a dinner party tonight," Mrs. Appleton announced to Danny and Claire the next morning. "Mrs. Robertson will tell you all about it and what you need to do. I was given warning only last night. Barely enough time to plan the menu and shop for it!"

"This soon?" Danny asked as she started filling a plate. She wasn't going to miss a full breakfast today. "Doesn't it take time to send out invitations for parties?"

"Usually," Mrs. Appleton agreed. "But not when it's just family coming."

"Oh," Danny replied, not all that interested. "Well, I'll be sure to stay out of the way."

"No, you won't. You and Claire will both be serving. So will Carlton."

Danny had been doing just fine with her speech until she heard that. "Serving wot?"

"The food and drinks, of course."

"That ain't me job," Danny pointed out reasonably.

"It is when we're short on staff," the cook countered, much to Danny's dismay. "Every hand will be needed with some fifteen to twenty guests expected."

"So it's not just 'is family?"

"It is. The Malorys are a *big* family. But not all of them are in London at the moment. The Marquis of Haverston, head of the family, rarely comes to town, I'm told. And the earl's two daughters aren't in town either; they're on their country estates with their husbands. One is married to a duke, you know."

Royalty, Danny thought. The bleedin' nabob was related to royalty! And Mrs. Appleton was sounding so proud, to be able to mention it.

"I'm feeling sick," Danny said.

"The devil you are," the cook snorted.

"This will be a good test of your resource-fulness, my dear. With a little instruction, you'll do just fine."

That was doubtful, but Danny said no more on the subject. The breakfast didn't sit well with her, going down on a nervous stomach, which she now had, so she didn't eat her fill after all and headed upstairs to start her routine. Maybe if she avoided the housekeeper for the rest of the day, the woman would forget about giving her new instructions and Danny wouldn't be forced to serve royalty that night.

In her nervous state, she managed to clean the entire upper floor by noon—except for Jeremy's room. He was still in it, so she wasn't going near it.

By midmorning, Mrs. Robertson had found her and took her to the large dining room for that promised instruction. There really wasn't that much to learn, just whom to serve first, how to pour wine without gaining notice, to watch the glasses and re-fill them as needed. The men would appar-ently serve themselves drinks prior to din-ner. She'd only have to fetch a tea tray if the ladies requested it. She was to stay on hand, though, in the parlor, in case there were any other requests. She just had to stay unobtrusive and not draw any attention to herself.

"And look your neatest," Mrs. Robertson had warned before she sent Danny back to her cleaning.

Danny blushed. Claire had snidely mentioned her wrinkles that morning, too. She was going to have to give up her habit of sleeping in her clothes, obviously.

"Danny, come here, please."

She sighed mentally. So much for avoiding Malory. He was the only one left upstairs, and he *still* hadn't left his room. But obviously, he was no longer sleeping in it. He'd opened his door to call her and had left it open.

She peeked her head around the corner of the doorframe. He was still abed, lying on it, his arms crossed behind his head, looking so damned comfortable and relaxed. He wasn't fully dressed. He was wearing just a white lawn shirt, fastened only halfway up his chest, and buff-colored breeches. No shoes or stockings.

Lazing the day away, that's what she used to do before she got a *real* job. Bleedin' nabobs. And how was she supposed to clean his room if he wouldn't leave it?

She was making excuses for her annoyance when, the truth was, seeing him lying in bed set her pulses racing. God, she wished he wasn't so damned handsome that her fingers itched to touch him.

"Don't you have something to do during the day that would take you elsewhere?" she said more sharply than she should have.

Her voice drew his attention to her and his cobalt eyes widened in surprise. He even sat up on the edge of the bed. "Good God, you're beautiful!" he exclaimed.

Danny would have been pleased to hear Carlton say so, but Malory's flattery didn't impress her, since she knew his motives. Besides, she wasn't at her best, so she snorted. "You're a bleedin' liar. I've been told twice already today that I'm wrinkled beyond salvation."

"Wrinkles can't hide potential, dear girl. What you wear doesn't detract from your amazing bone structure, doesn't change the unique color of your hair, doesn't alter the violet clarity of your eyes. But since I was already familiar with all that, what I probably should have said was, 'Good God, you've got nice breasts!' "

Her face went up in flames. But she couldn't call him a liar this time, not when she'd spent ten of those thirty minutes yesterday in front of his mirror admiring just how nicely she filled out her new blouse.

She scowled at him though, flustered enough to slip back into her street talk. "Mentioning me breasts ain't proper, is it?"

He grinned unrepentantly and assured her, "Only in mixed company."

Her lips flattened out. "Then ye talk to all yer servants like ye do to me, eh?"

"No, just those I hope to get extremely intimate with. By the by, this is a comfortable bed. Would you like to try it sooner rather than later—like now?"

She should have known better than to ask questions that would encourage him to be more outlandish. "The only thing I'll be doing with that bed is fixing the covers on it after ye get out o' it."

"I'm wounded." He sighed.

"Yer lazy. Go do something so I can clean yer room."

"But I am doing something. I'm recuperating from last night's entertainment, and resting up for tonight. And besides, your job doesn't require a room to be unoccupied. You can clean around me." He turned on his side, bent his elbow to rest his head on one hand, and grinned at her again. "Just pretend I'm not here."

Right. As if that were even remotely possible. But she could try not to look at him. Bleedin' hell, that wouldn't work, because she'd know he was watching her. And even if he wasn't, she'd think he was and be glancing at him to find out, and . . .

"I'll wait."

"You can't," he seemed happy to tell her. "I'll be resting here until dinner."

She gritted her teeth, ripped the duster out of her apron pocket, and turned toward his small writing desk with the intention of attacking it with her feathers. She gasped instead, seeing the hat lying on it. It hadn't been there yesterday.

"Me 'at! Why do ye still 'ave it?"

There was a shrug in his tone. "I kept it as a keepsake of an—interesting experience."

"I've missed it."

"Too bad. Belongs to me now."

She glanced back at him curiously.

"Why? You wouldn't be caught dead wearing it."

"Don't intend to wear it. Don't intend to give it up either. So if I find it missing, I'll know where to look, won't I?"

"I've given up stealing."

"Glad to hear it. Then I'll consider my hat safe." That got him a glare, to which he only chuckled. "Cheer up, luv. It really doesn't go with skirts, you know. Frilly bonnets are what you need now."

She snorted. "I'll wear these bleedin' skirts, but those silly lady hats aren't for me."

He tsked. "You're thinking like a man again."

"So shoot me."

She went on to attack the desk as she'd intended, but it was rather deflating to find no dust on it yet that she could scatter about the room. She was careful not to touch her—*his* hat. She had a feeling he was silently laughing at her for having gotten into such a rotten mood over a hat. As if she cared.

When she took a moment to really look at the room, she was glad to see she'd done such a good job on it yesterday that there was barely anything to do to it today other than pick up a few clothes he'd dropped here and there. She gathered those and started to leave with them, keeping her gaze well away from the bed.

"Hell's bells, Danny, you aren't thinking of depriving me of your delightful company already, are you?"

He truly sounded disappointed. A ruse, no doubt. Still, she found herself stopping at the door to say, "You have guests coming tonight. There's a lot of work that needs to be done before they get here."

He sighed. "Ah, yes, my first foray into entertaining on the home front." Then he added somewhat snidely, "Mimicking your betters again, are you?"

She stiffened, realizing he was referring to her speech. "No, actually, Mrs. Robertson has been coaching me."

"Good God! And you caught on that quickly? Amazing."

He was being derisive, so she didn't bother to tell him that the way she used to talk was coming back to her more and more. She still had too many lapses when she got nervous or angry for him to believe her, so she changed the subject instead.

"I'm surprised you're having a party this

soon. I've barely gotten all the dust and grime off the new furniture."

"I assure you it wasn't my idea."

She lifted a brow. "Let me guess: your cousin?"

"Of course."

Since he sounded annoyed at the moment, Danny's mood improved a lot. She even flashed him a cheeky grin. "Cheer up, mate. I was told it's just your family coming. No need to impress family, eh?"

"On the contrary. I could care less about impressing mere acquaintances. It's my family that needs to think I'm getting along fine or they'll join forces to find out why not and proceed to correct the matter."

"You're a grown man. Why don't they let you muddle through on your own?"

"Because they love me, of course."

Chapter 19

~~~

Because they love me, of course. Danny couldn't get those words out of her mind. Must be nice to have that kind of family. Her "family" had never really felt like family. Members joined Dagger's band between the ages of five and ten, so there was no birth bond to generate a feeling of true closeness, and they usually left between the ages of fourteen and seventeen, to set off on their own. Rarely did any that left come back to visit. Once gone, gone for good.

Danny had enjoyed helping the younger children and had even had a few favorites over the years, but still, none that felt like brothers or sisters to her. Lucy was the only one she'd really developed a closeness to. Lucy was like a sister. But once Lucy had started whoring, she didn't have much time to spare for Danny.

But she was going to start a family of her own. That thought had been in the back of her mind now for quite a few years, though never seriously until now, since her masquerade had restricted her options in that regard. Hard to go looking for a husband if you looked like a husband yourself. She was herself now, though, or trying to be, so there was nothing to stop her from getting married as soon as the right man came along. And then finally, she'd have a real family.

The Malorys didn't arrive all at once; they trickled in over several hours prior to dinner. Regina Eden and her husband, Nicholas, were the first to arrive, probably because they lived only a few houses away.

Regina stopped short when she saw Danny in her dark blue skirt and white blouse, a light blue apron this time giving her even more color. She said only, "Famous. My eyesight must be going. I can usually recognize my own sex, no matter what they're wearing."

"Was pro'bly my hair, ma'am. The rakish male style, you know."

"I suppose." Regina sighed. "Just feels deuced awkward, having made such a colossal mistake."

"Beautiful chit," Danny heard Nicholas Eden remark to his wife as they moved off to join Drew on the other side of the large parlor.

"*You* weren't supposed to notice," Regina chided him, though in an amused tone. "But I'm sure Jeremy did."

More and more Malorys arrived after that. Carlton was letting them in. Danny did have to fetch a tea tray, and still another as the evening wore on. She caught their names in snippets of conversations that she over-heard. She also caught many of them look-ing her way curiously.

The two ladies who had joined in the shopping expedition yesterday turned out to be Jeremy's cousin and his aunt by mar-riage. The dark-haired cousin was Kelsey, married to Derek, one of the big, blond, handsome Malory men. Derek's father, Jason, was the marquis who rarely came to town.

The copper-haired beauty was Roslynn,

married to Jeremy's uncle Anthony. This
chap bowled Danny over when she first saw
him. Anthony looked so much like Jeremy it
was uncanny, just an older version. It must
be odd, though, knowing exactly what you
will look like when you get older. But then
the older version was so bleeding handsome, it was no wonder Jeremy fairly
reeked with confidence. He knew he had
many, many years of the amazing sexual
appeal he possessed to look forward to.

Another uncle arrived, the earl Mrs.
Appleton had mentioned. Edward Malory
was a jovial sort from the blond side of the
family. About ten years or so older than his
brother Anthony, Edward had a large family
of his own. His wife, Charlotte, was present,
and their two grown sons, Travis and
Marshall. They had three daughters, too,
apparently, all married, and none expected
tonight. Two of the girls lived in the country,
but the youngest, Amy, had sailed to
America with her husband, Warren, who
was one of Drew Anderson's brothers. They
were expected home sometime that summer, but no one knew for certain when.

Because it was only going to be family
and close friends, Anthony and Roslynn's

young daughter, Judith, had been allowed to come to dinner. With such handsome parents, it was small wonder that Judy, as she was called, was such a beautiful child. She had her mother's red-gold hair and those amazing cobalt blue eyes that her father, Regina, and Jeremy possessed. She was precocious, too, and quite frank in her remarks, as children tended to be.

She came over to Danny before dinner was served and after staring up at her for a few moments said candidly, "You're very pretty."

"So are you."

"I know." But the girl sighed as she said it, as if she wasn't pleased by it. "I'm told it will give m'father grief when I grow up."

"Why?"

"Because of all the suitors I'll have."

"So many?" Danny asked.

"Yes, hundreds and hundreds. Uncle James doesn't think m'father will be able to deal with it very well. Thinks he'll make a"— she paused to lean forward and whisper— "bloody arse of himself."

Danny choked back a laugh. "But what d'you think?"

"I think Uncle James might be right."

Danny couldn't help but laugh and wished she had better restraint. She ended up drawing every eye in the room to her. She could have withstood that, despite the embarrassment it caused, except that she'd drawn Jeremy's eyes, too.

He'd been making the rounds, chatting with each of his family as he or she arrived, and doing a good job of ignoring Danny at her station next to the door. But he wasn't ignoring her now and his eyes were fairly eating her. And they were all talking about her now. She knew it, sensed it, even caught a snippet of conversation here and there, though not enough to figure out what they were saying about her. It was highly embarrassing to know she had temporarily become the center of attention.

Across the room, Anthony whispered to Jeremy, "Get her set up in her own place. It will cause dissent among your servants when it's found out that you're bedding her. Jason might have gotten away with it for over twenty-five years, bedding his house-keeper, but he had a secret entrance to Molly's room. Doubt this house has it set up so conveniently."

"I'm not, bedding her that is."

"What a whopper," Anthony chuckled. "You wouldn't pass up a prime article like her."

"Don't intend to," Jeremy grumbled. "It just ain't happened yet."

Anthony lifted a black brow. "Losing your finesse, dear boy?"

Jeremy frowned. "I'm beginning to think so. I have to constantly remind m'self that she's unique."

"Uniquely beautiful, I couldn't agree more. But that isn't what you meant, is it?"

"No. As it happens, there isn't a bloody thing about her that can be called typical. Her background, her habits, everything about her isn't what you'd expect."

"She can't be that far off the mark, youngun," Anthony disagreed.

"You'd be surprised. Yesterday she talked like a street urchin. Today I caught her talking like an English tutor! And she thinks like a man. In fact, until a few days ago, she wore pants for most of her life. But as soon as she gets into a skirt, she wants a husband," Jeremy added on a mumble.

Anthony coughed. "You?"

"No, she knows I'm a confirmed bachelor, which is why she'll have nothing to do with me. She wants a *respectable* husband."

Anthony laughed. "Well, the pants part convinced me, but now we're back to typical. Most women do want respectable husbands."

Jeremy raised a brow. "When she's not the least bit respectable herself?"

"Ah, I see. Trying to move up in the world, is she? Well, if you really don't stand a chance of winning her over, then perhaps you should consider getting rid of her, to avoid temptation as it were."

Jeremy finally grinned. "Malorys don't give up that easily."

In another corner, Edward asked his wife, "Does the maid look familiar to you?"

"Can't say that she does," Charlotte replied.

Edward's brow knitted. "Can't place her, yet it seems I *should* know her."

"So you've probably seen her in passing, perhaps on the street or in one of the shops. Pretty gel like that would make an impression."

"I suppose." He sighed. "Though it's going to nag me now until I recall where I've seen her before."

By the fireplace, Travis remarked to his brother with a sigh very like his father's, "I suppose Jeremy's already staked his claim."

Marshall chuckled. "Course he has. Damned if I'd make her play the part of maid, though."

"Maybe she likes being a maid."

"More likely she hasn't realized yet that she don't need to lift a finger to do anything other than keep our cousin happy. That lucky dog. *Where* does he find all these beauties? I never see him at a gathering that the prettiest gel there isn't trying to gain his attention. Emily Bascomb has set her cap for him, of course, and she bowled me over, she did," Marshall confessed. "Was considering courting her, even had her interest—until our cousin showed up and caught her eye."

"I know what you mean," Travis said. "Wish Jeremy would get married already. Deuced hard to get anywhere with the ladies, with him around. Had the same problem with Derek before he married."

"We'll be old and gray before Jeremy ever considers marriage. Damned if I would either if I looked like him and had women throwing themselves at me all the time."

And in the center of the room, sitting on one of the two new sofas, Regina said to Kelsey, "Can't imagine what Jeremy is thinking, to install her in his house. I think Uncle James is going to have to have a talk with him, about flouting convention."

"It *is* a bachelor residence, m'dear."

"Yes, I know, and if he wants to keep his mistress here, I doubt the servants would raise a brow. And as long as he's discreet about it, it won't make the gossip mills. But he's hired her to his staff, so there will be problems in the lower quarters. *He* might not have to deal with that, but the poor girl will."

Kelsey patted Regina's hand. "I think you should let him muddle through this one on his own. He's never had his own servants before. He'll get the hang of it. His father and uncle certainly did. Notorious rakes that they were, I'm sure they ran smooth households."

If Danny knew that every Malory in the room thought that she was Jeremy's mistress, she wouldn't have been embarrassed, she would have been furious—and caused a scene guaranteed to get her fired, blackmail or not. But she was blissfully unaware of the conclusions that the Malorys had reached about her. And although she *did* guess that she was being talked about, which embarrassed her, Percy's arrival took her mind off it.

He stopped by her as he entered the room, frowned for a moment, then said. "Ah, I have it! Twins. Met your brother. First-rate chap. Did me a good turn, for which I shall be eternally grateful."

Danny wasn't sure what to say to that. Correct the mistake he'd just made and risk having him blurt out that she'd been wearing pants a few days ago?

Jeremy saved her from having to answer at all. He knew what Percy was capable of spilling and obviously didn't want it spilled in front of his family.

"You're late, old chap. Barely enough time for a drink before dinner. Come along and we'll fix that."

"Don't need a drink," Percy replied. "Looking forward to finding out if you got lucky with a cook, though. But by the by, *where* did you find the twin sister of our little cutpurse? Don't tell me you went even deeper into that den of thieves than the tavern we found that night?"

Since Jeremy had already led Percy halfway into the room, there weren't many who didn't hear what he'd just said. Jeremy put his hands over his eyes with a groan.

Danny decided it was a good time to go see if dinner was ready to be served.

Chapter 20

Tyrus Dyer's luck was improving already. He'd given the matter a good deal of thought, several days' worth, and had decided if he was going to kill the wench proper he ought to get paid for it proper this time. He wasn't going to be greedy about it. Getting his luck back was the better reward. But as long as he was going to kill her anyway, why not get paid for it as well, he'd reasoned.

So he went to find the lord who'd wanted her dead. He remembered where he lived. He hadn't been sure he would, as he had only been there twice before. But he recognized the house. And the lord was at home.

That's where his luck was improving, because the chatty servant who let him in told him that his master lived in the country now and rarely came to London anymore, perhaps only once or twice a year. That he'd just arrived a few days ago for a brief stay to conduct some business left Tyrus incredulous that he could get so lucky. In fact, the lord was due to return to the country in the morning. Another day of debating and Tyrus would have missed him completely.

Of course, the nabob might not see him when he heard his name. They had parted association with bad feelings, after all, because of Tyrus's failure. The man might even try to kill him again. But Tyrus reasoned that incident had been spawned by anger, and the lord had had fifteen years to calm down about it.

He was made to wait though, for nearly three hours. Deliberate he didn't doubt. But he wasn't leaving, if that was what the lord was hoping he'd do. He was going to demand a lot of money to finish the job he'd been hired to do all those years ago. That was worth a little wait.

The hour was approaching midnight when the servant finally came to take him to his master. He was in an officelike room toward the back of the house, sitting behind a desk. Standing on either side of him were two men who looked like street thugs. Tyrus's palms began to sweat.

He had to wonder now if he'd been fooling himself. Perhaps he wasn't as lucky to find the lord at home as he'd first thought. Had he been kept waiting so those thugs could be summoned to kill him?

Before the lord could give an order to have him removed, permanently, Tyrus blurted out, "Wouldn't 'ave come 'ere if I didn't think you'd want to 'ere wot I 'ave to say."

"Sit down, Mr. Dyer."

Tyrus let out a sigh of relief and grinned cockily as he took the seat across from the desk. The two thugs, though they kept their eyes on him, were expressionless. "You remember me, do you?"

"Unfortunately, I do, at least your name. I must admit I wouldn't have recognized you. Your appearance has changed drastically, hasn't it?"

Tyrus's lips twisted in annoyance. The nabob was referring to his hair, of course. Forty-two years old, not a wrinkle on his face, yet his hair had turned pure gray a number of years ago. While the nabob hadn't changed much at all. He must be nearly fifty now himself, yet looked much younger.

"Runs in the family," Tyrus lied. "You've faired well, m'lord?"

"Extremely well—no thanks to you."

Tyrus wasn't sure if he should be relieved to hear that. If the nabob wasn't desperate anymore to get rid of the girl, then he wouldn't be paying for it. But on the other hand, if his pockets were pleasantly plump these days, then he might just pay even more than Tyrus had planned to demand, to get the job finished.

"The hour is late," the lord said tiredly. "State your business, Mr. Dyer."

Tyrus nodded. "I've found the girl, the one that got away. She's still alive."

"Yes, I know."

Tyrus's hopes just plummeted. "You know?"

"There was a commotion on the street the other day near my bank. I was close enough to see what the trouble was. Couldn't quite believe my eyes to find the girl the cause of it."

"I know wot you mean. Doubted m'sight, too."

"I'd almost forgotten about her. I would have had her declared dead all those years ago when she never surfaced, but I got—convinced—that wouldn't be a good idea."

"You didn't follow 'er?"

"Certainly I did, but I lost sight of her a few blocks away."

"I didn't. I know where she lives."

The lord had been sitting back, giving the impression he wasn't all that interested in the subject. He sat forward abruptly now, causing Tyrus's hopes to soar again.

"Where?"

Tyrus chuckled. "You don't think I'll be giving you that sort o' information for free, d'you?"

The lord sat back again, gestured at his two companions, who immediately started moving around the desk. Tyrus nearly knocked his chair over in his haste to get out of it. He nearly fell, but recovered nicely and came up with a pistol in his hand. The thugs stopped immediately as he waved the gun between them. They weren't expressionless now, they were looking quite angry.

Nervously, Tyrus demanded, "If you still

want 'er dead, I'll be doing it, and you'll be paying me twice wot you promised before, 'alf now and 'alf when I tell you where the body is. I ain't taking no chances wi' you this time, m'lord."

The man laughed. "Not a penny without results. You've already proved how incompetent you are, Mr. Dyer. You'll have your payment, but only if you succeed this time."

Tyrus was happy to settle for that. Aye, his luck was definitely improving.

Chapter 21

Mrs. Appleton was so happy that her first dinner party was such a success that she poured herself a glass of wine to celebrate—and poured one for Danny and Claire, too. Claire declined. She was still washing dishes. But Danny only had to check the dining room and parlor once more, to make sure they were back to looking orderly before she retired, so she chugged down her glass.

The cook shook her head at Danny in disgust. "Now that was purely a waste I hope to never see again. That used to drinking, are you? Or do you just not know that good wine should be savored?"

Danny didn't blush—well, not much. But she did regret having drunk the wine that quickly, tasting it after the fact, as it were. She was used to cheap wine, not this fine stuff with such a heady flavor.

"Can I 'ave another taste then? Missed it the first go-round, I did."

Mrs. Appleton laughed. "Yes, I suppose you've earned it. You did good tonight, lass, very good indeed. Didn't spill or drop anything. The mark of a good maid is, she's never noticed. Of course, you'll never aspire to that with the way you look, but you can still manage to be the best maid on the block if you work at it."

"And wot's wrong with the way I look? Mrs. Robertson picked out these togs, ye know."

"Bless you, child, you must know how pretty you are. That face of yours will always draw attention to you. There's simply no help for that. But as long as you do your job well, you can overcome that flaw. Now run along. You've earned some rest and morning will come around quick enough."

Danny left the kitchen with a grin on her face. Who but a domestic would consider a pretty face to be a flaw?

The last guest had departed the house quite a while ago, so Danny had been able to collect all the dishes from the dining room in peace. She didn't expect to find anyone there when she passed through it to give it one last quick inspection, but there was Jeremy back at the table, a decanter of wine in front of him and a half-empty glass in his hand. He didn't look happy. He looked quite miserable and didn't even notice that she'd entered the room.

Danny was torn between wanting to ask him what was wrong and wanting to slip back out of the room before he noticed her. She chose the smarter option and turned to leave.

"Don't want to join me?"

"No."

"Too blunt," he tsk-tsked. "Shouldn't be blunt with a man in the doldrums, you know. Any excuse, even a lame one, would have sufficed."

Danny tried to concentrate so she'd be able to answer him properly, but the wine she'd drunk herself made it too difficult. "Ye want to be lied to then?"

He thought about that for a moment, then said, "Well, no, 'spose not. But excuses aren't considered lies, they are considered polite whoppers."

"Are ye foxed, Malory?"

He blinked at her, then staggered to his feet to pose in an offended manner. "Course not. Never been foxed a day in m'life."

Danny snorted. "That's wot they all say. So wot excuse d'ye 'ave, eh? Yer party was a success. Ye should be pleased, not drowning in yer cups."

"Would be pleased if I didn't know that at least three members of m'family, possibly four, and I know exactly which ones, are going to go straight to m'father and chew his ear off that I'm failing miserably at my first foray into property ownership."

"Ye 'ave a smashing party and think yer failing? Aye, yer foxed to the gills."

Jeremy finished off his wine, set the glass down hard on the table, and admitted, "Isn't about the party, dear girl. It's Percy and his bloody big mouth. And if you knew m'father, you wouldn't want him annoyed with you."

"Ye 'ave a nice family. Even I could see that. Yer father can't be worse than the rest o' them."

He laughed. She waited, but that was apparently his answer.

She shook her head at him. "Go to bed and sleep it off, mate."

He scowled for a moment. "I would, except I can't seem to find my bed."

"Eh?"

"I tried, really I did. But I kept finding beds that weren't mine. I'd recognize m'own bed, you know. So there was nothing for it but to come back here and find a chair instead."

Danny rolled her eyes, marched over to him, grabbed his arm, and pulled him out of the room and toward the stairs. He got harder to pull though when she started up them. She glanced back to see him frowning.

"Don't think I can manage those again," he confided. "Not without help."

"And wot d'ye think I'm doing, eh?"

"But if you should let go for some reason, I could lose m'balance. Course, a broken neck would probably make m'father go easy on me."

Danny was starting to get amused. When Jeremy Malory was drunk, he was pretty funny. And harmless. The sensual glances that always undid her were missing. The nervousness she always felt when she was around him went away completely. She didn't even mind touching him at the moment.

"You want to sleep on the couch then?"

"When I've a perfectly good bed upstairs?" he said indignantly. "No, perhaps if you let me hold on to you, that would work?"

Her violet eyes narrowed suspiciously. "Hold on to what?"

"Your shoulder, of course. What the deuce did you think I meant?"

She blushed slightly, grabbed his waist, and pulled his arm over her shoulder. "This better?"

"Much."

They made it up the stairs with no mishaps. He *was* leaning on her a bit hard, but despite her narrow frame, she was strong and could support him well. He didn't let go of her when they reached the upstairs hall, though, even seemed to be leading her down it. She decided it would be quicker to get him to his room if she said nothing and just got him there. But he still didn't let go of her at his room and apparently wanted assistance right to his bed.

Danny's suspicions returned, particularly

when he got clumsy right next to his bed and fell onto it, dragging her down with him. That she ended up beneath him didn't help her to extricate herself quickly. Jeremy at a dead weight was quite heavy. She still shoved and bucked to push him off her, but it was wasted effort.

"You better not have fallen asleep, mate," she growled. "Let me up now or—"

"Be still," he admonished with a groan. "I think I'm going to puke."

Danny went very still. She'd forgotten for a moment that he was drunk. She felt bad now, for her suspicions—for all of five seconds. He'd turned his head toward her when he'd spoken, lifted it slightly now, and put his lips right on top of hers.

Danny turned her head aside. She was going to give him the benefit of the doubt, that he hadn't meant to do that. But his lips grazed her neck now, sending shivers up her spine, and she heard, "You must know that I want you. I've made no pretense about it. There is such pleasure awaiting us, luv. Don't fight it anymore."

Before she succumbed to it—desperately now, because his words had such a weakening effect on her—she turned her head back to tell him what he could do with his offered pleasure and got trapped again. She tried to resist, she really did, but all she could do was forget every single reason why she shouldn't be kissing him. She'd always wondered what it would be like. Lucy had told her about sloppy kisses, wet ones, drunk ones, and the right ones, those rare instances when a kiss could stimulate her sexual urges.

Danny knew well the latter was happening to her. She even knew why. This was Malory, after all, and she was already attracted to him more than she'd ever been to any man before. And he might be drunk, but his kiss didn't reflect that at all, far from it. In fact, she wouldn't be a bit surprised if this first kiss of hers was the most fantastic kiss she'd ever get, that she'd never find another one as powerful or sensual again.

She should have ended what he was doing instantly, before she got a good taste of him. It was going to spoil her for all time, she was sure, because how could any man compete with the best, and she was being shown the best. But ending it was the last thing she wanted to do at the moment. She just couldn't muster the willpower to do so, when her every sense was being manipulated so expertly, when all she wanted to do was wrap her arms around him and never let go.

And she had the odd thought that if this was how he kissed when he was drunk, heaven help her when he wasn't.

"God, you taste good!"

She'd been thinking the same thing. His lips were so velvety soft. Or maybe it was because hers were soft and the combination of the two meeting made for a perfect meld. His breath wasn't fumed with alcohol at all, was rather heady in scent. His taste was exotic, beyond her capability to describe. And she was feeling things other than the kiss, delightful sensations, all new to her, all highly pleasant.

One of his legs had slipped between hers. The pressure there was exquisite because he wasn't keeping his leg still; he was moving it against her loins in the most erotic way. And he'd gathered her so close, holding her to him as if he weren't already pressed fully to her, one hand behind her back, the other cupping her bottom, actually pressing her even harder against his thigh. Heat was swirling madly there, about to explode . . .

"Hell and tarnation, Jeremy," Drew complained out in the hall, his tone as disgruntled as his words. "You could at least close the blasted door."

Drew's door was then slammed shut. And Danny had no trouble getting off the bed now. She didn't just shove this time, she balled her fingers into a fist and knocked it hard against Jeremy's ear. He howled and moved off her right quickly.

She shot off the bed and didn't bother to look back, just hissed on her way out the door, "Ye'll be getting no 'elp from me the next time yer foxed, mate. Ye can bleedin' well sleep on the floor."

Chapter 22

The next morning, as Danny was on her way downstairs to clean the lower rooms because nothing was left to clean upstairs until the two slugabeds rose for the day, a knock came at the front door. Carlton wasn't around to answer it. She knew that he'd left the house with Mrs. Robertson earlier to help her with a few errands, and it didn't look as if they'd returned yet. She still didn't approach the door immediately. In her current mood, she wouldn't make a courteous butler.

She wasn't angry at Jeremy over what had happened last night. Drunks were drunks, after all, and did stupid things while they were at it. But she was angry at herself. *She* had no excuse for what she had let happen. She could think of any number of ways she could have extricated herself immediately from that kiss last night, but she hadn't used them simply because she didn't really want to. And that's what infuriated her. Knowing better hadn't counted. Knowing what that kiss would have led to hadn't counted. Nothing had counted but the pleasure Jeremy Malory was capable of handing out.

Claire wasn't showing up to answer the front door. And the pounding got a lot louder, indicating the impatience of the caller.

With an annoyed sigh, Danny finally yanked it open and snapped, "They're all sleeping, come back later."

"I beg your pardon?" the man said in a sardonic tone that implied he wasn't doing any such thing.

Danny's palms began to sweat. The large fellow standing there on the doorstep was quite likely the most intimidating man she'd ever seen.

He was big, solid big, with hefty arms and an extremely wide chest of hard muscle, but

he wasn't much taller than she was, probably just short of six feet. Somewhere in his
midforties she would guess. And it was impossible to tell if he was an aristocrat or not.
His bone structure indicated he was, but he
was dressed too casually: no cravat, a white
lawn shirt opened at the neck, a black coat,
buff trousers, and black riding boots. His
blond hair was much too long, though, for
him to be a member of the ton, who prided
themselves on being fashionable. It was so
long it rested on his shoulders in thick
waves, giving him the air of a pirate. His expression, though, said clearly this was not a
man to cross. He fairly reeked of danger,
which was probably why she was suddenly
so nervous. She'd never encountered anyone who exuded such an aura, didn't doubt
for a moment that he could be utterly ruthless if provoked—and deadly.

She was tempted to close the door on
him and lock it. She might have, too, if he
hadn't brushed past her into the entryway,
where he now stood with his arms crossed.

She cringed since she was forced to put
him off. "They really are still sleeping. Which
one o' them did ye want to see?"

"Jeremy."

"It's doubtful that one will be up anytime soon. 'E got foxed to the gills last night and is sleeping it off."

A golden brow rose quite high. "What utter rubbish. Jeremy foxed? That's an impossibility. He was weaned on strong spirits. The youngun is quite incapable of overimbibing, I do assure you. So go wake him and tell him to get his arse down here."

Danny ran up the stairs, forgot to hike her skirt and tripped a bit, hiked her skirt high, and finished running till she was out of sight. She wasn't running to get to Jeremy, just to get away from that fellow. But upstairs in the hall, after a long sigh of relief, it sank in what the man had said.

Malory was incapable of getting drunk? So all that nonsense last night had just been a ruse to get her upstairs and into his bed? That bleeding bastard! How dare he trick her like that?

She didn't knock on his door, she was too angry for that. She marched in and found him on the bed, wide-awake, just lying there looking smug and self-satisfied. He was surprised by her unannounced entrance, though, and sat up. His expression even turned wary when he noted hers.

She stopped in front of him, her hands on her hips, and shouted, "Ye son of a bitch! Ye ever try tricks again to get under me skirt and I'll gullet ye. And I don't care if I get fired for it!"

"What tricks?"

"Being foxed. Ye weren't drunk last night. Yer incapable o' being drunk!"

He actually grinned. "I did mention that, didn't I? Definitely recall doing so."

"And that ye couldn't find yer bleedin' bed on yer own? D'ye recall mentioning that, too!"

He chuckled. "Danny, luv, you leave a man few choices. So I was getting desperate enough to take advantage of the conclusion you drew. A few minor fibs, but it was well worth it to finally taste you."

"Was it?" she snarled just before her fist cracked against his cheek.

She'd expected him to move out of the way. He'd done that easily enough before. She didn't expect to have her knuckles throbbing now. But it was very satisfying that they were.

"D'ye still think so?" she asked him smugly. "And that's letting ye off lightly, mate. Keep yer kisses to yerself from now on!"

She marched back out of the room and ran straight into a brick wall. Well, that's what it felt like. The intimidating chap she'd left in the entry hall had come upstairs, his patience gone, apparently.

"Run along, wench," he told her. "I'll be taking over where you left off, you may depend upon it."

That sounded too ominous by half. Malory was about to get more than a black eye, she'd wager. Couldn't happen to a more deserving scoundrel.

Chapter 23

Jeremy dropped back on his bed with a groan, recognizing that voice outside his room. He'd thought he would have another day or two before his father returned to town. But George had no doubt dragged him back as soon as she'd gotten word that her brother's ship was in. And to go by what James had just said, Jeremy had been right last night in thinking his wonderful relatives were too concerned about his behavior to keep it to themselves. Either Percy's remark had been relayed to James, or he'd been told that Jeremy was bedding his upstairs maid. Probably both. Though how the deuce they'd gotten to James this quickly boggled him.

"Hiding behind a black eye, puppy?"

Jeremy sat up and pointed to his upper cheek. "Take a look. Her fist landed here, but my eye does smart a little. Think it will turn black?"

"What I think," his father said, "is you've bloody well lost your mind, tangling with a wench who throws punches instead of slaps."

Jeremy grinned. "You don't think any such thing. You saw her. You know exactly why I'd want to tangle with her, no matter what she throws."

"Beside the point," James said, but he still came over to the bed, took hold of Jeremy's chin to tilt his head at a different angle, and examined the rapidly bruising area on his upper cheek. "Won't be a full shiner, but you might have enough bruise there to put off Albert Bascomb's girl, so she'll tilt her cap elsewhere."

Jeremy flinched and exclaimed, "Hell's bells, you even heard about *her*?"

James moved his large frame over to one of the two stuffed chairs in the room and got comfortable. "Let me tell you about my morning, dear boy. I manage to get to the family home by midmorning, much to George's delight, only to find Eddy boy burning a hole in the carpet of my study with his impatience to see me. Thirty minutes later the elder marches off, unsatisfied with my replies, of course."

"Naturally," Jeremy grinned.

His father was unique to the Malory clan, always had been, going his own way and breaking convention as he pleased, the black sheep of the family, as it were. He'd been disowned by his brothers for over ten years when he took to pirating on the high seas. He was back in the fold now, but he still bucked convention.

James simply enjoyed being different. Even names had to be different for him. Most of the family called Regina "Reggie," but James insisted on calling her Regan, much to his brothers' annoyance. Even his own daughter, Jacqueline, he called Jack, much to *her* uncles' displeasure.

"Then Tony shows up with the prediction that your staff will soon be abandoning ship because you're bedding one of them," James continued.

"I would have thought at least *he'd* understand," Jeremy said.

"Oh, he was quite amusing for the most part. My brother took to fatherhood rather well and now *thinks* like a father, don't you know."

"Which means he's forgotten what it's like to be young and unshackled?"

"Exactly."

"But you haven't—"

"We'll get to that, puppy," James cut in. "And then Regan, the dear puss, walks in before Tony's finished and proceeds to add yet a new subject, said Lady Bascomb to be exact, to this growing list of concerns."

"How the deuce did she find out about that chit? I only mentioned it to Drew and Percy—never mind. Percy and his bloody big mouth."

"Actually, the Bascomb girl is spreading the rumor herself that she'll be married to you before the end of the year. But as it happens, Regan overheard her telling a friend that she was going to have you—one way or another."

"One way or another?" Jeremy frowned. "And what the devil does that mean?"

"Exactly what you think it means. There

will always be a few rotten apples in the bunch who will lie and manipulate to get what they want. *Are* you pursuing the lady?"

"She's a debutante, her first season out. I avoid them like the plague."

"I thought as much. I'd advise you to keep your distance from her then, a very far distance, though even that might not help. False rumors tend to condemn a man just as easily as the truth does."

"I can keep away from the social scene for a while, until she starts casting her eyes elsewhere. The young husband-hunters aren't known for their patience, seem to think they *have* to get married their first season out, which doesn't really give them much time to work their wiles for the most part. And now that George is back in the city, she can see to dragging her brother about to those fancy affairs that all the debutantes flock to."

"Bite your tongue, puppy. That means I'd get dragged to them, too."

Jeremy chuckled. If there was one thing his father detested above all else, it was London's social whirl. "Fortunately, Drew's preferred form of entertainments are more in line with mine, places where he can be guaranteed a wench for the night. He'll make his excuses to George as he always does."

"That's *after* she gets her way a few times. My dear wife always does, you know. But never mind, I've already got my own excuses lined up to avoid joining my wife and brother-in-law. Now—" There was enough of a pause that Jeremy groaned inwardly, knowing what was coming. "What in the bloody hell were you doing entering the very bowels of this city's criminal element?"

"I didn't," Jeremy was quick to assure him. "Well, only the edges, but that was for a very good cause." He quickly explained the problem Percy had had and how he'd elected to solve it.

When he finished, James grinned. "Stole them back, eh? Don't think I'd have thought of that."

"No, you would have invited Heddings into the ring for a round or two."

James shrugged. "Does work wonders, don't you know. I don't think I like the fact that he had one of Diana's trinkets, though. Stealing from m'niece feels like he stole from me, damn me if it doesn't."

"Well, we cleaned him out, or rather, our

thief did. I managed to return those pieces we recognized to their rightful owners and had the rest delivered to our nearest magistrate. Hopefully, he can figure out what belongs to whom and get it back to them."

"Didn't want to just turn Heddings over to them?" James asked.

"Couldn't do that without admitting we'd found the jewels in his house while robbing him."

James coughed. "Quite right. I suppose they *would* require proof of where you found the stolen baubles. Well, maybe he'll see the error of his ways and steal no more, now that he knows someone is onto him."

"But he doesn't. He probably just thinks he got robbed by a common thief and nothing will come of it. Very unlikely that he'd think the thief might recognize any of the pieces, or even know he was stealing already stolen property."

James sighed. "I suppose I'll just have to kill the fellow then, to make sure he doesn't rob any members of my family again."

Jeremy coughed now. "You really don't need to get involved. I intend to keep an eye on the chap. I was going to find out his haunts and start frequenting them m'self.

I'm not sure how he's stealing, but I plan to catch him at it. No trouble a'tall then, turning him in."

James was silent for a moment. His next remark indicated he'd let it go for now. "By the by, how'd you manage to hire your thief's sister if you didn't go back into that den of thieves?"

Jeremy wished he could lie to his father for once, he really did, but he never had and he wasn't going to start now. "My new maid *is* our thief. And I didn't have to find her again, she came to me, since I was responsible for her getting kicked out of her gang."

James raised a brow. "I take it your chum Percy don't know that?"

"No. She masqueraded as a male, has done so apparently for most of her life. Percy never saw the woman in her, so when he saw her again last night, he concluded it was her twin brother he'd met before."

"I see. Bloody hell—no, I don't. You've hired a common thief to your staff?"

Jeremy flinched at the raised tone. "There's nothing common about that wench. Did you really look at her face? She's got such fine bones she could be a princess! She talks like a guttersnipe, but she would, since that's where she was raised. But she's an orphan. She has no idea where she came from or even what name she was born with. But she wants to better herself. I've no doubt she can, because she's smart as a whip. Her speech has even improved in just the few days she's been here. She sought me out merely because she blames me for losing her home."

"*Was* that your fault?"

"Apparently. I didn't exactly give her a choice about coming along with us that night. Her little band of pickpockets had their rules to abide by, and she ended up breaking a number of them by helping us."

"So you hired her because you feel you owe her?" James asked.

"Course not," Jeremy said, and with a blush added, "I hired her because she gave me no choice in the matter. She threatened to go to Heddings and tell him all."

James frowned. "Let me get this straight. Instead of extorting money from you to keep silent, she demands you put her to *work?* I thought you said she was smart?"

"She is. A good job is part of her plan to better herself."

"Money would have done that," James pointed out dryly.

"I know. Deuced odd that she didn't go that route instead. But then I'm beginning to think it was just a bluff."

"Probably. If she's as smart as you say, then she must know that confessing to Heddings would implicate herself as well."

"Exactly. But she's working out rather well as a maid. Didn't think she would, but she is, and besides, I still mean to bed her."

"Then why the devil don't you do so and then send her on her way?"

"Because I doubt once will be enough, and, well, she isn't interested in a pleasant tumble."

"Good God, don't tell me a thief and blackmailer is holding out for marriage!"

"No, she just wants nothing to do with me."

James rolled his eyes. "What an odd statement. I'm sure you believe it to have said it, but you'll never get anyone else to believe it."

"It's true. I just haven't found out why yet."

"Did you think to ask her why?"

"That's putting too many cards on the table, ain't it?"

James snorted. "To go by why she socked you, I'd say you've already tossed the whole deck on the table. Ask her, deal with it, bed her, then get her out of this house. Aside from the fact that she'll probably rob you blind if you keep her here long enough—"

"She's given up stealing."

"Sure she has," James replied dryly.

"No, really, she claims to hate it, and come to think of it, that's probably why she didn't demand money from me. She'd see that as stealing."

"Regardless, set her up elsewhere if you want to enjoy her for a while, but get her off your staff. You can even install her here if you must, but do it right. Keeping her as a maid and bedding her as well is going to make for a very unhappy household."

"Is that *your* thought on the matter, or what got whispered in your ear this morning?"

James chuckled. "Malorys don't whisper complaints, youngun. But you're right, doesn't matter to me if you want to muck up the hearth and home with contention. What I *do* object to is having the elders breathing down my neck about it, Jason in particular. So satisfy the rest of the family that you're not bucking convention and managing your household splendidly, then they won't go running to Jason about it, and I won't have to listen to any more of his rants."

Jeremy sighed. "Reggie's the only one who comes by so often. I wonder if I could bar her from my house. D'you think a butler could stand up to her and keep her out?"

James laughed. "Not a chance, not that you'd really want to. The little darling does her fair share of manipulating and match-making, but always with the best intentions, and she's usually right on the mark. Bloody shame she had to marry a bounder like Eden."

Jeremy grinned. His father got along well enough with Nicholas Eden these days, as long as he always won their verbal skir-mishes, which he usually did. Those two went way back, to the high seas actually. Jeremy had been injured in the sea battle between the two men, which was why James had given up pirating. Nick had sailed away unscathed *and* thumbed his nose at them, which you just didn't do to James Malory.

James finally got even, trouncing Nick soundly—right before his wedding to Reggie, which he almost missed because of it. Nick in turn landed James in jail for it, which turned out for the best, actually, since James was able to arrange the "death" of the pirate Captain Hawke, the name he was known by on the seas, when he escaped, allowing him to come back to England for good.

"Speaking of butlers," James said as he got up to leave, "how would you like to borrow one of mine?"

"Hell's bells." Jeremy grinned in delight. "I've been hoping you'd suggest that."

"Borrow, puppy, not keep, so you're still to look for a permanent man. Artie suggested it, actually. Since he and Henry share the job at my house, it really doesn't give them both enough to do."

"Which one do I get?"

James laughed. "Both of them, of course. They'll take turns here as they do at home. Those two old sea dogs have been sharing the job for so long, I wouldn't doubt they think that's the normal way it's done."

Chapter 24

~~~~~~

Jeremy found Danny in the parlor, dusting one of the tables, over and over, so deep in thought she didn't hear him enter the room. He wondered if her thoughts were about him. He wondered if she was still furious. He wondered if she would blacken his other eye if he turned her around and kissed her again.

He coughed instead to draw her notice. She spun around and seemed more surprised than she should have been to see him there.

Her question indicated why. "You're still alive?"

Jeremy mulled that over for a moment.

"Expired from a black eye? No, don't think I've heard of that one."

"Weren't referring to wot I did," she mumbled. "And your eye ain't black."

"Yet," he corrected cheerfully, causing her to scowl at him. He chuckled. "Very well, I give up. Spit it out, wench. Why were you expecting my demise?"

"That visitor ye 'ad," she almost whispered in her nervousness. "I hid in the kitchen till 'e finally left. Scared the bejesus out o' me, 'e did. Was easy to tell 'e'd slit yer throat without batting an eye. There's not many men who are that ruthless, but 'e 'ad that look about 'im, if ye know wot I mean. And 'e was mad at ye."

Jeremy started laughing. Danny was back to scowling. "Wot d'ye find so funny, eh?" she demanded indignantly.

"You're talking about my father, dear girl."

"Sure I am," she scoffed. "Wot a clacker. 'E looked nothing like ye."

"No, he doesn't, but he *is* my father. James Malory, Viscount Ryding, fourth born of the elder Malorys, ex-rake, ex-pir—er, never mind, but he's now a devoted husband, and father of four with more on the way."

She believed him finally, even commiserated, "You poor man. I'd 'ate to 'ave a father that frightening."

He grinned. "He's not, really, well, not once you get to know him."

She humphed. "Well, obviously 'e didn't rip ye to pieces as I figured 'e were 'ankering to do—more's the pity, if ye ask me."

That easily her own anger was back in place. Jeremy coughed. "Let's have a chat, Danny."

"Let's not."

"You haven't figured out yet that you need to humor your employer at all times?"

"Not bleedin' likely when my employer is a randy buck only interested in getting under my skirts."

"Devil take it, you have to work on this bluntness of yours, really you do."

"Why?"

"Because—"

He stopped short. She was right. It was one of the things about her that was unique and he didn't want to change her in that regard. Besides, right now he was after frankness from her, and he wouldn't get that if she started prevaricating as most women tended to do when they were asked pointed questions. And he intended to ask a few of those.

"So you have brothers and sisters, do you?"

Jeremy's hopes soared high. She hadn't waited for him to answer her question, and her curiosity was an excellent indication that she was more interested in him than she pretended to be.

"Twin brothers and a sister, actually," he told her. "All quite young still."

"Why weren't they at your party? Or your father for that matter?"

"They were visiting my uncle Jason in the country. He's head of the family and doesn't come to town very often. So if we want to see him, we go to the family estate at Haverston. But children that young aren't usually allowed at adult gatherings anyway."

"Not even when the gathering is all your own family?" she asked.

Jeremy grinned. "We've tried that. There are a *lot* of youngsters in m'family now. It's quite like a battlefield when they all get together."

She chuckled for a moment. "I've been in a few o' those m'self."

"Have you? There were a lot of children in your band of misfits?"

"Mostly all children, and all o' them orphans like me. Dagger supplied the roof and food and taught us how to make do."

"You mean, how to steal."

"That, too."

"He was your elected leader, I take it? The one who kicked you out?"

She nodded curtly and turned away, going back to her dusting—with a vengeance. A touchy subject, apparently. It was probably still too soon after her ousting from that band for her to want to discuss it. He was surprised she'd said as much as she did, when she'd refused to talk about any of it before.

"Have a seat, Danny," he suggested agreeably. "There are a few more things I'd like to ask you. Might as well get comfortable."

He'd indicated the sofa. She stared at it a moment then shook her head. "Wouldn't be proper, would it? You have a seat. I'm fine right 'ere."

"What I'm going to ask you is rather—intimate. Really, sitting down would be most appropriate."

"So ye can sit next to me and try yer tricks again? I'm onto you now, mate. You might as well give up."

"Not a chance, luv."

It wasn't intentional, but Jeremy's look turned so sensual, Danny actually gasped and quickly glanced away. She even started fanning her face with her duster, apparently not realizing she was doing it. When she did, she made another sound, close to a groan.

And Jeremy was met with a dilemma. Should he take advantage of having just aroused her or proceed with his plan to get to know her better? Much as it went against his instincts, he was forced to opt for the latter. He simply wanted more from her than immediate gratification. And he was afraid that even if she succumbed fully, she'd later see it as his taking advantage of the moment and be so furious with him, this time, that she'd quit her job and leave.

A moment later she said rather breathlessly, "I'll sit. But you sit somewhere else, eh."

Jeremy grinned. Progress, definite progress. But when she moved to sit on the sofa, she sat on the end farthest away from him. He sighed and moved to the other sofa across from her.

"This won't take long, will it?" she asked, sounding somewhat annoyed now that she'd given in. "I've more work that needs doing."

"It could, but it probably won't. And don't worry about your work when I detain you. If you don't finish today, I'll accept the blame."

"Wot do you want to know then?"

"Let's start with your age?"

"Thought I'd already mentioned that."

"Fifteen, was it?"

"Ten actually. Just tall for my age."

He burst out laughing. She didn't share his humor so he tried to curb it quickly and asked, "So you were orphaned when you were what? Two or three?"

"I'm guessing closer to four or five, might even 'ave been six."

"So you're closer to twenty? Might even be twenty-one?"

She nodded. It was curt though. She still wouldn't relax and he wasn't sure how to fix that when he was the one making her nervous. He'd been hoping she'd open up and forget that she'd rather be anywhere other than having a conversation with him.

He tried a different route. "Was Dagger the one who taught you to steal?"

"It were Lucy. She were the one who found me and took me in."

Two *were*s that close together reminded him that he'd meant to help her with her vocabulary. "*Was* instead of *were*."

"Eh?"

"You used the word *were* twice. The correct—"

She cut him off indignantly, "I know I don't talk good enough to be a maid in a fancy house like this. Mrs. Robertson is trying to help, but she gets distracted easy and goes off on some other subject."

"I'll teach you."

For some reason that garnered a scowl. "Teach me wot?"

He chuckled over her overly suspicious mind. "Anything you like, dear girl, but what I was referring to was your speech. It *can* be corrected, you know. Had to have m'own corrected as well. That doesn't surprise you? Oh, I see, you don't believe me."

"And wot did ye talk like?" she asked, her tone scoffing. "Me?"

"Not quite." He grinned. "But close."

She snorted. Apparently, she still wasn't buying it. "Were ye stolen then as a babe? Raised amongst thieves?"

"I was raised in a tavern on the docks, Danny, and if you snort again, I'll come over there and squeeze your nose shut. It was where my mother worked for many years and where I stayed after she died. I'm a bastard, don't you know," he added cheerfully.

"Ye aren't joking, are ye?"

"Not a'tall. And roll that *u* off your tongue, m'dear."

She blushed, but only slightly. "When did ye-ur father take you in then?"

"I was sixteen when he found me, or rather, I found him. He didn't know I existed."

"Then how'd you know who he was?"

"Because my mother was so taken with him that she talked about him at least once every single day and described him so perfectly, I knew him the moment I saw him. Bowled him over, of course, when I told him I was his son."

"And he believed you?"

Jeremy chuckled. "Well, there were a few

moments of doubt, extreme doubt actually, not that I wasn't related to him, but that I was his. He *knew* I was related, couldn't miss that, when I look just like his brother Tony. But after I told him about my mother, he actually remembered her, and the time he'd spent with her."

"So wot you're saying is, you didn't become a nabob till you were sixteen?" she asked incredulously.

"Indeed."

"But you act like one so bleedin' perfectly."

He laughed. "Quite acquired, dear girl. All of which proves my point, don't it?"

"That I can learn to talk like you?"

"Exactly."

"I used to," she admitted.

"Eh?"

She laughed now. It was such a delightful sound Jeremy caught his breath. And she didn't keep him in suspense, adding, "Talk like you."

"Really?"

"A few times it's come back naturally to me, but most times I have to think about it first, and when I'm nervous or angry, I forget about even trying. It was so long ago that I talked proper that it just doesn't seem familiar to me now."

"Sure, you're ancient, I know."

She grinned but said no more, which drove his curiosity through the roof. "So you weren't born in the slums?"

She shrugged. "I don't know where I was born. I lost my memory when I was young. Lucy found me, like I mentioned, and took me home with her. She weren't more'n twelve or so herself. It's hard to remember that long ago, but I recall she said I talked too fine, that I wouldn't fit in unless I talked like her, so she fixed that—probably like you've been doing," Danny ended with a grin.

"Where were you when she found you?"

"In an alley."

"You don't remember how you got there?"

"Sure I do. Miss Jane brought me there. She died though, the same day Lucy found me."

"Who was Miss Jane? Your mother?"

"She said she weren't, that she was a nurse. She w-was with me after the blood. I think she took me away from it."

Jeremy sat forward abruptly, exclaiming, "Good God, *what* blood?"

Danny frowned. "That part o' my memory ain't clear, and I remember nothing from before then. I had a nasty gash on the back of my head. Lucy said it was bad enough to leave a scar. I've never seen it m'self."

"So you have no memory a'tall of your parents?"

"None. I have dreams though. One is nice, of a pretty lady. She's so pretty and dressed so fine, she's like an angel. I told Lucy about it, and she figured she were an angel, that I were dreaming that I should have died and the angel were looking for me."

"Was," he corrected almost automatically. "Did she look like you, the angel?"

Danny blinked. "How'd you know? I never told Lucy that. But she did look like me some, at least, her face did. And her hair was white, but done up real fancy. She wasn't old, though, not a'tall."

"She's probably your mother, Danny."

She snorted. "Sure she is. She was dressed too fine for that. My thoughts on the matter are more likely. She's what I want to be."

He gave that some thought, then had to

concede, "Possibly." He grinned. "And not an unreasonable goal either. I wonder what you'd look like in silk and with your hair in an elegant coiffure—God, never mind. I can imagine, and you'd have me groveling on the floor kissing your feet and promising you the world."

She laughed. Again, he caught his breath. Her violet eyes fairly sparkled when she did that. Her whole face changed, glowed, making her even more beautiful than she was, and he hadn't thought that was possible, she was already so lovely it hurt.

"I am appalled at the notion m'self, so why are you laughing?" he demanded with mock sternness.

"Because when you're silly, you're *really* silly, mate. Kissing my feet, eh? Will I need to remove my boots first?"

He blinked, looked down at her feet. "Well, damn me, you *are* still wearing boots. Did Mrs. Robertson forget about that part of your new wardrobe? You should have some comfortable house shoes, m'dear. After all, your job requires you to be on your feet for most of the day. Although, come to think of it, I'd much prefer you be flat on your back all day. Care to switch jobs?"

"Not bleedin' likely." She was back to snorting.

He raised a brow. "You're not even curious what the other job entails?"

"Being one o' the 'boys' for fifteen years means I know how you gents think." She stood up stiffly as she said it and added as she marched out of the room, "Keep that in mind, mate, 'fore you insult me again."

"Now wait—I didn't—"

Jeremy gave up. She was already gone. Blister it, how the devil had he erred so quickly? She'd been laughing only a moment before.

He sighed, then a grin came slowly to his lips. Their talk might have ended on a distinctly sour note, but he'd made great progress nonetheless. He'd gotten her to relax with him a little, *and* he'd made her laugh. The next step would be joking, teasing, more laughter. Then he could progress to some legitimate stolen kisses—well, perhaps he should wait until his bruises healed. After all, she was a woman who threw punches instead of slaps.

Chapter 25

"Lucy!" Danny gasped when she got to the door after being told she had a visitor. She threw her arms around Lucy, gave her a big hug, but one look at her friend's expression when she stepped back had her adding, "What's wrong?"

"Let's go for a walk, eh? I don't feel right, being in a place like this."

Danny understood. Lucy wasn't just a whore, she dressed like one and was so out of place in this neighborhood. She was surprised Lucy had made it this far without someone trying to run her off.

"Let's go over to the park," Danny suggested, taking Lucy's arm and leading her across the street. "How'd you manage to get here?"

Lucy grinned at that point. "Found a hack. The driver were so pleased to do me, 'e were more'n willing to bring me up 'ere. In fact"—she turned to blow a kiss to the hack driver, who was waiting just down the block— "'e's going to wait and take me 'ome, too."

"I didn't expect a visit this soon. I haven't even been gone a week yet."

Danny had used some of the coins Mrs. Robertson had given her to hire a chimney sweep, to take Lucy her new address. Mrs. Appleton had written it out for her, and the lad had been more'n pleased to run the errand, since he didn't get as much work in the summer as he did in the winter.

"It's wonderful to see you though," Danny said as they sat down on a bench, the street still in sight.

"I were worried that ye wouldn't find a job soon, with all the trouble ye 'ad before when ye went looking. But it appears ye landed a right nice one. Look at ye. I barely recognized ye in yer fancy clothes. And it bowled me over it did when the driver pointed me to that 'ouse. Ye like it 'ere? Cor, 'ow could ye not!"

"It takes getting used to, but the people are very nice and helpful. They're even teaching me to talk better."

"I noticed, and not better. Ye used to talk so fine, it 'urt me ears."

Danny chuckled. "No, it didn't. You were forever pinching me when I'd slip up, when you were teaching me."

"I never pinched 'ard, just didn't want ye getting kicked out 'cause ye didn't fit in. Though truth to tell, I always figured ye wouldn't be with us long, that yer family would find ye and take ye away from us."

"Did you really?"

Danny had hoped for the same thing. For many years, she had cried herself to sleep for parents she couldn't even remember. But when she was old enough to think about it logically, she had to conclude she had no family left, other than the one Lucy had brought her to. If there had been any-one, even a distant relative, wouldn't Miss Jane have mentioned it and tried to get to them?

Reminded that she'd gotten kicked out of the gang anyway, just years later, had sobered them both. "It were time ye go on yer own, Danny, and look 'ow well it turned out."

"I know, but I still miss all of you."

"Ye can visit from time to time. Be good to rub it in Dagger's nose, 'ow well ye've done on yer own. Speaking o' 'is nose, 'e got it broke."

Danny blinked. "Well, good for him. I've no sympathy a'tall for him at the moment. But you didn't come all this way just to tell me that."

"Actually, I did," Lucy said, uneasy now. "I weren't there when it 'appened, so didn't get a look at the man who broke it, but 'e slapped Dagger around good, to get 'im to tell where ye went."

"Me?"

"Aye, course Dagger couldn't tell 'im wot 'e didn't know. That boy who brung me yer address found me on the street, so Dagger didn't know I 'ad it."

"But the man was looking for *me?*"

Lucy nodded. " 'E didn't give a name, or why 'e was searching for ye. 'E scared Dagger, though, and ye know Dagger don't get scared by much. And that scared me, 'cause if 'e could 'urt Dagger just to get to ye, then 'e likely means to 'arm ye, too. And Dagger knows now."

"What?"

"That yer a woman. The man called ye 'the white-'aired wench.' "

Danny flinched. "Was he very angry?"

" 'E were too busy moving us to a new place, so that bloke don't find us again, and nursing his nose and other bruises. Were 'ard to tell if 'e were angry over wot happened or over yer deception."

"You think it's someone I've robbed?"

"I can't think o' any other reason. But ye were always so careful not to be seen."

"I know, but—" Danny broke off as it occurred to her who it might be.

"Wot?"

"That lord I robbed that night, his servant got a good look at me. And although I talked my way out of there, he would've known the next day that I was the thief, when the lord's jewelry came up missing. Turns out he were a thief himself, that lord, so he'd probably know how to go about hiring some street thug to track me down."

"That don't sound good," Lucy said nervously.

"No, it don't."

Chapter 26

Giving it more thought after she left Lucy, Danny had to doubt the person looking for her had been hired by Lord Heddings. He'd asked for a female, but Heddings's servant that night had given no indication at all that he'd seen through her male disguise. So they'd be looking for a white-haired man, not a woman.

And besides, she remembered having the feeling that someone was following her home that morning. They must have lost her, asked around, and finally found where she lived. She'd passed through some nice areas getting home that day. So it could have been no more than some nabob who'd recently been robbed. Seeing her passing through his neighborhood, he could have decided she was the culprit and followed her for some payback. She'd lost her hat by then, and it was much easier to tell she was a woman when she wasn't wearing her hat. Or he could have followed her all the way home, but seeing where she lived, decided not to confront her himself but to hire some tough to teach her a lesson instead.

That made more sense and wasn't really worth worrying over. The gent would never find her where she was living now. So she got back to cleaning the upstairs and didn't give it another thought.

Lucy's unexpected, though welcome, visit had thrown Danny off schedule a bit. It was late in the afternoon when she finally got around to cleaning the downstairs rooms. Thinking it was empty, she entered the parlor, but did an about-face upon seeing Jeremy and his cousin Regina Eden sitting on the sofa. She didn't get back out quickly enough, though.

"Come in, Danny. You can clean around us," Jeremy told her.

"It can wait," Danny assured him.

"At this late hour? Don't be silly. Go

ahead and finish up, then you'll be done for the day."

She would be, too. The parlor was her last room to see to. And it didn't need much cleaning today, hadn't been used since she'd sat on that same sofa yesterday.

This was the first time she'd come across Jeremy since then. He'd gone out last night, went out again early this morning, and had only just returned. Oddly, the house didn't seem the same when he wasn't in it. She couldn't exactly tell why, but it was definitely noticeable, by her anyway. Maybe because she couldn't completely relax when she knew he was around. No, that *should* be why, but it was the opposite. She couldn't seem to relax when he wasn't there.

She was still slightly annoyed with herself for letting her guard down with him yesterday. The trick he'd pulled on her the other night was clue enough that she could never do that again. And yet yesterday all they'd done was talk. She'd learned a few interesting things about him.

He was a bastard. Imagine that. Who would have thought, with him living in a grand house like this, and in the nabob part of town—and with such a huge family, all of whom had obviously accepted him without question.

Born and raised in a tavern. It still boggled her mind. It brought him down to her level, it did. His mother had been no different from what her parents had probably been. And why had he told her that? You'd think it would be something he'd want kept secret.

"You still have her dusting?" Regina said to Jeremy as Danny crossed the room to clean the mantel above the cold fireplace. "Or does she just love to dust?"

"Don't start—" Jeremy began, only to get cut off.

"I swear, Jeremy, I would have thought you of all people would know how to treat a mistress properly."

Danny glanced over her shoulder in time to see Jeremy kick his cousin and glare at her. The lady merely tsked and changed the subject, which seemed to be back to what they'd been discussing before Danny'd arrived.

"You can't avoid this ball, Jeremy, really you can't. And it's a perfect opportunity for you to set matters straight. Emily started a new rumor last night, that she actually had a lovers' rendezvous with you. You *do* know what that means, don't you?"

"Means she's a bloody liar."

"No, *we* know that, but no one else does. It means she's already moving on to the last resort, and the season's barely begun!"

"Hell's bells, I've barely even looked at the chit!" Jeremy complained. "I don't understand why she's picked me, when I haven't given her even two minutes of my time, let alone indicated I'd like to know her better."

"What dealings *have* you had with her?"

"None worth mentioning. She had someone introduce us, as I recall, don't even remember who, but I was already leaving that party, so I didn't say more'n a few words to her. And she approached Drew and me the other night, but again, I barely even glanced at her. You'd bloody well think she'd want *some* clue that I was interested, before she started this campaign to get me leg-shackled."

"Famous! Denial doesn't help us here, Jeremy. You know very well that there isn't a young unmarried female in this whole town who wouldn't jump at the chance to catch you. Emily Bascomb is just *doing* something about it, whereas the others just wait around hoping to gain your notice."

Danny glanced back again, in time to see Jeremy blushing. Fascinated by their conversation, she knew she should move on to a different piece of furniture, but she didn't want to remind them that she was there.

"If you know so much, puss, tell me why the rush?" he complained. "I only clapped eyes on the lady for the first time last week. D'you think she has to get married? Already enceinte?"

Regina frowned, then shook her head. "No, highly doubtful. I think she just fell head over heels for you and has decided no one else will do for her now. And her impatience stems from being spoiled. I *have* learned that much about her. Found an old chap who's known the Bascombs for many years. He mentioned that she's an only child, so her father spoiled her beyond redemption."

"But to blacken her own name in this campaign? That's a bit much, ain't it?"

"Well, that can only be for one reason," Regina said. "She wants her father to hear about it and take matters into his own hands. Now do you see why you need to attend this ball tomorrow night?"

"No. My attending if she is there is just going to—"

"No, no, you won't be going there alone. I ran into an old friend of our cousin's last night."

"Which cousin?"

Regina tsked impatiently, "Diana, not that it matters. The point is that her friend's younger sister is also having her first season."

"Do I know her?"

"No, don't think so."

"Then what are you getting at?"

"I'm sure she would agree to have you escort her to this ball if we present the plan to her. And if you devote the entire evening to her, it will prove without a doubt that your romantic inclinations are directed elsewhere. Particularly if you ignore Emily completely in the process."

"Easy enough to do, but the chit isn't going to get her own hopes up, is she?"

"No—well, probably. They all do, if you just happen to glance at them. But we *would* explain fully that she'd merely be helping you out of this horrid situation which is escalating far too quickly. And she would benefit from your attention. It will quite raise her on the ladder, as it were, since it will draw her to the attention of every other young buck. They'll want to know what *you* find so fascinating about her."

Jeremy chuckled. "You overstate the effect I have, puss."

"Rubbish. We both know that your appearance at any social gathering quite stirs up the pot. Mostly everyone wonders if you've taken after your father and uncle. Those two rakes did leave their mark, notoriously, before they quit the social scene. You, however, have managed to avoid any scandals thus far, so no one knows what to make of you yet."

"I do try." Jeremy grinned.

"We know you do," Regina said, patting his hand. "I suppose you learned from Derek's example, to keep your affairs strictly private. Of course it helps that you choose your women from the ones who don't feel a need to brag about it to anyone who will listen. And don't you dare mention my Nick's bad luck in that regard."

Jeremy hooted with laughter. "Never entered my mind, old girl. Although, come to think of it, his bad luck with Lady Eddington turned out to be your good luck. Doubt you would have met him otherwise, or been forced to marry him, if Lady E. hadn't crowed to her friends that he'd meant to abduct her, but abducted you instead."

Regina scowled. "Thank you for *not* mentioning it. Now *as* I was saying, if you show up tomorrow night with this young debutante and spend the entire evening devoted to her, it will hit all the gossip mills that you're courting her and should quite undo the gossip Emily is spreading. And Emily will be forced to back off—"

"That is if she believes it," Jeremy cut in. "This sister of Diana's friend, she's prettier than Emily?"

Regina frowned. "Well, no, actually. Famous! All my brilliant thoughts on the matter wasted. You're quite right, it won't work. Emily will easily see it for the ploy it is. It won't put her off a'tall, will more'n likely double her own efforts."

"Well, it would work if you can find me a chit who is prettier than Emily. No easy task, I know. The lady is quite stunning."

Regina sighed. "Devil take it, Jeremy, if you think so, then *why* aren't you interested in her? *She's* probably wondered the same thing, *and* thinks you're just playing hard to get. She could think she's merely doing you a favor, to hurry things along with these lies she's spreading."

"One simple answer, puss. Give it just the tiniest bit of thought and you'll come up with it."

Raising a black brow, Regina said in a droll tone, "Because you've decided to spend your life without a wife?"

"Exactly. So I keep my eyes and hands off debutantes, and any other young misses on the marriage mart. There are quite enough women to enjoy without risking my bachelorhood."

"Spare me the details, please," Regina said, rolling her eyes now. "And we can forget about my brilliant idea. There simply are no other young hopefuls this go-round who can even come close to Emily Bascomb in rank and looks. The lady is hands down the reigning belle of the season."

Jeremy did some hand-patting now. "I'm sure you'll think of something else, puss. You always do."

Regina sighed. "But we're running out of time. She's already claimed you've had a lovers' rendezvous, when you haven't. But that little on-dit is going to reach her father eventually, then he'll be calling on *your* father, and you know how that goes."

Jeremy grinned at her. "My father will laugh in his face and tell him to go buy her a husband elsewhere, that I ain't for sale."

"Then he'll just move on to Uncle Jason, and you know very well Jason won't laugh over the matter."

Jeremy cringed now. "Very well, we are down to desperate measures. Your plan was a good one. Just think of some other chit to play the part who is at least somewhat comparable to Emily."

Regina shook her head again. "I hate to say it, but we just don't have a sterling crop of young hopefuls this year. The only other girl who even comes close is already engaged. In fact, I can't think of a single unmarried woman in all of London who—well, hmmm."

"What?"

"I should rephrase that. There is one, and I'm looking at her."

Danny swung around to see whom Regina was talking about and found the pair on the sofa staring at her now. She started blushing. She'd been following their conversation avidly. She didn't need to ask what Regina Eden meant. She'd just been given an amazing compliment and was still absorbing how nice it felt.

Jeremy glanced back at his cousin and with a frown said flatly, "No."

"But she's perfect!" Regina exclaimed. "She quite outshines Emily Bascomb by far."

"No."

"And why not? Yes, yes, I know, she'd have to keep her mouth shut, of course."

"It's not that—"

"Course it is," Regina interrupted. "For her to speak at all would quite give away the ruse. Can you keep your mouth shut, Danny?" Danny said nothing, prompting Regina to add triumphantly, "There, you see, she can."

"Reggie, I love you, but you've gone half-baked on this idea now. She can talk well enough when she's not nervous, b—"

"She can?" Regina interrupted again in surprise.

"Yes, though there's no guarantee she wouldn't slip up. But she doesn't have attire for a ball, and there's no way a gown of that sort could be done up between now and to-morrow night."

"So I'll lend her one of mine."

He lifted a brow. "Did you grow an extra seven inches last night?"

"So we'll add a hem. Stop being so negative, Jeremy, you know this will work, especially if she can mimic her betters."

"It won't. She can't dance. She—"

"How d'you know I can't dance, eh?" Danny cut in now. "Maybe I've attended those masked balls in convent gardens. Maybe I'm a right fine dancer."

"For a man," Jeremy countered impatiently. "Ever try it as a woman?"

Danny blushed again. Actually, she'd never danced in her life, but she resented him taking that for granted. And this idea was starting to sound like fun. Attend a fancy high-class ball? Something she'd never dreamed possible. And what a perfect opportunity to meet a man who might fall in love with her and want to marry her! Not a lord, of course. She knew she couldn't aspire that high. But surely it wouldn't be just lords at such a gathering. Other well-to-do, respectable men would be invited, men without titles who weren't as restricted in whom they married.

And she *had* attended a masked ball before at the gardens—well, not actually attended, but looked on from a distance wishing she could. The people at it seemed to be having such a rousing good time. And those balls weren't just for the nabobs, far from it. Anyone could go to those and pretend for a night that they were someone other than who they were.

"So she won't dance," Regina was saying to counter Jeremy's last objection. "Sprained ankle and all that."

"So she can't talk, can barely walk. Sounds like she should be in a sickbed, not showing up at a ball."

Regina scowled at him as she insisted, "She lost her voice on a particularly exciting fox hunt in the country earlier this week. She's recovering nicely, but still pampering the vocal chords. Twisted her ankle at the same hunt, don't you know. She *would* have declined this ball, but she didn't want to disappoint you, when you were *so* looking forward to showing her off tomorrow night. And since she's only in town for the weekend—"

"I catch the drift, Reggie. And just who are you going to pass her off as being?"

"Perhaps she can be distantly related to Kelsey. Kelsey does come from all sorts of titles, though they rarely get mentioned since she married our cousin Derek. But I'm sure she wouldn't mind claiming Danny as a relative."

"Related to a duke is a bit much, don't you think?" Jeremy said.

"No, no, one of the lesser titles, of course. And very distantly. Perhaps her parents moved to America and she grew up there—no, I know, Cornwall! Just in case her thick accent gets noticed. This *is* going to work, and splendidly. No one, and I mean no one, is going to doubt that you've been courting this lovely girl for the last several months, so you couldn't possibly have been rendezvousing with Emily Bascomb. Must have been some other lucky chap."

Jeremy shook his head at his cousin, but he did so in amazement. "How do you do it, Cousin? You simply boggle me, 'deed you do."

"Rubbish," Regina scoffed. "And I'll be taking her home with me to get her ready. Come round with a carriage tomorrow night to pick us up at precisely nine p.m. We only want to be fashionably late, nothing more."

"Us?"

"I'll be going with you, of course. She must have a chaperone."

"When did you become my guardian angel, puss?"

"When Amy asked me to keep an eye on you while she was gone."

He rolled his eyes. Amy wasn't just their cousin but his best friend, and she worried about him far more than was necessary.

"Far be it for me to put a damper on your amazing scheme, but don't you think you should ask Danny if she's willing to rescue me from Emily's clutches?"

"Oh, dear," Regina sighed. "Yes, I suppose." And to Danny: "Are you up to the task at hand, m'dear? Jeremy here really does need rescuing, or he'll be dragged to the altar through no effort of his own."

Danny grinned. "I'm right handy at masquerading."

Regina blinked. "Why, yes, you are, aren't you? Well, come along then. We've a lot to accomplish in very little time."

Chapter 27

Regina Eden was simply amazing. She was a whirlwind of activity, instructions, and nonstop chatter. She did drag Danny out of Jeremy's house and down the street to hers and took her straight up to her bedchamber, not giving her any time to gape at the magnificent town house they were rushing through. Regina immediately summoned her maid, Tess, told her what was required, and between them, they pulled out from Regina's wardrobe countless gowns of the like Danny had never before seen. When they finally settled on one, Danny barely got a look at it before Tess sent another maid off to work on it.

The next order of business was shoes, but those that matched the gown simply wouldn't fit Danny's feet no matter how they tried to stretch them, and there was no time to have a pair made. So Regina sent a footman around to her relatives'. Danny wasn't sure whose white satin slippers showed up before dinner, but they were only slightly short at the heels and her toes weren't nearly as scrunched as they had been when trying on Regina's shoes.

There was no break for dinner. Regina had trays brought up to her room, and Danny got to eat from hers while Tess tried to figure out what could be done with her hair. No easy task. In fact, this turned out to be the toughest of their problems. Such short curls simply didn't want to be tamed. And a good number of them had to be cut even shorter, to even out the butchering Lucy had done.

Regina finally produced a tiara and Tess exclaimed, "This will do it! I can divide the curls now and control them like this. It's as close as we'll get to a contained look."

"Famous! I knew you could do it, Tess. I'll want it looking just so tomorrow."

Danny didn't get a chance to see it herself before the tiara was removed and she was shown to a guest bedroom, where Regina told her to get right to sleep. They had a *lot* more work to do tomorrow, and she'd be woken early.

A guest bedroom! She couldn't believe it, couldn't believe either that Lady Regina was going to such bother to save her cousin from marriage to a beautiful heiress. If someone like that didn't tempt him to put the shackle on, then Jeremy obviously hadn't been exaggerating when he'd said he was going to remain a bachelor the rest of his life. Which was too bad, she thought with a pang of sadness. For him to go to such lengths to avoid marriage just proved he wasn't the man for her.

She was excited, though, at the prospect of his seeing her transformation into a lady tomorrow. She'd be attending a ball with him! He was even going to pretend to be courting her. For a short while reality would be suspended and she could do some pretending of her own—that the whole glorious evening was for real. . . .

She was awakened earlier than she expected the next morning. It seemed as if she'd barely gotten to sleep when a maid was knocking on her door and coming in with a platter of breakfast. She'd only eaten half of it when Regina walked in complaining, "Not done yet? Well, do hurry. You shouldn't need to dance tonight, but just in case something goes wrong and you end up having to, I've decided we have enough time for a little instruction in that regard."

"You're going to teach me to dance?"

"Not me, dear girl, Jeremy is. I've already sent for him."

Danny couldn't help snorting. "You won't get him out of bed this early."

"Yes, I know." Regina sighed. "But he will be roused, since I've mentioned it's an emergency."

"Is it?"

"Course not, but that will get him here in quick order. Now, I suppose I should tell you a little bit about this ball. Lady Aitchison is having it, and that means it is going to be the premier ball of the season, because her parties are all the rage, yet she only has them every four years or so."

"That mean there will be a lot of people there?"

"Yes, it will be an immense crush, with

the very cream of London society in attendance. All the young debutantes this season, all the young men who *do* want to get married, their mamas and papas and other assorted escorts, and a few scoundrels like our sweet Jeremy whom you should avoid."

"He's not a scoundrel," Danny said, though she'd thought the same thing herself more'n once.

"Course he is, though a lovable one. Why look what he's doing to you? He makes you his mistress, but still has you cleaning his house!"

"I'm *not* his mistress, nor will I ever be!"

Regina blinked at the vehement tone as well as the words. "Really? Oh my, I do apologize then. I thought, well, the whole family thought, well, blister it, it's rather obvious he wants you to be, and Jeremy has never failed to obtain a woman he wants."

Danny was blushing by then, because she'd come close to succumbing to his seduction herself and had to constantly remind herself of her goals and that Jeremy Malory wasn't one of them. But Regina didn't notice the blush and, as usual, went from one subject to the next seamlessly.

"Come along, then. I've already had the parlor cleared so we'll have room to work."

The work wasn't just dancing. As soon as they got downstairs, Regina told her, "Now, let me see how you walk. No, no, you aren't wearing britches anymore. Take small steps. That's better, but, no, don't walk with your whole body, just your legs. We want it to look like you're gliding across the room without really moving a'tall.

Danny slowed down and took smaller steps. "Perfect!" Regina exclaimed.

Danny grinned. "Do *you* walk like this?"

Regina chuckled. "Well, I do try, really I do. But truth be known, I used to be a bit of a tomboy. I was raised with my cousin Derek after my mother died, and I enjoyed the freedom that boys have. Course, you must know what I mean. Isn't that why you wore britches?"

"No, where I come from, girls work on their backs, and at young ages. I didn't want to be forced into that line o' work, so I lived the life of a boy."

"Oh my." Regina was blushing now. "No one knew?"

"Only my friend Lucy."

"Reggie, where are you?" Jeremy suddenly called from the hall.

"In here!"

He appeared in the doorway, his expression quite disgruntled and turned on his cousin. "D'you know what time it is?"

"Yes, and half the morning is already wasted. You're going to teach Danny to dance."

"I am?" He crossed his arms and leaned against the doorframe. "I thought she was going to have a sprained ankle?"

"She is, but it's mostly recovered, merely a bit tender. We're not making her limp, after all. And this is just a precaution. What if King George shows up and asks her to dance?"

Jeremy rolled his eyes. "That's stretching it, Reggie, 'deed it is."

"That was merely an example of why she needs to learn to dance. Don't be difficult. This is your ankle we're saving from the shackle."

He glanced at Danny and his eyes widened slightly. "Cut your hair, did they? Looks very nice."

Danny blushed becomingly. "It will be fancied up for tonight."

"Heaven help me if you get even more beautiful." Then he grinned and said to his cousin, "Damn me, I don't suppose you'd leave us alone for this instruction, Reggie?"

"Not a chance. This isn't an excuse for you to manhandle her, so behave!"

He sighed. "Don't we need music for this?"

"I'm going to hum, and if you laugh about my humming, I'll box your ears, see if I don't."

He crossed over to Danny and extended his hand. "Are you ready to be taught, luv?"

He said it in such a way that she humphed. "To dance and nothing else."

"More's the pity," he whispered as he drew her a bit closer and began to waltz with her about the room.

She keenly felt his hand on her back, his other warm against her palm. The room was large. Regina was on the far side of it, so she couldn't hear Jeremy when he began to fluster Danny with his whispered comments.

"I love touching you. D'you think she'll notice if I put my hand on your derriere?"

"*I'll* notice," Danny gasped.

He chuckled. "But you'd like it, wouldn't you?"

"No. And don't you dare! We're supposed to be dancing."

"But I can make love and dance at the same time," Jeremy whispered. "I promise you."

Danny sucked in her breath and was barely able to reply, "What a whopper. Now stop it!"

But, of course, he didn't. Leaning slightly closer he whispered, "Shall I tell you how it can be done? You only need to hold on tight and wrap your legs about my hips. We'd both have to be naked, of course."

She tripped, was surprised she hadn't done so sooner when she suddenly couldn't concentrate on anything but him and the images he was drawing in her mind. He gathered her closer till she regained her balance, which *didn't* help, only made her distraction worse.

Regina had stopped humming. Danny became aware of that when she noticed a servant had come in to speak to the lady. Jeremy must have noticed as well that his cousin wasn't paying attention to them because his mouth was suddenly on Danny's neck, kissing her hotly, then moving over her ear where his tongue laved deeply. Oh, God, the feeling was amazing. Her knees went weak, but she didn't need the strength to stand. Jeremy was holding her so close her feet were off the floor! And she was clinging to him. She couldn't help it. The feelings he aroused in her made her want to get even closer. . . .

Regina's loud throat-clearing drew them apart again, but slowly. Her feet back on the floor, Danny tried to regain her composure. Noticing Jeremy's grin helped in that regard. That scoundrel! He knew exactly what he'd just done to her senses and was puffed-up pleased about it.

Jeremy took pity on her and got serious after that, told her to follow his lead, and she actually learned a thing or two about dancing before he was done.

Danny had thought they would continue after lunch, but she got sent back to bed instead, with Regina warning her to sleep, not just rest, because they would be up until the wee hours of the morning. Danny was sure that she was too excited by that point to actually fall asleep in the middle of the day, but all the information and instructions that had been thrown at her had quite worn her out, and she was asleep within moments of lying down.

Chapter 28

~~~~

Danny slept so soundly she was disoriented when she awoke and keenly disappointed. She assumed that she must have been dreaming that she was going to a ball. But then the knock came at the door and she opened her eyes to find she really was in Regina Eden's house, really was going to a ball.

A bath was drawn for her after her nap, and then it was time to get ready. She was led to Regina's room again and set before the vanity so this time she could watch Tess work her wonders with her hair. Regina was being dressed as well by another maid, yet all the while she was giving last-minute instructions that Danny barely heard, she was so fascinated by what was happening to her appearance.

Tess was using a jeweled tiara with a large amethyst at its center to tame her curls. With the tiara as a dividing point, the short curls left at her temples were twisted to look like ringlets, and the rest was combed in such a way that it resembled a short style many women had favored a few years back. Then in quick order, they were tossing petticoats over her head and draping her in the most exquisite ball gown.

The dress was basically a pale lavender silk. It had two layers of tulle lace ruffles toward the hem. To the second layer the maid had attached another border in white silk, over which violet lace was added. Once the same violet lace was added to the short puff sleeves, a narrow layer to the low, wide décolletage, and a half inch to the top edge of the long white gloves that she was also to wear, the entire effect was as if the ball gown had been created just so to begin with.

They had had to cut the shoulders, since the waist had been a bit high for Danny to begin with, Regina having a shorter torso than hers. But with the insertion of more white silk and violet lace that blended in with what had been added to the sleeves, it now fit her snugly about the waist as it should.

The entire ensemble was so fancy, Danny was reminded of the dream she'd had of the beautiful angelic woman. It had come true. For one night, she would be that incredibly beautiful woman. Danny simply couldn't stop staring at herself. Regina had to liter-ally drag her away from the mirror to go downstairs when they were done.

"Close your mouth, Jeremy, do," Regina complained when they found Jeremy wait-ing in the foyer for them.

He didn't, and he wouldn't stop staring either. Danny started blushing. She had a feeling he hadn't even heard his cousin's admonishment. Deep down, though, she was so pleased she could barely contain it.

He looked splendid himself in his formal black togs. His coat was open, the frilly white cravat tied loosely, giving him a rakish look. His raven black hair had been combed back, but it wouldn't stay. It fell over his temples and about his neck. His expression thrilled her.

He was shocked by her appearance, no doubt about it. She'd been shocked as well, so she understood why he could do nothing but stare.

Regina had to nudge Jeremy several times. When he finally paid attention to her, he dug in his feet and said adamantly, "She ain't leaving this house looking like that."

"And what's wrong with the way she looks? I'll have you know—"

"She's too bloody beautiful and you know it, Reggie."

She stared at him wide-eyed. "Well, that was the point, you daft boy."

"Not even close. Didn't expect her to look like this. She'll cause a sensation the likes this town has never seen. She stays home, and that's my last word on it."

Regina tsked at him in annoyance. *"You* stay home. *She's* going to the ball. Come to think of it, you don't really need to be there to accomplish what we're after. I can spread the word quite easily without your attendance. She has to be there, though. The rumor won't fly without the proof staring them in the face."

"You aren't listening, Reggie."

"No, *you* aren't. This is quite out of your

hands now. I'm going to save you despite yourself. Come along, Danny, and get in the coach."

Jeremy followed them, of course. And continued his objections all the way to the Aitchisons' home, which wasn't all that far. The ball was taking place in one of the mansions near the first Malory house Danny had visited.

Regina had stopped listening to Jeremy as she was quite annoyed with him now. Danny did, too, for that matter. She was disappointed that he was making such a fuss and didn't quite understand his reasoning. She was too pretty? Was going to cause a commotion because of it? She'd thought that had been the idea, to dispute the false rumors that Emily Bascomb was spreading.

Riding with Jeremy in a coach again also brought back memories of the night she'd met him. Jeremy must have guessed what she was thinking from her expression because he whispered to her, "Quite the change from the last time we rode together, eh? You're rather good at bolting from coaches. Feel free to do so anytime now."

She gave a soft snort at his suggestion. The man was determined to be in a rotten mood and predict dire consequences for tonight's agenda.

But reminded of what they'd done that night, she whispered back, "D'you think he'll be there?"

Without having to ask whom she meant, he said with a shrug, "Wouldn't matter if he is. It's his servant that would recognize us, not him."

Regina stopped Jeremy once more, just before they entered the Aitchison mansion. With a finger poked in his chest, she snarled, "If you don't stop with the doom and gloom, I'll never speak to you again."

"Do you promise?" he asked.

She ignored that and added, "And if you *are* going in there with us, then do your part and act appropriately smitten, or this entire farce will be pointless. Now get hold of yourself, Jeremy. The performance is about to begin."

The moment was at hand and Danny was finally hit with a large dose of apprehension. Regina had drilled her with a long list of dos and don'ts while they were working on her gown. She was afraid she was going to forget every one of them now. And then she was simply struck dumb by the sight of a high-fashion ball in full swing. The lights, the colors, the most exquisite ball gowns twirling about the huge room. She'd never seen anything like it in her life.

Her mouth must have dropped open, because Jeremy hissed in her ear, "Stop looking like you've never seen anything like this. You are supposedly gentry tonight and accustomed to such entertainments."

"Yes, but I 'ave"—she paused to cough, then continued—"*have* done very little socializing, *hav*ing only just finished my schooling."

"Reggie feed you that line?"

She blushed. "Yes, and a lot more."

"Why?" he groaned. "You aren't supposed to be talking at all."

Danny shrugged. "I suppose she figured I'd make a mistake or two."

"Or three or four. This was *such* a bad idea. I've simply lost my mind, no other answer for my agreeing to this. And it's your fault, you know."

She swung around, wondering how the devil he could blame any of this on her. "How's that, mate?"

"I want you so much, I simply can't think at all clearly anymore."

Danny's mouth dropped open again, to the accompaniment of a vivid blush. Her knees had gone weak, giddiness swirled in her stomach, and an image of them twirling about the dance floor without a stitch of clothing on popped into her mind. . . .

Why did he have to say things like that, that got her all mushy inside? And now, of all times, when she was on display to half the ton?

Regina moved closer to whisper, "Don't upset her now, Jeremy. Let her have her moment of glory. She's quite brought the house down."

Danny swung back around. Sure enough, the music was still playing, but the dancers had all halted, every single one of them staring her way. Her blush deepened. So did Jeremy's groan.

"I warned you she'd cause a sensation," he told his cousin in disapproval.

"And I'm pleased you were right. If you haven't noticed, Emily *is* here, and at this precise moment she's looking daggers at our Danny."

"Our Danny? When did she get to be *our* Danny?"

"I take credit when it's due. *You* might

have found her, but *I* helped to make her shine, dear boy. Now stop looking like you're annoyed with her. You're supposed to be in love. Do your part. Or do I need to instruct you how it's done?"

He rolled his eyes at her, but he did start grinning. And he warned Danny, "We're about to be overwhelmed. Remember, no talking if you can help it. 'Yes,' 'No,' 'Nice to meet you,' 'Good-bye.' That should do you fine. Do a lot of head nodding, goes a long way in a conversation."

He wasn't joking about being over-whelmed. It had only taken two people whose curiosity simply wouldn't allow them to wait before approaching them, then twenty more followed suit right behind them. Regina Eden proved once again how amazing she was. She fielded all the questions, made the statement about the lost voice and sore ankle as she'd planned to, and kept Danny from having to do any more than smile and extend her hand in greet-ings, at least for the most part. A few peo-ple were persistent and managed to get a word or two out of her, but it seemed more like a competition on their part, so they could tell their friends, "Well, she spoke to *me!*"

She didn't try to keep track of any of the names she was hearing in the introductions, didn't expect to see any of these people ever again. She was playing the part of a young miss fresh out of the schoolroom who just happened to have caught Jeremy Malory's eye and was making him seriously consider giving up his bachelorhood. She was Danielle Langton, with repeated mentions that she was distantly related to Kelsey's family.

Of course *that* became a source of conversation as it was remembered that Kelsey came from The Tragedy. Apparently her mother had shot her father over his gambling debts, then killed herself, both being an accident. She hadn't meant to shoot him or fall out the window afterward, but then that's why it had been termed The Tragedy.

Nothing was stated as fact, but the ton ended up assuming Danny was a Langton from Kelsey's side of the family, assuming she was engaged to Jeremy already, assuming she belonged among them. That several older gentlemen swore she looked familiar to them, Regina explained as a phenomena known as "if they hear it enough times, they believe it and begin to think they always knew it."

Jeremy had also relaxed and stopped complaining, after watching how smoothly Regina handled all the questions. One handsome young man came back though and must have missed the part about the sore ankle. Danny had been introduced to him she was sure, but she couldn't remember his name.

He flashed her an engaging grin. "I intend to shoot m'self if you won't allow me the first dance, Lady Danielle."

Jeremy didn't give her a chance to reply to such an outlandish statement. "You won't have to do that, Fawler," he told the fellow. "I'll be happy to oblige in that regard. She won't be dancing with anyone but me. Now move along."

The expression on Jeremy's face was so unnerving, the fellow didn't say another word; he simply backed off rather quickly.

Even after the last person moved on and she was finally standing there alone with Jeremy, the room was still buzzing about her. She'd played her part well, though, and was feeling mighty triumphant about it.

"Would you like to try dancing?" he asked her when they had a few minutes with no one else nearby.

"And muck up a good performance?"

"I didn't spend an hour twirling you about Reggie's parlor for you not to at least try it while you're here. If you trip a time or two, your sore ankle will be blamed. You know there's not much to it. You just need to follow my lead again."

She did want to try. It looked like such fun. So she nodded and let him lead her out to the dance floor. And for a short while, she forgot about where she was and all the people watching her.

His grip was firm, his palm against hers warm, the skin slightly rough. Was the rest of his skin like that, too? she wondered. Her hands almost itched to find out. And that image was back in her mind, of the two of them twirling around the dance floor, her legs wrapped tightly around him, both of them naked, the music filling her, him filling her, oh, God . . .

"What's wrong?" Jeremy questioned, hearing her gasp.

"Nothing," Danny lied, and desperate to get her mind off lovemaking, she asked,

"That chap wasn't serious, was he, about shooting himself?"

"Course not. I'm sure he tells all the young misses that. Flattery of that degree is bound to work for him occasionally. I prefer to stick to the truth, so what I would have said would have been, if you don't make love with me soon, I'm going to shoot m'self."

She blinked at him, then burst out laughing. "You call that the truth?"

"Well, stretched a little, but the sentiment was apt. I *am* getting desperate, dear girl."

She caught her breath. It was there in his eyes, not so much desperation, but passion hot enough to burn. She glanced away, was desperate herself to bank those fires of his before she succumbed to them.

To get him thinking along other lines she asked, "Who taught you to dance?"

"My father's first mate."

She looked back at him in amazement. "He had a woman for a first mate?"

"No, his nickname might have been Connie, but Conrad Sharpe is a six-foot-tall, red-haired Scot, and if you could have seen him pretending to be a female for an hour to teach me how to lead in a dance, you would have laughed your arse off."

She chuckled. "I can imagine."

"But I know he didn't have as much fun teaching me as I had teaching you."

She blushed. "Behave, Jeremy."

"Never!" he whispered in her ear.

He continued to tease her and make her laugh. He was such a good dancer, and he was so handsome tonight—cor, he was always handsome—but tonight in his black, fancy togs, exceptionally so. He made her feel special, dancing with him, made her feel as if she really did belong there. She couldn't remember when she'd had such a good time. And she couldn't deny it anymore. Jeremy might be pretending tonight to be in love with her, but she was beginning to suspect that she wasn't pretending on her part at all.

Chapter 29

⁓ ⁓

Jeremy might have relaxed enough to do his part as the evening progressed, but he still wasn't liking it. The only thing palatable about the evening was that Danny seemed to be having such a good time. He didn't begrudge her that at all. He simply hated sharing her.

She was his was the way he saw it, and every time another man got near her he felt the most primitive urge to protect what belonged to him. Which was insane. She wasn't his a'tall, she was his maid! He'd *like* for her to be more than that, but she wasn't cooperating in the least.

He went to fetch Regina and Danny some

champagne. They'd had to twist his arm. He had *not* wanted to leave Danny alone for even a minute. Unfortunately, his glance passed over Emily on the way and he noticed her casting sad eyes at him. Good God, was she going to play the wounded lover now? And still insist he'd bedded her when he hadn't?

"I do believe you are quite ready for bedlam," a voice he knew all too well said behind him.

Jeremy cringed. His father. He hadn't noticed James's arrival, hadn't noticed much of anything all evening other than Danny.

"I know."

"What the devil could you have been thinking, to bring her here?"

"It wasn't my idea. Think I wanted to share her with the ton and have every randy buck around ogling her? Not bloody likely."

"Who then? Or do I even need to ask?"

"You don't. Reggie, of course."

"My dear niece has come up with some very odd manipulations during the course of her interfering-in-every-little-thing career, but I can't fathom the reason for this one."

"Pro'bly because only a woman would think of it. She figured the only way to get

Emily to back off was to show her that I was interested in someone else, and she couldn't think of anyone who could outshine Emily other than—"

"I get the idea, but wouldn't a 'Get lost, wench' have sufficed for this troublesome young lady?"

"Reggie didn't think so, didn't think anything would make Emily find a new target. But this farce is more for the gossip mills, since Emily has been spreading the tale now that I've bedded her."

"Bloody hell!"

"Exactly. But there will be an opposite view now. After all, why would I pursue a mere daisy when I've been courting a rare white rose."

"Courting?" James choked.

"Just for effect," Jeremy assured him. "And we won't have to repeat this performance. Danny has made such a smashing impression, the ton will be talking about nothing else for weeks. Now what are *you* doing here? I could have sworn you said you had your excuses already prepared to escape being dragged along to these things?"

"Changed my mind. Wanted to have a

look at this conniving chit who is trying to maneuver you to the altar. By the by, which one is she?"

Jeremy looked to where he'd last seen Emily. She wasn't there. He then glanced back to see that his stepmother, George, had Regina's attention for the moment, which left Danny unobserved by either of them, and alarm bells went off when he saw who'd taken advantage of that.

"Good God, Emily is confronting Danny."

James raised a brow as he looked in the same direction. "This should prove interesting. Don't think I've ever watched two women throwing punches, and considering where your Danny comes from, that's a distinct possibility."

Danny's hackles rose when the lady pinched her arm to gain her attention. She was beautiful. Blond hair arranged elaborately in a perfect coiffure, a stunning white ball gown, which seemed to be the favored color for young debutantes, this one trimmed in powder blue to match the lady's azure eyes. Those eyes were narrowed in a baleful scowl though. In fact, so much hate was pouring out of them, Danny was stunned for a moment.

"I don't know who you are, but if you think you're going to steal him from me, you are sadly mistaken," the young woman told her.

It clicked then, who the lady was. Regina should really have pointed her out to give Danny some warning. Not that she could have avoided this, when she hadn't noticed the lady approaching her.

After that unnecessary pinch, though, she didn't pull any punches when she replied, "Ah, you must be Emily of the many lies."

"I beg your pardon?"

"You're making a fool of yourself, lady. He's onto you, his family is onto you, and after tonight, the entire town will be onto you. Your lies will only serve to bury you in your own shame."

Emily gasped, a high blush rising up her ivory cheeks. "I don't think you quite understand. He *is* going to marry me. My father will see to that."

Danny raised a brow. "Based on a lie?"

"I see you've been misinformed. I'm not a liar. He is, though, if he's trying to deny that he trifled with me."

"Is that what you call having a few words of conversation?" Danny asked innocently.

"Is *that* what he claims?" Emily looked incredulous, and it didn't seem the least bit contrived. And then she added with a sigh, "I should have known he couldn't be trusted to keep his promises. After all, his father was the most notorious rake this town has ever seen, his uncle Anthony a close second, and obviously, Jeremy is endeavoring to follow in those same footsteps."

Danny had no comment for that. She wouldn't be a bit surprised if some of it was true. She knew Jeremy had no intention of getting married, had heard him say it. And obviously he took his pleasure where he could find it. His trying to get under her own skirts was proof of that. She didn't think he was that callous though, to make promises he had no intention of keeping. He could have seduced the lady, yes, but Danny doubted he'd done it with anything more than a quick tumble in mind.

Danny hadn't expected the lady to seem so sincere either. She was quite believable. Either she was very, very good at lying, or she was telling the truth.

Danny pointed that out. "If he's as despicable as you say, why do you even want him?"

"I don't anymore," Emily insisted. "But I have no choice in the matter now." Then she explained in a whisper, "I suspect I'm enceinte."

"How can you know that already? He only met you last week!"

"I said suspect," Emily hissed in annoyance. "I won't know for certain for another week or two. And I hope I'm wrong, I really do, but unfortunately, I doubt it. So you can see now why you're wasting your time and are headed for nothing but disappointment."

Danny shook her head. "No, what I see is you're deluding yourself. Buck up and accept your loss. Getting your father involved will just add to your own shame. And for what? He still won't marry you."

"What a dense twit you are! You don't know how these things are handled. When the heir to a fortune is involved, it goes beyond personal preferences. Believe me, Jeremy will have no more say in it than I will. It will be quite out of our hands."

Danny didn't even know this lady and she was beginning to seriously dislike her. "Go away, wench. You've given me a bleedin' headache."

Emily gasped in outrage. "Well, I never!"

Danny nodded in agreement. "Likely the first truth out of your mouth."

Emily opened her mouth for a rejoinder, but changed her mind and quickly hurried off. Danny found out why when Jeremy said behind her, "Are you all right?"

She turned to give him a sour look. "That were tough work, mate, keeping all them *h*'s and *u*'s in line for that much talking. Give me a bleedin' headache, she did."

"Here, this will help," he said, handing her one of the champagne glasses he was holding. "I'm sorry you had to deal with that. I'm amazed she had the nerve to approach you. She wasn't spiteful, was she?"

"She was very believable, was what she was."

"Your appearance with me at your side hasn't made her change her mind a'tall?"

"Not a chance. I'd wager this has merely forced her hand. She's likely to move up her time schedule now."

"Bloody hell."

"Buck up, mate," Danny said cheekily. "You can always move to Africa."

He burst out laughing, then wound down enough to say, "I rather like it here. And at least Reggie's plan was half successful. The tongues will be wagging in a different direction now. Shall we further that along and dance some more? Might as well enjoy the rest of the evening, as long as we're here."

She humphed, though she was grinning at him. "I'm onto you, mate. You just want an excuse to put yer hands on me again."

"Never think so," he protested, but his own grin said, Absolutely! She might have given him the idea, or he might have already had it, but they didn't remain long on the dance floor. A few twirls around and then he was dancing her off to the side of the room where plants and potted trees had been arranged to resemble a small garden.

He was giving the impression of trying to be discreet, but he just couldn't contain his ardor any longer. The foliage only concealed them from half the room. The other half got a full view of Jeremy being most indiscreet.

"This should do it," he said, just before he kissed her.

Danny was taken by surprise. A man and a woman didn't kiss in public unless a wedding date had been announced, and even then it wasn't considered acceptable behavior. Only a scoundrel like Jeremy would ignore such rules. His remark meant this was part of the plan and she should go along with it. Danny might have argued the point, but she wasn't given a chance and besides, she'd been too close to Jeremy all evening, had felt his hands on her, had been seduced by the sensual promise in his eyes.

Just a few moments, she told herself just a few . . . Oh, God, she didn't want this kiss to end. Heat spread along every nerve of her body, steamed up between them so swiftly, if she'd been wearing spectacles they would have completely fogged over. The fluttering in her belly spread, too, lower to the juncture of her thighs when it throbbed deliciously.

She was at the point of wanting to rip his shirt off and press her mouth to his warm, muscular chest, to unbutton his trousers and feel his heated flesh, but she had just the tiniest measure of sense left. If she didn't stop him now she never would.

She gasped out, "Stop!"

"Must I?"

He said it so simply. She was trembling with passion while he didn't sound the least

bit affected by what had just passed between them. But then she met his eyes, and
it was there, the promise of what could have
been, and what could be, if she'd just let it
happen.

Chapter 30

It was hands down the nicest time Danny had ever had in her life. She'd never thought she would go to a ball, let alone the grandest one imaginable. She was still bubbling over with pleasure and champagne on the way home. She knew she'd drunk too much. She'd felt light-headed after two glasses, but then she'd gone on to have two more. It just wasn't the same as that fine wine she'd had the other night. Champagne went down too easily and its potency snuck up on her.

But that was all right. She'd soon be in bed to sleep it off. And she was sure her intoxication hadn't caused her to slip up on her performance tonight. Jeremy would have said something if she had, and after Emily Bascomb's visit he hadn't left her side for the rest of the night. Well, he had let her dance once with one other gentleman, though she wished he hadn't. All other men he'd chased away, but this one he couldn't.

She had *not* enjoyed dancing with James Malory. That fellow still scared the pants off her, though he did try to put her at ease with a few droll remarks designed to make her laugh. He hadn't succeeded.

She pitied his wife, Georgina, whom she got to meet briefly. George they called her. Nice lady for an American, and very pretty.

Jeremy helped her out of the coach. His hand lingered on her waist as he led her into his house. She thought nothing of it. She was still floating in contentment, still savoring how much fun the evening had been. She vaguely noted that she was climbing the stairs. That was all right, she worked up there. No, actually . . .

She stopped in the upstairs corridor. "I'm thinking I made a wrong turn."

"Not a'tall," he disagreed, pointing out, "you're going to need help getting out of that gown. It's fastened rather tightly up your back."

It was, too. She remembered Regina's saying she'd have to get one of the servants to help her out of it. But they were all asleep at this hour.

"Would you lend me a 'and then, mate?"

"Certainly, as soon as I light a lamp so I can see what needs undoing. You'll need one to get to your room as well."

"One what?"

"Lamp, m'dear. Didn't look like any had been left burning downstairs other than in the foyer."

Danny nodded. Jeremy led her into his room. She waited while he lit a lamp, then turned her back to him so he could loosen her gown enough for her to slip out of it. She sighed dreamily while he worked at it and shivered in turns, as his fingers brushed against her skin.

"So you enjoyed yourself tonight?"

"Too much, I'm thinking," she admitted with a grin. "I like dancing."

"So do I—with you."

She giggled. "Don't be using any o' those seducer lines on me, mate. Remember, I'm onto you."

"That was no line, Danny. I can't remember ever enjoying dancing so much as I did tonight."

She wished she could believe him. It still warmed her to hear it.

Glancing over her shoulder at him, she said sincerely, "Thank you for teaching me."

"It was my pleasure, but the lessons for the day aren't over."

The gown was loosened. He'd helped her out of it while they talked, so it didn't occur to her yet that she shouldn't be dropping it in his room, but hers. She was simply having trouble concentrating on two things at once, three, actually. He'd kept touching her as he'd worked the gown off her, and she'd managed to notice every single brush of his fingers against her bare skin.

But she shouldn't have glanced back at him. She'd been doing fine until she met his eyes and got lost in the deep, pure blue of them. And in those eyes as well was his expression, everything he was feeling, passion so hot she felt the heat of it wash over her. Or was that her own heat that was swiftly rising?

He turned her toward him. He placed one hand on her neck, his thumb tilting her chin up. This breathless moment ended in an exquisitely tender kiss. One kiss. What could it hurt? And it felt so bleeding nice.

She didn't notice his other hand on her back until it pressed her closer to him, and still closer, until she was so close she could barely breathe. Yet that felt exquisite, too. Deceptive, that tender kiss. He didn't need to be overwhelming her with his passion when her own was doing a right handy job of it.

But now he kissed her again. By slow degrees this kiss became much more erotic, his tongue delving into her mouth, finding hers, capturing it, sucking it forward until she groaned into his mouth. She had to grip his shoulders, her knees turned so weak. And his hands moved, one sliding through her curls to cup the back of her head, keeping her mouth under his control, while the other slid down her back to caress her derriere. Then abruptly both his hands were on her bottom as he lifted her to his loins.

Oh, God, there was no help for it after that. Too much heat was escalating between them. And Danny was tired of trying to fight it. What he made her feel was so wonderful, she couldn't recall why she wasn't supposed to enjoy it.

Somehow he got them on the bed without breaking that kiss. Danny became a little more dizzy, lying down, but after a few moments, she no longer noticed. She noticed Jeremy's hand on her breasts though, squeezing them gently, teasing her nipples, which had already hardened under his manipulation. She'd never paid much attention to her breasts, other than regretting when they got so plump, which made it harder to keep them flattened. She had no idea they could tingle at a touch or cause fascinating sensations elsewhere. And the kissing never stopped. It got so hot, there should have been smoke in the room.

Danny was approaching an erotic state of no return and she didn't care anymore. She'd lost her chemise and petticoats. She had a vague memory of them sliding off her to the floor soon after Jeremy had started kissing her, probably because he had unfastened them at the same time he'd done her gown. Something else she hadn't noticed. Or that he'd taken his own coat and shirt off. She simply had no idea when or how he'd done that, but she became instantly aware of it when he hugged her closer at one point and she was scorched by the heat of his bare skin on hers.

He removed her drawers now, by slow, agonizing degrees. Was he afraid she'd stop him? Not a chance, when she had such an amazing urge to feel his naked body against hers. But that removal was one long caress, his hand hot on her thigh, her calf as he bent her knee, her ankle, the drawers merely hooked on the back of his wrist as he explored her long limbs.

She didn't know what to do with her own hands other than to hold on to his hair, because she really didn't want him to stop kissing her. The trouble was, she didn't know *what* she wanted, but she wanted it now.

Jeremy must have known. He didn't make her agonize much longer with the primitive urges that had been overwhelming her from the start.

He put her arms around his neck and told her, "Hold me tight, luv, tighter."

She did just that, squeezing for all she was worth as he covered her body completely with his just as she'd been dying for him to do. And then she felt the sharpest pain.

Danny screamed, yanking his hair until he raised his head. "What in the bleedin' 'ell did you do that for?"

Jeremy was staring down at her as if she'd lost her mind, but then he smiled gently. "Danny . . . luv," he started to explain, but broke off to kiss her instead, deeply, with the same passion he'd bestowed on her earlier.

Did he think that would mollify her? Well, it *did* distract her.

"That wasn't part of lovemaking, other than the first time," he continued. "An initiation as it were. But it's never going to hurt you again. Really it isn't." And then he sobered and demanded, "And how is it that you were still a virgin?"

"What was I supposed to be, when I've been a lad all these years?"

"Well, I thought—never mind." His expression turned infinitely tender. "I'm rather glad you were."

"Am," she corrected.

"Were," he stressed with a slight cringe, as if expecting another clobbering.

And she did explode, eyes wide. "You

bleedin' bastard, you've turned me into a whore!"

"Good God, where'd you get that ridiculous notion? You can't be a whore if you only make love with one man. That's about as far from whoredom as you can get—well, other than remaining a virgin, which is moot now."

"Then what am I?"

"M'dear, you are the sweetest thing this side of creation." He bent to lick her nipple. "Beautiful beyond compare," he added before he went on to lick and suck her other nipple. "And the only thing you should be worrying about is how often we can do this."

He leaned up and grinned at her again. Danny had drawn in her breath, fighting the urge to pull him back to her breast. He didn't understand what he'd done to her. He figured it was a trifling thing, this initiation as he called it. For him it was. For her it was utterly earth-shattering.

"Ye don't get it, mate, but I wouldn't expect ye to. Now let me up."

He didn't move other than to caress her cheek with his finger. "You know you've loved everything we've been doing. *Why* would you want to deny yourself such pleasure. It gets better, you know. You may depend upon it."

"I don't doubt that a' tall," she replied with a sigh. "But I might be able to salvage this if I *don't* find out just how much better."

"You have *got* to be joking. The damage is done, Danny. Let me prove it to you, that it was more'n worth it. You could be wrong, you know. Whatever it is you're thinking, you could be absolutely wrong. And then you will have missed out on this."

He moved inside her, showing her what "this" was. Oh, God, the heat came back so swiftly, it spread clear to her toes. No trace of pain was left, just the deepest, most delicious pleasure. He continued to move in her, must have thought she didn't get the point. She'd stop him in a moment, just another moment. But before she knew it she was moving with him, and then it was too late. It came upon her suddenly, bloomed up, had her gripping him to her for dear life, then oh, God, the most sublime feeling burst and spread, lingering deliciously as he continued to drive his point home.

She didn't want to let him go. Even when it seemed that he'd found his own pleasure, she didn't want to lose the least bit of contact with him. He answered her wish in his own way, moving off her, but pulling her back into his arms.

Wisely, he didn't say a word, didn't gloat that he'd been right, didn't do anything but hold her close and caress her back gently. He did sigh in contentment. She couldn't miss that. Then he fell asleep.

She wished she could do the same. She wished he hadn't been right. But more than that, she wished she hadn't been right either.

Chapter 31

❧

Danny woke by slow degrees, a luxury she hadn't experienced for quite a while. She was probably late for work. She wondered if Claire had been looking for her when she'd gotten no response from her room. Did the rest of the staff know where she'd spent the last night? Maybe not. Maybe they assumed she'd spent the night at the Eden household again, since they hadn't seen her since she went off with Regina.

She was holding at bay what she felt about last night. It wasn't easy when she was still in Jeremy's bed. He'd probably sleep the morning away. He usually did. It wouldn't be that hard to sneak out of there without waking him.

But she didn't move yet. She felt more relaxed than she'd ever been, with the oddest feeling of contentment, which she wanted to savor just a little while more. Which was crazy. Her world had been turned upside down. She should be frantic, at the very least furious. She was neither.

She couldn't blame Jeremy for what had happened. He'd been trying to get her in his bed since she'd started working for him. He'd made no pretense about it. She couldn't blame the champagne, either, when the pain he'd dealt her had sobered her quickly. She could blame herself, but for what? Wanting him so much that she just didn't want to fight it anymore?

And, oh, God, making love with him had been so nice, even nicer than she'd imagined it would be. She'd worried that it would be added to her small list of cravings. She'd been absolutely right. It was going to be an irresistible craving now—with him.

Ah, well. She wasn't one to cry over her lot or endlessly bemoan her mistakes. She'd have to find another job, though. Jeremy would only have to look at her now and she'd probably lead him to the nearest bed.

"You aren't pretending to be asleep, are you, when I know you're not?"

Danny opened her eyes to find that he was lying on his side next to her, elbow bent, head resting on his hand, grinning at her. She hadn't felt him move into that position and realized he must have been watching her before she woke.

She wished she'd thought of that. Staring at him at her leisure would have been quite pleasant. Just looking at him now was rather thrilling, considering he was still naked and covered only to his waist. She knew now that his skin was smooth and tight over thick muscles. His hair was mussed—God, he was so damn sexy when it was. One lock had fallen half over his eye, making her want to push it back.

"A bit early for you to have your eyes open, ain't it, mate?"

"When I knew, at least hoped, that you'd still be here? Barely slept a wink."

She laughed. She loved his humor. And there was no longer any reason to restrain her own. He seemed surprised, though, by her agreeable mood.

His grin widened. He even said, "No wonder you got away with a boy's disguise so long. You snore!"

She blinked at him and then snorted. "What a rotten thing to say."

"You think so? I thought it was better than mentioning how much I loved making love to you. Wasn't sure you wanted to hear that just yet."

"I don't," she agreed, then added lightly, "I should sock you."

"Yes, I suppose you should." He sighed. "I'd let you again, too, if you feel you must."

"Let me?" she asked incredulously as she sat up.

He grinned again, but she had the feeling he hadn't been joking. And his gaze had moved down to her breasts when she sat up. It didn't cause her to blush, but it did remind her that she should be getting dressed and out of there.

With that thought in mind, she left the bed. He didn't try to stop her, probably because he was too busy staring at her body. She found her underclothes where he'd dropped them and began putting them on, then the beautiful ball gown. She wasn't going to have him fasten it, when she'd just need someone else to undo it again when she got downstairs. So she went into his dressing room and grabbed one of his coats.

"I'll be borrowing this long enough to get down to my room," she said as she came back out, stuffing her arms in the sleeves.

Amazing how big that coat was on her. Jeremy didn't seem *that* big, yet obviously he was. And glancing at him now, with his bare chest above the cover, she could see that he really was broader of chest than he seemed when dressed. It shouldn't have surprised her. She was used to having clothes conceal her own shape.

He was also looking damn pleased with himself. Well, why not? He'd gotten what he'd been after. And it hadn't changed *his* life any. It appeared that the woman got the short end of the deal, in the matter of "first times." Not bleeding fair, she was thinking.

Which was why she gave him a sour look when she asked, "Did you get me foxed last night just so you could bed me?"

"No, you managed that on your own if you'll recall, though if I *had* thought of it, I probably would have. By the by, you don't have to work anymore. You can stay here, do as you like, spend your time as you please—as long as you spend some of it with me. Or if you'd prefer to have your own residence, that will work just as well. Someplace close by where I can visit."

"And you'd pay for it?"

"Of course."

"What would you prefer?

"I'd prefer you never leave this bed."

She had a feeling he was serious. And he was talking about making her a mistress. She should be pleased. Lucy would jump at a chance like that and worship the bloke who offered it. She would be thrilled to service one man exclusively. But Danny didn't see it that way, found it about as distasteful as going out and selling her body for coins on the street.

She didn't tell Jeremy that. She wasn't even going to tell him she was leaving. Just pack up her things, grab her pet, and take off was the smartest way to go about it. She didn't want to have to explain why or risk the chance that he would talk her out of it. She didn't really want to go, after all, now that she craved him. She was going to be miserable, working somewhere else.

She moved over to the bed, nudged it

with her knee. "Never leaving this is unrealistic, mate."

"Not a'tall!" he disagreed, then frowned a bit suspiciously as he pointed out, "You're being awful calm about this, after the fuss you made about it previously. Realized the objections you had, whatever they were, were silly, did you?"

"Not silly. But I understand why you don't get it."

"Then why don't you explain it to me."

"I'd rather not. You wouldn't understand, when you can't even figure out how you've turned me into a whore."

He sighed. "There's that word again. Do I need to find you a dictionary?"

"That I can't read? Sure, that would be real helpful."

He grinned at her sarcasm. "Why do I get the feeling that you equate *whore* with *prostitution?* Yet neither would apply to you. We made love. It was the most incredible experience of my life, I don't mind telling you. A whore spreads herself around, mainly, because she enjoys the variety."

"Sort o' like you?"

He coughed. "If you insist, though there's another word for it when it applies to a man.

But in either case, no money exchanges hands. Now come here." He patted the bed next to him. "Let's greet the morning properly."

She almost laughed. It took every ounce of will she had not to crawl back into bed with him just then, to shake her head instead.

"Why not?" he asked simply.

Why not? Because to do so would be to completely give in and not have any will left of her own. But she wasn't going to admit that she craved him as much as she did. With him looking so damned sensual lying there, she wanted to be kissing him, not arguing with him. She liked him too much, that was the problem. But the damage was done, so why couldn't she enjoy him for just a little while? Not for long, a few weeks, maybe a month, at least until he lost interest in her.

"I was going to leave," she told him. "I still should. Playing with temptation once was one time too many. But I'll stay for now. Just don't be tempting me every time I turn around. And I'll be keeping m'job, thank you. Doing nothing means you're paying my way, which means you're paying for bedding me. Don't try to deny it. I don't pay you for it and you don't pay me for it. Got that, mate?"

On her way out the door, she realized that Jeremy hadn't had to talk her into staying. She'd done that just fine on her own.

Chapter 32

Danny was cleaning the parlor when Jason Malory, the Marquis of Haverston and the head of the entire Malory clan, arrived later that week. She shouldn't have been there to run into him. A downstairs maid had finally been hired yesterday who *should* have been there. But the new girl had been insulted by the new butler Henry and had quit in a huff barely four hours after she started.

Henry was actually one of two new butlers at the house. A Frenchman who tried to speak English, he was really quite funny. But the new maid hadn't thought so. He swore he'd only tried to compliment her.

She must not have understood English with a French accent.

Henry had shown up first, then the very next day, his friend Artie had arrived to do the butlering. They were actually going to share the job, had apparently been sharing it for years at James Malory's house. They were both old sea dogs who used to sail under James when he captained his own ship. When he gave up sailing, they elected to stay with him. But since he didn't have enough jobs to go around, they'd agreed to share the butler's job.

What they hadn't done was actually learn how to properly butler. They figured they did just fine at it, but Claire had been complaining about their rudeness, and even Mrs. Robertson had been heard to mumble a bit under her breath about their unorthodox approach to the job.

Danny didn't mind the loss of the new maid. She still didn't really have enough to do to keep herself busy for the entire day. Even with the downstairs added to her list of duties, she was finished long before dinner. And with Drew moving over to his sister's house for the duration of his visit, all but one of the upstairs bedrooms was empty, which meant less work for Danny up there.

Then there was Jeremy. If *he* had his way, she'd be spending most of each day in his room. If she had her druthers, she would, too. But she had to draw the line some- where, and lazing the day away in his bed didn't get her work done. As it was, if he found her upstairs when he awoke, he usu- ally got his way. She was a pushover when it came to his style of persuasion. That sexy voice of his lowered to a deep timbre when he was aroused, and his expression prom- ised such wicked delights. Hell, just looking at him was all the persuasion she needed, he was so bleeding handsome. So although she had determined not to make love with him every single day, she was doing just that, and one day, more'n once.

He wanted her to sleep with him each night, too, but she managed to dredge up enough willpower to find her own bed each night. Actually, it was more like escape to her room before she ran into him again. And even then, he came down to her one night and spent the night in her bed. She hadn't really had the least desire to kick him out.

But she *had* insisted he not do that again. And much to her own frustration, he didn't.

She'd had to do some serious thinking about staying. Doing so meant she'd have to put her goals aside for the time being. That wasn't going to be easy, when she wanted them so bad. But she'd reasoned a month wouldn't be too long a delay, and during that time she'd be saving her pay, so when she did leave, she could afford to let a flat while she looked for a new job.

When she did leave—God, that was going to be so hard. Never see Jeremy again? The thought nearly brought tears to her eyes now, how much worse would it be a month from now? But what if he fell in love with her during that month? It wasn't an impossible notion. She could fit into his world, she'd proved that the night of the ball. He might even defy convention and marry her then. And that was the deciding factor that convinced her to stay for now. That slim hope, that Jeremy could be more than just a temporary diversion, that he could be the man for her.

Jason Malory wasn't alone when he arrived. Jeremy's father was with him. The two brothers looked very much alike. The elder was a few inches taller, but they were both big, blond, handsome men. Jason was a little narrower of build, whereas James's arms and chest were more muscular, reminding Danny of some of the brutes she'd watched in street fights.

James Malory still frightened her, more than any other man ever had, and for no good reason that she could think of. The overall feeling she got in his presence was that he'd as soon kill you as talk to you. Which was why Danny kept her back to them both after a single glance.

Fortunately, she'd learned the phenomenon of being "invisible" to the nobles. Mrs. Robertson tried to explain it to her one night. The upper crust, living in houses full of servants, tended go about their daily lives without "seeing" the underlings who worked around them all day, every day. Unless, of course, one of the nobles wanted something, then every single servant in the house would become visible to them again.

It was the case with these two Malorys—she hoped. And it seemed to be when she heard the elder ask as they entered the parlor, "By the by, who is this relative of Kelsey's that I've been hearing so much about since I got to town? Didn't think she had any that I didn't know about. Is Jeremy really courting her?"

Danny sucked in her breath. That she was the subject of their conversation appalled her. She'd never get out of there unnoticed now. And the Marquis of Haverston wasn't likely to take lightly the scam they'd pulled off. He'd probably be furious with them all for duping the ton like that. Nor did James try to avoid answering.

"No, she's just one of Regan's inventions, conjured up to try to counter the Bascomb rumors."

"Blister it, James, must you—"

"Give over, old man," James cut in dryly. "It's just a bloody habit, calling her that. Wouldn't hurt for you to accept the fact that she's Regina, Reggie, *and* Regan."

"You forgot Eden."

"Intentionally, I do assure you."

Jason sighed. "And that's another thing. It's high time you and Tony let up on Nick already. He's made her an exemplary husband."

"Course he has. We'd kill him otherwise."

Danny's blood turned cold, but Jason was apparently going to ignore that remark altogether and asked again, "So there is no such relative?"

"No," James replied. "Just a wench our niece found who's much prettier than the Bascomb chit. She didn't have very far to look."

"Prettier? I was told Emily Bascomb is a raving beauty. That was the excuse I've been hearing for why Jeremy couldn't keep his hands off her."

"My son picks his women well, which is why you haven't heard of any more scandals from him since he finished school. I already told you he ain't touched her. You didn't need to hear it from him."

Danny held her breath, though it still seemed as if they hadn't really noticed her. But at least James hadn't stated that the "wench" who had been found was a mere maid. Now if she could just slowly work her way to the door and disappear for real. She started inching in that direction, still keeping her back to them.

"So her father actually went all the way to Haverston to pay you a visit?" James asked next.

"Yes, and I don't mind telling you, that was a very embarrassing conversation, particularly since I had no prior warning about these scandalous rumors that have been making the rounds."

"Rumors the lady started herself, and all lies," James assured him.

"Be that as it may, you know very well the damage a few rumors can do, lies or not. The girl's reputation is quite ruined now."

James actually laughed at that point. "When she ruined it, and deliberately, mind you? Since when do we dig strangers out of the holes they dig for themselves? This is her father's problem, not yours, not mine, and certainly not Jeremy's, who's barely even spoken two words to the chit."

"It became our problem when it's simply her word against his."

"Then why don't you let me see to this?" James suggested mildly.

"How? By shooting the chap?"

"Think you have me pigeonholed, do you?"

"I'm sorry. That was uncalled for."

James nodded, accepting the apology. Danny caught that as she moved a few more inches toward the door. But then Jeremy burst into the room, having been fetched by Henry. He managed to notice her first with no difficulty and even gave her a smile that she *hoped* his relatives didn't notice.

But then he said, "Hell's bells, I hope this visit ain't what it looks like, Uncle Jason."

Jason Malory cleared his throat. "Albert Bascomb came to Haverston yesterday."

Jeremy groaned and dropped down on the nearest sofa. "Whatever he told you, it's all lies."

"So your father has informed me," Jason replied.

James added for Jeremy's benefit, "The chit has played her last card and painted the foulest picture of you, youngun, that you seduced her, promised her marriage, then tossed her aside as soon as you got what you wanted from her—and that she's now pregnant with your child."

"I knew she was already hinting at that. But if she is pregnant, it ain't mine. I never touched the wench, never even *thought* about touching her. Not that it matters, when she's obviously convinced her father."

"I see you already understand the gravity of the situation," Jason replied. "And to make matters worse, Albert Bascomb was a school chum of mine. Wasn't well liked.

Full of himself, if you know what I mean. He made a remarkable marriage, though. Courted a beauty in his neighborhood before she had a chance for a London season and got her to marry him. They had only the one child."

"And spoiled her rotten. I already know most of that. Reggie's good at ferreting out that sort of information and passing it on."

"Well, what you may not know is Bascomb, through his wife, has some very high connections."

"So what you're saying is I'll have to marry the wench?" Jeremy said.

"As a temporary measure. After it's proven that she isn't pregnant, we'll get it annulled, of course. So you will have to 'continue' to keep your hands off of her."

Considering the turn the conversation had taken, Danny couldn't help but turn and stare at Jeremy. He looked despondent, as if he had already accepted his fate. She looked despondent as well, though she didn't know it. Jeremy married was Jeremy out of her reach, and she hadn't gotten nearly enough of him yet to satisfy her craving. Whether it was a marriage in name only or not, it still meant he'd be off-limits to her.

And she wasn't about to stick around and deal with his wife, either.

James Malory didn't look despondent, he looked like hell warmed over. "You really should have mentioned these were your thoughts on the matter before we got here, Jason. You know bloody well I won't allow my son to be thrown to the wolves, as it were. Bascomb never should have gone to you in the first place. You ain't the boy's father."

"He probably came to me because of our prior association. And he knows your reputation. Frankly, the idea of his bringing this matter to you probably scared him to death."

James snorted. Jeremy sighed and said, "The problem is that Lord Bascomb is quite convinced I'm the culprit here. And he's convinced because he believes his daughter. Which is understandable. Why wouldn't he, after all?"

Danny took the moment of silence that followed that remark to blurt out, "Then he'll just have to be unconvinced, won't he?"

"How?" Jeremy asked her, having no trouble including her in the conversation as if she'd been in it from the start. "I've already disputed it. Fat lot of good that did."

"The lady has based her scheme on a lie, so why don't you counter it with some lies o' your own, eh?" Danny suggested logically.

As if he'd also known she was there all along, James replied, "How's that going to help? It's still her word against Jeremy's."

Danny was even more nervous, having to speak to James directly, particularly since he was still frowning. But for Jeremy's sake, she got out, "Weren't thinking o' having Jeremy do the countering. No, that wouldn't do a'tall. It's her lie against his truth, after all. But what if it were her one lie against two others—hmmm, no, make that three others for good measure?"

"What the deuce is she talking about?" Jason demanded of no one in particular.

Danny had no trouble answering the elder Malory. "Well, it's a matter of a child now, aye? She says it's his. You know it ain't. But I'm guessing there's no child a'tall. There's no way to prove that though, is there, least not for four or five months down the road, and she wouldn't be waiting for the wedding that long, would she now? And she could always lie again later and say she'd lost the babe—after she's married to Jeremy, of course."

"So where do these other 'three' come into play?" Jason asked.

"Three other men who claim they've bedded her. She'll deny it, but even she will see that three to one ain't good odds. Can you think of three men who would lie for you, mate?" she asked Jeremy directly.

"Certainly, but—damn me, that just might work," he said with a wide grin.

James started chuckling. "Indeed, dear boy, especially if all three confront her at the same time, with her father present to hear it. Brilliant solution, indeed it is. Surprised I didn't think of it m'self."

"I believe I shouldn't be hearing any of this," Jason said with a stern look, but then gave his younger brother a barely discernible nod of approval and added, "I'll leave it in your capable hands, James."

"Thought you might." James grinned.

Jason prepared to leave, but he stopped by Danny on the way out. He studied her face for a few moments, a frown growing on his brow.

He couldn't have helped notice the

duster in her hand, yet he said to her, "You are familiar to me, though I can't seem to figure out why. Have we met before?"

"Not that I recall, m'lord."

"Worked at Edward's house, did you? Or Reggie's? Is that where I've seen you?"

"No, this is m'first time working as a maid, anywhere."

"Odd. It's going to bother me now, till I recall where I've seen you."

Danny was starting to get uncomfortable. She hoped she'd never robbed the bloke, but it was possible. She doubted it, though. When she used to pick pockets, she'd rarely picked men of his size, who would have had an easy time keeping up with her if she'd had to flee. And he had a presence she wasn't likely to forget.

James must have been having the same thoughts because as soon as Jason left, he said to her, and in a most derogatory manner, "Lightened his pocket at some point in your previous career, did you?"

She blushed. Jeremy came quickly to her defense though. "Don't start in on her. She just saved me from a marriage made in hell. I'm bloody well pleased with her at the moment."

James rolled his eyes toward the ceiling. "You've been bloody well pleased with her since you found her. Be that as it may, her contribution to saving your arse does deserve some praise, but you ain't saved yet. So round up your three liars and bring them to me. I'll drill them on what they're to say, and what will happen if they muck it up." And then on his way out the door: "But for God's sake, don't pick Percy for one of them."

Danny was able to relax immediately after James left, even grinned at Jeremy. "Does your whole family distrust your friend Percy?"

"Not a'tall. They love Percy, 'deed they do, they just *know* him. I've no doubt had he been at the ball last week, he would have blurted out, 'Good God, Jeremy, what's your maid doing here!' "

She giggled. "He wouldn't have."

"Oh, he would, you may depend upon it. So we were damned lucky he was off in Cornwall for a couple days buying new horseflesh and missed that ball."

"Not that our performance that night did much good," she reminded him with a sigh.

He shrugged, but he also grinned. "Don't

worry about it, luv. We might not have accomplished the original goal, but we had
fun trying."

And a lot more fun afterward, but she
didn't point that out because he was already looking as if he had some of that fun
on his mind now, when he should only be
thinking about collecting some friends who
were willing to lie for him. She hoped her
suggestion would work, she really did.
Jeremy would end up getting married if it
didn't work. And she'd be looking for a new
job.

Chapter 33

Danny waited anxiously to find out how Jeremy's search had gone. When he came home that day, he didn't look discouraged, but he hadn't had much luck in rounding up three friends, at least, not on the spur of the moment. Most of his old school chums apparently didn't live in London and didn't visit often either. And he'd had only one thing to say about the young rakehells that he and Percy chummed about with who did live in London.

"Wouldn't trust a single one of them to keep his mouth shut about this matter after it's resolved."

And that would ruin the entire scheme if

Lord Bascomb heard about it later. Which was why Danny suggested, "Then maybe you shouldn't be looking for friends, but some men who lie for a living."

"I hope you don't mean of the criminal variety?"

She gave him a disgusted look that he'd think of that before anything else. "No, I meant actors, of course. It's their job to be convincing in the roles they play, ain't it? So they're good at lying—well, that is, if they're any good at acting."

"Damn me, they are, aren't they? Think I'll pay a visit to the theater district. And we should celebrate tonight, maybe a night on the town. I owe you for all these splendid ideas you've been coming up with, luv, 'deed I do."

"I don't know about that," she replied doubtfully, but he was already back out the door, so she wasn't sure if he'd heard her or not.

A night on the town? She had no idea exactly what that entailed, but she had a good idea she wouldn't have the proper clothes for going out with a nabob. The ball gown had been returned to Regina, only to have it returned back to her since it no longer fit the petite lady. But still, that was an outfit for only a grand occasion, not for a night of gallivanting around London.

She finished her work early that day. Nervous anticipation helped to speed her along. With nothing else to do, she offered to help Claire with her chores in the kitchen. She hoped it would improve the girl's attitude as well, since Claire had been decidedly frosty to her lately. Not that she'd ever been chummy, but still, there'd been a noticeable difference. It didn't help, though shedid finally find out why Claire was displaying such dislike for her now.

As soon as Mrs. Appleton left the room for a short break, after she got dinner started, Claire hissed at Danny, "You're such a slut. I knew you'd end up in his bed. You're just too pretty."

Danny was stunned, but only for a moment. She was too pretty? She gave Claire a critical look and finally replied, "You're not a slouch yourself, Claire. Well, you are, but I think you try to be. Why is that?"

Not surprisingly, Claire took offense and slammed down the knife she'd been paring the potatoes with. "None of your damn business."

Danny shrugged and continued cutting her share of the potatoes. "Course it ain't, but neither is what I do your business, so why'd you remark on it, eh?"

"It's wicked what you're doing."

Danny laughed. "In whose opinion? So I've been having a little fun with the nabob. In *my* opinion that ain't wicked as long as it's only with him. Might 'ave took me a while to figure that out, but I finally did. And it's only my opinion that counts. 'Sides, he ain't married. I ain't married. So who's getting hurt by it?"

"You will," Claire said simply.

That sobered Danny real quick. She'd already figured out that much for herself. He'd get tired of her eventually. She hoped she'd get tired of him about the same time, but the way she felt about him, she seriously doubted she would. But she *was* going to leave in a few months, to get on with her life and to find a man who would want to marry her, not one who never wanted to get married at all.

With a sigh she said, "I pro'bly will. But that's my concern, not yers."

"Yours," Claire corrected.

Danny stiffened. She'd made so many

mistakes with her speech in the parlor today that having it mentioned now had been bound to set her off. "Is every bleedin' person in this house going to correct me now?"

Claire assumed an offended stance again. "I thought you wanted to learn proper?"

"I do, but it ain't easy, thinking every word out o' my head, you know."

"Which is why reminders are necessary, so it becomes habit, rather than a chore."

The logic of that was too accurate to dispute. Danny even vaguely recalled Lucy doing the same thing when she'd taught her to talk like her all those years ago. Danny just wished she didn't mess up when she got nervous or upset, but Lucy had done a good job of drumming that "fancy talk," as she'd called it, out of her.

"I'm sorry," Claire added. "I didn't mean to change the subject."

Danny couldn't help laughing at that, considering the subject that had been changed had been what Claire called Danny's "wicked" behavior. "You should try being so wicked. It improves the disposition greatly."

She'd been joking, to show there were no

hard feelings, but Claire amazed her with the reply "I did."

"And?"

Such a long silence followed, Danny was sure Claire wasn't going to explain. But then she said, "I got to know my last employer well, too well. It led to the worst grief imaginable."

Danny wasn't sure what to say. Worst grief imaginable was an odd way to describe a broken heart, so maybe . . .

"Did he die?" she asked hesitantly.

Claire snorted at that. "Don't I wish."

Danny frowned. "So you hate him now?"

"No, I can't really say that I do. I'm not even surprised by what he did. If I want to be completely unselfish, then I can't even say I'm sorry for what he did."

"Blimy, what'd he do?"

Another long silence followed. Claire seemed to be fighting with herself, on whether to say any more. And the subject was obviously painful to her. Moisture had gathered in her eyes.

Danny was about to say forget it when Claire said, "It was just one time. A mistake. It shouldn't have happened. I didn't even like it—well, not all of it. And I shouldn't have got a child from *just one time,* but I did."

Good God, she'd had a baby and it died. No wonder she'd mentioned grief.

"Claire, you don't need to—"

"I was happy about the child," Claire continued, as if Danny hadn't spoken. "I didn't think I would be, but my life was an endless round of work and sleep, with nothing out of the ordinary ever happening to me. The child could have changed that, would have, too, if—if—"

Claire was crying in earnest now, though silently, large tears rolling down her cheeks. Danny didn't know whether to try to hug her, when they weren't close at all, or leave for now, so Claire could work on composing herself. Her urge was to hug her when so much grief was just pouring out of her.

Danny started to, then thought better of it again. They *really* weren't close, and Claire might take it the wrong way, might be completely offended if Danny offered sympathy. After all, the girl had given every indication of disliking her from the very beginning.

She opted instead to press more, thinking Claire might feel better if she talked about it. Maybe she'd never had anyone to grieve with her, to help her share her loss. It did seem as if she'd kept all this grief to herself.

"How did it die?" Danny finally asked.

Claire blinked and stared at her, a frown forming. "Die? He didn't die. They stole him from me."

Danny stared now. "Eh?"

"His lordship didn't believe the child was his, at first. He'd scoffed and said some really nasty things that boiled down to 'one time doesn't make babies.' That's what I'd thought, too, but I'd found out differently firsthand. But I wasn't going to try to convince him. I didn't want him to acknowledge the child or anything like that. I was mostly worried I was going to lose my job over it. And the rest of the staff did scorn me for getting with child without a husband to show for it."

"So you left?"

"No, I wish I had. But my aunt was still there. She'd gotten me the job, just like she did here."

"Here?"

"Didn't you know?" Claire asked. "Mrs. Appleton, she's my aunt."

Danny didn't know, and the two women

bore no resemblance at all, so she wouldn't have guessed. But she was more interested in the girl's story and asked, "What happened after the child was born?"

"His lordship's sisters came to see the baby. He'd mentioned it to them, you see, that I'd tried to pretend it was his. I don't know why he bothered to tell them."

"Maybe he thought you'd go to them about it and he wanted to warn them not to believe you."

"Possibly, though I wouldn't have. They weren't very nice ladies, either of them, so going to them about anything was unthinkable. Two bitter old maids was what they were. I avoided them whenever they visited."

"But they came to see your son?"

"Oh, yes, and insisted he was the very image of their brother when he'd been a baby. His lordship was their younger brother, you see, much younger at that, so they'd both been around when he was born."

"So they acknowledged him as family?"

"Yes."

"But wasn't that a good thing?"

"Hell no. They insisted I had to give my son to them to raise. You see, their brother was getting past middle age and had never produced an heir. They'd been frantic that he never would. But I'd supplied the heir. They could stop worrying and nagging him about it."

"So you just gave him up?"

The tears started again. "They didn't give me any choice. They were going to claim I'd committed all sorts of crimes and get me imprisoned if I didn't turn the boy over to them and agree to never see him again."

"Could they really do that?"

"Oh, yes, very easily. Who'd believe a lowly kitchen maid against two ladies and a lord of the peerage, after all?"

"But why'd they insist you never see him again. You were his mother!"

"Because they didn't want him to know that. He's their heir. They're raising him to be an acceptable member of the ton."

"Without a mother? Produced him out o' thin air, did they?"

"Oh, his lordship has a wife. I didn't know that, or I never would have—well, you know. But I wasn't the only one who didn't know. Don't think most of the staff did, either, she'd moved out so long ago. I assume they didn't get along well, so she refused to live with him. The sisters had mentioned she'd run crying back to her family."

"Why didn't she just divorce him?"

"The gentry don't do that."

"But they're going to claim the child is hers? She agreed to that?"

"The sisters can be very convincing." And then Claire leaned forward to whisper, "They were going to tell her that their brother would come to live with her again. I gathered she'd agree to anything to avoid that."

"They *told* you that?" Danny asked incredulously.

"No, but they discussed it in front of me, how they were going to handle it, as if I weren't there and hearing every word."

The invisible phenomenon again. Absolutely amazing, how that worked.

"I take it you weren't allowed to work there anymore, after that?"

Claire's lips started trembling again. "No, I had to leave that very day and also swear that I'd never come back or try to see my baby again. He's going to have a good life, though, the best schooling, the best of everything that money can buy."

"And to go by what you've said, a despicable family as well."

Claire sighed. "No, actually, they dote on him."

"How do you know if you never went back?"

"My aunt stayed there a while more, just to see how they treated him. They didn't know she was my aunt, so she didn't have to leave when I did. She said they adore the boy, that they're completely different when they're around him, like *nice* people. Even his lordship took to fatherhood well."

Danny began to understand that "unselfish" remark now. "So you think he's better off with them?"

"I know he is. What can I offer him, after all, other than the stigma of a bastard?"

Danny knew that stigma wasn't so bad, at least if one of the parents was noble. Jeremy was proof of that.

"Love?" she suggested.

"He's getting that aplenty. No, he's much better off with them. I just—just miss him. The sisters didn't show up until nearly two months after he was born. I got to have him that long and—and I wish now that I didn't. It would have been much easier giving him up if I'd never held him, or suckled him, or—"

The tears started in earnest again. Danny felt some of her own gathering. She did hug Claire this time. And she wasn't pushed away.

After their emotions settled down a little, Danny asked, "Have you thought of doing something different for work? You don't seem to be too happy with kitchen chores."

"I don't mind it so much. I'm just always thinking about my boy."

"Then have you thought of having more children? That might make it easier to bear."

"More bastards you mean?"

"No, I was thinking of marriage first."

Claire snorted. "And who'd have me?"

Danny rolled her eyes. "No one with the way you look and act now. But you have a pretty face, Claire. There's no need to be hiding it. I've a mirror in my room that doesn't get much use. Why don't we go and see if we can't do something with your hair? It's very ugly the way you wear it in that bun. And is there something wrong with your back that makes you slouch like that?"

Claire blushed and whispered, "No, I just have very large breasts that draw the wrong sort of attention."

Danny burst out laughing. "I see I'm not

the only one who needs some correcting. That sort of attention doesn't have to be wrong if you handle it right. If your goal is to have more babies, then your priority is to get yourself a husband first, so do yourself up as bait and catch one."

"I don't see you taking that approach."

"I need to better myself before I start looking for a decent husband. I'm doing that here."

"I wouldn't call dallying with Malory an improvement, especially if you intend to find a husband for yourself."

"That's true, but Malory is a prime exception to anything, if you know what I mean. He's so bleedin' handsome it's purely sinful. I tried to resist him, I really did, but now that I've stopped resisting, I'm damned glad I did. He's the type of man a girl just has to enjoy if she gets the chance to, a once-in-a-lifetime type of man."

"And it doesn't bother you that nothing will ever come of it?"

"When I have no expectation of anything other than a good time for a while? I'll be ending it m'self in a few months, if he doesn't end it first. I'll be sorry to see it end, sure, but as long as I know it does have to end sometime soon, I won't be falling on m'face with surprise when it does."

"That's a rather open-minded way of looking at it. Most women would never see it that way, you know."

Danny laughed. "I ain't been a woman for that long, Claire, so how would I know, eh?"

"You're that young?"

"No, I just wore pants that long!"

Chapter 34

Jeremy wasn't taking any chances where shackles of the matrimonial type were concerned. He rounded up seven actors and brought them all to his father's house that day. And he had a stroke of luck. On the way there, he caught sight of one of his old school friends passing by in an open carriage and chased him down.

Andrew, or Andy as his friends called him, Whittleby, Viscount Marlslow, had actually shared a room with Jeremy at one of the colleges he'd attended and had been his cohort in many of the antics that had gotten Jeremy suspended a time or two and, finally, kicked out of yet another school. Andy had proven back then that he could be trusted to keep his mouth shut. That was the main reason Jeremy had lasted longer at that school than the others. Andy had frequently covered for him. He was a good sort, always willing to help a friend out of a muddle.

Of medium height, blond-haired, brown-eyed, Andrew would be considered a Corinthian if he were a little taller. A handsome chap, he was still a bachelor. He'd retired to the estate that came with his title when he finished his schooling, so Jeremy hadn't seen him since then. He preferred a hands-on approach to managing his property, loved the outdoors, to go by his deep tan. And he was due to inherit a lot more property as well as titles when his father passed on, but that wouldn't be for many years. So he *was* a prime catch. Too bad Emily hadn't clapped eyes on him first.

After Jeremy explained the situation, Andrew agreed to be one of the liars. Jeremy had had no doubt that he would, splendid sport that he was. He'd even met Emily just a few nights ago and had thought about courting her himself until he'd heard the rumors that Jeremy was.

"Didn't think I'd stand a chance against you, Jeremy. 'Deed not, so I put those thoughts away. Regrettably, though. She's a damned fine-looking gel."

"You're welcome to her, if you don't mind that she's scheming, spoiled, and an adept liar who will apparently resort to any measures to get her way. She decided I was going to be her husband, and when I didn't pay her the least bit of attention, she began her campaign of rumors that were mild to begin with, but progressed to this latest farce that she's having my baby, when I've barely even spoken to her, much less touched her!"

Andrew seemed amused and explained why, "My mum used to be like that—well, not quite like that, but something of the sort. She'd spin the most entertaining tales for our neighbors, get them aghast, alarmed, on pins and needles, and be sitting back laughing to herself over their gullibility. And they never caught on. She just loved spinning tales."

"Not quite as damaging, but . . . I suppose being forewarned would make all the difference. So, you're still interested in Emily?"

"Oh, most definitely. I'll wed her if she'll have me, so I think I can be most convincing in that regard. Think her father will insist I marry her when *I* insist the babe she's carrying is mine?"

"Now there's a thought and just deserts, since that was her plan for me. Mention it to my father. He'll be handling this particular performance."

"Oh, I say, I finally get to meet your father? Splendid! Always wanted to, you know. Amazing reputation that man has, unparalleled in the ring, and in duels for that matter, and did you know . . .

Jeremy listened with half an ear as they continued to his father's house. He wasn't hearing anything he didn't already know about his sire, and the amusing part was, Andrew didn't know the half of it.

And then he was met with another unexpected stroke of luck. Drew had also volunteered to be one of their liars, and he already had his story lined up. Ironically, it was no more than his usual approach where women were concerned, so for him, it was merely a matter of inserting Emily's name in the tale. So it merely remained for James to pick a third from one of the actors Jeremy had brought along.

Jeremy was looking forward to the performance that would take place at the Bascombs', but when he mentioned it, James told him flatly, "You ain't going along, puppy. Your presence ain't required and would only give the chit an opportunity to test her own acting skills. The idea here is to surprise her enough that she blunders with her own story."

Jeremy was forced to accept that, but bloody hell, it wasn't going to be easy waiting in the wings to find out if the plan would work. But at least Danny could take his mind off it. Indeed, when he was around her, he could barely think of anything else.

It still boggled his mind, the change in her. She enjoyed making love, no doubt about that. Once she got over her objections, it was as if she'd never had any. What bothered him was her approach to their relationship: no ties, no obligations, just mutual enjoyment. It was almost *manly* how she wanted it handled.

Bloody hell, come to think of it, it was almost identical to his own usual approach with the ladies. But for once, he didn't want it that way. He would have liked to have Danny a little more committed than she wanted to be—well, actually, a lot more. He would have liked to spend more time with her each day than she was willing to give him, and not just in bed. It was becoming damned frustrating that he couldn't, that he had to keep their relationship a secret to avoid alienating his other household servants. If she were his mistress, he could spend all the time he wanted with her, could dress her accordingly and take her out to the many places where mistresses were acceptable. But she wasn't the least bit interested in that, much to his chagrin.

But at least she was there, in his house, accessible, well, for the most part. She wasn't around though when he got home. And when he finally gave up waiting and went down to her room, he heard female laughter coming from inside telling him she wasn't alone. Bloody hell. So much for their celebrating tonight. Of course, celebrating *was* a bit premature, when he wasn't quite out of the muck yet.

Chapter 35

The Bascomb town house was rather small, but then Lord Bascomb and his lovely wife came to London rarely, and many of the gentry these days were of the new opinion that letting a house sit staffed, but otherwise empty, was a waste of good servants. Of course they wouldn't admit it was a waste of good coin. That was merely an added bonus of not keeping a town residence. The new trend seemed to lean more toward renting a furnished flat if a trip to London was required, or merely staying in one of the grand hotels if the visit was brief.

Bascomb had business interests in town, which was probably why he kept a town house there. And they were putting it to good use for their daughter's come-out. And for all that it was small, it was grandly furnished with some exceptionally nice pieces and artwork. The Bascombs were rather rich, after all, just intelligently frugal.

James Malory paid his visit the next morning. He'd sent word the day before that he was coming, so his being kept waiting, and in the small foyer no less, he found rather amusing—for a while.

Albert was at home. The butler had informed James, after letting his master know James had arrived, that Albert was quite busy, so James might wish to return at a more convenient time. James had merely sent the fellow back with the message that he wasn't leaving.

"Rather rude of him, don't you think?" Andrew remarked after twenty minutes had passed.

"Probably just an indication that this entire matter has upset him," Drew suggested.

"I don't doubt he was upset," James replied with some annoyance. "Enough to hie off to Haverston and lay it all before my brother Jason."

"Then perhaps he just feels it's already

settled and would be a waste of time to discuss it further," Andrew suggested. "Which would again be rather rude of him not to at least say so."

"Jason might have given him the impression that it was settled," James allowed. "But I highly doubt it. Jason is good at telling a man what he wants to hear, but not really telling him anything."

Drew chuckled over that. "Wish I could figure out how that's done."

"With finesse, dear boy, a lot of finesse," James replied. "And you have figured it out, you just use it exclusively with women."

"Ah, *that* sort of finesse." Drew grinned.

Five minutes later James's patience ran thin and he told the younger men, "Come along, but wait outside the door until I call you."

The butler, standing guard outside his master's study, thought to stop James from entering it. It was a brief thought. A good look at James and he decided to open the door instead and announce him.

Albert had been reading some document at his desk. He glanced up and then sighed at the sight of James entering the room. "This really isn't a good time."

"So I was informed, though I doubt any time will be a good time for this, distasteful subject that it is. But considering you took this matter to the wrong Malory, you'll make time, won't you."

It wasn't a question by any means. Albert understood that and set his document aside. James had never met the chap before. He was rather distinguished looking, dark brown hair with lighter shades at the temples suggesting it would soon be gray. James was surprised it wasn't gray already with a daughter like Emily.

"There really isn't anything to discuss further, other than a date for the wedding," Albert insisted. "Have you come to supply that?"

James didn't answer. He pulled one of several chairs near Albert's desk to the side of it, so he'd have a good view of the performance when it began. It was a comfortable chair, which was a good thing. He had a feeling this wouldn't be a brief visit.

The silence unnerved the older man, enough for him to burst out, "Now see here. I *know* your reputation and I refuse to be bullied."

James raised a brow. "Come now, old

chap. Where d'ye get the idea that I bully? I either ignore or I—well, it won't come to that, I'm sure."

A flush rose up Albert's cheeks. "Then get to the point, Malory. What are you doing here?"

"Well, it's a strange thing about rumors. They tend to either titillate, amaze, or enrage, depending on one's perspective and involvement."

"I'm aware there are rumors of a highly embarrassing nature. Whoever spread them should be shot. But unfortunately, they happen to be true."

"I beg to differ. It's fortunate they aren't true a'tall."

"So your son intends to deny his responsibility? That's rather cowardly—"

"You will refrain from slander, Bascomb," James cut in. "I tend to take that sort of thing personally."

It was said in the mildest of tones and yet Albert still paled, but then blustered, "This is *your* grandchild as well as mine that we are discussing."

"If it were my grandchild, you can be sure we wouldn't be having this conversation."

"The truth will come to light on its own," Albert said confidently.

"Indeed it will, but it won't be the truth you're expecting, and it won't surface until it's too late. So I've brought you a few other truths to chew on."

"Is this where you make threats and promise to kill me?" Albert demanded.

James burst out laughing, not because of the question but because it was asked so indignantly. "I don't know what you've heard about me, Bascomb, but it was probably only half true, I do assure you. Another case of rumors not adding up, don't you know."

"I doubt that," Albert mumbled.

"Suit yourself. But as I was saying earlier, because of the rumors currently making the rounds, one of which has Jeremy all but married to your girl, my house was besieged this week by two outraged swains of your daughter's who weren't aware that Jeremy has his own residence now. They thought he could be found living with me. There was a third, but he *is* staying with me, unfortunately. Wife's relative. Hard to get rid of."

There was a cough outside the door, but

Albert didn't seem to notice. "And?" he asked with a scowl.

"Well, imagine my surprise when they each insisted that they have more right to marry Emily than Jeremy does, since they got to her first."

"Got to her? Just what are you implying?"

James lifted a brow again. "Do I really need to get vulgar in my verbiage, Bascomb?"

The man flushed with anger, stood up, and leaned forward, his clenched fists turning white. "If you think you can make these insinuations without the least bit of proof, Lord Malory—"

"And where is *your* proof?"

Albert flushed again, but this time because he got the point quite sharply. James let a moment pass for it to sink in more fully, that what Albert had instigated was based purely on the tale his daughter had spun.

James then said, "I would suggest you get your daughter down here to see what she has to say for herself. Actually, I insist."

"You insist? This subject is unthinkable for a girl of her tender years—"

"Rubbish. The subject is hers, created by her supposed indiscretion. Did you really think you could force my son to marry her and *not* have her tell her side of the tale to us? And I've brought my proof with me, all three gentlemen who claim to know her— very well."

"And you didn't bring your son? Why not? If Emily must be subjected to this embarrassment, then I'll hear what your boy has to say as well."

"He'll merely tell you he don't know the chit a'tall. So what is the point of hearing him say it? You are the one making demands here, Bascomb, not my family. Do keep that in mind."

Rigidly, Albert marched to the door to tell his man to fetch Emily. Seeing the three strangers there as well, he said curtly, "Come in. I'd prefer to hear what you have to say before my daughter arrives."

The three filed into the room. Only Drew made himself comfortable in the remaining chair by the desk. Andrew stood stiffly to the side, while the third moved over to one of the windows for better light. Actors always worried about the lighting.

Andrew didn't appear nervous, merely anxious. James had been surprised to hear that he still wanted the chit for himself. He would have wished him luck in the matter, but luck as he saw it would be that the lad wouldn't get the conniving chit.

The actor, William Shakes—James was amused every time he said the stage name to himself—was eager to perform. He saw this as an opportunity to test his acting skills on a more personal level. The Bascombs might have seen him perform, however, and recognize him as an actor. Which was why he wasn't going to lie about who he was.

It was pushing the limit, using the chap. Rather tawdry that a lady of Emily's stature would consort with a man out of her class. But then Emily Bascomb had deliberately tarnished her reputation beyond repair, so what was one more slip here or there?

Chapter 36

~

"Before these two coxcombs give their accounts, Lord Bascomb," Andrew began the
proceedings, "allow me to assure you that I
adore Emily and would dearly like to marry
her with your approval."

"And who are you, sir?" Albert asked.

Andrew offered an assortment of titles
and connections. Albert was impressed.
Even James was impressed since he hadn't
heard them all himself.

Albert admitted when Andrew was done,
"Know your father. Good man."

"Now see here," William began his performance with a disgruntled tone. "All those
titles don't change the fact that the child

could be mine. You might not find me as suitable for your daughter, m'lord, but I assure you she found me quite suitable."

"And who are you?"

"William Shakes, at your service. I'm an actor, sir, and a damn fine one. One of my recent performances was so sterling, in fact, that I was actually invited to attend a ball several weeks ago, which is where I met Emily. We hit it off splendidly, I don't mind saying. And we managed to find an empty room upstairs to, well, I'm sure I don't need to go into details."

Albert wasn't just embarrassed now, he was understandably furious. "My daughter consorting with an *actor?* Utterly preposterous!"

William ignored the rage, merely shrugged and remarked, "Hero of the moment and all that. She was determined to make my acquaintance *and* make my day, I might add," he said with a roguish wink. "I'll even marry her, if the child is mine. Would rather not get married just yet if it isn't. That's assuming, of course, that you'd accept me into your family. Know there are quite a few nobles who would consider me not quite up to stuff."

"At least you understand why you shouldn't even be here," Andrew said, glaring at William. "She'd never agree to marry you. Her father would likely disown her if she even hinted at it."

"But what if the child *is* mine," William countered. "You can't just ignore that fact."

"Which of us sired it is rather irrelevant since it might not ever come to light," Andrew insisted.

"How's that?"

"It could take after its mother entirely. But I'm willing to marry her and raise the child, whether it turns out to be mine or not."

"Now that's too bloody noble even for a noble," William sneered.

"Not a'tall," Andrew disagreed. "I simply want her for my wife."

Andrew's statement had a calming influence on Albert. The older man regained some of his composure, now that the options weren't sounding so completely abhorrent. But then he caught sight of Drew, sitting there so relaxed and even grinning, and he stiffened again.

"You find this all amusing, do you?" Albert demanded of Drew.

"All this?" Drew said, shaking his head.

"No indeed. That these two fellows have been at each other's throats since they found out that Emily favored them both, well, yes, I do see some humor in that."

"And just who are you?"

"Drew Anderson. I don't think Emily realized that I'm a member of Jeremy's family, when she batted those pretty eyes at me. Not many know that my sister married Jeremy's father. We're Americans, after all, and ship's captains, my brothers and I, so we don't get to London often. I'd just docked a few days prior to meeting Emily, so I hadn't heard the rumors yet either, that she and Jeremy—well—"

"Get to the point, man."

"Certainly. I travel a lot, and I'm not one to turn down a pretty wench when her intentions are so obvious. I take my pleasures where I can find them, you understand. Always have, probably always will."

"I suppose you're claiming the child as well?" Albert demanded.

"Hell no!"

Albert frowned. "Then what are you doing here?"

"I'm here because although I didn't actually make love to the girl, it was damn close.

We'd gone for a stroll in the garden at some party my sister drug me to and found a nice secluded spot. Another minute or so and I'd be forced to admit the child could have been mine. But we were interrupted just as I was about to . . . well, anyway, we dressed quickly and got back to the party. She promised to meet me later to finish what we started. I showed up at the rendezvous, but Emily didn't. Waited a damned hour, too," Drew added with some disgruntlement. "She would have been worth it. And then the next day I hear she's to have Jeremy's baby. Hate to say it, Bascomb, but I don't doubt she is with child, with the way she's spread herself around."

Albert was red-faced with fury again by the time Drew finished. James couldn't blame him. He would never have put it quite so bluntly, whether it was true or not. Typical of Americans to be so bloody blunt.

And that was when Emily Bascomb walked into the study. She'd entered with a smile, expecting only her father to be there. Such an exceptionally pretty girl. It was too bad she was so spoiled she believed she could have anything she wanted—at any cost.

Her smile vanished at the sight of her father's rage. But when she noticed James there, her eyes flared briefly with alarm before she assumed an inscrutable look. James sighed to himself. This might not be as easy as he'd thought, if she could conceal her emotions that easily.

"I wasn't aware we had guests, Father."

"We don't. I would not by any means call these gentlemen guests."

Andrew flushed over that remark, which caught Emily's eye. She must have decided to play the gracious lady for the moment, because she said to him, "Lord Whittleby, how pleasant to see you again."

"The pleasure is all mine, m'dear," Andrew replied with an adoring look and a flourishing bow, causing the girl to give him a brilliant smile.

"So you *do* know him?" Albert demanded.

Emily frowned over her father's sharp tone. "Well, certainly. We were introduced last week at a soiree, then again a few nights ago. I wasn't sure he would remember me," she added coyly.

"Oh, he remembers you," Albert said in a

derogatory tone. "And wants to marry you, thank God."

"I'm flattered," she began, then went very still when the rest of her father's remark sunk in. "What d'you mean 'thank God'?"

Andrew was quick to reply first, "Whatever happens here, Emily, please be assured that I would consider it an honor to marry you."

"Again I'm flattered, sir, but—"

"You are fresh out of 'buts,' Emily," her father interrupted sharply. "Jeremy Malory doesn't want you and denies ever touching you."

She sighed. A bit overdone, in James's opinion. Too much dejection.

"I warned you that he would deny it, irresponsible rake that he is." And then she turned toward James and with an owlish look, as if she'd only just noticed him there, "Oh, I beg your pardon, Lord Malory. But then everyone knows *where* Jeremy got his habits from."

James burst out laughing over that remark. She was on the defensive already. She'd have to be dense not to realize something had gone wrong with her plan, with her father's anger so obvious.

"Yes, I'm damned proud of the lad, particularly of the fact that he doesn't lie."

"To *you,* maybe," she sneered. "But he's lied about this matter—"

"Enough, Emily," Albert interrupted. "Do you or do you not know these men gathered here?"

Her back stiffened again. James had a feeling that she wasn't used to having her father angry with her, that that alone was disturbing her the most. She probably didn't know how to handle it, at least, not with others present.

She glanced about the room, admitted, "I know most of them, yes."

"The American here?" Her father wanted confirmation.

"Well, yes, I do recall meeting him. It's hard to forget a man as tall as he is."

"And handsome," Drew added with a roguish grin and a wink for her.

"Fie, sir, don't be so full of yourself," she took a moment to rejoin in the typical form of flirtation.

"And this one?" Albert asked, pointing at William.

"No, I don't believe I've ever seen him before," Emily said mildly.

William assumed an angry pose himself. "I like that," he said indignantly. "It was fine and dandy to dally with me, as long as your father never found out about it, eh? Now you're going to deny it?"

"Deny what? I don't *know* you. What else is there to deny?"

"Good God, d'you really not remember? You were a little foxed at that ball, but I've never heard of a woman not remembering something like this. Or have you slept with so many men that you can't keep track of them all?"

Emily gasped in outrage, her face flaming. William had overdone it. Getting vulgar was guaranteed to offend, true or not, so her reaction couldn't be judged merely on the statement implied.

And she turned her offended outrage on her father. "Is this what has you upset? A stranger comes here and tells you the most outlandish lies and you believe him! And I've never been foxed in my life—well, that one time at Mama's birthday party last year, but you already know about that, and no men were around."

"Your drinking habits aren't an issue, sweetheart," Drew put in. "I'm not here to claim your baby is mine, though you'll have to admit it was a close thing."

She swung around with another gasp to face Drew. "My God, you, too? What is this, a conspiracy cooked up by the Malorys?" And then she turned to her father again, her expression imploring. "Papa, I swear they're lying!"

"All three of them?" Albert said in a tired voice as he sat down behind his desk. "One I could have doubted, even two, but all three?"

Emily glanced at Andrew, gave him a hurt look. "Surely not you, too?"

He flinched at her portrayed disappointment. There was a distinct possibility that he might break down and confess all. He did still want to marry her, after all. And since *she* knew he was lying, he'd have a bloody hard time working around that if he got his wish and Albert did give her to him. However, he must have recalled that this little scenario was exactly what she'd planned for Jeremy, that they were merely throwing the same lies she'd started back at her, so she was hardly in a position to carry a grudge.

"My main concern is the child," Andrew told her. "Which could be my heir."

"We *both* know it's not yours!" she snapped. "So stop this nonsense."

"We know nothing of the sort. I understand your need to make denials. But don't forget that I still want to marry you. I'm willing to raise the child, whether it's mine or not, and willing to overlook your"—he paused to glance at the other men—"many indiscretions."

Again her face flushed severely, but no embarrassment was left, only pure rage, and she turned it back on her father. "You have subjected me to these horrible accusations, none of which are even remotely true. Can't you see what they're doing here? This is a complete farce, a conspiracy contrived by Lord Malory there, I don't doubt, just to get his son out—"

"Enough!" Albert snapped. "Don't make me any more ashamed of you, girl, than I already am."

That had to hurt. She did draw in her breath before she said, "So you're going to believe them instead of me?"

She managed to get some tears rolling and to look utterly devastated. Drew's expression wavered. He was a sucker for tears. Andrew turned around so he'd be less affected. William rolled his eyes, recognizing a fellow performer.

Fortunately, Albert knew his daughter well and her tactics. "I know you're capable of lying, Emily. It's a bad habit you got into growing up. And I know you do it very well. I just never dreamed you could lie about something like this that has such irreparable consequences."

She stiffened. The anger was back so quickly, it was apparent it had never left, had merely been briefly concealed for her moment of melodrama. She chose to direct that anger at James now, having decided he was responsible for ruining her plans.

"I know you instigated this, Lord Malory. But you didn't give it much thought, did you?" she said scathingly. "I can't imagine how you thought you could pull this off, when I can prove they're all lying."

James lifted a sardonic brow. "And how would you do that, m'dear, when it's your word against theirs, three to one as it were— no, make that four to one, since Jeremy has also branded you a liar?"

"Jeremy be damned, I can prove it because I'm still a—"

She realized what she'd been about to say and cut herself off, but James pounced on the opening she'd supplied. "A virgin?"

James stood up. Emily took a step back, realizing belatedly just whom she'd verbally assaulted. But James was no longer interested in the chit. She'd done exactly what he'd hoped she would.

"My apologies, Lord Bascomb, that this visit was necessary," James said.

Albert nodded stiffly. His expression was self-explanatory. He was embarrassed over the whole affair, now that he realized to what lengths his daughter had gone to entrap a husband.

"By the by," James added, "in case it hasn't occurred to you yet, she's the one who started the rumors and escalated them. I wouldn't recommend shooting her, but I would recommend some discipline. The girl can't go around deciding other people's futures on a whim. My family is done with yours. See that it stays that way. After you, gentlemen," he said to his companions.

Drew and William filed out of the room.

Andrew didn't move. "Go ahead, m'lord. I believe Lord Bascomb and I still have much to discuss. Emily's reputation still needs salvaging, after all."

"I'll salvage my own reputation, thank you very much," Emily snarled, and marched out of the room herself.

James lifted a brow at Andrew. The smile he got in return said Andrew was still staying. The boy must be in love, to still want the girl after witnessing her theatrics and temper firsthand.

Chapter 37

Back at Jeremy's town house, Danny was upstairs dusting that morning when the screaming and shouting started. She thought there was a brawl out in the street at first, it was that kind of noise, some cheering, some shrieking. When she realized the noise was coming from directly below her, she rushed downstairs to find out what was wrong.

The commotion led her to the kitchen. Claire was there. She was holding a pot in her hand, as if it were a weapon. Carlton was there. He had a broom hefted over his shoulder. Danny would have guessed that those two were having a rather serious fight, except they weren't facing each other. Mrs. Appleton was there, too, but she was ignoring the uproar, just standing at the stove adding some spices to the stew she was cooking for lunch.

Carlton was bending over, looking under the cupboard. Claire's eyes were moving wildly about the room, searching for something.

"What's wrong?" Danny asked, wondering if she should pick up a weapon, too.

"A rat got in," Claire said. "I found it in the pantry. It ran in here."

"A rat? In a neighborhood like this?" Danny said doubtfully.

"Not unheard of, m'dear," Mrs. Appleton remarked with a glance over her shoulder. "They'll go where there's food, and we have a well-stocked house."

"And the aroma o' yer food, lass, would lure 'em all the way from the docks," Artie, the butler, said cheerfully as he came in behind Danny.

That got a blush out of the cook. Danny was marveling over that when Claire shouted again, "There! It's behind the dry sink."

Carlton leapt in that direction and thrust

his broom under the long piece of kitchen furniture to flush the rat out. It worked. The rodent dashed for the next nearest place to hide, the big cast-iron stove that Mrs. Appleton was standing in front of. She still didn't move, was just stirring her pot of stew, which made it difficult, but not impossible, for Carlton to get his broom underneath the stove.

"Stop it," Danny said, but no one was listening to her at the moment.

Claire was shouting suggestions and warning Carlton not to miss again—he'd gotten in one swipe of the broom when the rodent had dashed for the stove. Artie was laughing quite loudly over the footman's antics.

Danny started to give another warning, but the stove wasn't close enough to the floor for the rodent to feel safe under it, particularly with the broom swishing toward it. It ran out in the open this time. Carlton straightened and raised the broom over his head for a good whack, and Danny dove straight at Carlton, knocking them both to the floor.

"You missed the rat, Danny," Artie snickered.

"Weren't aiming for it," she snarled, and sat on top of Carlton's chest to keep him supine long enough for him to listen. "He's m'pet," she told the incredulous footman. "You try to kill him again and I'll be coming after you with that broom, see if I don't."

He looked up at her wide-eyed, more amazed that she was sitting on him than that she kept rats for pets. "Didn't know he was yours," Carlton offered.

She nodded, accepting that, was about to get off him when Jeremy walked in, having been drawn by the noise as well, and said, "You're fired, Carlton."

Danny glanced toward the door to see that Jeremy wasn't smiling. In fact, his expression indicated he was dead serious. "What's he fired for?"

"For trespassing."

That was an odd way to put it, but she understood what he was getting at. Carlton did, too, because he dropped his head back on the floor with a groan.

Danny tsked at Jeremy. "He wasn't. I knocked him on his arse because he was trying to kill my pet."

"Then he's fired for that, too," Jeremy said.

Carlton groaned again. "You ain't fired, man, so stop with the groaning," Danny snapped as she got to her feet. She spared a glare for Artie as well, who was back to laughing his arse off.

"You actually keep a rat for a pet, Danny?" Claire finally got around to asking.

And Jeremy said now, "Oh, good God, a rat? Carlton, you're no longer fired."

Danny was getting quite irritated by that point. "He ain't a rat, he's a mouse."

"Danny, that thing was huge!" Claire disagreed. "It can't possibly be a mouse."

"So he's a little fat. I feed him good is all. But he's not a rat."

"Do you even know the difference between a mouse and a rat?" Claire asked.

Danny thought about that for a moment and had to admit, "Probably not. He's still my pet, whatever he is." She bent down so the large pocket on her apron opened against the floor. "Come here, Twitch."

She hadn't seen where he went to hide this time, so it took a moment for her to see him poking his head out from under the dough box. She didn't have to call him again. The moment he saw her looking directly at him, he scurried across the floor and went straight into her pocket.

"I'll be damned," Artie said. "Ayep, that's definitely 'er pet."

"Didn't know a rat could be tamed," Claire added in amazement.

"Mouse," Danny mumbled.

Claire chuckled. It was a rich sound. Most of them had never heard it before.

All three men were staring at Claire now. Jeremy raised a questioning brow. "What'd you do to yourself, lass? You look—softer."

"She's a raving beauty now, ain't she," Carlton added. He might actually have thought so, or he might merely have been making an effort to further relieve Jeremy's jealousy.

Claire didn't blush though, probably because she didn't believe him. But she grinned and told him, "Don't be filling my head with nonsense."

The change in the girl really was startling, but then confidence was an amazing thing. For Claire it softened all her rough edges, allowed her to flirt and tease and not take it seriously. She'd stopped slouching, too, and she really *did* have big breasts, which was the first thing Carlton had clapped eyes on this morning when he'd seen the "new" Claire. Getting her hair out of her face, dressing her in some of her prettier blouses and skirts that she'd buried in the bottom of her trunks, just those simple changes made her look so different, she was barely recognizable.

But confidence had finished off the new package, was responsible for the smiles, the laughter, both of which altered her expressions and showed off a pretty face. She wasn't a raving beauty by any means, was a bit on the plump side, but all in all, she was a pretty girl who would have no trouble attracting men now.

Danny was mostly responsible for cracking Claire's shell, and she was right proud of that. They'd spent hours together last night in her room, then in Claire's room, talking and laughing while they changed the way Claire looked. They'd formed a bond. Danny felt she had a close friend now and she'd realized just how much she'd missed having one since she'd left home. Someone to talk to about things that mattered. Someone to share triumphs and failures with.

"You children need to get back to work," Mrs. Appleton said, mindful that the master of the house was still there. "You can play with Danny's pet some other time."

Danny rolled her eyes and headed to her room to put Twitch back in his box. He must have gotten comfortable with his new surroundings, to make him go exploring farther than her room, timid as he was.

She didn't expect Jeremy to follow her, with everyone watching. She did expect to talk to him later about his burst of jealousy. That was really too bad of him, making it so bleeding obvious to the others that he was her lover. Not that any of them hadn't guessed—well, maybe Mrs. Appleton hadn't—but still, he'd as much as said to Carlton, "Get your hands off her, she's mine."

That had been quite annoying at the time, but in retrospect, she was rather thrilled by Jeremy's display of possessiveness. Maybe he cared about her a bit more than his natural sensuality implied. Then again, maybe he got jealous over all his women.

Unfortunately, that was probably more like it. Most men did fly off the handle, after all, if another man made obvious overtures to a woman they were currently sleeping with. She'd be a fool to make more of it than what it was, just a natural male instinct.

"You don't have any other pets in here, d'you? Snakes? Spiders? More rats?"

Danny swung around to find Jeremy leaning against her open door, arms crossed, ankles crossed. So he *had* followed her. And *that* was too bad of him, too.

As for his question, she snorted at him. "He's not a rat, just a very fat mouse."

"If you say so, m'dear."

"And he's a coward."

"I believe all rats are cowards when things one hundred times their size swing brooms at them."

She grinned. "You're probably right."

He moved away from the door. Danny gasped. His relaxed pose had been deceptive. She saw it now, the heat in his eyes, the intensity. She had a feeling he hadn't recovered yet from that burst of jealousy. And the hard grip of his hands as he clasped her head just before he kissed her lent proof to it.

He wasn't hurting her, far from it. He was overwhelming her though with his passion, his tongue ravaging her mouth, his hands moving down to lift her up against him so she could feel his arousal. It was almost intimidating, his aggression, but thrilling, too, that he wanted her this much. It sparked an equal boldness in her that made her press one hand against the back of his dark head while the other slid down his back, barely reaching the curve of his buttocks to press him even closer.

With a groan of pleasure, he yanked her skirt up, and somehow got his hand inside the back of her drawers, curving it under her till he could reach her moist warmth. Oh, God, his fingers thrust inside her, again, again, in and out, his wrist pressed firmly between her cheeks, his arousal grinding against her from the front. She was so over-whelmed with erotic sensations that she cried out and climaxed within seconds. If he weren't still holding her so tightly to him, she would have crumbled at his feet.

His mouth slid across her cheek to her ear, his tongue delving there as well before he said, "I want to feed you cheese in bed. Your mouse is welcome to share. I want to pour champagne over your naked breasts and lick them until one of us is drunk. I want to drape you in fine silks and pretty baubles. I want more time with you, Danny." He leaned back, and that possessiveness was there in his eyes now. "Be my mistress. I promise you won't regret it."

She couldn't think at the moment, so wasn't about to reply to something that important. But she wasn't about to send him away either, despite everyone's knowing he'd followed her here. She was too inflamed herself. . . .

"You might want to close the door," she suggested in a husky tone.

He turned to do just that, only to have Artie appear. "Yer pa is here, and yer uncle. Don't know if they've got good news for ye. They're at each other's throat as usual, so it were hard to tell if they're bringing good tidings or not."

Jeremy sighed, not over Artie's remark, but because he hadn't gotten the door closed soon enough on intruders. Danny's sigh was even louder. She needed to sit down. She needed a cold bath.

Jeremy didn't take that into account when he said, "Come along, Danny. You might as well hear firsthand how your idea panned out."

Chapter 38

"And how would you have helped the situation?" James was asking his brother as Jeremy and Danny arrived in the parlor. "You're a married man, or have you been in the doghouse so long you've forgotten that fact?"

"Ain't in the doghouse," Anthony replied. "And I'd never forget that I'm married to the most beautiful woman under creation."

"Have to disagree, old chap," James remarked. "George is much prettier."

"George is an American," Anthony rejoined, as if that didn't count.

James sighed. "*Some* things have to be forgiven, don't you know."

"Besides"—Anthony got back to the subject they'd been bickering over—"you missed the bloody point like you *always* do. Think you do it on purpose, don't you?"

"Me? Deliberately try to annoy you? Wherever would you get that idea?"

Anthony hooted with derision. "*As* I was saying, I wasn't suggesting I should have been on hand for the performance, since, as you so aptly pointed out, that wouldn't have helped a'tall. What I was getting at was I should have been consulted before the performance."

"Why?"

"Because he's my nephew. Because I *am* known to have moments of genius and might have contributed nicely to resolving the issue."

James rolled his eyes. "If we had still been stymied on a course of action, you probably would have been consulted— eventually. But we had a splendid plan, so it wasn't necessary to gather more suggestions. And *genius* my arse," he added for good measure.

Jeremy decided that was a good opportunity to interrupt their typical bickering: "*Splendid* as in *successful* I hope?"

James glanced at his son and even smiled. "Indeed, lad. It went very well."

"Despite the fact that I wasn't consulted," Anthony mumbled.

"So Emily admitted she was lying all along?" Jeremy asked his father.

"Better than that, she admitted she's still a virgin. Slip of the tongue, as it were, but then that *was* what we were hoping for. It was close though, since she did accuse us of a conspiracy against her on your behalf. *She* knew it was exactly that, but at least her father didn't, and we were able to plant the seed firmly in his mind of her lack of maidenly morals, before she arrived to deny it. We also had the added bonus that he was already aware of her tendency to lie, since she'd been doing it from childhood, apparently."

"I can't believe it went so well," Jeremy said, beaming with relief.

"It might not have," James was forced to admit. "I think your friend Andy was the deciding factor."

"How so?"

"If he hadn't assured her father right up front that he still wanted to marry Emily, then Bascomb might not have been so easily swayed to doubt her. And had her father stood with her on the matter, then she might not have lost her temper to allow the slip."

"Even though it was three to one?"

"Could have been ten to one at that point. As soon as she tossed 'conspiracy' on the table, that put a new wrinkle in it. But the odds *were* mentioned, and that was when it got out of hand for her. So three to one was sufficient. And we know who you can thank for that."

Danny started blushing immediately when all three pairs of eyes turned toward her. She was thrilled that her idea had worked, that Jeremy wouldn't have to marry a woman he didn't want to marry. Actually, she was thrilled because that still left him a bachelor whom she could enjoy for a bit longer. But she hated being the center of attention as she'd just become, was completely embarrassed by it.

"It weren't nothing," she mumbled.

"Wasn't," Jeremy whispered beside her.

She stepped on his foot. "That, too."

He said to his father, "Indeed, and I'm going to buy her a kitten as a token of my appreciation."

"You call that an appropriate gift?"

Anthony hooted, turning to his brother to add, "What *have* you been teaching the lad?"

"Actually"—Jeremy frowned thoughtfully, changing his mind—"cats don't like rats, do they? Think I better make it a puppy instead."

Danny stepped on his foot again, much, much harder this time. "Don't you dare mention my pet to them," she hissed at him.

But his father wanted to know, "What the deuce do rats have to do with it? And for once my brother is right. A pretty trinket would be a more appropriate token, don't you think? Always worked for me."

"Did I hear that correctly?" Anthony jumped on James's remark. "You said I was right?"

"Put a lid on it," James mumbled.

But Jeremy explained, after he moved away from Danny to protect his feet, "She'd throw trinkets back at me. The wench won't accept gifts."

"So it's like that, is it?" James said, staring at Danny. Then he said to Jeremy, "That why she's still wearing an apron, too?"

Danny's embarrassment twisted the

spike at that and she replied hotly, "My choices are mine to make, mates. Don't be trying to tack the title *mistress* to me. I ain't one and won't ever be one. I pay my own way and will take my pleasures on my own terms."

"Here, here!" Anthony cheered. "Good God, I wish more women thought like that. They don't, you know. Come to think of it, only a man would."

The hot blush was firmly back in place. Danny threw up her hands in disgust and stalked out of the room, snarling, "Bleedin' nabobs."

"Well, damn me, didn't mean to insult the chit," Anthony said.

"You didn't," Jeremy replied. "She just don't like being reminded that she spent the last fifteen years or so living *and* thinking like a boy."

"So James wasn't pulling my leg for once?" Anthony asked curiously. "She really did pass herself off as a lad for most of her life?"

"By choice. It kept her out of a whore's shanty, is my guess."

"Ah, so that's why." Anthony nodded.

"Smart girl. But it must be deuced hard dealing with her, if she thinks the way you do."

Jeremy burst out laughing. "You don't know the half of it, Uncle Tony."

Chapter 39

Teasing Danny was sometimes detrimental to his health, so Jeremy decided to wait until the afternoon before he approached her again. Besides, that gave him time to locate a gift for her that she'd have a hard time refusing. He also had a plan to give them some time alone together, and the time of day played a part in it.

So later that day he tracked her down and found her changing the bed in one of the guest rooms. God, it was hard being near her with a bed at hand, it really was. Hot desire shot through him every bloody time. Of course, it really didn't matter if a bed was at hand or not. Danny simply had that effect on him no matter where they were.

He stood in the doorway and cleared his throat to draw her attention. She glanced at him and frowned. She was obviously still annoyed with him for bringing up their relationship in front of his relatives, had probably been saving up a good chiding for him, but whatever she'd been about to say was forgotten when she caught sight of what he was holding—in each hand.

"Oh, you didn't," she said as she approached him and grabbed the snow-white kitten from his left hand. "I'm not keeping it," she added as she put the kitten to her cheek to cuddle.

"Didn't think you would" was all Jeremy said, and managed not to smile.

With her eye on the tiny puppy in his right hand, she stressed, "I'm not keeping him either," as she held out her other hand to take the puppy from him.

"Course not," Jeremy agreed.

She moved back to the bed to set them both down on it. They sniffed at each other for a moment, then the puppy curled into a ball to sleep, while the kitten sat next to it and started licking a paw. They were nearly identical in size, probably no more than a few weeks old.

"I've heard they'll get along splendidly, if raised together," Jeremy remarked, coming to stand behind her to observe the small creatures.

"You think?"

"Should work with rats, too."

She groaned and complained, "You're a wicked man, Jeremy Malory."

"Thank you. I do try."

She glanced back at him. "Can you just say you bought them for yourself?"

"But I did!"

"Very well, then you won't mind if I take care of them for you?"

"Wouldn't mind a'tall, luv."

She beamed at him and sat on the bed to pull the kitten into her lap to gently pet it. "They are adorable, aren't they?"

The only thing he found adorable these days was her. Come to think of it, he hadn't even glanced at another woman since he'd clapped eyes on Danny. But to keep the mood light, since he still had his other plans to introduce to her, he merely nodded.

"As much as I'd like to dress you up for a night on the town," he mentioned casually, "it occurred to me that we'd need a chaperone, which wasn't part of the plan. So I settled on a nice picnic."

"It's past lunchtime, if you ain't noticed."

"But not past dinner, is it? And who says picnics are only for lunch? I was thinking an early dinner picnic, next to a nice pond, flowers scenting the air. Now tell me that don't sound like a nice way to celebrate? And you *do* owe me a celebration. You were single-handedly responsible for extracting me from the depths of hell. Now while you might not think that is cause for celebration, I do, and I'd much rather do it with you. So how's a picnic sound?"

"Sounds pretty nice, actually. I've never been on one. There's a pond in the city?"

"I was thinking of something a bit more secluded, where we won't be interrupted by people who recognize me. And I know of a nice spot just outside London, not far a'tall. I've already ordered the carriage brought round, and Mrs. Appleton has agreed to keep an eye on the babies in the kitchen till you're back. She's also got the basket of food prepared. So grab your jacket and we'll be off."

He left the room before she could think

up some reason why she shouldn't accompany him. And thirty minutes later they were leaving London behind. He'd only lied a little bit about the distance they'd be traveling. The pond he had in mind was near an inn more than an hour away. His father usually stayed the night there on his way back from Haverston if he got a late start. And having an inn nearby was crucial to Jeremy's plans, since he hoped to be spending the night in it with her.

But she didn't really notice the time it was taking them to get there, since she'd never ridden up on the driver's perch of a carriage before and was enjoying the unobstructed view. He also kept up a steady stream of light conversation, telling her how he'd gone through hell and back trying to find those two pets for her, when in fact the kitten was from a litter at Reggie's house, and the puppy from a litter at Kelsey's house, the ladies having mentioned them when they'd taken him furniture shopping.

The pond really was a beautiful setting at that time of the year, flowers in a myriad of colors dotting the landscape around it, several ducks floating about in it, one with a small train of three ducklings following it.

And Mrs. Appleton had outdone herself on such short notice: the food was varied and delicious, with several bottles of wine included.

They ate, they laughed, they even had some meaningful conversation. Despite Jeremy's wanting to keep the mood light, goals somehow got mentioned, and Danny grew serious when she admitted, "I had a goal many years ago, one that was unrealistic though, since I had no way to accomplish it."

"What?"

She was lying on the blanket they'd spread out near the water, her head resting on his thigh. In one hand she had the stem of a daisy that she was lazily twirling about, her wineglass in the other.

"I wanted to get the younguns into a more stable environment."

"The ones who lived with you?" he asked, his fingers casually moving through her curls.

"Yes. I had sorely felt my lack of schooling, so I figured the other children did, too. I wanted to get them that, get them supplied with a steady flow of food, too, so they wouldn't have to steal anymore."

"Sounds like you wanted to set up a real orphanage for them."

His fingers moved down to her cheek, and then on to her earlobe and her neck, his touch still casual. He noticed her shiver though and drop the daisy without noticing. And it took a moment for her to answer him.

"Well, I was too young at the time to have figured that out. It was just a goal I had for a year or two," she ended with a shrug.

Jeremy was hesitant to mention it, but did anyway. "Would you let me set something like that up for you?"

She frowned. "You mean you'd pay for it?"

"Something like that."

"That'd be a gift, wouldn't it? With a really big 'beholden' factor. No, it ain't your goal. It was mine, but even now, I still don't see how I could accomplish it, not on a maid's wages."

He coughed and said, "I *could* raise your wages."

She laughed at that point. "Not unless you're going to raise everyone's wages, you won't. You snuck in one gift on me, mate. I'm going to let it pass, but don't be doing it again, eh?"

He reached for her empty hand, brought

it up to his mouth so he could nibble on her fingers.

"You make it deuced hard, luv. You see, I have this overwhelming urge to give you things." He drew one of her fingers into his mouth and sucked on it for a moment. "I don't know why. Never been plagued with such an urge before." He bit the pad of her second finger. "And it's rather frustrating— no, actually, *very* frustrating, come to think of it."

She was looking up at him now, said a bit breathlessly, "You've got nothing o' the sort."

"And how would you know, when you've probably never had such an urge before?"

"Actually I have," she admitted. "Every time I used to see something I wanted, I always thought to m'self, Lucy would probably like that, too. Of course, that was because I care about her. She has been like a mother, a sister, and a best friend to me. So what you're trying to tell me in your odd nabob way is that you care about me?"

"Oh, good God, if you haven't figured that out yet, I think I'll throttle you. Better yet . . ."

He dragged her up until she was lying in

the crook of his arm and lowered his mouth to hers, tasting her deeply, thoroughly, with a passionate urgency he could not control. He loved tasting her, loved touching her, feeling her trembling in his arms as she was now. He began unfastening her blouse, but his finesse and his patience were deserting him, and he cupped her breast through the cloth instead. She put her hand on his cheek. That inflamed him further, but her groan . . .

Using every ounce of willpower he possessed, Jeremy pulled his mouth away from hers. "Damn! If it weren't for the promise of a comfortable bed at the inn near here, I'd make love to you right here on the grass. I think it's time to leave, luv, I really do."

Chapter 40

It was nearly fully dark by the time they packed up the remnants of their picnic and got back into Jeremy's carriage. What little remained of the setting sun was hidden behind a thick bank of clouds and the trees along the road. If it weren't for those trees, which acted as a kind of fence, they might not have stayed on the road, since the carriage wasn't designed for country jaunts, at least not at night.

The well-lit inn was a beacon though, off in the distance, and when they finally reached it, Jeremy relaxed again. He didn't mention what *could* have happened out on the road, where highwaymen prevailed at night, where the slightest wrong turn could have ended them in a ditch. Sleeping in an open carriage alongside the road would have been a rotten way to end a most enjoyable day.

Arm in arm, they went upstairs to their room. Danny hadn't questioned why they would be staying at an inn instead of returning to London. Nor did she question why he'd ordered just one room for them both. She probably understood about the dangers of the road, but as for the single room, either she was as eager for some lovemaking as he was, or she figured it wouldn't matter out here in the country where no one knew them.

Which wasn't exactly the case. The innkeeper recognized Jeremy and called him by name. He had been a guest there enough times over the years for the man to remember him. One of the other guests in the common room recognized him as well, or seemed to. Actually, the fellow was staring at Danny, and with an expression that indicated he was seeing an angel—or a ghost.

But the couple didn't notice, and again Jeremy's finesse went right out the door the moment he closed it behind them. Lighting the lamps could wait. Undressing fully could wait. Jeremy fairly tossed Danny on the bed and was kissing her so deeply, she wouldn't have been able to get in a word of protest. But she wasn't protesting in the least. In fact, he wasn't sure which of them was the more heated with desire.

Danny found Jeremy's lack of control incredibly erotic. He tore out of his coat and tossed it. She'd been carrying hers and dropped it when he tossed her on the bed. He ripped open the cuffs of his shirt and merely pulled it over his head. She quickly unfastened her blouse, afraid he'd rip that open next if she didn't. Her chemise he merely pulled down, then he gripped both her breasts and buried his head between them with a groan, suckling one until she cried out for mercy. His mouth, so hot, trailed up to her neck and kissed and sucked her there as well. Then he moved to her ear, where he rasped out, "Touch me. I love it when you touch me."

He rolled over and sat her on his loins to give her better access to him. Her hands moved over his chest, pinching his nipples lightly. He groaned when she bent down to

lick one and became so aroused that he
nearly unseated her. Yanking her skirt up
out of the way, he slipped his hands inside
her drawers and gripped her derriere, grinding her loins against his. But it wasn't
enough for her, it was a mere tease. She
wanted him inside her, hard and hot and
buried deep. She couldn't wait any longer.

Her mewling said so. His hand gripped
her hair, leading her mouth back to his as he
rolled them over again, his other hand taking her drawers off as he did. And then she
had her wish, he was inside her, such heat,
driving hard to her depths, and she ex-
ploded around him, sucking him in even
deeper, her cries of pleasure lost beneath
his lips, continuing as he thrust again and
again, until his own cry ripped through the
room.

Jeremy's heart was still pounding hard.
Without a doubt, that had been the most
spectacular climax of his life. So that's what
happened when anticipation built for hours
upon hours?

No, he'd experienced anticipation before.
It had never been like this. It was Danny. For
some reason, she was affecting him like no
woman ever had before. And it wasn't just

the lovemaking. This wanting to be with her, every minute of the day, when he knew bloody well he couldn't, was such a keen frustration, he wasn't sure how to deal with it.

Jeremy was loath to move away from her even for a moment, but he finally finished undressing. He even got up and lit some lamps since the hour was still early and he wasn't the least bit tired yet.

"We didn't bring anything to sleep in," Danny pointed out as he rejoined her on the bed.

"Yes, we did," he said, pulling her close to him again. "I don't know about you, but I'm sleeping in your arms. You're welcome to try sleeping in mine."

"If you think that will work, I suppose I'll trust your judgment." She curled into him to get comfortable. "It feels odd, being at an inn when I'm not here to rob the guests."

He chuckled. "I don't need to lock you in, do I? You can restrain yourself for the duration?"

"I'm considering it. Guests get noisy, after all, when they find out they've been robbed. Don't think I'd care to be awakened by the commotion."

She said no more. He waited nearly a minute before he lifted his head to see if she was grinning. She wasn't, not even a little.

"You *were* joking, weren't you?"

"Course I was, mate," she assured him. "But while we're on the subject of restraint, you need to be practicing some of your own."

"Bite your tongue. You hold me off enough as it is. Any more and I will go quite insane."

She snorted. "No, you won't, and I didn't mean that kind of o' restraint. I meant your jealousy."

"Jealousy!" he exclaimed, then added indignantly, "I've never been jealous in m'life."

"Then what'd you fire Carlton for this morning, eh?"

"Oh, that," he said with a shrug. "That was—well, that was, hmmm, I'm not sure what the bloody hell that was, but it certainly wasn't—"

"It was. *And* it was silly. You didn't even pause to find out why I was sitting on him before you fired the poor man. You might as well trust me, Jeremy, because the only way this works for us is for it to *only* work for us. See my point?"

"Not in the bloody least."

She released a long sigh. "I've made an exception for you. If I start making love to every Tom, Dick, and Harry, then I'll have turned into what I swore I'd never be. So there won't *be* any other man for me. When we're done, I'll wait for marriage to some bloke, but I won't be testing the waters first, if you catch my drift."

He pulled her closer. "Danny, luv, I seriously doubt 'we'll' ever be done."

She didn't reply immediately. He found himself holding his breath until she said, "Unless I get offered a better job."

He sat up. She pushed him back down. "I was joking, mate. Cor, learn the difference, eh?"

He frowned. "I believe I know the difference, and you weren't joking in the least. What job would tempt you away from me?"

Again, it didn't seem as if she was going to answer him, but finally she sighed and said, "Wife and mother. I've made no bones about it. I want my own family. You've already got a family, a large one, so you have no hankering for a new one. But I'll be moving on eventually to accomplish my goals."

He held her to him, tighter than necessary. He didn't like being reminded of her goals, but her "eventually" could be years off, might never even arrive, so he wasn't going to worry about it now, while their affair was progressing nicely.

A while later he confessed, "I'm not sure how I'm containing how happy I am just now."

Danny had been drowsing off, but hearing that definitely woke her up. She leaned up to stare at him. "Are you really?"

"Wouldn't have said it if I wasn't. But I do wish you'd start sharing my bed at home. It's not as if the staff doesn't know I've staked a claim. I made that perfectly clear this morning, didn't I?"

Her eyes narrowed on him. "If you tell me that silliness was deliberate, I may just pinch you—hard."

"Well, no, not deliberate a'tall." And then he grinned. "But it worked out rather well, don't you think?"

"I think we better leave things as they are. You keep trying to turn me into a mistress. Stop it. I've told you my terms. Equal all the way."

"Yes, but what's that got to do with sleeping together nightly? *Sleeping,* Danny. I truly do love just holding you in my arms."

She smiled at him and snuggled back down. "This is kind o' nice, ain't it? I'll have to give it some thought." And then as she drifted off to sleep a bit later, she mumbled, "You make a nice nightgown, mate, 'deed you do."

Chapter 41

An inn wasn't a good place to do it. Tyrus came to that conclusion when midnight rolled around but the lights were still on in the girl's room. He still couldn't believe he'd found her again, after he'd lost hope that he would. He'd been so confident, after visiting the nabob, that he'd get the job finished this time. Then to find she wasn't where he'd thought she'd be, where he'd seen her go the day he'd followed her. She'd been kicked out and they didn't know where she'd gone. And London was too bloody big to just hope he might run into her again, so he'd given up.

He hadn't gone back to tell the lord

though, didn't want to own up that he'd failed yet again. But he'd found her again! And he wasn't going to lose her this time; he was going to finish the job tonight.

He'd figured he'd have a few hours' wait, so he'd swiped a bottle of rum out of the innkeeper's stock to take up to his room. He hadn't figured the couple wasn't there to sleep. He should have though. The girl had turned into a prime piece, just like her mother. And the gent she was with had had his hands all over her.

Still, they had to sleep sometime. He doubted they'd head back to wherever they came from in the middle of the night. So he waited, and waited. Every ten minutes or so he'd open his door just enough to see if the light was still coming from the crack under hers.

It was too bad the girl was with a Malory. That family was so notorious, even he'd heard of them. That they were all bloody lords wasn't the problem, but rather that they weren't men to cross. Prime shots, he'd heard, masters at dueling, masters at fisticuffs—masters at evening scores. So he'd try not to hurt the bloke, just hit him enough to knock him out.

With his rotten luck, he'd probably kill Malory, too. But not if he killed the girl first. As soon as she was dead, he'd have his luck back.

~~~

Danny had the dream that night, the bad one. She shouldn't have. It had only ever plagued her when she was nervous about something, frightened, or just plain uneasy, none of which applied that night. But it woke her, as it usually did, when the club swung toward her head.

After a single shiver to shake the dream off, she turned to move closer to Jeremy. For once, she had someone to gain comfort from. Not that she thought to wake him. Just being near him, touching him, was comfort enough.

But she was awake enough now to have no trouble hearing the soft rap on the door and the woman's voice asking, "Jeremy, are you there?"

Danny stiffened. A number of things ran through her mind, none of them nice. And she was none too gentle in shaking Jeremy awake to hear about it.

"What?" He sat up immediately.

"There's a wench at the door calling for you," Danny fairly snarled.

"The devil there is. Were you dreaming?"

And outside the door again: "Jeremy, I hear you in there. Are you decent enough for me to come in?"

"Oh, good God," he said now in surprise. "Amy?"

"So you *do* know her, eh?"

Danny's tone was angry enough that he guessed, "It's not what you're thinking. That's my cousin."

"Sure it is," Danny said as she put both feet to his backside and kicked him out of the bed.

"Blister it," he said, gaining his balance before he landed on the floor. "It really is."

He flicked a match to relight the lamp by the bed. Danny's gasp drew his eyes back to her, and then to the man she was staring at. He looked just middle-aged, though his hair was pure gray and long, clubbed back with straw. Straw? He was tall, skinny, and dressed like a beggar, his clothes threadbare and riddled with holes.

The man had frozen where he stood when the match flared to life, several feet away from the edge of Danny's side of the bed, looking as amazed as they were. He had a club in one hand and a pillow in the other, which he had probably intended to use to stuff their belongings into. He had liquor fumes coming off him, an indication that he wasn't thinking clearly.

"Amy!" Jeremy called out. "Get back from the door, because I'm about to throw something through it—unless you have a gun, in which case you can come in and use it."

"I don't carry guns," the woman called back. "Warren does, though. He's putting our horses in the stable. He'll be here in a moment."

Jeremy was already on his way around the foot of the bed to get to the intruder. The mention of guns had put some panic in the man's eyes and had him leaping across the bed to get to the door and out of there. Danny caught hold of one of his feet as he shot over her. She lost her grip though, with the momentum he'd gained. It did cause him to tumble headfirst to the floor on the other side of the bed, but he didn't stay there. Fast for his age, he scrambled to his feet again and ran out the door.

Jeremy charged after him, with no

thought for his nakedness. Danny quickly got her skirt and blouse on so she could follow. The door was still wide open. The woman in the hall didn't try to peek in through it. If she really was Jeremy's cousin, then she was probably standing out there with her back turned.

Jeremy came back just as Danny finished dressing. He looked nothing but disgruntled, which started her laughing.

"What the deuce are you laughing at?" he asked, his tone as annoyed as his expression.

It was such a comedy of errors, on everyone's part, she couldn't help it and said, "You just chased that thief down the hall buck naked."

"And scandalized me!" Amy called out in an indignant tone from the hall.

"He would have been gone if I'd grabbed my pants first," Jeremy pointed out logically.

"So chasing him naked helped?" Danny asked. "You caught him?"

"No," Jeremy mumbled. "He took the quick way down the stairs, tumbled the lot of them, and damned if he didn't get right up and keep on running. I draw the line at scampering about the countryside naked, thank you very much, particularly without my boots on."

"Never mind boots, have you got your pants on yet?" Amy asked.

Jeremy rolled his eyes and reached for the pants Danny was holding out to him. A few moments later he said toward the door, "Get your arse in here, puss, and tell me what the devil you think you're doing, banging on my door in the middle of the night?"

Amy poked her head around the opening now, and seeing that he was at least halfway decent with his pants in place, she came in and said huffily, "I didn't bang. I was very quiet about it, I'll have you know."

"She was, too," Danny added, sure now that the woman was his cousin.

It was the tone he'd used, and what he'd called her, that had convinced Danny. But seeing the woman now left no doubt whatsoever. She bore the same midnight black hair as Jeremy, the same deep cobalt blue eyes with the slightly exotic slant to them. She was stunningly beautiful, too. Was their entire family like that?

"What are you doing here, Amy?" Jeremy

wanted to know. "For that matter, when did you and Warren get back to England?"

"We sailed in this afternoon, or rather, yesterday afternoon. And I got this feeling—"

"Good God, never mind," Jeremy cut in with a groan. "Forget I asked. I don't want to hear about it."

"Oh, be quiet," Amy said as she got comfortable in one of the upholstered chairs the room offered.

Jeremy looked about the room for his shirt, since he'd sent it flying when he'd taken it off. He was trying his best to ignore his cousin. Danny sat down on the bed, having a feeling she wouldn't be getting back to sleep anytime soon.

"We docked this afternoon, or rather, we rowed in. Warren's ship is probably *still* waiting for docking permission. But as soon as my feet touched the dock, I got the strangest feeling that you were in some sort of trouble. So we went straight to Uncle James's house, only to find out you'd acquired your own residence while we were gone, so you weren't there. By the by, how are you liking that?"

"Splendidly, thanks. You didn't tell my father about your feeling, did you?"

"No, no, I managed not to. But then we expected to find you at your new town house. Was quite annoyed to hear you'd gone off for the day. But at least you had the presence of mind to tell your housekeeper where you were going, in case you were needed."

"What sort of trouble, Amy?"

"Nothing specific, and actually, it leaned more toward danger than trouble. You weren't planning on tackling anything of that sort, were you?"

"Anything dangerous? No, nothing like that on the agenda this week."

She gave him a sour look for the dry reply. "Don't scoff at this. You know my feelings are *never* wrong. I wouldn't have dragged Warren out here when we'd only *just* got home if it were just a mild feeling—"

"Course you would have."

She tsked over his interruption and continued, "But this was a strong feeling. She's not planning on killing you or anything like that, is she?"

Danny blinked, since the woman was looking directly at her as she said it, and quite suspiciously at that. Jeremy started laughing.

"She kills me with pleasure, but other than that, no," he got out between chuckles. "This is my—friend, Danny. Danny, meet my imp of a cousin, Amy."

"Is that what they're calling it these days?" Amy said, rolling her eyes.

"I wasn't painting it up nicely," Jeremy insisted. "She refuses to be my mistress, refuses to be my lover, for that matter. She'll only be my friend. Well, and my maid. Insists she earns her own keep."

Amy smiled at Danny. "How refreshing. A servant who doesn't jump at the chance to laze about. Nice to meet you, Danny."

Danny nodded curtly. She didn't like being discussed in such frank terms. And it was the first time *she'd* heard that Jeremy considered her a "friend." She wouldn't exactly call him that, but then, what would she call him, when he was much more than just her employer? Partner in lovemaking? Cohort in pleasure? Was there even a name for their particular relationship?

"Nothing is amiss, puss, other than your arrival interrupted our getting robbed," Jeremy went on to assure his cousin.

"So that's what that was about?"

"Yes. Not exactly a dangerous occurrence, since the chap was only carrying a club. But you *did* interrupt it, so I'll wager that's what your feeling was about."

Amy looked doubtful for a moment, but then conceded, "I suppose he might have awakened you, there could have been a scuffle, which you could have gotten hurt in. Yes, I suppose that could have been it."

"Does that mean we can get some sleep now?" Warren said as he came through the doorway.

"Welcome home, old man," Jeremy said, giving his cousin by marriage a jaunty smile. And to Danny, he explained, "This is the second Anderson to have married into the family, the first being his sister, George—"

"Georgina," Warren corrected by habit.

"Who married m'father," Jeremy continued. "Warren used to be the most bitter man alive, now he's one of the happiest, thanks to my cousin here."

Amy stood up and made a flourishing bow. "I do take all the credit."

Warren was extremely tall. Danny didn't see much of his brother Drew in him, except for the height and the golden brown hair the men had in common. Warren's eyes were a lime green and filled with warmth when he glanced at his wife.

"This is my friend Danny," Jeremy introduced again.

"Another male name?" Warren replied with a shake of his head. "What is it with you Malorys and your propensity for giving your women manly nicknames?"

"This one wasn't my doing." Jeremy grinned. "It's her actual name, though *I* think it's short for Danielle."

"It ain't," Danny mumbled.

"And how would you know when you can't remember?" Jeremy countered.

"I just know," she insisted.

Her terse tone prompted Warren to say, "I believe we could all do with some sleep."

"You got us a room?" Amy asked.

"Across the hall."

"Splendid," Amy said, and to Jeremy: "We'll see you in the morning then. We can ride back to the city together. And I want to hear everything that's been happening while I've been gone."

Warren pulled his wife out the door before she could think of anything else to say and closed it behind them. Jeremy joined Danny on the bed again.

"Are you all right?" he asked carefully.

"Why wouldn't I be?"

"Well, I assume you aren't used to being on this end of getting robbed. Not all that pleasant, is it?"

"Don't be censuring me on what I was forced to do all these years. I never liked stealing. I hated it."

"But you did it anyway."

"I come from the slums, mate. D'you realize how few choices women who can't read or write, who can't even talk proper, have?"

"I see why you have such an aversion to that 'word,' " he replied, careful not to say it.

"Well, that *is* what most of them end up doing, whoring or stealing."

He put his arm around her shoulders. "That's not what has you upset at the moment. Admit it. Being the victim has you realizing how all your victims must have felt."

She rolled her eyes at him. "Not even close, mate. And we didn't get robbed, nor would we have. I was awake. I would've heard that bungler tiptoeing about the room if I didn't hear the knock on the door first, or I would've smelled him. He reeked of rum, if you didn't notice. He was doomed to fail. A good thief knows better than to steal when he's foxed."

"Very well, I give up guessing." He sighed. "What turned you sour?"

"I ain't sour. I just realized, listening to you, that we have no definition, you and me. You called me your friend, but you paused before you said it. You don't really think of me that way, now do you?"

"Well, if you consider the definition of *that* word, then, yes, I do. What is a friend if not someone you feel close to, someone you like being with, someone you can confide in and share pleasures with." He grinned wickedly. "Of course, not the sort of pleasures *we* share, but you get the idea. Now we ain't best friends—yet. But we're getting there."

She was surprised, asked him, "You ain't pulling my leg, are you?"

He pushed her back on the bed so he could lean over her. "I will never joke about *us,* Danny. Now, I haven't done much confiding, other than things you could have heard from anyone. So here's a little tidbit for you. Amy *is* my best friend, and you'll be seeing a lot of her, since she visits often—when Warren isn't dragging her off to America. I'd like you to get to know her better. You'll like her. Actually, you can't help but like her. She's a sweetheart. Just never bet with her, over anything.

"Why?"

"Because she never loses."

"She's that lucky?"

"No, she's that gifted. It's those 'feelings' she gets. She's never wrong about them. So consider yourself warned in advance. If she wants to bet with you about something, run the other way."

Chapter 42

Jeremy had been right about Amy Anderson. It was impossible not to like her. She was vivacious, refreshingly frank, funny, and capable of an endless stream of chatter. Danny sat in the carriage next to Amy while Jeremy drove them back to London, and Warren rode his horse alongside. Somehow, Amy had managed to get Danny's entire life story out of her, all that she could remember anyway, including her goals. And Amy hadn't been surprised in the least, merely interested. Amy did cast a few glances at Jeremy's back, and Danny had to wonder if he was listening. But he never joined the conversation, so she doubted it.

They were approaching the outskirts of London when Amy suddenly said, "We're being followed."

Jeremy stopped the carriage immediately, proving he had been listening all the while, though Danny hadn't said anything he didn't already know about.

"Who?" Jeremy asked his cousin, then realizing she couldn't possibly know that, he asked instead, "They mean us harm?"

Danny was about to point out Amy couldn't know that either when the lady replied, "Most definitely."

Danny became distinctly uncomfortable at that point, as Warren rode off to see if he could ferret out anyone behind them or hiding alongside the road. She'd had the same feeling, that someone was following, but she'd discounted it, since she'd felt it more than once since moving uptown, and nothing had ever come of it. But with Amy having the same feeling, and since her family certainly didn't doubt her, Danny wondered if she should mention that this wasn't the first time.

She held her tongue. It simply couldn't be related. The two times she'd felt she'd been followed in the city had no doubt been due to that thug Lucy had told her about, the one who'd been trying to find her. Whoever was following them now would have nothing to do with her, was probably just some highwayman who'd missed his chance to stop them before they got too close to the city.

Sure enough, Warren came back shaking his head, having found no one. And Amy relaxed again, announcing, "The danger has passed. I do believe you scared them off, Warren, whoever they were."

They continued on their way as if nothing out of the ordinary had happened. Danny was amused. The two men took Amy's pronouncements as gospel. She said they were no longer in danger and so they thought nothing else about it.

Jeremy merely dropped Danny off at home before he took Amy home. He mentioned that he probably would be late getting back, since he had some business to attend to, something about carpenters he had to hire for one of his uncle's properties that needed renovations.

Danny got right back into her cleaning routine as if she hadn't spent the night out with the master of the house. The house hadn't picked up much dust while she was gone though, so she finished her work before dinner. Jeremy returned about that time and interrupted her dinner with a summons to the dining room where he was having his.

"Have a seat, luv. Have you eaten yet?"

"I was eating."

"Fetch your plate then and join me."

She'd sat down next to him. She wasn't getting back up. "You know that ain't proper."

He sighed. "I won't keep you then. Just wanted to let you know I'll be gone for the weekend."

She sighed now. "You know you don't have to keep me apprised of your schedule."

"Why are you throwing up a wall between us again? I thought we agreed we were friends. And friends do tell each other what they're up to."

She looked down to avoid his gaze. Was she doing that? Trying to put more space between them in preparation of her leaving? Probably. It wasn't going to be easy to walk away from Jeremy Malory. But the sooner she did so, the less it would hurt.

To put off that unpleasant thought, she said, "So what are you up to, mate?"

"Aside from the Crandle house party, I'm up for anything *you* have in mind."

"Crandle? Ain't that where Percy got fleeced?"

Jeremy didn't answer. He stood up, came around behind her chair, and drew her to her feet as well. And before she knew what he was going to do, he was kissing her so deeply her toes curled. She didn't know how long he continued to do so. Every single thought went right out of her mind as it usually did when she tasted him.

She wrapped her arms around his neck and kissed him back. And then he was setting her back from him, and she didn't have to guess that he was angry.

She hadn't sensed it in the kiss, but it was definitely there in his expression as well as his tone when he warned, "That's going to happen every time you play at indifference with me. Don't do it again. I bloody well don't like it."

She hadn't been pretending indifference about his plans for the weekend, she'd been desperately trying to ignore what he made her feel every time she got near him. Which was pretty pointless. She should have realized that by now.

Annoyed with herself *and* with him now, for the way he chose to get his point across, she stabbed a finger in his chest. "I wasn't pretending anything. I was trying to keep from pouncing on you and dragging you off to your room. I thought you'd want to finish your dinner first."

He blinked at her, then burst out laughing. "God, no, you can pounce on me anytime you like, dear girl."

She snorted. "Sit down, mate. The impulse has passed. And you can tell me why you're going to a party where Lord Heddings is likely to be."

He tsked, but took his seat again. "Because he *is* likely to be there, of course."

She frowned. "You're going to try to catch him stealing, aren't you?"

"Certainly. Aside from what he did to Percy, the man stole from my family. If I don't see to his apprehension, then m'father is going to step in and kill him. In the end, I'm sure Heddings would prefer my approach."

She rolled her eyes at him, *hoping* he was just exaggerating about his father. "Did it occur to you that he might not work alone? That he might employ others to do the stealing for him?"

"You're thinking like a thief, m'dear. Think like a lord instead—"

"Exactly. Would a lord really risk doing the dirty work himself when he could hire others to do it and just sit back and rake in the spoils? I mean, the man employs servants who walk around with pistols in the middle of the night. That should tell you something."

"That was deuced odd, wasn't it?"

"More like a normal butler used to blokes of the nasty sort showing up at all hours of the night—ourselves excluded, of course," she thought it prudent to add.

"Naturally. But I hope not. I'd prefer to catch him red-handed. Much more satisfying."

She sighed. "You'll be careful?"

"Aha!" he pounced immediately. "Finally going to admit you worry about me, eh?"

"Not a chance, mate," she grumbled. "It's my wages I worry about." Then she teased,

"Maybe you should pay me before you leave for your weekend party."

"No, but I'll make *you* pay for that remark."

He did, too, most pleasantly.

Chapter 43

〜

Danny had left the lamp in her room burning low for the pets. She'd taken them to bed with her, but didn't expect them to sleep the night through with her, so she wanted them to have a little light if they wanted to play a bit before settling down again.

It was the kitten's tail, swishing against her cheek, that woke her from the dream, though not soon enough. She relived it once again, the club falling toward her head, then the burst of pain. It hurt. She'd never had pain in her dream before, just the memory of it . . . oh, God, she wasn't dreaming.

He swung the club again. She saw him clearly, a middle-aged man, gray, straggly hair, and then she saw another image of him, younger, black-haired, with the same dark eyes filled with deadly intent. He was the man who'd hurt her before, the one who'd disrupted her life and stolen her memories. She hadn't recognized him at the inn, but it was so clear to her now that he was the man from her past. And he was still trying to kill her . . .

She couldn't move far with the covers hampering her, but she got out of the way of that second swing of the club, heard it slam against the pillow next to her bed. She fought with the covers to get her feet loose, didn't think she could avoid the next swing unless she rolled out of the bed. But she was afraid she'd be even more tangled then, helpless, so her only real chance would be to fight him and wrest the club away from him.

She turned back to try to intercept the next swing, but Jeremy was suddenly there and tackling the man to the floor. He punched him, again and again. She'd never seen Jeremy like that. He seemed determined to kill the man with his bare fists.

"I don't think he feels that anymore," she said.

Jeremy glanced back at her. He'd been holding the man off the floor by his collar, so each blow would land squarely on his face. He let him fall now and came to her side. He lifted her face, examining it intensely.

His voice held a frantic note as he demanded, "Where'd he hit you?"

"My head, but I think I deflected the worst of the blow with my arm when I raised it to move the kitten away from my cheek."

He inspected her head now, found the small lump forming. She winced as he touched it, but said nothing. It was starting to throb, though not extremely. Her forearm actually hurt more.

"The skin didn't break," he told her. "You'll probably have a bit of a headache though for a day or two. We should have some ice in the house to put on that. I'll have Artie fetch some after he gets rid of the trash."

He went to the door to shout for their butler, but came right back to the bed and finally sat down next to her so he could gather her in his arms.

"I don't believe what just happened," he said. "You're all right, though, right? Tell me you're all right."

"I'm fine. But how did you know he was here?"

"I didn't. Some noise woke me, probably him robbing the rooms upstairs. But once I was awake, I thought of you all warm and cozy in your bed and decided my bed was rather lonely. Amy must have been right. He followed us from the inn."

"He followed *me*," Danny corrected. "If he was upstairs, it was to find me. He's the same man who tried to kill me when I was a child, the same one who killed my parents."

He stared at her incredulously. "You didn't know that when you saw him at the inn?"

"No, I didn't recognize him at all then, not until I saw him with that club raised over his head tonight. I should have known, though, that he wasn't there to rob us that night. I'd had the feeling I'd been followed recently, since I came uptown, but I managed to lose him."

"Until he found you again at the inn and followed us back?"

"It looks that way."

"You think he was just tidying up loose ends, because he knew you could recognize him?"

"But I couldn't. I didn't remember him at all until tonight."

"But he wouldn't have known that, would he?"

"No. Look out!" she screamed as the man loomed up behind Jeremy's back.

Jeremy swung around, but her warning must have changed the man's mind about attacking them, because he bolted out the door instead—and ran into Artie by the sounds of the butler's complaint. Jeremy hurried to the door, told Artie to apprehend the fellow, then came back to Danny.

He wasn't leaving her alone with a madman in the house. "Artie will catch him. He can be quite ruthless when warranted."

Danny felt that Jeremy's confidence was a bit misplaced until the butler came back and announced, "He's dead."

"Blister it, Artie," Jeremy complained, "I wanted to question him, not bury him."

"I didn't kill 'im," Artie said with a shrug. " 'E dove back out that window 'e broke to get in the 'ouse and landed on a sharp piece of glass.

Danny started to cry. She was silent about it and turned her head aside so the men wouldn't notice, and fortunately,

Jeremy left with Artie to see to the body and to summon the authorities, so she had time to get her emotions under control. But she couldn't manage it, the tears kept pouring, because she'd realized too late that that fellow could have told her who she really was. But now he couldn't.

Chapter 44

"You're coming with me and that's final," Jeremy said.

"You get really silly when you're worried, mate," Danny replied. "That chap was a loner. No one else is going to break in here and try to kill me."

"You don't know that for certain, or have you remembered more?"

They were in his bedroom. Jeremy was packing for the weekend trip to the Crandle house party. He'd almost talked himself out of going that morning, he was still so worried about her. But he'd mentioned that Crandle wasn't known to throw a great many parties, just a few per season, so it might be a long time before he had such a prime opportunity again to observe Heddings and hopefully catch him at some wrongdoing. Danny had to convince Jeremy once again that she was fine, that he shouldn't change his plans on her account.

She thought she'd succeeded. He'd agreed. But apparently not completely, since he'd just summoned her to his room to inform her that she would be accompanying him.

"I've remembered nothing else," she told him, answering his question.

But she was still quite amazed that she'd remembered her name, not all of it, just the first name. It had come to her that morning just after they awoke in each other's arms, and she'd blurted it out, "My name is Danette," and then she'd laughed. "A far cry from Danielle, eh? And don't be calling me that. It sounds too foreign for my liking."

"I think it's rather pretty," he'd said.

"Too bad. It's mine and I choose to forget it again."

But she wasn't going to forget it. And she had hope now that more memories would come back to her. Because she'd taken another blow to her head? Or because she'd come face-to-face with her worst night-mare? Whatever the reason, she had confidence now that she *would* remember more.

"You're still coming with me," he insisted. "Or do you prefer cleaning house to going to parties?"

She snorted at his logic. "I'd prefer being realistic, if you don't mind. I don't belong at such parties and you know it. Look at the fuss you made about my attending that ball."

"But you did splendidly there."

"So? What's that got to do with another party? I don't have the clothes for it either. I have that one ball gown—"

"Which will do just fine."

"For both days? You gentry wouldn't be caught dead wearing the same clothes two days in a row, mate."

"It will have been in the only trunk that was salvaged when they all got dumped in the river. Quite understandable."

She stared at him, then laughed. "Who would believe that whopper?"

"Anyone I mention it to. You don't think the gentry suffer simple difficulties like having baggage come loose from its strapping and roll down a hill into the river? I assure you, the same mishaps that bedevil the general populace can bedevil the upper crust, too."

He got his way, the scoundrel. Despite all her objections, he was able to talk circles around her, cajole, tease, and otherwise browbeat her in his nabob way.

Her last warning was, "You know, mate, if you don't stop making me pretend to be a lady, I might like it and work on getting m'self a lordly husband, rather than just a respectable one."

But that didn't work either, merely had him replying in a casual tone, "I haven't shot anyone lately. I suppose I'm overdue."

That shut her up quickly. He was joking, of course, but she still hadn't liked the sound of that, which reminded her too much of his father. He *was* James Malory's son, after all, and although he was mostly just a lovable scoundrel as his cousin had termed him, there could be another side to Jeremy that he didn't allow her to see.

~~~

"I never thought I'd see the day, Jeremy," Amy said, "that you'd fall in love."

Amy and Warren had come with Jeremy

and Danny to Lord Crandle's party. That had been decided when Jeremy stopped by to borrow their coach and he'd been reminded that "Danielle" should have a chaperone.

"Bite your tongue, Cousin," Jeremy replied. "You ain't seen it yet."

Amy raised a brow at him. "Don't tell me you're going to be the last one to know?"

She started laughing then, causing him to grit his teeth. They were dancing, the first opportunity they'd had to talk alone since she'd returned to England. A trio of musicians had started playing after dinner, and with Warren keeping Danny occupied teaching her to play cards, Jeremy had let Amy drag him onto the dance floor.

Lord Heddings hadn't made an appearance yet, and he might not show at all. Amy had agreed to pose as the "temptation," wearing some of her best jewelry for the duration of the visit. Fat lot of good that was going to do if the thief didn't show up.

"You see, you can't even keep your eyes off her for two minutes," Amy said triumphantly, as if she'd just made her point.

Jeremy snorted. "She's a raving beauty. Of course I'm going to stare at her every chance I get. I'd have to be blind not to want to."

"It's all right to love her, you know. She comes from good family."

"If I were going to love her, I wouldn't give a bloody damn where she came from, and how the devil do you know about her family? No, never mind. Forget I asked."

"Don't worry, it's not one of my 'feelings.' You just have to watch her, listen to her, to know she's got good breeding in her background."

He gave a hoot of laughter and said, "You wouldn't be saying that, puss, if you could have heard her talking just a few weeks ago. Right out of the gutter she sounded, and was, for that matter."

"Exactly," Amy said triumphantly. "You don't really think someone like that could learn to speak so well in just a few weeks, do you? Unless it was how she used to speak. She said as much, that her friend Lucy taught her to talk like a guttersnipe. Did you never wonder where she came from before she got adopted by that riffraff?"

"Course I have, but that's all I can do, when she can't even remember her full name. And she's sure her parents were killed by that bastard who tried to kill her. They'd have searched high and low for her otherwise. So even if her memories do return, she has no one to go back to."

"Don't sound so hopeful," Amy huffed. "She could have distant relatives other than those *you've* created for her. And even if she doesn't, that does *not* mean you're going to get to keep her as your maid forever. The girl has goals, Jeremy, if you didn't know, and you've only supplied one of them in giving her a job."

"I know about her damned goals," he grumbled. "Bloody hell, did she tell you her whole life story on the way back to London that day?"

Amy grinned at him. "You know I have a way of getting people to open up. There's no prevaricating when you're around me."

"More's the pity."

"I don't know why you're protesting what is so patently obvious, scamp. And you *could* supply her other two goals, though come to think of it, you don't really fall under the heading of *respectable,* do you?" Amy feigned a sigh. "Forget I mentioned it."

Jeremy scowled. He hated when Amy got

in a teasing mood. Like her two more notorious uncles, she went for blood.

Fortunately, a change of subject walked
in the door. "Ah, there he is finally."

Amy followed his gaze. "Lord Heddings?"

"Yes, and why don't you go introduce
yourself, puss, and let him get a good look
at all those baubles you're wearing. You
and Warren *were* given a room of your
own, right? I doubt he'll take the chance of
sneaking into a room if it's being shared."

"Yes, we have our own room. Crandle
has a standing arrangement with his two
closest neighbors to help him with any extra
guests when he runs out of rooms. It's fortunate we arrived early, or we probably
would be staying elsewhere. I take it you'll
be sharing a room yourself?"

"Of course. With a half dozen other bachelors at last count. And Danny was put in
with the single young misses. Hadn't considered that when I dragged her along," he
added with a frown.

"Don't worry, she'll do fine."

He was glancing about the room now,
having noticed that Danny was no longer
where he'd left her at the card tables with

Warren, was nowhere in sight. Heddings was heading to the card tables, though.

"Intercept him before he settles in at one of the tables. He's known to spend all night gambling. I'll go see where Danny's gone off to."

She'd gone to bed, according to Warren. This early? She'd mentioned a headache, which made Jeremy feel like the worst cad, for having forgotten the knock on the head she'd taken. She'd said she was fine, but the wench was probably as good at lying as she was at stealing.

He bounded upstairs to check on her. This early in the evening, the room she was sharing was likely to have only her in it. He knocked. She opened the door, was still dressed, had probably just gotten up there herself.

"Why didn't you tell me your head was still hurting?" he admonished rather sharply.

"Because it wasn't. It was trying to concentrate on the cards that brought the headache on."

He gave her a suspicious frown. "You wouldn't lie to me, would you?"

"Of course I would. Thieves are good at that, you know."

His scowl got worse. She chuckled. "I was joking, mate. Cor, you're touchy lately."

He sighed and leaned against the doorframe. "Crandle has a very nice garden, I was told. I was hoping to show it to you later."

She raised her brow at him. "That'd be better suited to the daytime, wouldn't it? So I could actually see what you're showing me?"

"Well, no, you don't have to see anything for this."

He'd no sooner said it than his arm snaked out and pulled her body flush with his, and his mouth covered hers. He wanted to devour her, but he restrained himself, just barely. The kiss was sensual, God, he loved the taste of her. She kissed with her whole body, not just her mouth, pressing into him.

He broke off abruptly before he lost all sense and carried her to bed, a bed that wouldn't be private for long. He stepped back. He was actually trembling!

"I'm sorry," he said. "I shouldn't have done that."

"No, you shouldn't have," she replied breathlessly.

He groaned inwardly, almost grabbed her

back. He stuffed his hands in his pockets rather quickly instead and got the subject off kisses and how much he wanted to make love to her right now.

"Heddings showed up finally," he said.

"Well, that worked out rather well, didn't it?"

"How so?"

"If he doesn't know I'm here, he won't know to look for me in the morning. He'll be doing a head count before he tries sneaking into any of these rooms. *If* he's going to try it."

"You still don't think he will?"

"I think he's too smart to do the stealing himself," she reasoned.

"I disagree. I don't think he can resist the temptation."

"But look what he risks if he's caught."

"Exactly. Some men would find the danger of that exciting. But I'll allow we could both be right. He might not take the risk often. However, with Amy's jewels as the bait, he's more likely to try it. She travels too much these days, being married to a ship's captain. So if he wants her baubles, he'll need to grab them while he has the chance."

"But how would he know she's not often in England?"

"Because she's going to tell him, dear girl. Amy is quite as good as Reggie at setting up a plot. She's going to mention that although she and Warren only just returned home, they're going to be leaving again in a few days. She's even going to hint that they might not return this time, that Warren's been talking about a new trade route that would bypass England. And she's going to leave the baubles in her room tomorrow. So it will be now or never."

Danny shrugged, conceding, "Well, if he's that stupid, as I said, it's a good thing then that I came upstairs before he noticed me. I'll just remain up here in the morning and keep an ear open for him to make his move. If he's going to do it, it will be after he's assured himself that all the guests are accounted for downstairs."

Jeremy shook his head at her. "You aren't going to be doing the catching here, m'dear, I am. If or when he comes upstairs in the morning, I'll give him a few minutes and then follow—"

"And miss him in Amy's room if he's quick? Finding him in the hall here or in his own room won't prove a bleeding thing, now will it? Your timing would have to be too perfect."

"Her jewels being missing will be proof enough."

"Not if he hides them somewhere up here. He could even toss them out the window there at the end of the hall to one of his accomplices waiting below for just that. She's going to miss them, after all, which means a search will ensue. So he won't keep them on his person."

"Bloody hell, you're coming up with too many variables. *Must* you think like a thief?"

She grinned at him. "You can do the catching as you planned to. I'll just be up here to point you in the right direction."

"And miss the rest of the party yourself?"

"I didn't want to be here in the first place, mate. But, no. If he doesn't make his move before noon, I'll be coming down for some lunch. I'm not going to starve myself to catch your thief."

Chapter 45

Danny would have regretted her decision to wait upstairs the next morning, since she got hungry not long after waking. But she'd gone to sleep early, so was awake before any of the other young ladies she was sharing the room with, and likely the other guests as well. So she took the chance to slip downstairs for a bite to eat and got back in her room without running into anyone other than the servants.

She used the same excuse of a headache to remain behind in the room when the other girls started waking each other to go down for breakfast. They hadn't brought their maids with them, were apparently

used to helping each other dress at weekend gatherings like this one. And they were
all envious of Danny, having heard the rumors that Jeremy Malory was courting her,
and thinking them confirmed since she'd arrived with him and his relatives.

She'd had to listen to each of them gush-
ing about how handsome he was, how
he was the most eligible bachelor in all of
England. She'd managed to refrain from
laughing. Bachelor, yes. Eligible, not a
chance.

Alone again, she got comfortable near
the door so she could listen to the comings
and goings in the hall as the rest of the
guests headed downstairs for the day. She
wasn't about to lie on the floor to watch the
feet passing as she'd done in Heddings's
house, since one of the young ladies might
return for something and end up banging
the door against her head. But she felt safe
in cracking the door open just a smidgen
and leaving it like that. With Amy's room just
across the way, the crack gave her a clear
view of the only room that mattered.

And she didn't have long to wait. A well-
dressed gentleman in his middle years
came into her line of vision. Tall, distin-

guished looking, with black hair turning silver at his temples. He stopped at Amy's
door, glanced both ways down the hall, then
tried the doorknob. Finding it unlocked, he
quickly slipped inside.

Danny was amazed. She hadn't really
thought he'd be that stupid, but Jeremy had
been right. Unless that hadn't been Lord
Heddings. But who else could it have been?
She'd met most of the other guests last
evening at dinner, and that man hadn't been
one of them. He was also dressed too fine
to be a servant. And his caution before entering the room spoke clearly that he was
up to no good.

She listened closely to hear Jeremy coming up the stairs, but no other sound came
from the hall. She hoped he didn't give
Heddings too much time. She wasn't sure
what she should do if the lord left Amy's
room before Jeremy arrived. And what if he
hadn't even seen the man come upstairs?
Heddings was going to get away with it if
Jeremy didn't hurry. She could accuse him.
After all, she'd witnessed him enter Amy's
room. But fat lot of good that would do if he
disposed of the jewels first.

The door opened again across the way

so silently, she wouldn't have heard it. He didn't leave the room immediately either; he was looking down the hall first, then he poked his head around to look down the other way. Finding no one about, he fairly flew out of that room and closed the door again, leaving it as he'd found it, then hurried farther down the hall, out of Danny's view.

Danny had mere seconds to decide what to do. Maybe she could just detain him long enough for Jeremy to arrive.

She stepped out into the hall and said, "Wait up, Lord Heddings."

He turned around to face her. She was looking to see if anything was in the hall that he could have put the jewels in temporarily. There wasn't, not even a vase. And the window at the end of the hall was still a long ways off, so he had to have the jewels still on him.

But then she noticed that he was staring at her quite incredulously. So he was going to play the innocent, was he? She snorted to herself. He should have waited until she actually accused him.

She did that now, warned him, "Give it up, m'lord. I know what you did."

"So he failed again to get rid of you?" Heddings replied, his tone filled with disgust. "Still as incompetent as he was fifteen years ago? But whatever he told you, you can't prove it."

Danny felt poleaxed. She couldn't breathe. He wasn't talking about the theft he'd just committed. He was talking about the man who'd tried to kill her, twice, and his own involvement in it.

And then she really couldn't breathe, because his hands were suddenly around her neck, squeezing, and she heard him snarl, "I'll finish this myself."

She fought with his fingers, tried to pry them loose, but too quickly her own were tingling, losing strength. A haze was clouding her eyes. The last thing she saw was the hate in his . . .

Jeremy came around the corner at the top of the stairs. He sighed to himself when he saw Danny standing there in the corridor in front of Heddings, her back to him. He'd warned her to stay out of this. It would be nice, it really would, if she'd pay attention to him occasionally.

He'd almost reached them when Danny

slumped to the floor at Heddings's feet. "What the hell?"

"She fainted," Lord Heddings told him. "Mentioned she hadn't eaten yet today and not much yesterday. I'll fetch some smelling salts."

Jeremy knelt down to pick Danny up and get her to a bed, but he couldn't help seeing the red surrounding her neck with the low cut of her gown. So much emotion welled up in his chest he couldn't breath for a moment, then it released in a keening cry. He gathered her limp body to his chest. He rocked with her. Pain was ripping him to pieces. He hadn't felt such loss since his mother died.

"Jeremy?" Warren said hesitantly, putting a hand on his shoulder.

Jeremy looked up. He couldn't see Warren clearly through the moisture in his eyes. "He killed her," he said simply, his voice choked.

Warren bent down, tried to take Danny from him, but Jeremy wasn't letting go of her, continued to rock with her in his arms. Again Warren said hesitantly, "Jeremy, I don't think she's dead. She's still warm."

Jeremy went still. He looked down at her

chest, but it wasn't moving. He put his ear to her mouth, heard the barest rasp of breath.

"Oh, God!" he cried, and squeezed her even tighter in his relief.

Warren wasn't hesitant at all this time, said sharply, "For God's sake, Jeremy, you're giving her no room to breathe. Let her go."

That snapped Jeremy out of it. And a new emotion took over, one so primitive it was all-consuming. "Take care of her for me," he said, handing Danny to Warren. "I'll take care of him."

"You've caught him, and for more than stealing. Let the authorities handle—"

Warren didn't bother to finish since Jeremy wasn't there any longer to listen. He ran down the hall to the only room with an open door. Heddings was just climbing out the window. Jeremy charged toward him, yanked the man back inside so forcefully, he was tossed across the room. Instead of getting right up, though, Heddings scrambled to get the pistol out of his pocket that he'd fetched from one of his bags, the reason he hadn't escaped immediately.

Jeremy didn't notice the gun, he was too busy getting to Heddings again. He heard the shot fly past him. Couldn't miss that. But he ignored it, too, that primitive rage still in complete control of him.

He reached him, kicked the pistol out of his hand, and started pounding him. He wanted to hurt him, not knock him out, not kill him, though he didn't care at that moment if that was the result. The man had to pay for hurting Danny, that was the only thing in Jeremy's mind.

He had to be pulled off him. Warren was probably the only man there who could have managed it, as enraged as Jeremy still was. Others were present though, having been drawn by the pistol shot. And he hadn't killed Heddings. He'd broken a good many of his bones though and damaged his face badly enough that it would never look the same.

Jeremy left Warren there to explain to the other guests what had happened and went to find Danny. Warren had placed her in his own room. Amy was there, sitting next to her on the bed. And Danny was sitting up, rubbing her neck. Sure now that she was going to be all right, he directed some of the rage still riding him at her.

"You accused him, didn't you?" he said angrily.

"Well, yes, but he thought I was accusing him of something else."

"What do you mean?"

Before she could answer him, Amy stood up and shoved Jeremy back. "Now isn't the time to be questioning her. Open your ears, Jeremy. Can't you hear how faint and scratchy her voice is?"

He stared at Danny. The redness on her throat was fading, but bruises would probably appear there in a few hours. He felt immediately contrite, knelt down next to her, took her hand in his to bring it to his lips.

"I'm sorry. Amy's right. You need to rest your throat. Don't talk for now."

"I'll talk if I want to, mate."

Jeremy threw up his hands over that stubborn remark. But Amy said reasonably, "We should leave her alone so she can rest."

Jeremy didn't want to leave her alone for a second, wanted to get her back home where he could care for her himself. But he nodded at his cousin. And he still had to talk to the magistrate himself, to make sure Heddings got charged with more than just theft.

But Danny had too many questions of her own to watch them leave without getting answers. "Wait a minute. What happened with Heddings?"

Jeremy summed it up nicely, or tried to, so she wouldn't have to ask any other questions. "He's unconscious at the moment. And he won't be trying to escape out any more windows. I believe he broke at least one of his hands when he tried to block one of my punches."

"You knocked him out?"

"Something like that. The magistrate has already been sent for. He'll probably want to question you as well, but I'll make sure he keeps it brief."

"He was going to kill me," Danny whispered. "And not because I caught him stealing. He knows who I am. He knows that other man who attacked me, too. I think he's the one who sent him."

"So you recognized him?"

"No, not at all. There's nothing about him even vaguely familiar to me. But he knew me as soon as he saw me. He can tell me who I am."

"*If* he will. I doubt he'll be very accommodating under the circumstances, luv."

Chapter 46

At Danny's behest, Jeremy confronted Heddings before he was escorted away. After the local magistrate had congratulated Jeremy, the fellow confessed that they'd been onto Lord Heddings for quite some time now, but had never been able to prove anything against him. He did work with others, as Danny had guessed. Apparently, he'd spot the jewelry at the parties he went to, get the owners' addresses, then send his men to steal the items. He didn't usually try to take the jewels himself.

He'd come under suspicion when he got greedy for more than just money. Most of the jewels he merely sold off, but those from prominent people, he'd wait a few months, then approach the owner of the bauble, say he'd heard of their loss and happened to have come across a piece that looked like it in a pawn shop, so he bought it on the chance that it might be the piece. These he gave back without charge, earning favors instead, favors that wouldn't do him a bit of good now.

Amy's jewelry was removed from Heddings's pockets before he regained consciousness, and with enough witnesses that the lord wouldn't be talking his way out of the crime. He was well and truly caught, and furious about it when he did wake. The rage probably kept him from feeling the worst of his injuries. It also kept his mouth shut on the subject of Danny.

"You tried to kill her. Why?"

"So she's not dead? Too bad."

Jeremy had to be pulled back again, was going to slam his fist in the man's face once more. Heddings laughed at him, confident that the three constables waiting to drag him away would keep Jeremy off him.

"Why do you hate her?" Jeremy demanded.

"I don't hate her. I don't even know her."

"So you just try to kill pretty young girls for the hell of it?"

Heddings snorted. "It's who she is, Malory, that matters."

"Who is she then?"

Heddings seemed surprised. "She didn't tell you?"

"She doesn't know."

Heddings started laughing again. "Now that's rich. Almost makes this worth it, to know that."

"Who is she?"

"If I knew, do you really think I'd tell you?" Heddings sneered. "Not a chance. That information would go with me to the grave *if* I knew, recompense, as it were."

"You're lying."

"No, I'm done talking to you." And to the constables, Heddings said, "Get me out of here, or get him out of here. I really don't care which."

Jeremy considered trying to talk his way into a few minutes alone with Heddings, but he didn't think it would work at that point. And besides, he was sure now that no matter what he said or did to Heddings, the man wouldn't cooperate.

He was forced to return to Danny with the

bad news. She'd been ordered to stay in bed the rest of the day. One of the guests was a doctor. He'd packed her neck with cold cloths and given her a balm to soothe her throat. A maid was there to change the cloths as they warmed. Jeremy sent her out of the room, closing the door after her.

Danny sat up, asked hopefully, "What did he say?"

Jeremy sat on the bed next to her, cupped her cheek with his hand. "Does it really matter who you are, luv? You've gone through life this long without knowing."

She slumped back on her pillow. "You're right, it's not important."

"I didn't say that—"

"No, really, you're right. It's not like I have family or anybody waiting on me to come home. If I did, they would have looked for me, wouldn't they? Or Miss Jane would have mentioned taking me home, but she never said anything about going back, which would indicate there was nothing to go back to. So he wouldn't tell you who I am?"

"No."

"But he knows! I know he knows. I saw it in his eyes, his expression. It fairly bowled him over to see me standing there in the hall."

"I don't doubt he does know, but he's decided it's a fitting revenge to keep it to himself. After all, we were personally responsible for his downfall. He's going to prison because of us."

"What if you promised to get the charges dismissed for him?"

He smiled gently. "It's too late for that. There's a house full of witnesses here who know he tried to kill you, several of them who've been robbed in the past and are sure now that he was responsible, after Amy's jewelry was found on him. Besides, he was already under suspicion, has been for many years now. There'd just been no proof to charge him with. We supplied the proof."

Jeremy would be trying again though, he just didn't want to get Danny's hopes up, in case he failed. But he'd give Heddings a few weeks to realize just how much trouble he was in, then dangle the offer of reduced charges in exchange for the information he wanted.

She sighed. "Well, at least you accomplished what you came here for."

"And nearly got you killed."

She flinched at the admonishing tone. "I was only going to detain him. You were taking too long to get up here," she admonished right back. "He could have dumped the jewels, and then where would you be?"

"I'd be fine. And you'd be without bruises around your neck."

She frowned at him. "How was I to know he'd recognize me and attack me for something that had nothing to do with the jewels he'd just stolen? What were the bleeding odds of that, eh?"

He grinned. "Nothing I would have bet on. Now get some rest. We'll go home in the morning."

"I'd rather go home now. I'm fine. Don't I sound fine? Just a few little bruises to show for my folly. I'd rather get back to work than lie here and dwell on what I could have learned today."

Put that way, he had to agree.

Chapter 47

~~

Danny waited four more days, long enough for the last of the tenderness to leave her neck. She didn't want any discomforts slowing her down. She was also waiting for Jeremy to be gone from the house for more than just a few hours, and Percy helped her out there. He came by that week to invite Jeremy to some horse races that were taking place a good hour's drive away from London. She didn't *really* think he would try to stop her from leaving, but she wasn't taking any chances, which was why she didn't want him to know about it until she was long gone.

As soon as Jeremy left the house that

morning for the races, Danny went to her room to gather up her few belongings. It didn't take her long. She would have left the ball gown, since it was too bulky to lug about the city for very long, but Mrs. Robertson's seamstress wasn't that far away and she figured she could get a few extra coppers for it from her, maybe even a few pounds. Every little bit was going to be needed until she got a new job.

She didn't think it would take long this time, though, finding a job. She had experience now, and her speech had improved so much, she didn't even slip anymore when she was nervous. She could probably get another maid's job in this part of town, but that would be too close to Jeremy. The middle-class area of the city would do her just fine and be the easier place to find a husband, too, maybe even a gentleman, at least a man who wasn't so lordly it'd be unthinkable for him to marry a servant.

She wished she could write Jeremy a note. She didn't want to go without leaving him an explanation. That was going to be a new goal for her. As soon as she could afford it, she was going to find herself a tutor to at least teach her to read and write. As an alternative, she dragged Claire to her room for a few minutes to leave a message with her.

"It's time for me to move on," she told her friend. "I'll be spending a few nights at my old home, if they'll let me, while I look for a new job. Or I'll rent a flat."

"Why must you go?" Claire complained. "We'd only just got to be friends."

"That won't end with my going. I'll keep in touch. I might even come visit from time to time." Danny wouldn't, couldn't afford to risk seeing Jeremy again after she was gone. "Or better yet, you can come visit me. I'll let you know where I get settled."

Claire sighed, but then asked suspiciously, "You're not pregnant, are you?"

Danny shook her head. "No, I was lucky in that regard. But that would become an issue if I stayed longer. And although I don't think he'd try to take the baby from me, I'd have an even harder time leaving with one."

"So why leave at all?"

"Because I've fallen in love with the man, Claire, and he's tempting me to put my goals aside for him."

"He doesn't know you're leaving, does he?"

"Of course not. He'd have no trouble talking me out of it. He's good at that, talking circles around me. So don't be telling him where I'm going. But I do want to leave him a message, if you wouldn't mind."

"Certainly."

"Tell him for me that I said thank you for improving my lot, that I'm much more confident now that my goals will be realized."

Claire raised a brow. "You really think he's going to want to hear that? Or doesn't he know what your goals are?"

"You're right, scratch that second part. Tell him instead that I'll miss him, but I have to get on with my life. And tell him—" She had to pause, was feeling her throat close up. "Tell him I don't regret being his friend."

"Eh?"

"He'll understand. Now I have to go. Watch over my pets for me?"

"You're not taking them?"

"Only Twitch. The other two, he shouldn't have given to me in the first place." Danny hugged Claire. "I'll miss you. I'll miss all of you."

"Bloody hell, I think I'm going to cry. Go on then, if you're going. And good luck."

Danny ran upstairs one last time before

she left. Jeremy had warned her never to touch it again, but too bad, she was taking her old hat with her. Not to wear. It would look silly with her skirts. But it was hers, and she wasn't leaving anything behind.

She paused in his room to give it one last look. She touched his bed, his pillow. The tears started.

She didn't want to leave. She'd said it to Claire, but that was the first time she'd put it into words. She loved Jeremy Malory. It wasn't supposed to happen. She thought she'd be able to leave before it did. But it was too late. She wanted to spend the rest of her life with Jeremy. He could fulfill all her dreams—if he would. And, dear God, what if he would? How could she leave without finding out?

It would mean confronting him and spilling her guts, and risking what she'd feared, that he'd try to talk her out of going. He couldn't. Her resolve was firm now. But it would rip her up if he tried, make it that much harder . . .

Danny waited, went through an agony of indecision. But in the end, that tiny hope that Jeremy loved her, too, enough to defy convention and marry her, kept her there until he got home.

She let Claire know that she wouldn't have to give him any messages for her after all, and why. "You've got more courage than I would have under the same circumstances," Claire said. "Good luck, Danny."

She didn't need luck, she needed her one small hope to be realized.

Jeremy returned in time for lunch. Percy was with him. They were laughing as they entered the house. Danny savored the image from where she stood in the doorway to the parlor. She wasn't holding her sack; it was on the floor just inside the doorway where she could grab it quickly.

It must have been her expression, though, that made Jeremy's expression turn serious and tell Percy, "Run along to the kitchen and let them know you're hungry, old man. I'll be along shortly." He approached Danny then, put his hand on her cheek. "What's wrong, luv?"

She stepped away from him, moving back into the parlor. She wasn't going to be able to say what she had to if he was touching her. He followed her into the room. He was going to reach for her again. She put up a hand to stop him.

"I'm leaving, Jeremy."

"I just got home. Where are you off to?"

She realized he'd been drinking, for him to mistake her meaning like that. But he wasn't foxed. Jeremy Malory was incapable of getting drunk.

"I'm not going out on an errand. I'm leaving for good."

"The devil you are. It's too soon."

"Actually, I shouldn't have stayed this long. But don't misunderstand. I don't regret my time here with you, not a'tall. I—I'll miss you." She had to pause, was feeling her throat close up. "But I have to get on with my life."

"Don't do this, Danny."

"Then give me a reason to stay! Living my life sharing only half of yours isn't what I want for myself. I want a real family, and children who aren't bastards. I won't get either here unless you marry me."

There, she'd said it, put her heart on the table.

And he said nothing.

Even his expression was inscrutable for once. For a man with such telling eyes?

That *was* his answer. He wasn't going to remind her that marriage wasn't for him. He was sparing her that. God, what a fool she'd been, to grasp and cling to such a small hope!

She wasn't sure how she got out of there without bursting into tears in front of him. But no sooner was she out of the house than the tears began in earnest. Thinking about leaving just wasn't the same as walking out the door and realizing she'd never see Jeremy Malory again.

Chapter 48

It took Danny a few extra hours to find where Dagger had moved the pack to. She knew the right people to ask. Back in the old neighborhoods, it was amazing how many people didn't recognize her at first. A few did and were dumbfounded, but most didn't recognize her at all, had to be reminded, and she'd known these people most of her life!

Had she changed that much? Probably. And it wasn't just the female attire. She was walking boldly into the most crime-ridden area of the city, confident that she could deal with any trouble that came her way.

Dagger was home. So was Lucy, who

squealed in delight when she saw Danny walk in the door. A few of the children were also there and demanded an equal share of her attention. It was a good ten minutes before she thought to look at Dagger to judge his reaction.

He'd said nothing yet. And he was just staring at her, as if he didn't recognize her either. But he *knew* she was a woman now, so he was probably trying to figure out how he'd missed that fact all these years.

Finally he said in a gruff voice, "Ye can't stay 'ere. There's a dangerous fellow looking for ye in these neighborhoods who means ye 'arm."

"Yes, I know." Danny moved to join him at the same old kitchen table where he could usually be found. That table always traveled with him. And she realized now that he treated it like his office, or his throne. He gave all his orders there, dictated his rules. He should have an office, a real one.

She said as much. "You should have an office, Dagger. Why did you never turn one of the bedrooms into one?"

He snorted. "Like we ever 'ave spare bedrooms. And don't be changing the subject."

She noticed his nose was a little off-center and nodded toward it. "Did it hurt a lot?"

"Bleedin' right it did. It were that fellow looking for ye who broke it."

"Yes, Lucy told me."

Dagger spared a moment to glare at Lucy, who shrugged as she joined them at the table, too. "So I knew where she were working. It's a good thing ye didn't, or ye would've spilled yer guts to that thug."

"It doesn't matter," Danny interjected. "He found me anyway. He's dead, though, so you don't have to worry about him anymore."

"*Ye* killed him?"

Danny shook her head, explained, "He did that on his own when he got caught trying to kill me and ran. And the lord who hired him, he's off to jail himself, so he won't be doing any more hiring."

"A lord?" Dagger exclaimed. "Wot the devil 'ave ye been getting yerself into, Danny?"

"Nothing. It was my past catching up to me. That lord, he knows who I really am. He wouldn't say though, the bastard, and I still can't remember. But I think he's the one who killed my family. I was supposed to die with them, but my nurse protected me and escaped with me. Then Lucy found me."

Dagger turned an incredulous look on Lucy. "Ye brought home a *nabob!*"

"I don't think I'm one of them," Danny was quick to deny. "That lord, he's as crooked as they get, a thief himself. If my family was associated with him back then, maybe they weren't so upstanding themselves. He did want us all dead, after all. To wipe out a whole family sounds like revenge no matter how you look at it."

Lucy snorted now. "She were a nabob. Dressed like it, spoke like it. And lords kill each other all the time for all sorts of silly reasons that don't bother us down this side o' town."

Danny rolled her eyes, was about to mention that not only nabobs talked like that, that even upper-crust servants did, but Dagger demanded of Lucy, "Then why'd ye bring 'er 'ome, eh? You bleedin' well knew better."

"Because she 'ad no one, and no memories, and was barely five years old. If ye think I'm that cold 'earted that I'd leave 'er

in an alley to fend for 'erself, then I'm thinking ye need yer nose broke again."

"But ye 'id wot she was, not just that she
were gentry, but that she were a female.
Why'd ye do that?"

"Because ye were going through one o'
yer desperate-for-money periods and were
about to force me to whore for coins. I was
furious wi' ye, Dagger, over that. And I didn't
want to see the same thing 'appen to
Danny. I wanted 'er to 'ave choices, and
men get more choices."

He was blushing by the time Lucy finished. "'Ow many times do I 'ave to apologize for that, eh?"

"Oh, shut up, Dagger. I made a good
whore as it 'appens. But I'm thinking o' re-
tiring. I've met a man who wants to keep me
exclusively to 'imself."

Danny grinned and guessed, "That hack
driver?"

Lucy chuckled. "Aye, 'e's sweet on me, 'e
truly is. Wants to get married! Who would've
ever thought, eh?"

"So I'm going to lose ye, too?" Dagger
said, looking crushed.

Danny thought that might be a good time
to introduce one of her old wishes. "Dagger,

have you ever thought of turning this into a real orphanage? We could get real jobs to support it, hire a teacher for the children, get them real beds. Lucy would probably help, too."

He was staring at her as if she'd lost her mind. "D'ye 'ave any idea wot kind o' money yer talking about, to run an orphanage? Teachers ain't cheap, are bleedin' expensive. And beds!"

"It *could* be done, Dagger. Think on it."

"Bah, where would I be finding a real job, eh? Ye didn't, did ye?"

"I did," she said, her tone turning defensive.

"Then wot are ye doing back 'ere?" he demanded. "Got fired already?"

"No, I left of my own accord. It was a good job, I really liked it. But I was getting too attached to my employer, so I thought it best to leave."

The moisture started gathering in her eyes again. She stood up, turned away from the table. Lucy was suddenly beside her, putting an arm around her shoulder all the while she was glaring at Dagger.

"I'm not here to stay, Dagger," Danny continued when she got control of her emotions again. "I'm just here to leave my things with Lucy for a few days while I look for another job. And I missed you all, and the children. I know you told me not to come back, but—"

"Hush, luv," Lucy cut in. "Ye can visit for as long as ye like. Ain't that right, Dagger?"

It was said in such a threatening tone that Dagger merely mumbled something under his breath, grabbed his hat, and left, probably to find the nearest tavern. But as soon as he was gone, Lucy turned Danny toward her, studied her tear-reddened eyes for a moment, then hugged her close.

"Ye poor lass, yer not pregnant, are ye?"

"No, at least, I don't think so."

"Then ye let yer 'eart get broken?"

"There was no stopping that. I thought if I left sooner rather than later, then it wouldn't be so bad, but I—I didn't think it would hurt this much."

"There's no chance for the two o' ye?"

"No, I told him I was leaving and why. He didn't try to stop me."

"Because he's upper-crust gentry?"

Danny shook her head. "He might have a huge family full of titled lords and ladies, but there's members of it who buck convention, even his own father. He just doesn't want to get married. He's one of those confirmed rakehell bachelors. All he wanted to do was make me his mistress for a while."

"I take it ye were 'aving none o' that?"

"None a'tall."

"Even though some men keep their mistresses for as long as they do their wives?"

Danny snorted. "He's not *that* type. Lucy, I swear he's so handsome he could melt butter with a smile. He's got women scheming and plotting to lure him to the altar by any means, while he'll go to any lengths to avoid it. But it doesn't matter. I want a family of my own. Jeremy Malory can't give me that."

Chapter 49

"I'm not surprised," Anthony was saying as the coach meandered through traffic late the next afternoon. "Saw it in the bone structure."

James snorted at his brother. "You saw nothing of the sort."

"Beg to differ, old man. Just because *you* didn't see it doesn't mean someone with a more discerning eye wouldn't. Maybe you need glasses in your old age?"

"Maybe you need an invite to Knighton's after we finish with this mess."

Anthony chuckled. Knighton's Hall was a sporting establishment that specialized in exercise of the brutal sort. Both brothers had been known to spend many an hour there in the ring perfecting their skills at fisticuffs.

"Be glad to take you on anytime," Anthony replied. "But fess up. You're just annoyed because *you* didn't see this coming."

"And how was it even a remote possibility that Jason would remember an obscure meeting that took place over twenty years ago? He'd only met the chit once back then."

Anthony laughed. "Because it annoyed him. He felt he should know her, so he bloody well wasn't going to stop thinking about it until he recalled why she looked familiar to him. I'm not surprised either that he hied himself back to London just to blister your ears over the matter."

"It wasn't my ears he was after. He went straight to Jeremy's house, but my lad wasn't home. Impatient as our brother is, I then became his second target."

"Don't envy you. Wouldn't want to have to tell *my* son that he has to give up such a prime piece."

James snorted. "You don't have a son. And I ain't telling mine any such thing. The youngun's a man now, he can make his own decisions on what to do about this mess. 'Sides, just because Jason says so? Not a chance."

Anthony grinned. "I've been having devilish good luck lately, to have been on hand for his tirade. I know bloody well you wouldn't have told me about it after the fact."

"Course I would have. Misery loves company, don't you know."

They didn't find Jeremy at home either, but unlike Jason, James knew whom to ask for his whereabouts.

"'E's gone to find the wench," Artie informed James. "She abandoned ship."

"They had a fight?"

"Don't think so. She's gone off to get a new job, according to the kitchen wench."

"In what direction did you send him?" James asked mildly.

"Didn't. The kitchen wench did, though. She told 'im the lass was going 'ome first, before she looked for a new job."

"And in which direction are you pointing me?"

"Ain't," Artie surprised them by saying

stubbornly. "Unless ye bring me along to watch yer back."

"Certainly. Wouldn't have it any other way. Now where's he gone looking for her?"

"Worse part o' town ye can imagine. The slums of the slums."

～～

"Have you thought about an orphanage, Dagger?"

"No," he mumbled. "Did ye even think it through? Wot 'appens if yer idea falls apart, eh? Ye give these younguns 'ope of a better life, then it gets taken away from them when we can't meet all the costs. Then ye've got a lot o' discontented younguns worse off than they were before. At least now they don't expect better, so they're 'appy enough as they are."

So he *had* thought about it. And she hadn't considered that aspect of failing. But he was being too negative. With that attitude, of course they'd fail.

"I found a good job this morning, first one I applied for, too."

"Wot's yer point?"

"The pay is better uptown. If you could get a job in the same area, we could start the orphanage there. It's a nice area of town, no gentry, mostly tradespeople."

"Forget it," he said angrily now. "I've never 'eld a real job."

"You have. You're an organizer, a manager, a foreman, and a host of other things you've been doing right here for years."

"I know wot I know and I don't try to reach for wot ain't possible. Be gone with ye. Yer goals are too fancy for 'ere. The only way ye'll get an orphanage is with government support or private support."

"If I could get the private support, would you be willing to run the orphanage?"

"Sure, ye set it up, I'll run it for ye." But then the sneering tone was back as he added, "So ye've rich friends now, do ye?"

He said that only because he didn't think she had a chance in hell of pulling it off. And maybe she didn't. But it wasn't something she was going to give up on.

"She does, actually."

Danny swung around and gasped at the sight of Jeremy filling the doorway. He was staring at her as if he wanted to grab her and shake her—or hug her. In fact, so much emotion was in his eyes she simply couldn't decipher exactly what he was feeling. But

he finally tore his eyes off her to glance behind him at the pack of children who had
gathered to ogle at a nabob in their part of
town.

He tossed one a coin, said, "Be a good
lad and watch the carriage for me. If it's still
there when I come out, there'll be another
coin for you. If it's not, I'll help you dig your
grave before I put you in it."

That brought Danny out of her daze. She
rushed to the door. "He didn't mean that,"
she told the boy who was standing there
with his mouth dropped open. "Just sit in
the carriage and give a yell if anyone tries to
take it."

Then she moved away from Jeremy again
before she swung around to demand stiffly,
"How did you find me?"

"I had to beat that tavern behemoth to
the ground and threaten to rip out his heart
before he told me where your cohorts in
crime were located."

"You tangled with *him?*"

"Well, no, sounded good though, didn't
it?" Jeremy said with a cheeky grin.

Danny didn't find that amusing, but
Dagger certainly did. He burst out laughing.
Jeremy continued, "As it happens, money

loosened his tongue without any coercion a'tall. Loyal bunch you have around here," he added dryly.

Dagger's laughter had drawn Lucy out of her room. She stared at Jeremy agape before turning an even more incredulous look on Danny. "Ye left *'im?* Cor, Danny, 'ave ye lost yer flippin' mind?"

Danny started blushing, but Jeremy flashed Lucy a smile and said, "You must be Lucy. I owe you a debt of gratitude, 'deed I do."

Lucy blinked. "Ye do? For wot?"

"For protecting the chit all these years until I could find her. Thank you. And you as well," he added to Dagger. "For giving her the boot out of here so she could find me."

Danny rolled her eyes. Dagger coughed. Lucy said, "Dagger, let's go admire the bloke's carriage for a bit, eh, and give these two a moment alone."

"Only a moment," Danny insisted, but they were already heading out the door. She then glared at Jeremy. "Why are you here?"

"I've come for my hat, of course. Warned you not to steal it."

That wasn't what she expected to hear, and even though she recognized he was

teasing, she angrily marched into Lucy's
room, dug the hat out of her sack, and
came back to throw it at him. He picked it
up, approached her, and handed it back.

"There. Now I've given it to you and you
can keep it this time." He no sooner said it
than he yanked her into his arms, whispering, "But I'm keeping you. God, Danny,
don't ever put me through such hell again."

He was squeezing her so tight she
couldn't breathe, but for a moment, she
didn't care, just savored the feeling of being
surrounded by him. But then reason returned and she pushed away. He let go, but
he didn't let her move so far away that he
couldn't grab her back in an instant.

"You shouldn't have come here," she told
him.

"I shouldn't have had to. And I would
have been here sooner, but the people
around here thought it amusing to misdirect
me for half the day."

"I wouldn't have been here anyway. I only
just got back m'self to get my things to take
to my new job."

"You can forget about any new job.
You're coming home with me where you belong."

Danny groaned inwardly. She'd never heard anything so nice. *Where you belong.* Good God, she'd known this would be too hard, if he tried to talk her out of her resolve.

She turned around, had to force the words out. "I'm not changing my mind, Jeremy. I want more for myself than you're willing to give me."

"If you hadn't run off so quick—"

She gasped, swung back around to cut in, "I didn't run off. I told you what would keep me there, but you ignored it. You let me go!"

He tsked at her. "Bowled me over, dear girl, is what you did, proposing like that. You really need to remember that you aren't wearing pants anymore. I was bloody well in shock if you must know."

"The devil you were. You knew it was going to happen. It's not as if I hadn't warned you previously what my goals were *and* that I'd be leaving soon to accomplish them."

"But your 'soon' was years off in my mind."

She snorted. "Then maybe *you* need a dictionary."

"Perhaps, but all I really need is you. Come home—"

"Don't!" she choked out, tears welling up in her eyes. "Just go, Jeremy. You didn't miss an opportunity to talk me into staying, if that's why you're here. It wasn't going to happen and still isn't. So just go."

"I'm here to apologize and to discuss marriage."

"To whom?"

"To me, of course, you silly girl."

She took a swing at him, aiming for his eye. She was furious. But he ducked, exclaiming, "Bloody hell, what'd you do that for?"

"That's nothing to joke about, Jeremy Malory. That was so bleedin' cruel, I can't believe you said that. Get out. And don't come looking for me again."

Instead of complying, he yanked her to him again, hard. And his arms wrapped around her completely so she couldn't do any more swinging, the scoundrel. Nor was he the least bit repentant.

He said in a jaunty tone, "Was that a yes?"

She squirmed to get at his eye again. He chuckled. "Bear with me, luv. I'd never planned to propose marriage to anyone, so of course I was destined to muck it up. But you should know me well enough to know this is one subject I would *never* joke about."

She went very still. He was right, he'd never joke about that. But she still couldn't believe he was serious, had to ask, "Why? I know you don't want to get married, ever. You've made that very clear. So why would you consider it now?"

"Because you're stubborn. Because it's what you want and I want to make you happy. Because I love you. Because the thought of going on without you rends me to pieces and I'd rather not experience that again, thank you. Because I want to wake up with you every morning, not just when I get lucky. Because you're everything I could want in a woman, Danny, so why wouldn't I want to marry you? Well, that's what I asked myself, and now we both have the answer. I didn't *know* I was in love with you until I thought I'd lost you. I would have figured it out eventually, but I'm rather glad to know it now rather than later. So will you marry me and let me be your family?"

She leaned back, staring at him in wonder. "You really mean it? You love me?"

"More than I can possibly express in mere words."

Anthony's voice intruded behind them as he and James walked through the door. "They told you not to interrupt them. Deuced embarrassing to hear that mush, ain't it?"

Jeremy turned, grinned at his father and uncle. "Congratulate me. She's agreed to marry me." But he whispered to Danny, "You will, right?"

"Yes," she whispered back, nearly bursting with the most profound happiness. "Most definitely."

"Well, I'll be damned," James said. "Don't think that even remotely occurred to Jason while he was having his tirade. It does solve the dilemma, however."

"What dilemma?"

"Jason knows who she is, lad."

"That she comes from here?"

"No, who she *really* is."

Chapter 50

Late-summer wildflowers filled the fields along the road through Somerset. It was far from London, a full day of riding plus half the next morning. Danny didn't notice most of the journey. She was in such a daze, her emotions ripped asunder.

There was the happiness. She'd never experienced anything like it. Jeremy loved her. He was going to marry her. He was going to fulfill all her dreams. It was almost more than she could bear, might have been, if the fear didn't counter those emotions. But the fear was overriding everything else.

She was afraid it wasn't true, that Jason Malory was mistaken. She was afraid if it was true, that her mother wouldn't still be alive. She'd last been known to be living in Somerset on her grandmother's estate, but no one had seen her since she'd retired there fifteen years ago. She could be dead, they could be making this journey for nothing. But Danny was also afraid that if Evelyn Hilary *was* still alive, she wouldn't accept Danny as her daughter. There was no proof, other than some vague resemblance. Why would a great lady, the daughter of an earl, the widow of a baron, accept some street waif as her own blood?

James Malory had come with them. He'd insisted. "The chit requires chaperoning, now that you know who she is," he'd told his son.

Jeremy hadn't liked hearing that, and Danny would have snorted herself if she weren't in such an emotional daze. They didn't know for certain who she was yet, they were only guessing. Just because the tragedy associated with Evelyn Hilary closely matched her own meant nothing. It could merely be coincidence.

"The lady wasn't there when her husband, Robert, was murdered. They had come to London for a brief visit, but she was called back to Somerset. Her grandmother had taken a fall, or something like that. The murders made all the papers, were assumed to have been committed by a madman who broke into their London house and went on a rampage of killing. Her husband, Robert, and several servants were killed. Their daughter and her nurse were never seen again, but the blood left behind suggested they'd both been killed as well and dragged off. That those bodies had been disposed of, yet the others left behind, was what prompted the madman conclusion. There was simply no rhyme or reason for such slaughter."

"Why is it you didn't recognize her?" Jeremy had asked his father. "Weren't you in London during that time?"

"Well, it was rather romantic actually," James said. "I recall being disappointed that I never got to meet Lady Evelyn. But as it happens, she had the shortest season on record, attended all of one party, which was where Jason happened to meet her. Apparently Robert Hilary was already acquainted with her and followed her to London to propose. She accepted and returned home the very next day. And they settled down on his country estate in Hampshire, where they had one daughter. Occasionally they visited London, but they didn't actually socilize when they were in town, which is why so few people remember Lady Evelyn."

Danny heard all of this with only half an ear. It sank in, but she couldn't really relate it to herself, not yet. The fear wouldn't let her.

Jeremy offered her comfort just by his presence, but more, he kept an arm around her for the entire journey. Without that, Danny would probably have fallen to pieces. The closer they got to Somerset, the more tightly the fear choked her. If she had been thinking clearly, she would have been running in the opposite direction.

The estate they finally arrived at was magnificient, three stories tall originally in the main block, with shorter wings off to the sides, dark gray stone covered with ivy. It spread out over immaculate lawns dotted with stately old oaks. It shot Danny's fear up a dozen notches. She'd never seen a building so big that someone actually lived in.

They weren't going to be let inside. Danny was glad when she heard that, that

Lady Hilary didn't receive visitors, for any reason. The butler was quite adamant. The name Malory meant nothing to him.

The door was about to be closed in their faces when Jeremy got annoyed and dragged Danny around in front of him—she'd been hiding behind his back. "I believe the lady will want to see her daughter," he told the man.

The butler, a rigid fellow, paled by slow degrees as he stared at Danny. Finally he said in a shaky voice, "Come inside. My lady is in the garden behind the house. I'll direct you—"

"Just point the way," James said, still irritated with the fellow.

She wasn't in the garden. One of the workers there pointed them to the skating pond just beyond a stand of trees, saying the lady often walked there.

Danny was holding back and had to be dragged along by the hand. She finally dug in her feet altogether. Jeremy stopped, lifted her face to his, saw how pale she was, and put his arms around her.

"I can't do this. Take me home," she pleaded with him.

"What are you afraid of?"

"She's going to hate me. She isn't going to want someone like me for a daughter. It's too late for her and me to be a family."

"You know that isn't true, but you'll never know for sure unless you face her." And then he added in a tender tone, "And if it is true—you still have me."

She melted against him. Her happiness, lingering beneath the fear, pushed forward again, surrounding her, giving her back some of her courage.

She let him lead her through the narrow stand of trees to the other side, where James had stopped to wait for them. Jeremy made an attempt to distract her, asking, "You don't recognize this estate?"

"No, none of it. It seems too big for someone to live in it."

"Actually, it's rather small."

"Liar."

"Really, nice and cozy."

She snorted at him, but then she caught her breath. A field of flowers spread out before the pond, and in the field walked a lady with white-gold hair.

"Oh my God, it's my dream, Jeremy. I *have* been here—with her."

He had to drag her forward again, her

feet simply wouldn't move of their own accord. James preceded them. Neither of
them were going to let her avoid this.

The lady was walking slowly through the
flowers, her back to them. She was so deep
in thought, she didn't hear or see them approaching.

James's first words startled a gasp from
her, and she swung around. "Lady Evelyn,
allow me to introduce myself. James
Malory, at your service. You met my older
brother Jason many years ago."

"I don't recall, but more to the point, I
don't receive visitors. Please go away, sir.
You are intruding on my privacy."

She turned away and walked on. She'd
barely glanced at James, didn't glance at
Jeremy at all, nor notice Danny hiding behind his back. She was serious about not
receiving and didn't inquire why they were
there or how they had gotten past her
butler.

"Can we leave now?" Danny whispered
in a trembling voice.

James heard her. "Bloody hell," he swore
softly, then called after the departing lady,
"We didn't come all the way from London to
be dismissed out of hand. Ignore me as you

will, but you might want to take a gander at my future daughter-in-law. She bears a striking resemblance—to you."

The lady turned around again. She didn't appear at all surprised by James's remark. Instead she appeared quite furious now.

"Don't take me for a fool, sir. I assure you I am not so gullible anymore. Do you think you are the first to come here to try and foist a daughter on me, in an effort to lay claim to my husband's estate? The first instance devastated me. The second attempt I was wary, but still willing to believe I'd found my daughter. After the third attempt, I lost all hope. Do you know what it's like to lose all hope?"

"Can't say that I do. But we aren't here to convince you of anything. There's no need. The wench is soon to be a member of my family. We take care of our own, so she needs nothing from you."

"Then what *do* you want?"

James shrugged. "I imagine she wanted her mother back. I'm beginning to think she'll do better without one."

The lady stiffened. Danny snarled at James, "Don't be assuming things for me, mate. And don't be insulting her either."

James raised a brow at her, said dryly, "Lost your fear of me at last, have you?"

Danny blushed, then hid her face in Jeremy's back again. That "We take care of our own" had endeared James Malory to her for all time. She really wasn't afraid of him anymore. But she still didn't have the nerve to face her mother.

Evelyn had heard her though, and although she couldn't see any more of Danny than her skirt behind Jeremy's legs, she gave him her full attention and demanded, "Why is she hiding?"

"Because she's terrified that you won't want her," Jeremy replied. "She lost her memory all those years ago. She's only just getting some of it back."

"Spare me, please," Evelyn said derisively. "That excuse has been used before as well."

Jeremy didn't reply to that. He turned around and lifted Danny's chin. "You're making this worse, you know. She's going to regret everything she's said."

"Or tell us to get lost again."

"So she does. Then we go home, get married, start making babies." He grinned at her. "If that's what she's going to say, luv, then let's get it over with. Delaying isn't going to change it one way or the other."

Danny groaned. He was right, of course. She was just prolonging her fears, and getting more and more sick to her stomach because of it. She stepped away from him, saw her mother's angry expression. It felt as if her heart just dropped on the ground.

But Evelyn had been expecting disappointment again, was still furious with them all for trying to dupe her. It took her a moment to look at Danny, really look at her, and then she was so shocked she couldn't speak. She was seeing herself twenty years ago, nearly identical, and the child she'd thought she'd never see again.

Danny had turned away, her worst fears realized. She put her arms around Jeremy and buried her face in his chest.

Her throat had closed off, she could barely get out, "Take me home."

She wasn't going to cry. She refused to cry there in front of Evelyn Hilary. Later—

"Danny!"

She looked back. Her mother was extending a hand to her. Her shock was evident now. She'd paled a ghostly white.

"Oh, God, Danny, it's really you?"

The tears started. Danny took a step toward her, then another, then ran the last few, was sobbing openly by then and even more when her mother's arms went around her, crushing her with her own emotion. The smell she recognized, the softness, it was coming back to her, how much she'd been loved here. She was home.

Chapter 51

It was a large parlor, utilitarian, cleaned as needed, but rarely used. They sat in it, Evelyn and Danny on the sofa, Jeremy in a chair across from them. James stood off to the side, by the empty fireplace, merely observing and remarking as needed—or not.

Evelyn held Danny's hand. She hadn't let go of it once since she'd first taken it to lead them back to the house. She was still crying off and on, every time she looked at Danny, actually, so she tried to keep her eyes on Jeremy instead. Danny was still crying off and on as well, and it didn't take much to set her off again. She had her mother back. She had her identity back, her real life back.

She was still waiting to wake up, was still so incredulous that everything that she'd ever hoped for had come true.

She'd already explained what had happened to her on the way back to the house. Evelyn had asked that almost immediately, wanting the whole story. She hadn't seemed that surprised when she heard it. It explained why she'd never been able to find Danny herself. She'd never thought to look in the worst of the slums.

"I thought you were dead," Evelyn was saying now. "After years of searching, I'd finally given up all hope. And then those impostors began showing up. They had your eyes, all three of them. They bore no other resemblance. Hair color might change over the years, appearance might change as well, but eyes don't. They'd had tutoring, obviously, from someone who knew my family very well."

"How many were there?" Jeremy asked.

"Three. The first girl was ten, she fooled me the longest. Five years passed before the second attempt. Then another two years before the last. I had the feeling that Robert's cousin was finding these girls and training them in what to say. He wanted

Robert's estate and title. After he tried to have Danette declared dead and failed, I think he resorted to creating a new Danny, one that he would have control of, or dispose of, to have substantial proof that she was dead."

"I was wondering about that," Jeremy admitted. "After fifteen years, she should have been legally pronounced dead."

"He did try and was furious when his petition got thrown out. My grandmother was still alive then, and she was close friends with the judge."

"This was your husband's only surviving relative?" James asked.

"Yes. He was a third cousin, though, and illegitimate, which was why the title would have passed through to Danny's children before it would go to him. But he could have gotten it if he could have had her declared dead before she started having children of her own. Do you have any?" she turned to ask Danny.

Danny blushed. "No, none yet."

"Soon though," Jeremy added with a grin.

Evelyn sighed. "I don't suppose I could

prevent this marriage? I've only just found her and already I'm going to lose her?"

"No, but you can come to London and live with us if you'd like," Jeremy offered.

"That's very generous of you," Evelyn replied. "But I couldn't intrude on newly-weds. I will however move back to London, if that's where you're going to settle, so I can see Danny often. I had our old house there torn down to the ground and never re-built. Knowing what happened there—" She paused to shudder. "But I could rebuild now. I still own the land."

"I have no memory of that house," Danny said.

"That isn't surprising. It was your first trip to London. We'd only been there a few days, which were mostly spent shopping or in the park, where your nurse took you to play. So you weren't in that house very long before the night the murders occurred. I would have died that night as well, I have lit-tle doubt, if my grandmother hadn't broken her leg. We were very close, she and I, and she was all I had left. My own parents had died when I was young, and my grand-mother raised me after that. So I couldn't rest until I saw for myself that she was all right."

"So you were here when it happened?"

"I hadn't even gotten here yet, I'd left London that afternoon. The news did come to me here though. I was destroyed. I nearly lost my mind. Robert was the love of my life. I'd known him since I was a child. His family estate is near here. I only went to London for a season to force his hand. We were already in love. It just took him longer to realize it. The possibility that Danny had escaped the mayhem was the only thing that sustained me during that time. But not knowing what happened to her was anguish in itself."

"I don't doubt that Miss Jane would have returned me to you, if she hadn't died herself," Danny said.

"Oh, I know she would have. She was a good woman. Which made it hard for me to keep up my hope. I finally suspected something had happened to her to prevent it. And you were too young yourself to find your way home. I never dreamed you had lost your memories completely."

"They've been coming back to me slowly, since I met Jeremy. I remembered that park

I had played in. I remembered my first name, though I didn't like it very much."

Evelyn laughed. "Neither did we. It was Robert's mother's name, though, so we were obligated to give it to you. But even he didn't care for it and was the first to call you Danny instead."

Danny smiled, but continued hesitantly, "And I recognized the man who did the killing that night, when he found me and tried to kill me again."

Evelyn paled. "When was this?"

"Just recently. He died himself in the attempt though, so we didn't find out who he was."

Evelyn sighed. "I'd always suspected it was Robert's cousin. He was the only one who stood to gain by Robert's death. And he'd always hated Robert. But there was no way to prove it. And he wasn't even in London when it happened."

"His name wouldn't happen to be Lord John Heddings, would it?"

"John Heddings, yes, but he's no lord. How did you know? You'd never met him. He never visited us after you were born, hating Robert as he did, and we never mentioned his name. I'd only met him a few times myself, before we were married. You could sense his animosity when he was around Robert. He never tried to hide it."

Jeremy explained, "He's been living in a grand house not far from London, and pawning himself off as a lord. Obviously, no one has bothered to check his background. But he's been a gambler and jewel thief for quite a few years, which is how he's been supporting himself in such high style."

"And he tried to kill me as well," Danny added. "We were trying to catch him stealing, because we knew he was a thief. But when he saw me, he recognized me, or rather, recognized you in me, so he knew who I was. He mentioned that other man, that he'd failed again to get rid of me, that he was just as incompetent as he'd been fifteen years ago. And he said he'd finish it himself, just before he tried to kill me. Jeremy showed up in time to stop him. I knew then that he was the man who'd sent that other one all those years ago to kill me. We couldn't prove it, though, and weren't aware that he had a motive."

"My God, so I was right," Evelyn said. "I'll have him prosecuted!"

"You'll have to get in line," James remarked. "The younguns have already had him arrested for theft as well as attempted murder."

"Then I'll make sure the charge is changed to murder. He's not going to get away with this, now that I know for certain he paid to have my Robert killed."

"Be assured his days are numbered, Lady Evelyn," James said. "My family also has a vested interest in this now, since Danny will soon be one of us."

"Ah, yes, another reminder that I'm soon to lose her. But until the wedding, she'll be staying with me. I don't suppose you'd agree to postpone the wedding?"

Jeremy was already groaning over that "she'll be staying with me" remark. To his future mother-in-law, he now said, "Not bloody likely."

Evelyn tsked at him. Danny grinned at him, though, before she told her mother, "I was about to say not bleeding likely m'self."

"So you love him then?" Evelyn asked softly.

"Oh, yes, with all my heart."

James rolled his eyes, said dryly, "Let's not get mushy before dinnertime, children. And do keep in mind it will be separate bedrooms for the duration. Have to take this chaperoning business seriously, don't you know."

Which had Jeremy groaning again quite loudly.

Chapter 52

～～

They were married in late August. The banns had been posted in Evelyn's shire, as well as in London, shocking the ton. It might have been rumored that Jeremy was courting the Langton beauty, but no one had thought he was *really* going to put the shackles on.

Danny learned that Regina Eden often came to the rescue when tricky situations arose, and explaining why Danny had been introduced to the ton as a relative of Kelsey Langton's, but was now Evelyn Hilary's daughter, definitely fell under tricky. But Reggie smoothly let it be known that she'd merely forgotten to mention that the Lang-

tons had adopted Danny and raised her as
their own since it had at the time appeared
she had no family.

It was a magnificent wedding. After thinking for so many years that she wouldn't
have the opportunity to arrange her daughter's wedding, now that Evelyn had the opportunity again, she outdid herself.

Danny was offered a new gown, in any
design of her choosing, or the gown Evelyn
had been married in. Never having thought
that far ahead, and actually, thinking she
wouldn't need a real wedding dress to get
married in, since her marriage aspirations
hadn't been that high, she chose her
mother's dress. It was too beautiful to pass
up, ice-blue satin and lace that was so soft
it felt like silk. And it fit her perfectly! It had
taken her a while to notice, during their re-
union, that her mother was exactly as tall as
she was. That was one of the reasons that
Evelyn hadn't wanted a season in London,
and why she'd left immediately after Robert
had proposed. She'd always been self-
conscious about her unusual height.
Robert, actually, had been no taller, so
Danny got all her height from her mother.

It was odd how their relationship developed over those weeks before the wedding. It was almost as if they'd never been separated. The warmth was there, the love was there, there was no hesitation in giving it. And Evelyn wanted to know every single aspect of the years she'd been denied. They talked endlessly together, sometimes into the wee hours. They laughed, they cried. More and more memories were recalled, of those first years Danny had spent with her parents. God, it was so nice to have her mother again.

While she was so happy she felt she'd burst with it, Jeremy wasn't. He'd all but been asked to leave! Told he would just be underfoot, told he would have Danny the rest of his life, that he could wait just a few more weeks, no, he wasn't happy in the least. But he sent letters to her each day, completely forgetting that she couldn't read them. Actually, she was to find out later that the fellow who had delivered the first one was supposed to tell her to save them, that Jeremy would read them to her after they were married, but the chap had been so dazzled by Danny's smile he hadn't mentioned that part. So Danny had her mother read the letters to her each day, and if

Evelyn did a lot of blushing over those readings, Danny was too engrossed and thrilled by the depth of Jeremy's passion to notice.

He loved her, really, really loved her. She wondered if she would ever stop being incredulous over that. And he was miserable over their short separation, said he even got foxed for the first time in his life. Well, actually, he said he was doubtful he did, but that his father, two uncles, and Percy all claimed he'd done exactly that, so he had to allow it might have happened.

Evelyn surprised Danny by sending for Dagger and Lucy, as well as all the children. She'd sent three coaches to collect them all and wasn't going to let them return to London. She'd decided to take up Danny's cause and support an orphanage herself. Robert had had two properties nearby, both of which belonged to Danny now, and one of them would be a perfect environment for children to be raised in. Dagger would run it, but under Evelyn's supervision.

They didn't get along well at first. He didn't like the thought of working with a grand lady. She resented that he'd gotten to raise her daughter. They did a lot of snapping at each other, but it calmed down after they finally got used to each other and worked out the details.

Jeremy's servants were also invited to the wedding. They were friends of Danny's, after all. Danny had decided to offer Claire the chance to change jobs, thought she might be happier working with children. And she'd been right. Claire jumped at the opportunity, and *she* and Dagger hit it off right from their first meeting. Dagger usually took getting used to, but Claire had too much confidence these days to be intimidated by him.

Dagger, in a fine suit for the wedding, had undergone a remarkable transformation. He'd shaved for the occasion as well and was humbled by his own appearance. Danny was reminded why she'd thought of him as "family" for so many years. She'd already forgiven him for kicking her out, especially since she would probably never have seen Jeremy again if he hadn't. And she'd amazed him by asking him to escort her down the flower-strewn path to the altar, to give her away.

Lucy, in fancy new togs as well, cried like a banshee during the ceremony. So did Evelyn. Danny shed a few tears under her lovely veil, too, but only because she was bursting with joy as she said the vows that joined her to Jeremy Malory. She might not have gotten the respectable husband she'd had in mind when she'd first determined to get one, but she'd landed one who was so much more than that, the most sought-after man in all of London, and he was all hers now.

He hadn't gotten to see her before the wedding. He'd arrived the night before, but she'd been sent to bed early and had been busy all morning getting ready. When she'd joined him at the altar was the first time she'd seen him in several weeks, so it was little wonder the kiss he gave her after they were pronounced man and wife was a bit prolonged and had to be broken up with numerous coughs that didn't work, and finally his father slamming a hand on his back to congratulate him. Bleeding well nearly knocked them both over.

Every single Malory had shown up for the wedding, so Danny got to meet those she hadn't met yet, including the children, since she'd requested that they be allowed to attend. The Malory family really was much larger than she'd thought, and she was one of them now, which was another wish of hers granted, to have a big family. In fact, between her mother and Jeremy, all of her hopes and dreams had been fulfilled, with just one exception, which she mentioned to Jeremy that night as they lay in the huge master bed in *her* house, her father's ancestral home, which was hers now until she had a son old enough to claim it and the title, baron, that went with it.

They'd just spent several hours making up for missing each other. The bedcovers were in disarray. She was lying against Jeremy's chest, his arms firmly around her. She wasn't the least bit tired yet. Neither was he.

"We'll have to air out this place a bit more. It's still a bit musty," Jeremy was saying.

Danny agreed. "It was only recently cleaned, had been closed down all these years." Then she thought to ask, "Did you want to live here?"

"No," he replied, then asked after a long pause, "Did you?"

"No, I rather like your house better. It's much easier to clean."

He sat up abruptly and frowned down at

her. "Don't even *think* of still cleaning that house, Danny. I mean it. Your days of wielding a duster are over."

She chuckled at him, pulling him back down so she could get comfortable again. "I was just teasing. I'm quite aware of my elevated circumstance."

He mumbled, "It's a bloody good thing I wasn't aware of it before I asked you to marry me, or I probably wouldn't have asked."

Now she sat up abruptly and demanded, "Why not?"

"Because, m'dear, your mother wouldn't have let me anywhere near you, so I wouldn't have gotten to know you, wouldn't have fallen in love, would still be going about my merry way blissfully unaware that I'd be miserable without you."

She thought about that for a moment and then laughed. "She would have welcomed you once she got to know you."

"Don't count on it, luv. She would have sized me up and decided a scoundrel like me wasn't good enough for her daughter. You *could* have aspired to a lofty title, you know, and *that's* the way mothers think."

"I'd like to be one to find out."

"One what?"

"A mother." Then she whispered, "I want a baby, Jeremy, your baby."

He groaned, pulled her back into his arms, said huskily just before he kissed her, "It's going to be my absolute pleasure to grant that wish, Danny, I do assure you."

"Since it's going to be my pleasure, too, can we work on it a little bit more tonight?"

"Tonight, tomorrow, every single day until you're puking your guts out, dear girl."

"I'm not going to have morning sickness. My mother said she didn't, nor her mother."

"Don't run in the family, eh? Well, that's one thing I'll thank your mother for."

"Doesn't," Danny said.

"Eh?"

"Doesn't run in the family." She beamed at him. "Now that was rather nice, correcting you for a change." Then she mimicked him, " 'Deed it was."

Jeremy burst out laughing.